DREAMS OF RIVERS AND SEAS

Tim Parks studied at Cambridge and Harvard. He lives near Verona with his wife and three children. His novel *Europa* was shortlisted for the Booker Prize. *Destiny* and *Judge Savage* were longlisted in 2000 and 2003.

ALSO BY TIM PARKS

Fiction

Tongues of Flame

Loving Roger

Home Thoughts

Family Planning

Cara Massimina

Goodness

Shear

Mimi's Ghost

Europa

Destiny

Judge Savage

Rapids

Talking About It

Cleaver

Non-fiction

Italian Neighbours

An Italian Education

Translating Style

Adultery & Other Diversions

Hell and Back

A Season with Verona

Medici Money

The Fighter

TIM PARKS

Dreams of Rivers and Seas

VINTAGE BOOKS
London

Published by Vintage 2009

2 4 6 8 10 9 7 5 3 1

First published in Great Britain in 2008 by Harvill Secker

Vintage
Random House, 20 Vauxhall Bridge Road,
London SW1V 2SA

www.vintage-books.co.uk

Addresses for companies within The Random House Group Limited can be found at: www.randomhouse.co.uk/offices.htm

The Random House Group Limited Reg. No. 954009

A CIP catalogue record for this book is available from the British Library

ISBN 9780099513360

The Random House Group Limited supports The Forest Stewardship Council (FSC), the leading international forest certification organisation. All our titles that are printed on Greenpeace approved FSC certified paper carry the FSC logo. Our paper procurement policy can be found at: www.rbooks.co.uk/environment

Printed in the UK by CPI Bookmarque, Croydon, CR0 4TD

Those familiar with Gregory Bateson and his work will realise that I have used elements from his life and writings to create the character of Albert James. Equally, it will be clear that only some aspects of their lives are similar: Bateson never lived in Delhi nor was he ever accused of any wrongdoing; then, unlike James, he married more than once and had many children. Readers who want to find out about his remarkable work should certainly not consult these pages, which are entirely fictional.

We go on doing research and thinking about all sorts of problems, as if we could one day reach the thought that would set us free.

Gregory Bateson

PART ONE

THREE ELEPHANTS

CHAPTER ONE

On reception of his mother's brief phone call announcing his father's death, John James took a deep breath, booked himself onto the first available flight for Delhi, had Elaine drive him to Heathrow, travelled towards the coming night and arrived at Indira Gandhi Airport to find the weather much cooler than expected. The funeral was to be the following morning. His mother was not in the apartment, but the elderly maid let him in and told him that Mrs James had gone as usual to the clinic. 'To clinic,' she said. 'Madam has gone to clinic.' John put his bag in the one spare room and sat on the bed. He stared at the bookshelves and sighed. Shall I take a shower? Suddenly he felt a loss of momentum, a faint giddiness. No, the important thing was to see Dad's body.

John stood up and went back to the kitchen where the maid was sweeping the floor. Did she have a phone number, he asked, for his mother? A mobile or work phone? The woman's head wobbled strangely as she looked at him. She seemed to have trouble understanding. John repeated the question. 'I need to phone my mother, at the clinic.' 'Clinic,' the woman said, her head still wobbling. She began to give directions for how to get there. She used her arms, miming a person going out of a door and turning right. John decided the walk would do him good and set off.

Outside, despite the cooler temperature, there was the same glazed and glaring light he remembered from other trips east, the same sour smell in the air, the same odd mix of frenetic traffic, roadside cooking, languid animals and persistent beggars. He liked it. He felt on holiday. I work too hard, he decided. This would blow away the cobwebs.

Somebody tried to sell him postcards of the old town, trinkets, necklaces, sacred images. He smiled and shook his head. But he couldn't find the clinic. The broad streets seemed one block of buildings after another, some at considerable distances, all enclosed by decaying red walls. There were big trees between the buildings and swarms of crows cawing in the foliage. John pulled a mobile from his pocket and texted Elaine: 'Can you believe it! Mum not home, and left no phone number. Now I'm getting lost looking for her. Wish you were here. Kisses. J.'

John's father had died of cancer, but the end had come unexpectedly soon. From what John had found out about prostate cancer, there should have been no immediate concern. Even in India, such things could be kept at bay for many years. Some Westerners actually went to Delhi for cheaper operations. And Dad could always have come back to the UK if he needed special treatment. 'John, your father died this morning,' his mother had said. He hadn't been able to gauge her voice. He had been in the basement lab at the Centre; the centrifuge was noisy and the signal poor. But she certainly wasn't crying. Mum was a tough one. And his own response had been quiet to say the least. He hadn't wept. He wasn't close to weeping. So all Dad's famous research has come to nothing; those were the first words that crossed his mind. It didn't upset him. Rather the contrary, as if something poignant had been sensibly cut short.

Only talking to Elaine, did he manage to feel the drama of it. 'Oh my God, John,' she cried. 'My God! John!' She forgot her own problems. There was the flight to arrange. 'How awful – you must check if your visa is still valid. It's so sudden. The poor thing, your poor mother!' Was she going to bury him out there? Surely not. And what about money? That John had nothing in his current account was common knowledge. He used his credit card to pay for the flight. 'What about the future, though: your poor mother, your allowance?' Elaine found a cash dispenser and insisted he accept £200, though she too was living off her parents.

Yet all this urgent talk, John sensed as they drove to the airport, was just buzz. His girlfriend was getting a chance to see how her man reacted in a crisis and to show how practical and sensible she could be. He adored her, but this was theatre. She was playing. Her vocation was theatre after all. Everything dramatic was fun for Elaine.

No, the only significant thought, he realised now, of these twenty-four hours that had followed his mother's phone call, had been the knowledge that he would never see his father again. The words had come to him on the plane. They had been showing a movie in Hindi about a man who was supposed to be marrying one woman but in fact was very evidently in love with another who, for reasons John hadn't grasped, was quite unsuitable. 'You will never see him again,' he suddenly found himself muttering.

The moment the words came into his head he felt a fresh alertness. It was much sharper than the phone call or anything Mother had said. Then, trying to picture his father, while at the same time watching the film, because the girls were pretty and he liked the brilliant colours and a certain charming artificiality you get in these Indian romances, he realised that there was no image of Dad in his mind: greenish-grey eyes, lanky, balding from the front, sandy hair, fine nose, a slightly distracted, sometimes aloof air. It wasn't much more than an identikit. Or not even. I won't see Dad again, he thought. And he decided that the first thing he must do on arrival in Delhi was view his father's body. He would see his dead father and fix the man in his memory for life to come. Except that now, wandering down a broad avenue of New Delhi with dry grass waving on the verges and here and there destitutes wrapped in rags, he couldn't find Mother's clinic; he didn't know where his father was.

It was fantastic that you could send text messages back and forth between India and Maida Vale, you could chat with Elaine 6,000 miles away, and yet you couldn't find your mother round the corner. The maid had seemed very confident. 'Straight, sir, just straight!' She had made a confident gesture with her hand, lifting the purple cloth of her sari. 'Just straight. Then left turn at the red light. Yes. Yes. Road very long, sir.' She wore a yellow blouse. Perhaps she had imagined he had a driver. 'I wish I could be with you too,' Elaine wrote back. 'Audition at the Rep today. Fingers crossed.' 'Good luck, Beautiful,' he replied.

I should ask someone, John decided, but there were no pedestrians in this part of town. A man squatting with his back to a tree simply shook his shawled head. He had his fingers in a bowl. Eventually an autorickshaw pulled in and began to follow him at a walking pace.

John turned. 'Is there a clinic near here?' he asked.

The vehicle stopped. 'Clinic, sir, which clinic?' The man's eyes were sunk in deep hollows. 'You are not well, sir? You need doctor?' He too had a shawl round his head, loose robes on his body. His wrists on the handlebar were uncannily thin. 'Yes, I take you, sir. Get in. I take you.'

John remembered that you were supposed to agree on a price first. 'Fifty rupees,' the man said. Only fifty rupees. It hardly seemed worth haggling. They swerved about through chaotic, honking traffic. When a jam forced them to stop, the driver shooed away beggars. A little girl moved her arms in a quite unnatural way. The driver shouted in Hindi. This really can't be what the maid meant, John thought, and in fact when he walked through mud and broken brick into the reception of a small private hospital they had no knowledge of Dr James.

'Helen James,' John repeated.

'No, sir. I'm afraid not, sir. There is no one of that name on our staff, sir.'

John took a regular taxi back to the apartment. The maid let him in. It seemed pointless recounting his adventures. Looking at his watch, he realised it was still very early, only lunchtime. I'm jet-lagged, he decided. He went to the fridge and found it almost empty but for two six-packs of Coca-Cola. He smiled. Even in these circumstances, Mum had remembered his Coke.

John opened a can, found some dry biscuits and cheese and went to sit on the sofa. The furnishings in the room were Western, but spare. It was typical of the Jameses. In all their travels there had never been any question of going native; they were largely impervious to the cultures they helped and studied; but nor did they seem to need the comforts that other expats demanded. John munched. The only impression of fullness came from the walls, which were stacked from floor to ceiling with books, box files, old audio cassettes, carefully labelled videos. I'll find a photo album, he decided.

He couldn't find an album. The folders were scientific journals, many of them photocopied. There were files full of notes, typed notes, handwritten notes. Some of them were very old. The videos were his father's work and wouldn't contain images of him, nor would the audio tapes have his voice. John knew these things. It was a family that produced generation after generation of scientists. If anything his father had been the least of them, too meditative to be a real achiever. A castles-in-the-air man. I will overtake him, John reflected. Perhaps I already have.

Eventually, he found a small black and white contributor's photo. 'Towards an Epistemology of Instinct', Dad's article was called. John peered at the grainy image. The paper was poor and yellowed. There was a wry grin on his face. John looked more closely. He remembered that grin. Or was it just a pained twist of the mouth? He took the photo to the window, but the image seemed to dissolve in the Indian glare. He couldn't make it out. Still, clear or not clear, it was definitely Dad. There was a way his hair had of falling in wisps, a mild cragginess about the jaw. Outside, in the distance, a column of smoke was rising above the apartment buildings, rather as if rubber tyres were burning on the edge of town. John went to take a shower.

CHAPTER TWO

Returning from an eight-hour shift at the clinic, Helen James came home to find her maid pointing excitedly at the bedroom, one finger over her mouth. 'Mr John is here! Your son, madam!' Helen opened the door to the spare room. John lay on the bed, fully clothed, his handsome face smoothed in sleep, a blond forearm on the pillow. What an improbable presence, she thought. He bore no resemblance really to herself or Albert, so lithe and so relaxed.

Helen had been very much tempted, two or three days ago, not to tell her son about this at all. Why tell anyone? She would definitely have preferred to wind up her marriage by herself. She would have preferred a funeral with no public but herself, or no funeral at all, the bare cremation. In a dream, not three weeks before, she had seen herself carrying her husband's body to a funeral pyre by the riverside – he wasn't heavy at all – laying him down on the mud at the water's edge while the crematorium wallahs heaped on the wood, then holding his hand and talking to him while he burned and sang and the river flowed by. An oddly Indian dream, she thought. When she woke he was shuffling back from the bathroom. She would have liked to cremate him herself, push the coffin into the furnace herself, collect the ashes herself, sweeping them into the skirts of her dress, and hide them herself, on her own, in a place that only she knew. Yes, yes, she had dreamed of doing that; she daydreamed. Yet the morning after the long and terrible last night she had called John on his mobile. 'Your father died this morning.' It was a duty. You can't deny a son the death of his father. John is a duty and a burden to me, she thought. She shook her head. What fine clothes he was wearing. He seemed unthinkably large and adult. There were two empty Coke cans beside the bed. 'We'll have to talk about money, my boy,' she muttered.

Helen changed out of her work clothes, then sat at the table in the sitting room looking through the newspaper and drinking tea. Every few moments she stopped, her head cocked, as if listening. These are fragile days, she thought, but in the end she would get through. The death of a partner is not the worst way for a relationship to end. Suddenly, Helen decided that she didn't want to eat alone with her son. She called a colleague, then woke the boy towards seven. 'John, love, we're going out to eat, do you mind?'

When John appeared in the sitting room, Kulwant Singh was already there. A Sikh. The young man had meant to ask at once how it had been, how his father had died so quickly when only a couple of months before the doctors had been talking of normal life expectancy; had he left any special message for his son? But Mrs James was already shooing them out of the apartment; there was a small place she hadn't been to for a long time, she said. 'I don't digest properly if I eat late.' She seemed so much her ordinary self that her son was taken aback.

Kulwant was a jowly, jovial, heavily built man recently returned from a trip to London and very much amused, he declared, by this marriage of Charles and Camilla. 'It is too funny,' he kept saying as they ate their meal, 'these old folks marrying, you know. It's too funny.'

Exactly as if he were in a pub with Elaine's friends in London, John began to get worked up about the complete idiocy of royalty.

It was incredible, he protested, that even foreigners were seduced by this soap opera.

For a moment the Indian doctor seemed offended – 'Indians are not ordinary foreigners' – he complained. Then he chose to be indulgent and chuckled. 'No, it's too funny!'

'How old are they, exactly?' Helen asked. She couldn't recall.

'Late fifties,' Kulwant said. 'Far beyond childbearing age, you see.'

'But who cares how old they are?' John insisted. 'It's the attention they get from the press that's so maddening and mindless, when anyone who's halfway talented is eternally ignored.'

'We must not speak only of talented people,' Kulwant laughed. 'There are so few of them!'

Eating quietly, Helen was grateful that no one had mentioned Albert. She herself was fifty-three.

'I like it here,' John talked enthusiastically as they walked a little way before finding a cab. Kulwant had hurried off in an autorickshaw. 'I like the way the air smells and the rickshaws and animals.' He was looking at a girl in a sari swaying side-saddle on a scooter. 'Are you going to stay?'

'Why shouldn't I?' Helen told him. 'I have the clinic. I have my patients.'

'I'm glad. We'll come and visit.' He meant Elaine.

'You didn't appear to like Kulwant very much,' his mother said.

'Oh no, he was nice. Just that it drives me crazy to think I'm sitting in a restaurant in the heart of the subcontinent eating whatever spicy stuff it was with a man in a bright green turban and all he wants to talk about is whether Harry was the butler's son and did Charles have the balls to murder Di.'

'So what did you want to talk about?'

'I don't know,' John laughed. 'The colour of his turban maybe. Are the colours symbolic or something?'

'Why didn't you ask?'

At this point John pulled a couple of coins from his pocket to get rid of two little boys who had been tugging at his sleeves. At once, a dozen more appeared. Poorly lit, the street was still busy. So many people seemed to be carrying things, in their arms, on their heads, with carts and bicycles, as if life were an endless to and fro of bulky packages. Many more squatted on the kerb. Helen shooed the boys away.

'I didn't want to offend,' John said. 'You know? I'm never sure what I can ask and what I can't.'

'Kulwant is busy arranging the marriage of his daughter,' Helen said. 'Unfortunately, the girl damaged a knee just when everything seemed settled. She was getting off a bus in traffic and a motorbike hit her. Quite near here, actually. They had to use the money they'd saved for the wedding to pay for her operation. These things aren't free here. So now the groom's family has turned cool.'

'Oh,' was all John could think to say. 'I thought they'd stopped arranging marriages.'

'Not at all.' Helen stopped on the kerb and waved for a taxi.

'How come the London trip, then, if he's short of money?'

'Financed by the drug companies, so that he'll prescribe the right things, to those who can afford them of course. If my patients only got what they could afford, they'd never be treated at all.'

Mother and son were silent on the drive back to their apartment, but when they were settled in the sitting room, John at last said: 'I was hoping to see Dad, tomorrow, before the funeral.'

Helen had gone to sit at her place at the room's big table. She sighed. 'I knew you'd want to, but I had the coffin sealed this morning.'

After a short silence, John tried: 'Can't they open it?'

His mother looked at her boy. The young man was so well made, with his grey, wide-set eyes, his soft thick hair. She sighed. 'It's not a nice sight, John. Best think of him as he was.'

'I'm not a child,' John protested.

'It's been forty-eight hours now,' Helen said. 'And he's not in a deep freeze. They usually do things right away here you know.'

'Mum, I spend all my time studying the difference between live cells and dead cells. We're in the same business.'

His mother didn't reply.

John turned to the window. 'How come it happened so quickly?'

'There were metastases.'

'So why didn't he fly back to England?'

'You know how he was, John.'

The young man felt thwarted. He had imagined himself sympathising with his mother. She would share with him how the end had been. His father would have left a message of some kind, some words for him to mull over. They would look at photographs together. Dad's had been a rich life, full of travel and ideas. They would feel consoled and close and talk about the future. Instead, the son felt frustrated, even angry. He walked into the kitchen, opened the fridge, took out a Coke and went to sit on the sofa opposite the television.

'You remembered the Cokes,' he said grudgingly.

'How could I forget?' she smiled. 'Tell me about yourself, John. How's the thesis going?'

'Pretty well finished,' he said. 'But the thesis is a detail compared with the research itself. It's a whole new approach to TB.'

'And this girl?'

'Elaine?' He softened. 'She's fine. Looking for her first acting jobs.'

'Well, let's hope this time,' his mother said.

John had a way of being left by pretty girlfriends. His mother would smile wryly. John didn't reply.

'And you finish when?'

'If things in the lab go well, this spring.'

'After which?'

'They'll take me on for the project we're doing.'

'You're sure?'

'I'm the best.'

His mother watched him. 'Don't you think it might be an idea to get some experience first? Often it helps your research if you've seen a few things. There are plenty of TB patients to study here, if you're interested. You know your father . . .'

'Mum,' John shook his head. 'In the field I'm in, just to understand all the information you need to make even the tiniest step forward takes a lifetime. You have to specialise, specialise, specialise. There's no time to fool around. And it's done in the lab, not looking at patients. You don't need to see the sufferers.'

They sat in silence, Helen behind the big table, John with his leg over the arm of the sofa, swirling his Coke round in its can as if it were cognac. Very soon, he knew, she was going to get up and say goodnight. All his life his mother had preferred to sit at table rather than in an armchair or on the sofa. Wherever they lived, one end of the sitting-room table would have her papers and correspondence, more recently her laptop, a couple of magazines: *Medical Digest*, *BMA News and Quarterly*. It was as if Helen James created a little office or nest of her own within the larger nest of the home.

And in the past, of course, Albert would have been present too, listening over and over to his audio recordings, watching the videos he had made, writing his interminable notes. When she wasn't in the clinic, when he wasn't off on his researches, it had been rare for the two of them not to be in the same room. They discussed his ideas. Dad was the one who had the ideas, sitting on the floor usually, sorting through piles of old tapes and books and notes. The whole house was Albert's office, and his kitchen and bedroom. He drew no boundaries.

'Listen to this,' he would say, and then they would argue some hypothesis back and forth – they rarely agreed – getting quite worked up sometimes, until she would get to her feet – she was a tall, graceful, angular woman – put aside a book that she hadn't really been reading, or a letter that hadn't quite got written, and announce that she was going to bed: 'I don't know about anybody else,' she would say, 'but this old girl needs to be fresh for the clinic in the morning.' She needed energy, she said, for her patients and their diseases. She had lives to save. It wasn't for the likes of her – but she was smiling – to spend her days idly videoing other people's conversations.

Afterwards, his father would sit up for another hour and more, or perhaps for half the night, playing and replaying the same four or five minutes of video, a conversation he had filmed, in the market, at the bank, in the hospital, at a religious ceremony, often in languages he didn't understand. And as he watched he would say, 'Ha!' Or, 'No! No, it's not that,' taking no notice at all of his son, never explaining quite what it was he was after or up to. It was a situation that had allowed John to get away with a great deal over the years.

'Well, I'm off to bed,' Helen James announced abruptly. She stood up. 'To be honest, John, I've had a difficult couple of months. I need to get my strength back. And we're short of staff at the moment.'

Her son stood up to embrace her. As he recalled, the places his mother worked in had always been short of staff. 'Didn't Dad say anything for me?' he asked.

Her eyes flickered away from his.

'I don't know,' he tried. He wasn't sure if he was asking too much. 'Some advice, some message?'

Helen James embraced her son and held him tightly. It was the first real contact. Each was looking over the other's shoulder. 'Your dad was ill,' she whispered. John pressed his cheek against hers. 'A couple of days before the end he said, "If John has time to come out, make sure he visits at least the Sufi tombs, and if possible takes the trip to Agra to see the Taj."'

'Oh God, that's so Dad!' John laughed, but he almost cried too. 'How can I? I'm leaving Thursday, Mum. Otherwise all the lab work will get behind.'

'Two days is plenty,' she said. She stood back and held him at arm's length. There were tears in her eyes, but she was smiling. 'You hardly need to hang about here with your old mum, do you?'

When his mother had gone to bed, John flicked through the TV channels. Why did I get so heated about Charles and Camilla? he wondered. He felt wide awake now and uneasy. What would happen at the lab if he wasn't there to keep track of things? He was the only person who was always present.

Going to the spare room, he took out his laptop and scrolled through lists of readings they had been taking. 'How did the audition go?' he texted Elaine. 'Everything okay, here. Mum making a big show of being in control.'

The girl did not reply. John pulled out a copy of a journal on communications theory. There was no wall space without its bookshelves and every book and magazine was covered with his father's scrawl. Some words were underlined, others crossed out. The comments in the margin spilled over onto the page. Not all of them appeared to have much to do with the text they had been written beside. On an article entitled 'Cybernetics and Invertebrates', Albert James had written: 'START AND END WITH BREATHING.' And then beneath that, in a tiny, heavily slanted scribble: '*drink every evening ceremonial substitute for thing that hasn't happened. But what thing?*'

John shook his head. It was the kind of distraction that had always prevented his father from producing anything concrete. Mother at least changed people's lives day by day with her diagnoses and medicines. Midway through an article on left-lobe anomalies in chronic schizophrenics, he found the note: '*Not to KNOW anything! Only observations, stories.*'

Again John frowned. Perhaps his father's real problem, he thought, had been his difficulty working together in a team, with other people, towards a shared goal, something essential these days given the sheer amount of spadework that was required to get to grips with anything. You had to be a link in a larger chain, contribute one thing, whereas Dad was always out on his own, trying to solve the whole world himself.

Not properly tired, John lay on the small bed, waiting for sleep. It was impossible to think usefully of his work without being in the lab. Breaking down the smallest particles and isolating even smaller ones, to manipulate them, even the most unimaginably tiny coils of DNA, RNA, ribosomes, every phospholipid: that was the way to progress. That was the way to put new drugs in the hands of people like his mother. Not scribbling queer thoughts over other people's publications. John felt uneasy. It was frustrating that he hadn't seen Dad's body. What did I come here for after all?

Suddenly he was dreaming. It was a troubled sleep. He was walking down the same broad avenues he had walked this morning, but wearing one ordinary, really rather elegant leather sandal, while the toe of his other foot was crammed into a tiny, white, child's shoe, a little girl's shoe, it seemed, which he was dragging along on the pavement because there was no way his foot would ever actually get inside it. And what irritated him enormously – it was an angry sleep – was that when the Indian man in the airport shop had told him that they only had one right-footed sandal in his size and that the best thing was to take that together with this strange little white feminine thing for his left foot, he had actually accepted this stupid solution. How dumb can you be! If there's one thing you need two of, John, and the same size, it's shoes! 'Symmetry!' Dad always used to say: 'At the heart of life is symmetry!' And shuffling along the broken pavement among the beggars and with car horns blaring and rickshaw drivers soliciting, he was torn between going back to the shop to protest, because he had actually paid £17 for the things – £17 of my parents' money! – and setting off instead to the Sufi tombs where he was to see his father's body for the last time.

'John!' A voice whispered. 'John. Time to get up.' His mother was shaking his shoulder. The funeral was at ten.

CHAPTER THREE

Elaine had reminded John he must take a black suit. John didn't have a suit. He had dug out a dark blue jacket. Elaine had helped him pack. He didn't have a tie either. 'I haven't worn a tie since school,' he said. He had laughed. But dressing now, he felt anxious. It would have been right to wear a tie for his father's funeral. Should he ask Mum if there was one in the flat? The hesitation surprised him. When did I ever worry about dress? Dad never cared. His father had scandalised many a prestigious audience by turning up to deliver lectures in an old tee-shirt. He always wore the same clothes. It was family legend, more memorable really than the kind of things he had talked about.

How had they dressed Dad for his coffin? John wondered. The thought stopped him. He breathed deeply. In his old jeans, with the zip that never stayed up? When he went through to the living room he found his mother wearing a very formal black dress. This too he hadn't foreseen. She had even found a black hat. Perhaps bonnet was the word. 'Am I all right?' he asked. 'How do you mean?' Helen James was putting papers in her handbag. She hadn't noticed how her son was dressed. Nor had there been any mention of breakfast. 'The driver is waiting,' she said.

Only in the car did it occur to John to wonder what kind of

funeral his mother had arranged. They were in India. He had no idea what an Indian funeral was like. He had never thought about his father's funeral. But it wouldn't be Indian, surely? 'Have you invited a lot of people?' he asked. Helen James seemed distant. She held her back erect. 'I wondered if there might have been an obituary somewhere,' he went on. It was still in the back of John's mind that he might insist on seeing the body at the undertaker's. He felt it was his right and he mustn't forego it.

'I beg your pardon?' she asked.

The car had stopped outside a place John imagined must be a hardware store but it turned out to be the funeral parlour. There were cars and autorickshaws double-parked and his mother jumped out and crossed the deep gutter to speak to a rather distinguished elderly man in a loose double-breasted black jacket, but rather incongruously wearing a yellow woollen hat and yellow gloves. It wasn't that cold. John saw her fussing with her handbag and pulling out papers, then rummaging to look for something else. They were gestures that took him back to childhood. He was aware of feeling simultaneously sorry for his mother, being widowed so early like this, and intimidated too. What was the point in my coming, if she didn't want me to see him? She saw death almost daily in her work of course. Then he realised four men were struggling to squeeze between the double-parked cars with a coffin swaying over their heads. A hearse, dilapidated yet oddly American-looking, had come round the corner and stopped in a third row, blocking the road, pumping out fumes. A din of horns began. A woman with a large basket on her head threaded the traffic. Drivers were shouting at each other while the four men struggled to get the coffin between the parked cars. The bulky, lacquered box seemed extremely cumbersome. Could he really ask them to open it?

'How much will it all cost?' John enquired when his mother climbed back in and slammed the door. The hearse was moving off ahead. 'I beg your pardon?' she said again. John couldn't tell if she was suffering or just distracted. 'I was wondering if it was expensive,' he repeated. 'Everything's expensive, dear,' she said.

They drove through the streets following the hearse in the always chaotic traffic. 'We're going to a Protestant cemetery to the north of town,' Helen James now explained. 'It's an old military place; a lot of the expats and local Christians use it. They've just added a modern crematorium because they're running out of burial space.' She frowned at a ramshackle block of low, brick buildings thronged with women milling around fruit carts. 'The Christians here are rather down on cremation,' she went on. 'They tend to insist on those parts of the Bible that suggest the body needs to remain intact until the day of resurrection. But probably the real hitch is that cremation is a Hindu tradition. It would be easier for the Christians to adopt it, if the Hindus did something else, if you see what I mean.' John recognised his father's kind of reasoning.

'And the funeral will be at the cemetery?' he said.

'There is no funeral,' Helen replied. 'As such.'

John fretted. This was not how his father's death should have been. But all his childhood had been lived in the knowledge that other families were integrated in the world in a way the Jameses were not. The Jameses were on the move, with a mission, always studying and helping wherever they went, but never really part of things. It was good when it came to impressing girls with the different places you had grown up. 'I don't know how you can settle for Maida Vale after the childhood you've had,' Elaine would shake her head. She herself had protective parents in Finchley; they were dead against her being an actress. John wanted to text her now, but it seemed inappropriate to pull his phone out sitting beside his mother as they followed Father's hearse through the clogged roads. A girl was walking in the gutter beside them, rolling a used car tyre with extended arms.

Apart from some exotic vegetation, the cemetery was remarkably English-looking: overgrown and ill-kept. The gravestones seemed positively Victorian with grubby angels holding scrolled tablets bearing elaborate black lettering. Even the weather had a raw and misty English feel, though the crows were definitely larger than London crows. As the car passed the main gate, the birds rose in a flapping storm, circling the graves, cawing so loudly they smothered the sound of horns on the road outside. Then John noticed two or three cloaked figures, apparently asleep among the tombstones. Here and there, on their haunches, women hacked at the rough grass with sickles. There were patches of broken red earth, abandoned sheets of corrugated iron.

The hearse followed a narrow track along the perimeter wall until it reached a clearing where a low cement building was topped by a conspicuous chimney. It's just me and Mum, John realised, as he climbed out. Already the undertaker's men were sliding the coffin out onto a bright steel trolley. The thought upset him. Dad loved people.

'Isn't there anybody else?' he asked. His mother was pulling a veil over her eyes, John hadn't noticed that the hat had a veil. She looked like a mourner in a film, tall and upright and gracefully contained in her suffering. John felt like an actor without a part.

Inside the crematorium, a dozen benches were unevenly lined in the cramped space. How damp it was. At the front was a low brick platform and against the wall a sort of counter with rollers leading to a purple curtain covering an aperture in the wall. Helen James and her son stood to one side of the door while the men wheeled in the coffin. It seemed improbable with its shiny finish and brass fittings. 'Isn't anyone going to say anything?' John asked. But his mother had already begun to walk after the trolley which clattered and squeaked across the concrete floor. The undertaker's men were talking and chewing.

Almost in a panic now, John followed. That his father was

actually shut away in that box seemed inconceivable. I should have seen him lying in it, he thought. I should have said goodbye. Why were there no flowers? India was full of wreaths and garlands. Why hadn't Mother arranged for the body to be flown back to London? For some reason he was frightened now that the coffin would just be dumped on the rollers and slid directly through the purple curtain, on the other side of which, surely, the cremation furnace must lie. Dad would be cancelled out without anything being said.

Helen James went to sit in the front row. Now John saw there was a large red push-button on the wall beside the curtain. He hadn't expected these feelings. He had never been close to his father. These last few years the man had come to seem an obstacle, an embarrassment. Stumbling into the pew beside his mother, he asked, 'Can I go and kiss the coffin?' He was sweating, but Helen James sat perfectly erect staring through the black gauze veil at the gleaming box now placed on the rollers.

Looking at her, John sensed that in her mind his mother was accomplishing some private ritual. She had known how these moments would be, she was prepared and concentrated, while he felt completely unanchored, his mind prey to a storm of feeling. I have nothing, the words crossed his mind. He left me nothing.

John thought he could see his mother's lips moving behind the veil. She was talking to Father. She has veiled her face to cut out the background noise, he thought, to have this last conversation with Dad in peace. And now she seemed to rock very slightly backwards and forwards on the pew. She is honouring some vow. He felt jealous. She was rocking backwards and forwards; it was a strange, trance-like motion. She is talking to him.

Then it occurred to John he must get to his feet, run out to the front, kneel before the coffin and kiss it. He would lay his forehead on the polished wood. He could see himself doing it. He could taste the polished wood on his lips. His eyes would be closed. His whole body was tensed now to make this dramatic gesture, to kiss his father's coffin before it slid into the fire.

But he mustn't. It would disturb his mother. This was her day, not his. He must not interrupt her last communion with her husband. John felt paralysed by a sense of inadequacy, and outrage too. He started to shake and had to put his face in his hands to hide the tears. He wanted and did not want to watch the coffin slide through the curtain. Who would press the button? Do it now, he thought, do it now!

Then a voice said: 'Mrs James?'

John's head jerked up. It was an elderly Indian in a dog collar approaching from the far end of the pew. Leaning forward, grey-haired and affable, the clergyman started to ask something in a low voice. A noise at the back of the hall prevented John from hearing what was said; there were footsteps and a buzz of voices. People were filing in and the noise had an odd, tinkling quality.

John twisted his neck. A dozen people in middle age, three or four of them white, together with some younger people, all Indian, including one very attractive woman, were walking up beside the benches. Two or three approached, as if to shake his mother's hand, but the fixity of her concentration on her husband's coffin must have deterred them. They nodded to John, presumably aware who he was, and arranged themselves on the benches behind. Meanwhile, the tinkling sing-song was growing louder, until, twisting again towards the back, John saw to his surprise that a crowd of young girls had begun to push through the crematorium door, held back for a moment by a buxom nun who frowned and hissed at their forwardness.

Peering in and pushing, the girls must have been fifteen or sixteen years old, all Indian, but wearing the kind of school uniforms that have long been a rarity in England: green blazers edged with gold, green skirts, green hats with golden ribbons, smart black, silver-buckled shoes that clipped and clattered on the hard floor. And as they advanced up the aisle in this bustle of green and gold, the atmosphere changed. The air in the place began to move and was suddenly perfumed. Beneath their hats, the girls' hair glistened, as if drenched in oil. Their eyes flashed, their skin was alive. The nun, also Indian, was shushing them now as they came forward, two by two along the aisle, each one clutching, John saw, a small transparent plastic bag, tinged with yellow. What was it about?

Helen James had not turned to look, but nor did she seem surprised. Solemn and excited, the girls came forward, curtseyed before the coffin, made the sign of the cross and sprinkled their yellow petals on the polished wood. Watching the scene, John felt a powerful sense of relief, and of yearning too. What small and dainty feet the girls had as they filed past to occupy the rows behind. Unexpectedly, he remembered the tiny shoe of his dream. Why didn't I have flowers to bring? he wondered. The coffin was thick with petals.

'The nuns and girls of the convent school of St Anne's,' the nun announced, standing on the platform, 'would like to express our deepest and most heartfelt gratitude for the work of Albert James in our small and humble community.' She smiled. 'He was very much loved. May he rest in God's peace and be ever and most warmly remembered.'

As she spoke, John watched the last pair of ankles pass. The young girl kept her eyes down and her hands pressed together as she hurried after her friends. So Dad was reduced to teaching school, he thought.

Now one of the older Indian men walked to the front and took the nun's place. He stood stooped in a long white kurta. 'The Theosophical Society of Delhi,' he said, blinking behind rimless spectacles, 'would like to wish Albert James an easy and peaceful return to the Great Circle of Being which was always the object of his most distinguished work.'

'Very true,' someone muttered.

Three other speakers followed. Earnest and pale, a hang-jawed Englishman said that as head of the British Council he had always relied on Albert to explain everything that was mysterious to him in India, which, needless to say, was a great deal. The Zoological Institute of the University of Delhi, announced a sober middle-aged Indian woman, was deeply indebted to Professor James for his contribution to various research programmes. 'We could rely on Professor James,' she said solemnly, 'to add unexpected dimensions to any project.'

'I'm here from the Delhi Drama School,' declared a young man in jeans. Bright-eyed and confident, he occupied the platform in a way the other's hadn't. 'Youth theatre that is.' He smiled. 'Yeah, well, we'd just like to take this opportunity to thank Albi, really thank him from the heart, for the fascinating way he had of thinking about drama. You know, he tried to teach a bunch of us a whole new way of interacting. Nobody was paying him and we were full of admiration. We learned a lot from him and had a good time together. Maybe one day we'll put what he taught us on stage. I hope so.'

Almost too pleased with himself, the young actor turned to pat the coffin. 'Thanks, Albi.' Then he tripped getting down from the platform. There was a titter from his friends.

'Mrs James?' the clergyman said. He had been standing behind the others and beckoned now to John's mother. All this had been planned, then, John thought: the flowers, the half-dozen telegraphic gestures of homage. He was very much relieved. Yet a feeling akin to guilt crept in at the thought that he himself had offered nothing. He hadn't been invited to speak, as if he were a stranger here.

Helen James walked forward, climbed the brick platform,

stood by the coffin. She turned, hesitated, austerely upright in her black dress and veil. 'What is there to say?' she asked. Her voice was low but steady. 'Albert was my life, my destiny' – she paused – 'and I his. I his,' she repeated. 'That is the truth.'

Helen James drew a deep breath as though about to begin a longer speech, then with a rapid movement she turned and pressed the red button on the wall.

The hum of an electric motor underlined the tension of staring eyes. The yellow flowers were swept across the coffin's shiny lid and sprinkled to the floor as it slid away beneath the purple curtain. The two colours, yellow and purple, seemed to form a dividing line through which his father was passing. John saw him going, saw his mother's lips moving beneath her veil, the petals falling to the floor. Behind him, one of the girls had begun to sob. Just before the coffin finally disappeared, Helen James lifted her hands to her face and pressed them against her mouth through the veil. There was the metallic click of the furnace door sliding shut, and then a dull roar. For a few moments the room sat still in the knowledge of the body burning. Then John was on his feet to hug her.

Walking out of the crematorium on her son's arm, Helen James felt she was stepping into a vast empty space. Albert was gone. She had passed a threshold. She was light-headed. Now she accepted these people's commiserations and condolences. She didn't know them well. Now she thanked the schoolgirls for having come. 'That was so kind of you. I'm very grateful.'

'Your husband was such a generous and learned teacher,' the nun said, bowing slightly and taking Helen's hand in both of hers. 'The girls were in adoration, Mrs James.' She had to speak loudly over the cawing of the crows. 'We were all in adoration.'

The midday air seemed to have grown whiter, milkier above the wheeling birds, and when Helen said, no, she hadn't planned a lunch, really she hadn't planned anything, she hadn't had time quite honestly and she was needed at the clinic of course, the guests from the university protested, they absolutely insisted on taking her and her son to eat. 'In memory of Albert. The very least we can do.'

'I'm game,' John said. It was a relief to be out of the damp gloom of the crematorium.

Helen hesitated. Then she saw it was a solution: 'Take us wherever you want,' she smiled. 'Will you come too?' she turned to the head of the Theosophical Society, then replied to his question of a moment before: 'He asked me to sprinkle them in the Yamuna. This is my son John; John, Dr Bhagwan Coomaraswamy, head of the Theosophical Society.'

'I'm afraid I really don't know what theosophy is,' John confessed and someone laughed.

The group were still sorting themselves into cars when a taxi appeared along the drive. The hearse had long gone. The schoolgirls were climbing into an ancient bus. A man got out of the taxi, a European, or American perhaps, wearing crumpled Western clothes. In the strangely empty state of mind she was falling into, Helen understood at once that he had just got off a plane. He was coming directly towards her, hand extended. She was caught off guard.

'You must be Helen James.'

He had a rather fleshy face, as of a boy who has aged without becoming adult. You knew at once he would be warm and enthusiastic and that it was the kind of warmth and enthusiasm that irritated. Instinctively, Helen raised her veil, then let it fall again. She looked at him through the gauze.

'I'm afraid I've arrived late,' the stranger said. He spoke with an American accent and looked up above the crematorium to where a steady grey smoke was winding off into the hazy air.

Helen James straightened. 'I'm sorry,' she said. 'I'm afraid, I don't . . .'

'My name is Paul Roberts. It's really too bad I'm late. My flight got delayed.' He smiled an apology. 'The fact is, I'd very much like to speak to you, Mrs James.'

Helen couldn't understand who the man might be or how, coming from England or even the States, he could possibly have known about the funeral. Now all she wanted was to be alone. It was only the need to find something for John to do that had prompted her to agree to lunch. The others were in their various cars, ready and waiting.

Yet automatically she asked, 'What about?'

'Oh, there's no hurry,' the man said. 'This is a distressing moment. Perhaps if you left me your phone number . . .'

Again automatically, Helen told him the number, but as the man keyed it into a mobile, she felt a growing resistance. 'Do please tell me what it's about. Then perhaps you could spare yourself the trouble.'

Paul Roberts seemed confident. 'Mrs James, I want to write a biography of your husband. I believe Albert James was a most extraordinary individual and that the story of his life will be a great inspiration to many people. His work needs to be collected, re-edited and republished. As I see it, the world hasn't even begun to understand what it owes to him.'

Helen felt she had been struck an unexpected blow.

'Of course,' the American was saying, and his face was alive with an earnest professional enthusiasm, 'you will understand that it would be of the utmost importance for me to have your blessing in this project, Mrs James, your authorisation, as it were. As his wife. Such a mandate from yourself would open doors. The work would take on the credibility a great man deserves.'

Helen James was struggling not to hear, not to take the words in, while at the same time she was hearing them perfectly, she understood exactly what he was saying. The roar of a motor sent the crows cawing into the air. It was a prepared speech, she thought. All around the city threw up its haze, its strange, sour, burning smell, through which, very occasionally, the sun floated ghostlike.

Paul Roberts had stopped talking. He waited expectantly.

'We can speak on the phone,' she muttered.

CHAPTER FOUR

Nothing was said about Albert James over lunch. They had been taken, very simply, to the university canteen where they served themselves on tin plates with rice and dhal, then sat on benches either side of the busy plastic-topped tables. The president of the Theosophical Society spoke of a new biography of Annie Besant, while the younger folks, joined now by other friends, were arguing heatedly about the government's plans to reserve college places for lower castes. The relationship between an individual and his surrounding ethos was at once undeniable and elusive, the theosophy man was saying. His small old face was smoothed of any expression. 'In that sense,' he added, 'it is not unlike the relationship between father and son, don't you think?'

Across the table, Helen James ate as though performing a duty. John wasn't following the conversation. The young woman beside him, the beauty of the group, had begun to ask about his research and he eagerly started to describe the complex experiments his team was working on. He had become interested in the purely technical challenge, he explained, that so many experiments presented today. Above all you had to isolate the tiniest particles welded to each other in the most complex ways.

A small, dark girl and her earnest, bespectacled partner joined the conversation. The point of this present project, John told them, was to establish every, but really every condition that was required to support the life cycle of a certain tubercular mycobacterium after it had moved into the dormant state following initial infection: nutrients, protein production, cell-wall resistance, environment, conditions for replication and so on.

'What you mean,' the earnest man proposed, 'is that you are looking at every possible way of killing the bacterium.'

But now a message had arrived on John's mobile. He felt the vibration in his pocket. 'Audition a disaster,' he read. 'Director a shit.' John sighed and put the phone away.

'Well, yes and no,' he answered the man with spectacles. 'We're looking at how we can avoid reactivation of the dormant bacterium that about one third of people on the planet carry. Really, one third. So obviously we're studying the conditions required for dormant life and reactivation so that someone else can consider ways of denying the bacterium those conditions.'

Then John explained that he personally was just one of a long and by no means linear or lineal chain of researchers seeking to develop a drug to nail this bacterium, or prevent it reactivating, but in the simplest, least toxic fashion. That was the progress they were aiming for: non-toxic prevention. No side effects. He would reply to Elaine later, he thought, some consoling message.

One team, he said, studied the life cycle of the thing, how it passed from active to dormant and vice versa, another its biochemistry, its cell structure – 'to identify vulnerabilities, targets if you like' – another studied what substances might efficiently attack those targets or in some way compromise one or more of the many conditions essential for its survival. Then someone else studied the toxic effect of those substances, someone else again thought about how to deliver and package them, and finally someone considered how to manufacture them.

'Nobody begins to understand it all, you see,' John concluded as if repeating a profound truth. 'I mean, I don't think it would be possible, really, to understand everything about even the most ordinary pharmaceutical project today. Nobody even tries. It would be like trying to hold the whole world in your mind.'

As he spoke, the Indians were flatteringly attentive, so unlike Elaine's theatre friends. John smiled, sipping from a cup of disgustingly sweet tea. There was a pause. 'The triumph would be,' the theosophy man was heard to say into the relative silence, 'as your dear Albert once wrote, I believe, to reach a point where one has no more biography than God Himself, can you imagine what liberation? To be utterly without a personal history.'

As he spoke these words, Helen James pushed her chair back, stood up and announced that she had to go. The clinic was always under pressure, she said, during these cold spells. John also wiped his mouth. His mother looked pale. 'No, no,' she told him quickly. 'You stay here, darling. It's so lovely to hear you getting excited about your work. So encouraging. Oh, John is eager to visit the Sufi tombs,' she announced to the rest of the table. 'If someone has time, perhaps they could take him this afternoon.'

There was an immediate buzz of offers. People seemed polite to the point of irony. 'I'll take you,' the woman beside him said. She had a wide forehead, very fine dark eyes, but strangely narrow cheeks around pursed, full lips.

For a moment Helen held her gaze. 'Thank you, Sharmistha. John: I'll see you this evening, dear. Thank you everybody,' she repeated, 'thank you so much, you've been very kind,' and she hurried out.

'Poor old Helen,' someone said after a brief silence. 'She works so hard.'

One of the more elderly white men, three or four places down the table, leaned across to ask, 'How is your mother taking it, John? Is there anything we can do?'

John was surprised. He swallowed his food. Mother's motto, he said, had always been, Battle on regardless. Then he found himself telling an exemplary anecdote of how, in New Guinea – and this was big-time family legend – Mum had just gone on with her normal work at the clinic when the local tribe, complaining that Dad had put a spell on a girl that had caused her to lose her baby, had threatened to cut off and shrink her, his mother's, head, not Dad's, since it seemed that the way to take revenge in that part of the world was not to kill the man who had offended you, but his wife.

'How very convenient!' someone chuckled.

'Well, these people were so surprised when Mum just went on running her surgeries and distributing medicines as usual that they left her alone. They sort of realised she wasn't part of their world, I suppose. They couldn't faze her at all.'

'And Albert?' someone said more soberly. 'That must have been when he was writing *Wau*. How did Albert respond?'

'Oh, I wasn't born then,' John told them, 'I've only heard the story.' But he added: 'Dad was always anxious about everything, which was why he collected so much information but never actually did anything.'

It was a cruel remark, and at once John felt he ought not to have said this on the day of his father's funeral.

The theosophy man was watching him. 'There is more wisdom in what you say than you imagine, my boy,' he said in his slow clipped accent. He smiled very faintly behind thick lenses.

It was some years since John had been called 'my boy'. He pushed his chair back and felt ready to go.

The woman his mother had called Sharmistha must be twenty eight-ish, John thought, and quite short he realised now, but charmingly shapely, and she had brought along one of the older European men who turned out to be German. Were they in some sort of a relationship? John didn't care. He still hadn't replied to

Elaine, who was used to receiving answers to her text messages at once, especially when some setback threw her into depression. On the other hand, it was the day of his father's funeral.

'For New Delhi, you need a good fast taxi,' the German was saying brightly, 'but in Old Delhi an autorickshaw is really the only way to travel; they have a better chance of sneaking through the traffic.'

The fog was even thicker now. The air was damp.

'And I only brought light clothes!' John protested. 'I never imagined it could be like this here.'

'Women aren't allowed to go right into the tombs,' Sharmistha was saying, as if to explain why she had had to bring Heinrich along. 'Are you cold?'

'A bit,' John said.

Even with the heavy tarpaulin hanging over the frame of the autorickshaw the air was chill when they started moving at speed. The driver had what looked like a towel wrapped round his head. When they stopped at a light, John moved the tarpaulin to one side and found three helmetless boys sitting on a scooter only inches away, one carrying a milk churn in each hand. They were shouting and laughing in the exhaust fumes.

Looking out, then, through the vehicles squeezing into the junction and overflowing onto dry mud beside, the pedestrians picking their way between trucks and buses, a donkey cart piled high with scrap metal, John was struck by the frenzy and density of life here. Why had his father always chosen such places? Why had he never lived in a sensible town where you could get things done?

'I'm sorry, I should have asked you what you do,' he turned to Sharmistha. 'I've only talked about myself.'

'Heinrich is in psychiatry,' she said. 'He's been in India twenty years.'

The man leaned forward and smiled. They were cramped in the autorickshaw.

'But I'm not really at the university,' Sharmistha went on. 'I just write for scientific magazines and so on. At the moment I'm working with some people in the zoology department who are studying a spider that produces an unusually strong kind of silk. I'm writing a book about it for them.'

John made an effort to arouse some interest but was suddenly distracted by her perfume. He hadn't noticed it before, something sweet and strong that drew him powerfully.

'The team I'm working for,' she was saying, 'is mainly interested in the chemical processes by which the spider makes its silk. They are attempting to reproduce it synthetically. But your father was interested in patterns and layers of communication. That was how he got involved. He was convinced the whole web-making process was essentially a communicative structure.'

'He would be,' John replied.

'And why are you so eager to see the tombs?' she asked. 'You have heard all about them?'

'Not at all.' John realised he was feeling ill. 'Apparently Dad said I should go and see them, and the Taj Mahal. It's in a town near here, isn't it? God knows why. I only came for his funeral.'

There was a brief silence, then Heinrich leaned forward again. He had a high, bony, solemn face, a strong German accent. 'It is because the Taj is another tomb,' he said, 'the most famous tomb in the world. It is your father's way of inviting you to think how death is celebrated.'

'That's right!' Sharmistha laughed. She was shaking her head. 'That's him! That is just the way your father did things, inviting others to think.' Then in a lower voice she added: 'It was very strange, you know, John, listening to you talk at lunch, because it was like listening to your father again. Yes! The same manner, the same voice, also sometimes the same facial expressions, even if you have very different faces. Albert was always very excited too about what he was doing, you know, though of course he would never have said the things that you said.'

John didn't know how to respond to this. 'How do you mean?' he eventually asked, but the woman didn't reply. They had arrived.

John had expected something grand, so when they climbed out of the rickshaw at the Red Fort he supposed it must be that. It seemed frighteningly solid and ugly with its huge ramparts; a great stronghold of death. Instead, Sharmistha took him by the arm and they set off in the opposite direction, through streets so crowded and confused and narrow, he felt alert, threatened.

'Wonderful, isn't it?' Heinrich said.

Boys sat on broken walls and men wrapped in white gowns squatted on the ground in the thick of the passers-by where gaudy little temples were side by side with food stalls and carpet stores, a cluttered window advertising mobile phones.

They turned into narrower and narrower streets, passages even, and perhaps because of the fog, or maybe it was later than John imagined, the air darkened and there were steps now and arches, until, under what looked like a small portico, they had to stop and a man wanted to take their shoes and put shower-caps over their hair. They couldn't go bareheaded to the tombs. They must turn their mobiles off.

John crouched and undid his shoes. Heinrich was explaining about the Sufi tradition and who were the holy mystics buried here and saying it would be wise to drop a banknote beside a tomb at the appropriate moment, a twenty or a fifty, to have one ready anyway, as a sign of respect, even though there was absolutely no obligation, but John was hardly listening. What am I doing wasting my time here? he kept thinking. He still hadn't had a proper talk with his mother. Perhaps I should have booked the very next flight back after the funeral.

Descending steps to the tomb compound proper, he became aware of the noise. Beside a small shrine a dozen men were sitting in a cement courtyard, swaying in white gowns to the steady beat of the drum, clapping their hands and singing tunelessly. Two smoking torches on the opposite wall made the place both darker and brighter than the day outside.

'I cannot go in here,' Sharmistha said, as Heinrich approached one of the small buildings. There was incense burning. A man stood on guard at the gate; a little boy tapped John's arm and said, 'Guide. Hello, sir. I am your guide. Twenty rupees.' John felt ready to hit him. For some reason that mindless chanting and drumming made him shiver. He hated it with all his heart.

Inside the tomb, a building no bigger than a small bedroom, four men were sitting cross-legged at the corners of a green mound that must be the grave of the most holy man. Heinrich began to circle the grave silently. It was as though a mound of cement or compacted earth had been painted bright green and then lavishly sprinkled with the same marigold petals that the schoolgirls had spread on his father's coffin. Another visitor was completely prostrate, blocking their path, murmuring prayers, actually kissing the ground, and evidently in an altered emotional state. And now John noticed that there was money in the shallow trough that went all around the tomb mound, quite a lot of money. But he was determined not to add any.

'The tomb is guarded every moment of every day, for all eternity,' Heinrich whispered.

John felt furious. There was a way, he was sure, in which his father had always been an utter fool.

CHAPTER FIVE

'Would I be right in supposing,' the biographer asked, 'that the truth about Albert's death is that he didn't want to be treated?'

Helen James had agreed to talk to the man. It was early evening in the lounge of the Ashoka Hotel. She had immediately felt better that morning when she had packed John off to Agra to see the Taj. She was proud of the boy, but he seemed superfluous. Then she had found herself disoriented at the clinic. It was distressing. She was aware of working without concentration or sympathy. All her life, wherever Albert got funding for one of his projects, she had offered her abilities, free of charge, at some local clinic. Her energy was never less than boundless. Under the glint of her rapid eyes, the sure touch of practised fingers on sore skin, even men and women of the most alien cultures surrendered their scepticism. *Wagan*, they called her among the Iatmul: witch doctor.

In the early years in Kenya and in New Guinea she and Albert had set up the clinics themselves and worked together: she examining infected wounds, listening to ugly coughs, distributing medicines, he doing all the lab and paperwork. Helen was a doctor, Albert a biologist. That was the thrust of their marriage, initially. They had both been eager to leave England. Each had needed the charisma of the other to make the break and each knew that the other could only be won and held by this willingness to leave everything behind. They would give their talents to the world's poorest. No other explanation for their travels was required.

Then Albert backed off. Over a period of five or six years he had begun to doubt the wisdom of it. Switching from biology to anthropology, to kinesics, proxemics, cybernetics, he had developed his famous theory of non-manipulative study: any established culture is wiser than its foreign visitors and would-be benefactors; the clinic saved individual lives but it altered habits of mind, community traditions, attitudes to sickness and death; they were changes that would have incalculable consequences down the line. He wrote papers about delicate, self-correcting cultural ecologies – he was himself a delicate man – about complementary personality differentiation in complex social dynamics. Anti-establishment intellectuals loved him.

At that point, Helen had had John. It was a difficult time for her. An impetus had been lost. From being a couple, or a team, they were supposed to become a family. Did we ever achieve that? she wondered. Helen missed her work, the work she had shared with Albert. She missed healing people. And she couldn't help her husband with the things he was doing now. Intellectually, he had moved away from her. Nor could she become a local woman; they were both agreed that a European could never be part of a pre-modern culture. Your Western consciousness blocked you. John, of course, had had to be sent to schools back in England. The boy came and went. So Helen began to use her medical skills in clinics run by local people along local lines, taking instructions from others. That was hardly intrusive, she protested.

Helen came to life in her work. She beamed at the native women, intimidated their suspicious menfolk. Examining a suppurated eyelid, pressing home a syringe, she was in command.

Albert had seemed pleased with the compromise. 'The choices I make apply to myself,' he said, 'and to no one else.' At this point he was studying the relations between spoken word and physical gesture, between patterns of communication and collective ethos. Sometimes he would sit in Helen's clinic for hours, talking to patients at random. He made sketches, took notes. A breakthrough paper was written: *Prayer and Courtship Postures in Christian, Hindu and Muslim Cultures*. The conference invitations began. Neither felt the need for another child.

In these local clinics, Helen had worked below her potential, seeing more patients than one could possibly give proper attention to. She had often been without the necessary diagnostic tools, without sophisticated medicines, without adequate facilities for care, without an interpreter. She had been thrown back on her intuition, which sharpened enormously. She could smell illness. 'Albert studies the local ethos and pathos,' she would laugh on rare social occasions, 'while I pander to the vulgar desire to stay alive.'

Yet there was never any question of her withdrawing her devotion to her husband. Rather the contrary. Their travels had meaning now because of his brilliance: the theories he was developing would have resonance for what began to be called globalisation, the merging of all cultures. We were one of those special couples – this was the first thing she must tell this would-be biographer – who are totally dedicated to each other, because they have a higher goal. The mission came first, even if they had different ideas as to what the mission was. That was what made their marriage so sound.

But do we really want a biography? Helen worried today as she saw her patients at the clinic. She picked her way through the bodies in the waiting room. There was a man with a very severe testicular hernia. Helen couldn't focus. Something wordless was gnawing behind these thoughts. Examining a deep abscess in a boy's neck, she framed the question: how old is a woman, a widow, at fifty-three?

She had agreed to meet Paul Roberts at his hotel because she didn't want him to see Albert's books in the apartment. It would be difficult to stop the man going to the shelves and picking things up. She must go through everything herself first. But she had no desire to go through her husband's work. She felt tired.

'Who was that?' John had asked the previous evening when she put the telephone down after the biographer's call.

'Just someone I have to meet,' she told him.

Her son had watched her. The boy was sprawled on the couch with his Coke in his hand. He had turned the television on. Whenever John came home from school – home being Afghanistan, or Laos, or Zambia – there had always been a fridgeful of Coca-Cola for him. Helen loved his crude young appetite and it disturbed her. She wanted to be strict, she wanted to have him eat local vegetarian dishes, to understand that money doesn't grow on trees, she wanted him to spend some time in the clinic where only the poorest of the poor came. She wanted to rub his young well-educated face in filth. And she wanted to spoil him and enjoy his youth and complacency. He seemed a stranger and she herself felt strange when he was here.

'Tell me about Dad,' John asked again.

Helen said she couldn't talk. 'He died right here,' she sighed, 'in our bedroom. You know he always said: You can't balance the life equation without death.' She frowned: 'Maybe next time you visit I'll be ready.' Then she added: 'He had a lot of pain, though he never let himself be nursed. You know how he was. At the end, he really wanted to die.'

As she spoke, John's eyes never left her. It was uncomfortable. The boy was trying to get close. She wanted to embrace him, but knew she wouldn't. Nor would she ever press him to come and see the work she did at the clinic. 'The truth is, John love,' she told him abruptly, 'we've hardly any money. You know. It's a problem. Now your father's various grant incomes will dry up of course and I'm afraid there's almost nothing in the kitty. You'll have to support yourself as soon as possible.'

It was an exaggeration, but it did the trick. 'Albert didn't have any insurance,' she explained. She was sitting at her place at the big table. 'You know we never thought about that kind of thing.'

'But how much money is there?' John demanded. His mood changed. He became alert and aggressive, constantly shaking the empty Coke can as if to check whether there was any left. 'I mean, if I've got to find other funds, I need to know when.'

'You should go and see your grandparents when you get back,' she said. 'I'm sure they can help.'

Mother and son had argued then. It was unexpected and unpleasant. Helen certainly hadn't meant to argue the very day of Albert's funeral, but the boy was stubborn.

There was no way, he repeated over and over, that he was going to go crawling to Granny Janet to ask for money. 'The fucking old witch.'

'There's my father as well,' she responded primly.

'Granddad Jack's fucking gaga!' John objected. With extreme belligerence, he began to tell his mother that she should get in touch with her mother herself. 'You do it. You're her daughter.'

'But she dotes on you!' Helen cried.

'Maybe ten years ago,' John said. 'You can't cut yourself off from members of your family for half a lifetime and then go crawling to them for money!'

'John, John, John,' Helen laughed, 'don't exaggerate! You should thank God you're not out on the street with a begging bowl in your hands.'

She paused and looked hard at him. 'Why have you always

been scared of people, John; scared of working, scared of asking for things? Granny Janet would love to help.'

'I'm not fucking scared!' he objected. He insisted on swearing. His mother never swore. 'And I work about fourteen hours a day, for your information.'

'But not for money. You've never done a stroke for money in all these years.'

'Well, nor have you! You're proud of not working for money.'

'But I don't need any. And what I do is different.'

'Everybody needs money.'

Helen smiled indulgently. 'Really, I don't, John,' she said. 'As long as I work at the clinic. People are generous. They pay in kind. Life is cheap here. And I don't need cans of Coke at every meal, or smart shirts and trousers.'

'It's the rent that costs,' John objected. 'You have no idea what London's like now. I don't have a car. I never eat out. Actually, I never drink Coke at home either. Only when you get it for me. I live like a monk.' There was a long pause. 'Dad should have thought of this,' he accused her.

'Oh for heaven's sake,' she laughed. 'Just because you have to fend for yourself, it's poor Albert's fault.'

John had shaken his head and turned away from her to the television where a tubby BBC man in a turquoise shirt was interviewing Moroccan shopkeepers about the shortcomings of democracy.

'Your father risked everything,' she said, 'to take his study in unconventional directions. You can't imagine how difficult it was for him to find funding for some of his projects.'

Helen paused. She appeared to reflect. 'And we certainly weren't depending on parental assistance at your age. When we went to Kenya we had nothing. A tent and a typewriter and that was it.'

'Only because you hated your mother,' he said.

'I didn't hate her. We just didn't get on.' And she added: 'Your father's parents weren't poor either, but we never took money from them. We made a clean break.'

John changed channel. He stared at a programme in Hindi that seemed to be about traditional theatre, or its disappearance perhaps. Helen watched him. She was right on the edge. If he keeps up the pressure, I'll go and say something, she thought. But the boy held back, like an animal unable to use its energy. He didn't know what move to make. Then she wanted him out of the house. She wanted her work in the clinic and that was that.

'No fucking way am I going to crawl to Granny Janet,' he finally repeated.

Helen burst out laughing. She even clapped her hands.

'And if we're so short of cash,' he rounded on her, 'what's the point of paying for a driver and a hotel for me to go to see some old shit monument I don't give a damn about? The Sufi stuff was gross. It was primitive! I'd rather go home. I've got work to do in the lab. Serious work.'

'I've already arranged it for tomorrow,' she told him calmly. 'Your father was very keen for you to see the Taj. These things don't cost much here.'

'I won't do it,' he repeated. He was interrupted by the beep of a message arriving on his phone. He pulled the thing from his pocket, frowned and got up. 'Anyway,' he said, 'goodnight, I'm still jet-lagged, I'm going to bed.'

After a few minutes, Helen had followed him, knocked, gently pushed open his door and asked, 'Let's talk about nice things, John. Tell me about this girlfriend. I suppose she's the one sending the messages.'

'I've already told you.'

Helen had waited at the door.

'She's into theatre,' he said. 'But I already told you. Actually, Elaine must be the funniest person I've ever met. I mean, she can mimic any voice. Even better than Dad could.'

'Not monkey calls, though.' Helen lifted an eyebrow.

'No, not monkey calls,' John smiled. Albert James had published a famous study on meta-communicative signals in monkey communities. He did hilarious imitations. 'But on the phone she can really make the craziest voice sound completely convincing.' He frowned: 'It's just that she's having trouble getting a first break after drama school. Her father's always on at her about a proper job.'

Helen watched him. 'That's a hard life, I imagine, the theatre, films.'

'You should meet her, Mum.' John looked up, suddenly enthusiastic again. 'She's very pretty. You'd like her.'

It was a characteristic of all members of the James family that they would drop an argument in a matter of moments. Nobody ever said sorry.

'You know your father's brother wanted to be a playwright,' Helen said.

'Right,' John frowned. 'Actually, Mum, that's the kind of story I have to be careful not to tell her . . .'

It was remembering this comment of her son's that the following afternoon almost the first thing Helen James said to Paul Roberts was: 'You can't understand Albert, Mr Roberts, without thinking about his brother, John. That's where you should begin.'

'The one who killed himself?' the American replied.

Helen was taken aback by this brusqueness. 'Among other things,' she said dryly. Just being in a hotel like the Ashoka restored her to the sort of rebellious, anti-establishment identity she felt most at home with. Its flaunted luxury was obscene. Yet she couldn't help but be impressed by the American's staying here. It meant quite an income.

They were at a low table in the Bamboo Room with soft-footed waiters bowing and scraping. Helen had ordered a tea and been confronted with the silly rigmarole of a dozen brands on a silver tray. Indian music drifted from the neon-lit wall draperies, never really listenable but never absent. The upholstery too aimed to evoke something local, yet that Westerners could feel comfortable with. Paul Roberts asked if his guest minded his ordering a gin. 'I'm a little nervous,' he laughed. His face had an Irish set to it, she thought, florid and earnest and a little stupid.

Certainly he was precipitate. No sooner had the drinks arrived with the inevitable nuts and biscuits and gleaming teaspoons and folded white napkins, than he asked: 'Since you've told me where I should begin, am I to take it, Mrs James, that you're happy for me to do this book? Can I count on your help?'

Helen had put on a simple, very elegant, grey wool dress. She had been conscious of dressing for an occasion, without really knowing what sort of occasion. An occasion without Albert.

'I know nothing about you,' she said politely. 'I'm a little surprised, frankly, to find an admirer of Albert's staying at the Ashoka.'

'Oh?' the American raised an eyebrow. 'I left in a hurry,' he said, 'the Indian Tourist Board booked for me.'

Helen watched him. Could he have been a student, perhaps, when Albert taught briefly in the States?

'Mrs James, I've been corresponding with your husband for some time, by email. We had, er, kind of explored the question of a biography. I wasn't aware that he was ill. I had no idea. He didn't say anything about it.'

She sipped her tea.

'He didn't tell you about our correspondence?'

'No.'

'I can show you the emails,' Paul Roberts said, 'though, like I say, we were only at an exploratory stage.'

Again Helen said nothing. There was a powerful energy coming from the man, a coercive and rather naïve energy. He wanted to be liked, but only because she was Albert's wife, of course.

'The idea,' the American continued, leaning forward rather urgently, 'was for a biography that would give equal space to his thinking and his life, you know, showing how the one grew out of the other, and how relevant that thinking is to the contemporary world.'

Helen left a pause. 'Tell me something about yourself,' she eventually asked.

'What can I say?' The American sat back. He had full, satisfied lips, a rather wide nose, ruddy cheeks. 'My father was an evangelical clergyman. Grew up in Albany. I'm the black sheep of the family, I guess. Graduated in philosophy, at Harvard. A few postgrad courses mixed with freelance journalism, till I got on the *Globe*, the *Boston Globe*, that is, and eventually travelled for them as foreign correspondent. In the last few years I've published a couple of books. A sort of novelised biography of Gandhi, you know, one of a collection of potted biographies for Harcourt Brace, and then a travel thing: *Evenings in Asia*. When they were both successful, I sort of dropped the day-to-day journalism. Just luck, I guess. Anyway, it was thanks to that success that I was able to get a publisher interested in Albert James.'

At this point Paul Roberts again leaned forward across the lacquered table, looking directly into Helen James's eyes: 'This book, though, Mrs James, will be *far* more serious than the other two. This is the book I want to write. You see, I truly believe your husband was one of the most important individuals of our times. I mean, he was at the heart of the modern contradiction and he knew it. Communication, consciousness, intervention, non-intervention, the mental ecology of global living, inside or outside: the problem is to get people to understand what Albert had understood.'

Helen James felt a sharp pain. Tears were coming. She stood

up. 'Thank you, Mr Roberts. I will go away and think about it.' She picked up her jacket from the back of the chair.

The American was alarmed. 'Mrs James! Please stay. I do apologise. Perhaps it is insensitive of me. I—'

She turned. He too was on his feet. He wore a smart blue suit but without a tie. His face was full of a sort of pained vivacity, like a dog that has expected approval and now finds himself being shut in his kennel.

'I need to use the bathroom,' Helen said.

She found the toilet area at the bottom of a long flight of stairs, cavernous and clad in white marble. She must wash her face, cool her eyes. 'I'll cry alone, with Albert,' she said out loud, 'when I scatter the ashes. Not with anyone else.'

A young, dark-skinned girl slipped off a stool and hurried over to run the water in the sink for her; a pretty girl with thick hair in a tress. She inserted the plug and tested the temperature. The taps were polished brass. The girl offered her a fresh bar of pink soap on a porcelain dish, then fetched a soft white towel and held it ready across outstretched hands. A girl for my son, Helen thought. There are so many young girls. She looked at the smooth dark hands drying her own, at the maroon and gold of the colonially inspired uniform. The girl had understood she was upset.

'Is it okay, madam, you are needing anything else?'

Helen opened her purse to give a tip. She could slip out of the hotel now if she wanted; she hadn't left anything in the lounge. She could spend the evening alone, start looking through Albert's things. So many things in the apartment had gone dead. So many places felt empty. She hovered, checking her face in the bright mirror. The bathroom was very lavish. The marble was white as icing sugar. Her face seemed faded, veiled.

'Does madam need some powder?' The girl came back. 'We have lipsticks, madam.'

Reluctantly, determinedly, Helen climbed the stairs back to the Bamboo Room.

They talked for two hours. First he must tell her why he was the black sheep of the family, she said. 'Oh, because I *divorced*,' Paul Roberts laughed. He had an explosive laugh. 'Divorce was sort of unthinkable in the environment I grew up in, you understand? Only wicked uncles divorced, only witches tempted them. But I'm sure you know what puritan New England is like. Then I smoke! Alas, yes. A real compulsive. And smoking is of the devil. Not to mention studying philosophy. The divorce was just a confirmation in the end.'

Helen smiled. 'And did you remarry?'

'Sure, and divorced again!' The American laughed even louder.

'How sad.'

'Not at all.'

'And do you have children?'

'Three. Two by number one, one by number two. A kind of neat symmetry if you're willing to confuse the logical types.'

This was Albert's vocabulary. The man was performing. 'I'd like a vodka,' she told him. She didn't smile. 'A vodka and lemon with plenty of ice.'

'My pleasure,' he grinned and raised his hand.

When the drink arrived she told the younger man that she had never really liked India. She had been happiest in the least contaminated places: New Guinea, Borneo. She wouldn't use the word primitive. After the USA, however, Albert had felt it was important to be at the point of greatest attrition between traditional and modern, the melt line, he called it, or confluence: which meant India.

As she mentioned the USA, she looked at the journalist carefully. He only said: 'I was based in Delhi a while for the *Globe*. Bewildering place.' Helen drained the vodka in one and felt better. Without asking her permission, Paul Roberts ordered another.

'What Albert wanted to do,' Helen said, 'was establish a cybernetic model that would allow us to predict how different cultural systems would absorb the influx of Western ideas and transform them. Even the way a clinic is run, for example, is completely different here from in Europe.'

The American took this as a cue to talk about the time he had covered the stand-off between Islamic and Hindu fundamentalists at the temple marking Krishna's birthplace which of course was just a stone's throw – and plenty of stones had been thrown – from some important mosque. On two occasions he had come under fire.

'And having recently read *Prayer and Courtship Postures*,' he told her, 'I was constantly thinking, what would be Albert James's take on all this, you know? He would have grasped the underlying pattern behind the confrontation. It often surprised me, reading his stuff, that he never offered himself as a mediator in these situations.'

Helen stared at the man. 'The biggest mistake people make with Albert,' she said forcefully, 'is to imagine that he saw his thinking as in any way "useful". That's quite wrong.'

'I know, I know,' the American came back easily. 'I know he thought that. But his ideas changed my life. Maybe they weren't meant to be useful or to change anything, but they did. Ideas do. Or it could be this is just a lexical problem,' he grinned. 'I mean what do we mean by useful? Do you mind if I smoke?'

'Not at all,' Helen said. She hated cigarettes.

A waiter stepped from nowhere with a lighter. 'Why thank you!' Paul Roberts exclaimed. 'There's usefulness for you!' he laughed. He seemed quite vulgarly at ease now. He drew on his cigarette between full fleshy lips. Suddenly, his face clouded: 'Mrs James, I know I shouldn't ask, but the question is tormenting me. I mean, my having a correspondence with a great man who was dying, yet who never mentioned being ill. Can I ask you, did he take his non-interventionist ideas so far as to refuse medical treatment? Is that why it happened? Do forgive me if I'm being indiscreet again.'

She took in how rapidly the man moved from the infantile to the shrewd, from building up credit to drawing on it, overdrawing in this case. Very slowly, she replied: 'It depends what you call treatment. A lexical problem.'

'Touché,' Roberts said.

And again Helen suggested, 'I do think the place to start is with his brother John, and his father.'

Paul Roberts listened respectfully for a few moments while she talked about the circumstances leading up to John James's suicide. It was an old story. 'And yourself?' he eventually asked.

'I beg your pardon?'

'Yourself, Mrs James. You are surely the most important relationship in Albert's life? Thirty years together, isn't it? Maybe the place to start is you.'

Helen bit a lip. She finished her drink. 'I worshipped Albert and I had the privilege of making certain things possible for him. In return, he was the most faithful and fascinating companion a woman could wish for.'

A few moments later, when she stood up to go, Paul Roberts asked her if she knew where he could contact a certain Sharmistha Puri whom Albert had apparently been working with. 'Some project on spiders.'

'I have no idea,' Helen told him.

CHAPTER SIX

Ellie, this trip has been so frustrating. I've hardly spoken to Mum, I didn't see Dad at all, tomorrow evening I leave already. There were some people at the university in Delhi invited me over to look at what they were doing (with spiders!), some project Dad was involved in, but Mum insisted I be driven to Agra to see the Taj Mahal. While she works of course. Seems this was his idea. Dad had this thing that the only acceptable way to communicate with people was to send them messages by lateral thinking. So now I'm supposed to visit the place trying to imagine what Dad wanted me to understand. The story is that this faithful beautiful etc. etc. seventeenth century dusky princess died in childbirth and her sultan hubby dedicated a gigantic white mausoleum to her. Possible messages: sultan and wife were mum and dad . . . in which case, who or what was killed by childbirth? Er . . . everything my fault? Or alternatively: Yes, the rich and powerful can be unlucky, but improvements in obstetrics would have deprived us of a fantastic work of architecture. Dum-di-dum. And me thinking: Why didn't Dad scribble a goodbye letter? Why didn't he phone, for Christ's sake? I'm pissed off and I think I'm getting sick. There's something in the air that stinks here. Mum is going to spread his ashes in a river somewhere – it's so primitive – but I'll be gone by then.

John stopped. It was most unusual for him to write off the top of his head like this. Except for the small electric fans over every workstation, the crowded room might have been an Internet café on the upper Edgware Road. The people looked much the same, intent and elsewhere, with their bits of food in paper, their heads jerking up and down from keyboard to screen.

It's great that they called you from the theatre, especially after you thought you'd screwed up.

He stopped again. His girlfriend had sent three or four text messages in rapid succession: they had phoned her; she had gone to see the director; he was okay after all, rather sweet in fact. John felt again that he was in the wrong part of the planet. His body seemed acutely aware of this geographical dislocation.

Typing with two fingers, he started to say how much he was looking forward to making love to her again. He paused. He couldn't decide whether to write fucking or making love. There was a facile patter they used: the bald cavalier would once again rise and pay homage to the bearded lady, etc. etc. It was childishly stupid, but cosy. He yearned to be back in that cosiness. Had it actually been necessary to come to his father's funeral? He imagined Elaine's elastic body yielding to his; bliss; after which, all day in the lab with the centrifuge, the computer, the samples in the big fridge. That was the life that made sense. John broke off, opened another copy of Explorer, called up Google and typed in: 'Albert James anthropologist'.

The screen filled with entries. Most of them seemed to be references to articles in obscure journals of years before. Nothing recent. John's eye ran down them with a strange anxiety. This was what was left of Father. Virtual fragments. They might drift out here on the Net for decades, long after his ashes had been carried down to the ocean. Nothing ages or decomposes on the Net. On the third page he found: 'James, Albert: *The Originality of Sin*, paper delivered at the Theosophical Society, Zurich, 1989.' Remembering Dr Coom-whatever-he-was, John clicked and scrolled:

'And behold the world was symmetrical,' he read, 'and as such, largely redundant. Every animal had its mate. The female could be deduced from the male and the male from the female. Every living thing grew into its necessary shape. This was a world of specular form. That is why it was called a garden. Its symmetrical nature annihilated time. Every element reflected its other half in perfect stasis.'

John scrolled rapidly down the text. Dad had lost the plot even before the nineties. He checked his watch. Any moment now his driver would come to get him.

'... officially, of course, the Serpent tempted Man with the lure of knowledge. This is possibly the most extraordinary red herring in history. Or rather, it is *the* red herring that makes history possible. Consider, ladies and gentlemen: the real crime, surely, was not to eat the apple for *knowledge*. How could we feel ashamed of wishing for knowledge? The sin was to eat the apple – to *think* of eating any apple – for *a reason that had nothing to do with apples*, a reason that was *not* appetite, *not* part of the ecologically perfect symmetry of the garden. Behold, the beginning of magic and technique.'

What on earth was the man on about? John stared at the screen. All his life his father had been obsessed by the forms and shapes of things: of crabs and leaf veins, of beetles and crystals. 'The shape of behaviour,' he used to say. 'The shape of life.'

'The demon, then, is the impulse to use something for an alien purpose, to abandon ...'

'Mr John, sir,' a voice said.

John, turned. His driver had appeared together with a man wearing a smart grey suit. Mother had even booked a guide. John closed down the computer without sending the mail.

They had driven through a misty morning, now the sun was bright. Outside, the driver had parked in a street where mud and asphalt crumbled together around kiosks whose small and colourful products, mostly sold in foil and plastic, John couldn't figure out.

'We cannot go right to the Taj itself, Mr John,' the guide explained, 'because of spoiling from pollution. No polluting vehicle is to be allowed within a half a mile. It is a very sacred place. So we are proceeding to the parking, then you have three choices: you can go on foot, you may take a bicycle rickshaw, or, and I recommend, you may take the electric bus, which departs every fifteen minutes and is free of any charge.'

To irritate his guide, John chose to go on foot. He was feeling nauseous. At once he regretted the decision, because now, along a broad pedestrian avenue with high walls to each side, he had to deal with a pressure of hawkers such as he had never previously encountered. Everybody was selling souvenirs of the Taj, photos, ornaments, embroideries. The guide pressed on regardless. John shook his aching head. 'No, thank you, no thank you,' he muttered.

'Hello! You like elephant?'

A young man stopped him, actually blocked his path, chest to chest.

'Look, sir, green stone, hand-carved elephant! Hello! 600 rupees, sir.'

In his hand the man held an elephant perhaps five inches high, roughly carved in some glazed green stone. He was smiling brightly from stained teeth. John shook his head, but the peddler wouldn't move aside.

'Stone elephant! Only 600 rupees, sir.'

John smiled wearily.

'Bargain!' the young man insisted. 'Is very good price.' He was wearing a grey shirt, washed to tissue. They must be about the same age. John tried to walk away. The hawker protested. 'No, sir, hello, hello, you not understand. You think one stone elephant – but look, look! – inside *one* stone elephant, sir, *two* stone elephants!'

As if performing a conjuring trick, the young man slipped his hand from under the ornament to allow a smaller elephant of the same design to drop out of it. 'Not one, two stone elephants!' the man cried, feigning amazement. 'Two stone elephants, sir. Green stone. Hello. Very precious, sir. Only 500 rupees!'

'Really no,' John replied. 'Really, no thanks.'

But the young Indian had got the Englishman's eye and held it. His teeth were pink with betel, his eyes shone. The whole face was intense and mobile. 'You don't like stone elephants? 500 rupees, sir. I am giving the best price?' He laughed in disbelief. 'Look, one stone elephant' – he reinserted the smaller ornament in the larger – 'no, not one, sir, *two* stone elephants!' He pulled the smaller one out again. '400 rupees, sir,' he said.

'No, thanks. Very kind, but no.'

John tried to get away from the Indian's bright gaze. He looked towards his guide who had moved on a few paces. Dressed in European clothes, the man's accent had suggested time spent in the USA. His face was chubby, moustached, subservient, his hair neatly cut and creamed. Now he stood watching in the busy pedestrian avenue, a hint of mockery on his plump lips: this was why one shouldn't walk to the Taj.

John started to move, but the hawker wouldn't let go.

'Sir, sir, not *two* stone elephants. No!' He shook his head theatrically. 'Not *two* elephants. Sir! *Three* stone elephants! Three! 350 rupees.'

John couldn't detach himself. Something about the young man seemed to mesh with his feelings of sickness.

'You hold, you hold, please,' the peddler said, 'not buy, just look, sir, hold please!'

He thrust the larger elephant into John's hands, then from

under the smaller, he slipped a third elephant, a tiny stone creature no more than an inch high. 'Three stone elephants, sir! 300 rupees. Very good price for smiling elephant. The smiling elephant. God of happy family, sir. Domestic harmony. India. Three elephants sir. Shiva, Parvati, Ganesh. Family, sir. Sacred family. Three elephants.'

John was at a loss. The young man was looking him straight in the eye. His shirt was stained with sweat, his trousers tattered. Elephants, elephants, elephants. He seemed to be in the grip of some sort of intoxication.

'One, two, three elephants, sir. Green stone. Very precious. Only 300 rupees, sir.'

John pulled out his wallet, counted three hundred-rupee notes and handed them over. A group of Americans who had been standing a few yards away and following the pitch with interest burst into smiles and applause.

'But you keep the elephants,' John said tartly. 'Take the 300 rupees, but keep your elephants.' He tried to hand back the one that had been given to him.

The young man backed off. 'No, sir. Three elephants, your elephants, sir.' He had already thrust the money into his pocket and now wanted to push the two smaller elephants back where they belonged inside the larger. For a moment there was almost a tussle.

'I really can't carry all this weight around,' John protested. He didn't want the things. He felt dizzy. 'Take the money, it's a gift.'

'Your elephants, sir! Three elephants.'

John began to wonder how much English the boy knew. Shouldn't he be delighted to get his cash for nothing?

'Mr John!' The guide hurried back to join him. 'Mr John, please, you have paid for the elephants. You must take them. This man is not a beggar. He will be offended.'

John breathed deeply. Something in the air had exasperated

him. He hadn't wanted a trip to India, only to see his father's body one last time. He managed a tired smile and let the man push the elephants into his hands. They were heavy. 'Thank you,' he said.

'Thank you, sir, thank you.' The peddler was already backing off. 'Three elephants, sir,' he said, eyes widening in a farewell smile that must be mockery, John thought.

And now, as they approached the compound gates, the guide began to give him the rigmarole about the great love of the Sultan Shah Jahan for his wife Mumtaz Mahal, a name which means: the chosen one of the palace. 'These two were very much in love,' the guide repeated, 'even after nine years of marriage, when the beautiful Mumtaz—'

'Do you want to know my father's thoughts on love?' John asked abruptly.

'I'm sorry, sir,' the guide said. 'The beautiful Mumtaz—'

'My father,' John continued, 'believed the word "love" had a special linguistic function. It didn't denote anything real, but you introduced it into a relationship to put the other person under obligation. It was a sort of weapon, to have people accept a pattern you wanted to impose on them.'

'I beg your pardon?' the guide repeated.

They were standing in a queue now, leading to a rather modest gate in a sandstone wall. With a polite smile, the guide asked: 'And what does your mother say about this?'

'My mother?' John shook his head. 'Mum loved Dad to death.'

The guide laughed. John's head cleared a little. Meantime, the queue edged forwards. Foreigners, it seemed, must pay ten times more than locals.

'Because you have ten times the money,' the guide explained complacently.

John was still holding the elephants. 'What were those names the boy said?' he asked. 'When he talked about sacred families?'

'He is just saying very silly rubbish for tourists,' the guide protested. 'Shiva and Parvati are not elephants. Only Ganesh is the elephant, and only his head.'

'I'll give them to my girlfriend,' John told him. Not *one* elephant, not *two* elephants, sir, but *three* elephants! He could hear himself mimicking the peddler's accent for Elaine.

'You love your girlfriend very much?' the guide enquired. He was bantering now, as if John's account of the late Albert James's position on love had created a sort of complicity between them. But John answered: 'I do actually.' He was surprised to hear himself say this. He had never said it to her face.

Then he was told he must hand over his mobile to a guard. 'No telephones are allowed in the compound, because this profanes the sacred space,' the guide explained. 'It is distracting the mind. Maybe you start to phone your girlfriend, no?' He laughed. 'He will give it back, sir, don't worry.'

A few paces then and they were looking at the Taj Mahal. The famous white façade floated on a lake laid down as a mirror. There was the great central dome, the minarets to each side. Only now did John realise he had seen a thousand photos. He knew the place already and was not impressed. The guide once again felt obliged to launch into a long spiel: 'Since Moghul architecture permitted no additions after completion, the building had to be planned to perfection from the start. Hence the marvellous symmetry, you see, of the layout, the balance of—'

'What did you study in the States?' John cut in.

'I was beginning to study, but there was a problem with money, sir.'

'I'm sorry,' John said.

'You must take your time,' the guide told him. 'It is very beautiful. Stop as long as you want.'

John refused to admire the reflection of the façade in the captive water. He set off briskly toward the monument itself. It was irritating having to carry the elephants.

'I have never come with one who visits so quickly,' the guide was wailing.

'But that's better for you, isn't it?' John asked. 'You'll get home sooner.' 'Presumably, what your father wanted you to do,' Heinrich had remarked as they rode back in the rickshaw the previous evening, 'was to visit these two very different tombs one right after the other.' 'Of course! He wants you to look for some meaning in their comparison,' the perfumed Sharmistha had added. Why did I allow myself to be bullied into coming here? John wondered. Why am I always being treated as a student?

Now he had to take off his shoes at the door.

'You may tip the keeper of the shoes, but only if you want to,' his guide told him. 'It is not obligatory.'

John didn't. 'So shoes are like phones and car fumes?' he asked.

'They bring in dirt from outside, yes. This is a sacred place.'

'Logically, then, I should hold my breath,' John said. 'Start and end with breathing,' his father had written. What on earth could that mean?

Yet once inside the building John did finally stop and look. Despite the crowd, the pushing, the general profanation, the Taj was awesome in its ambition and paralysed whiteness.

'You see also the perfect symmetry of the flowers inlaid in many-coloured stones. How they are twining everywhere. This is amber. And the Arabic lettering also, you see – this is topaz – it has been specially adapted to be perfectly geometric, so it seems the words are coming from the same perfection as the flower patterns.'

For a few minutes John studied the walls and columns. He waited his turn to get close up to the inlaid letters. They meant nothing to him with their lavishly coloured dots and tails. What is language if you can't read it? All around, people milled and fretted while everything about the building itself was dazzlingly balanced and still.

'Looks like bacteria under an electronic microscope,' John told the guide with deliberate provocation. He would have liked to touch, but it wasn't permitted. Each separate pattern was fitted onto the next in unending spirals of repetition: grey flowers of bas-relief marble; red, blue and gold blossoms of semi-precious inlay. John's grandfather had been a botanist.

'And in the exact middle,' the guide was saying, 'of all these marvels, you see, this cenotaph . . .'

'With the lady's corpse.'

'No. Actually not. When it came to it, the sarcophagi of the princess, and later the sultan, were buried under the floor. For convenience. But the original idea was to be putting them in these inlaid tombs behind the jewelled screen. Here the stone latticing, you see, is of the most extreme delicacy, like the centre of a web really, an enchanting artefact that is second to none in the whole world.'

John hurried out. He would ask the driver to head straight back for Delhi. He didn't want to stay a night in Agra. He didn't want to see the fort he had been told about. He wanted to talk to Mother.

'You must see the river at least,' the guide insisted, 'and the mosque and the jawab.'

John agreed to walk behind the mausoleum for a glimpse of the river. 'A glimpse,' he insisted. 'And what's a jawab when it's at home?'

'A jawab is something you make only to be giving balance to something else,' the guide said. 'You see, the mosque is the mosque, on one side of the Taj, and the jawab is balancing the mosque on the other side, but it is not a mosque. It is not anything. But a jawab.'

John shook his head. They reached the parapet behind the mausoleum and looked down on the wide emptiness of the river valley and a serpent of water far away, meandering through sand-flats against a backdrop of low hills. The dominant colour was brown. Beside the river, miniature figures in brightly coloured saris – yellow, purple, green and gold – had scored fragile lines on the formless terrain.

'They are turning the ground to plant melons.' The guide wouldn't stop talking. 'It is very fertile there by the river. When the rains come everything grows very quickly.'

John stared at the tiny figures in their bright clothes, labouring through the afternoon. A camel picked its way across the water with a huge grey bundle on its back.

'What's it called?' he asked.

'I beg your pardon?'

'What's the river called?'

'This is the river Yamuna.'

'I really want to go now,' John said.

After he had recovered his mobile at the compound gate, he asked: 'Did the child die by the way?'

Again the guide didn't understand.

'The one whose birth caused the beloved princess's death.'

They had already boarded the electric bus. 'Gauhara Begum was the fourteenth baby of Mumtaz Mahal.' The man was pleased to have a last chance to show what he knew. 'Gauhara grew up and lived a long life. Mumtaz was the sultan's second wife,' he added, 'but his favourite.'

CHAPTER SEVEN

The drive to Delhi was three dull hours. John's mind was trapped. He couldn't follow the driver's chatter. It was long dark when he returned. His mother was sitting at her place beside the table under a sharp electric light. 'But the hotel was already paid for, love!' She seemed at once worried, yet – John couldn't understand – younger. Not wanting her to comment on the elephants, he hurried them into the bedroom. He needed a shower, he said. Now a message arrived from Elaine; she was eager to know the exact time of his return. But it was impossible to engage in the back and forth of text messages.

'Mum?' he came back into the sitting room. 'Listen . . .'

She was studying a number of papers spread across the table. 'Did you enjoy the Taj at least?' she asked, though without raising her eyes. She had put on her reading glasses.

'It was a great bore,' he said. He turned away, went into the kitchen and pulled a Coke from the fridge.

'What are you looking at?' he asked, coming back. He didn't sit.

'Old stuff,' she said.

'Tell me.' He was turning the can in his hands, licking the drops inside the rim.

'Oh, it's nothing that would interest you.'

'Yes, but what?'

She sighed, still reading. 'Just old stuff.'

John took two paces and slammed the Coke down on the tabletop beside her. 'Tell me, for Christ's fucking sake!' The drink splashed out onto the wooden surface.

'John!' Helen James was alarmed. She pushed her chair back, grabbed a pack of tissues. He retreated a step or two shaking his head.

'I'm sorry,' he said. He sat on the couch.

'John, what on earth was that about? It's just some old unpublished stuff of your father's that I wouldn't want to bore you with.' She hesitated. 'Since these trips have already bored you so much . . .'

Her son had his face in his hands. 'I feel ill,' he said.

Helen James waited. She seemed undecided whether to put her reading glasses back on. 'I hope you were careful about what you ate,' she remarked in a calmer voice.

'Of course. I've been feeling odd since I arrived.'

'In what way?'

He tried to think. 'In my head.'

'You shouldn't drink straight out of those cans,' she told him. 'You never know where they might have been stored. We've been getting more and more cases of leptospirosis since people started drinking from cans.'

Looking up now, John had the strange impression that his mother was alternately ageing and rejuvenating before his eyes, almost as a light dims, then glows. One moment she was old. There was a web of wrinkles round rheumy eyes. He must look after her. The next she was young again. Mum is so young, he thought. He shook his head. Desirable. She put on her glasses and bent over the papers again.

John waited a while, then said quietly, 'Mum, I'm not going to go and beg for money from my grandmother.'

She breathed in deeply. 'You hardly needed to rush back from Agra to bring that up again.'

'I think you should talk to her, she's your mother.'

Helen sighed. 'John, you're twenty-four. You're an adult. You're the one who lives in England and you're the one who needs the money. Plus there's the fact that my mother always liked little boys more than little girls. My brother more than myself. You more than her granddaughters.'

'But . . .'

John stopped. The anger of a moment before had drained his energy. Apropos of nothing, he thought: I must marry Elaine.

'What is this work of Dad's about then?' he asked vaguely. 'This stuff on spiders?'

'No, not that. This is something he did way back, on sex actually.'

'The Symmetry of Sex,' John laughed.

'Don't be mean, John!' Helen James smiled indulgently. 'Obviously, anybody who wants to say something definitive about communication has to talk about sex.'

'And spiders' webs.'

'John, the biggest communications system in the world is called a web. You know your father came at things from various angles.'

Again John had the impression that his mother was a young woman inside an old. She was mocking him. Or an old inside a young. One moment the skin was mottled and slack, then she smiled and it was firm and fresh. He would text Elaine the moment he was back in his room. Will you marry me? He would propose tonight.

'This paper is about the meta-communicative signals sent out by perfumes, how they mask and mimic natural pheromone signals.'

'Sounds interesting,' John said mechanically.

'What concerned Albert was when the artificially induced

meta-communicative signal, typical of contemporary Western cosmetics, sets up a relational context that runs contrary to the more direct messages in gesture or speech, causing unease or confusion in the recipient. The lady's smell invites, but her behaviour rebuffs.'

'Right.' He had finished his Coke and was licking the stickiness off the back of his hand.

'John?' she asked.

'Yes?'

'After all that determination to have me talk about it, you don't seem very interested, do you, love?'

He stared. Unlike Elaine, his mother never wore perfumes.

She said: 'Well, if it's okay with you I'll carry on reading. The fact is I've been wondering if we couldn't publish some of these old things.'

'I feel taken for a ride,' he said.

'I beg your pardon?'

He had spoken in a low voice. He smiled at her rather childishly, unable to repeat what he had said. She looked at him, puzzled, then suddenly pushed the papers aside, lifted the string of her reading glasses from her head and turned her chair towards him. 'John, there's something I really must tell you.'

She sat forward now with her hands between her knees, rocking slightly on her chair. Her tone had changed completely. 'John, there's a man wants to write a biography of your father. A journalist. An American. I talked to him about it this afternoon.'

John sat up. 'But that's wonderful!'

'Yes, isn't it?' She hesitated. 'Of course, I need to know how you feel about it.'

'Oh.' John felt dubious.

'I wondered if it might bother you, someone writing about Dad.'

He couldn't understand. 'Why would I be bothered? I might

find out something at last.' He burst out laughing. The unexpected news had returned him to himself. When his mother didn't reply, he frowned. 'I am a bit surprised, though. To be honest, I thought Dad had been rather forgotten.' He paused. 'Elaine's friends hadn't heard of him at all.'

'No doubt there are many people Elaine's friends haven't heard of,' Helen James said dryly.

'Sorry, Mum, I meant—'

'John, every week your father got at least one invitation to some conference or other. And he'll probably go on getting them for quite a while since he never wanted to publicise his illness. Only in recent years he didn't accept very often.'

'Oh. It's just you never hear of him. I mean in the papers, the science journals.'

'Your father was always on the fringes, John, you know that. And when newspapers did ask for interviews or comments he always refused. He hated newspapers. Even with the conferences, he'd say, "You go, Helen. You can give a talk far better than I can."'

'So why didn't you?'

His mother shrugged: 'Aside from the fact that people wanted to hear Albert not me, I had things to do myself, I was needed at the clinic.'

For a moment, she seemed to have forgotten what she meant to say and turned back to the papers on the table, only to find she hadn't got her glasses on, she couldn't read. John's mind too was casting about, as if a path had petered out in open country.

'You know, Mum,' he suddenly said, 'I gave *Behaviour in Patterns* to Elaine to read.' He laughed boyishly. 'I mean, one has to show off the family's intellectual credentials, right? Actually, it was the first present I gave her. Anyway, Elaine said, reading it, it was as if Dad had something tremendously important to say and then wrote the whole book to make sure no one ever found out what it was.'

Helen frowned. 'Albert's writing isn't easy for the uninitiated.'

'So I suppose if the biography explains Dad to a wider public, it wouldn't be a bad idea, would it? Maybe his books'll start selling and there'll be some money in it.'

For the first time his mother laughed with real amusement. 'Oh John, John, John!' She shook her head. 'You're incorrigible with this obsession with money! Do you remember when you used to say, "Hurry up and write something that sells, Dad, so I can live off the royalties."'

'It was just a joke,' John smiled.

Pushing her hair from her face, Helen leaned forward across the table. 'Do you know what this man said, though, John?'

'Who?'

'This writer who wants to do the biography.'

John waited, strangely happy.

'He said' – Helen hesitated – 'that he thought of Dad as a great and inspiring *individual*.'

'So? That sounds positive.'

'It's rather funny, though, don't you think, about your father of all people.'

When her son still couldn't see it, the mother said: 'Well what was the title of his first book, for God's sake?'

'Oh right!' John said.

Albert James had published *Mythical Individuals* in 1973. Having briefly caused a stir in anthropological circles, the book was widely written off as holistic nostalgia dressed up in modern jargon, only to be discovered some years later by enthusiasts in communications theory who believed James had been suggesting that complex social feedback systems took precedence over the dubious concept of individual identity.

'I mean, it hardly inspires confidence, does it,' Helen said, 'stressing Dad's *individuality*? The last thing we need is a *stupid* biography.'

'As long as he is appreciative,' John said, 'I don't see how it can harm.'

'Perhaps,' Helen James said. 'I haven't decided yet.'

He watched her. She was old again now. Her eyes were trapped under a mesh of wrinkles. In a moment she would get up and go off to bed. He felt an inexplicable urgency.

'Mum, really, I can't see how you could *not* want a biography of Dad. He was your whole life! It was a fantastic relationship you two had. A biography would keep him alive.'

'I'd rather people read *his* books,' she said curtly.

'But they won't, will they?' Without thinking, John asked, 'You're not worried about that business with the court case, are you?'

'I beg your pardon?' She smiled. 'Heavens, no! That was pure calumny.'

'Still, to the extent that it affected his career . . .'

While John was in the last year of boarding school, his father had been accused of having sex with an underage prostitute in Chicago. It was a highly improbable story.

'It certainly interrupted his work,' Helen agreed. 'In that sense a biographer would have to mention it. But the scandal was that it ever got to court at all. No, the problem as I see it is whether this man will do Dad justice at the intellectual level.'

'But you can't know that until he's written the book. At least he takes Dad seriously.'

After another pause, Helen James announced: 'You know I did go to some conferences to give papers for him.' She laughed.

'You did?'

'For a year and more. While we were in the States. It was quite a success. One in New York, in particular. Melbourne too. I just showed a few slides, said what Dad was up to, read a paragraph or two he had written. Actually, he got more responses that way than when he presented things himself. You know how he tended to digress.'

'I wish I could have seen you.'

'Yes, that would have been fun.'

'So why did you stop?'

Helen looked at her son. The boy was a burden. 'Oh I couldn't go on. I always felt I was simplifying things terribly. The way his mind worked went so much deeper than the words I used. Actually, I suppose my success was due to the fact that I was watering down his ideas. I made him more political, more topical, whereas he always steered away from any kind of practical application.'

'So? Nobody starts at the deep end.'

'Then there was the court case. He needed me around while that was on. I mean, for about six months he wouldn't answer the phone. He wouldn't go out.'

'Right,' John said. Again he had the same strange impression that his mother wasn't fixed. He wanted her to stay still.

'Then we moved out here and your father's work took a new direction again. It was quite a radical shift.'

John said nothing. There had always been this vast mystery attached to his father's work. But what had the man ever discovered or produced? Nothing.

'Of course,' Helen now added very brightly, looking at her son sprawled on the sofa, 'any biography of Dad is also bound to be a biography of the family, in a way.'

John cracked his knuckles. 'You think so?'

'Quite possibly the man will want to interview you.'

'That's okay. I'll just say it how it was. In the end I was away at school most of the time. I don't know anything.'

'Only during term.'

'Term was two thirds of the year.'

'We used to write.'

'The guy's hardly going to be interested in the sort of letters Dad wrote me. Anyway, I threw them all away.'

'And more recently?' Helen James asked.

John frowned. 'He hasn't written to me for years. He never emailed.'

'He didn't?'

'No.'

She sighed. 'I suppose it's the extent to which all these people want to look into one's private life that bothers me.'

'Which people?'

'Well, this biographer.'

Suddenly, John was irritated. 'What private life? I can't remember anything particularly private?'

'John, you're being hostile again.'

'I'm not hostile. I just don't understand. What did Dad ever do but work? Or you for that matter. You were always frantic to get hold of some medicine or other for some kid who was dying.'

Helen James backed down. 'Oh, well, I just feel a bit cautious, that's all. The man wants me to tell our friends whether they should speak to him.'

'Surely the key thing,' John said, 'is whether you let him see Dad's papers.'

'I've no problem with that,' Helen said, 'so long as I look through them first.'

'Well then. That should be enough for anyone. It'll take a lifetime just to put them in order.'

She smiled. She sat back. 'You're right,' she said. 'You're right, thank you. Sometimes it takes someone with an outside view to say the obvious.'

The boy couldn't remember his mother ever having responded to him in this way. He was delighted. 'Why didn't you tell me,' he asked softly, 'that I would be seeing the river where you plan to scatter Dad's ashes?'

'Oh,' she smiled. 'You didn't ask, did you, John? You never ask.'

As she spoke her voice cracked a little. At once he stood to embrace her, but she had let her head drop. She was digging her chin into her breast. Just one hand reached out to clasp his. 'I can't believe he's gone, John,' she muttered. 'I just can't believe it happened. I don't know what to do, or who I am, or how to live.'

Some time later, in his room, John wrote a message on his phone: 'Ellie, it'll sound crazy coming out of the blue like this, but will you marry me? I have realised I love you. Really. Please, marry me. Let's do it and be happy.'

The little screen glowed. He reread the message carefully. Were they the right words? He couldn't decide whether to send it or not.

Agitated, John paced back and forth round the small bedroom. When he stopped, he could hear his mother too was moving in her room, the room Dad died in. Why wasn't I invited to come before the end? You didn't ask, John, she would say. Should he ask Elaine? It was hard to think of words that weren't trite and hackneyed.

John pulled a book from off the wall. All his childhood, the rooms had been lined with the books Dad wrote, the books he read. This one was by a man called Aby Warburg: *The Ritual of the Serpent*. John glanced through the pages. There were black and white photos of primitive folk in skins and feathers, then reproductions of childish drawings where lightning over mountains was sketched as if snakes were flickering down from low cloud. In thick, wavy pencil, pressing hard, his father had underlined the sentence: 'Where human grief in its amazement seeks redemption, there we draw near to the image of the serpent.'

The boy lay on his bed and couldn't sleep. His hands wouldn't rest. He forced his mind back to London, to the lab. The work they were involved in was a question of deactivating the RNA of a dormant tuberculosis bacterium, of tricking the ribosomes into some unnatural behaviour so that the disease could never reproduce again. Should he send the message to Elaine or not? His mother continued to pace about the other room. John remembered how strange she had seemed this evening, alternately fading and glowing.

Send it! He grabbed the phone and pressed the appropriate buttons. As he watched, the little envelope flew away across the illuminated screen. Done it! He felt enormously pleased with himself. Yes! He got out of bed and was on his way to tell his mother, Mum, I've proposed! But he stopped. You should wait for Elaine's reply. Mother had always mocked when his girlfriends left him, as if he was bound to be a failure with women. What time was it in England? Early evening. He went back to bed. The phone would vibrate on the wood of the bedside table. It would be loud enough to wake him. The three elephants were there too, one inside the other. They would rattle. He had made his move.

John lay in the dark, waiting. Dad had started out as a biologist. What was it that led him astray? His degree was excellent, his PhD likewise. He had done some good work on amoebas. Apparently. 'The most challenging question we face when we seek to explain the origin of life' – Professor Wilson's lectures came to mind – 'is not the question of whether some casual collision of electricity and chemical substance could have *generated* living cells. We know it could. The real mystery is the moment the RNA begins to replicate and the casually made thing *reproduces itself*. Who knows how many millions of primitive cells lived and died before one began to extend life through time in the form of species, the pattern of generations? Perhaps it is here that we might find a set of targets to attack the cells we wish to destroy, to tell each cell it is only one, one life is enough. Then we can let the individual live as long as it likes. The pattern is broken and no harm can be done.'

John never had trouble sleeping. Not normally. He admired Professor Wilson, though the distance between concept and experiment was vast. It was strange that Elaine hadn't replied at once, he thought, to such a momentous message. She always had her phone handy. The first response will be some jokey de-dramatisation, he decided. But there was no doubt Elaine was the right woman.

John turned on the bedside light and found *The Ritual of the Serpent*. 'Written in mental hospital,' the preface began, 'as a form of penitence . . .' John shook his head. In the margin his father had written: '*Ecstasy of defeat and the final bow!*' It was weird how his father wrote things that had nothing to do with the pages he was reading. Beneath one of the drawings of snakes were the words: '*No chemistry, no knowledge*.' The phone buzzed so loudly, John started.

'So sweet of you, Jo, but maybe not a great idea right now. All kinds of things happening! Big party. See you tomorrow, Handsome. Good flight. Kisses. E.'

Some time in the night John got out of his bed, picked up the three elephants, crossed the sitting room, opened the door to his mother's room, stood at her bedside. The rhythm of her breathing rose with a slight snore. The stone object was heavy as he raised his hand. The two internal elements shifted slightly inside the larger.

'Albert,' his mother muttered. She seemed to have sensed a presence. 'Oh Albert!'

Helen sat up abruptly. John turned, rushed back into the sitting room and crashed the elephants down on the wooden table top.

PART TWO

DREAMS OF RIVERS AND SEAS

CHAPTER EIGHT

Everyone imagined that to sprinkle his ashes in the Yamuna she was going to Allahabad, or even the Yamunotri temple. Or at least to Agra, to the broad sands below the Taj. They didn't know Albert. 'The Yamuna *in Delhi*,' he had said. Her poor son hadn't even realised the Yamuna flowed through Delhi. 'Right in town,' he insisted, 'with the rest of the rubbish. Or from the Wazi Bridge if you like. Not the ghats, please. And not where the washerwomen work.' He wouldn't like, he laughed, to turn up as a speck on some office wallah's starched shirt.

'Your ashes will be the cleanest thing in the river,' Helen had told him. 'The place is a sewer.'

'So be it,' he smiled.

It seemed strange to her now that there had been those conversations. Thirty years together had ended. 'If only it could be done *beautifully*,' he had said. She had told him a hundred times he was mad, he must fight. But Albert had been determined. 'Before it's too late,' he said. He must have said it a dozen times: 'Before it is too late.'

Now for two weeks Helen had kept the ashes in the apartment, she had put off the trip to the river. Her husband's remains had been given to her in a small plastic box, not unlike the boxes, she remembered, that people bought ice cream in at American diners. And it turned out the administrative people at the crematorium had known Albert well. He used to go and observe the mourners at cremations, the same way he went to weddings, or to the stock exchange, the various temples, cricket matches, the zoos and game parks. He had asked for permission to make videos. It would have been for the new edition of *Postures*. Nobody understood the messages people communicated like Albert, and the thousand ways every message can be misunderstood. 'In every movement and gesture, there is always something beyond the necessary,' he said, 'its aesthetic aura.'

'Was it a hard death, madam?' the lady at the crematorium had enquired kindly. There was a long form to fill in. Helen had asked for a pen. 'My husband used to say death was only hard for the living,' she replied.

For two weeks she kept the ashes on the table. The small plastic box exactly covered the spot where John had smashed the ugly ornament he had bought. Why had he done that? It did not bother her that the table was damaged, but her son's behaviour had been frightening. For half the night the boy sat on the sofa shaking and repeating over and over that he felt ill, when clearly he wasn't; John didn't know what illness was. She had been so relieved when he was gone.

Now Helen James took advantage of people's assumptions and announced that she would be away from the clinic for two days to accomplish a ceremony that in fact would require no more than a few moments. When had she last taken two days off? All her life she and Albert had lived in countries that attached the utmost importance to sacrament and ceremony. They had gone to the Third World to alleviate poverty and Albert had ended up studying people's ceremonies and accepting poverty. She felt he did accept it. There was always a continuum, he claimed in the preface to *Postures*, between how a society prayed, how it made love, how it killed; but Helen and Albert had had no ceremonies of their own. They didn't pray and they would never have dreamed of killing.

Then after his withdrawal from medical work, each had kept going in his or her different way. Helen would always be animated by suffering or injustice, always saw herself most clearly when reflected in the eyes of a feverish child or infuriated by some ritual mutilation, some pointless taboo that left a man dying by the side of the road. Then she was a rebellious daughter again, fighting selfish parents, her callous, opportunist brother. But Albert had imagined a world where everything was balanced in some magically self-correcting system of individual impulse and collective feedback. 'The catastrophes we experience in our lifetimes constitute only a fraction of the rhythmical pulse of the universe,' he wrote. On his bad days, though, he feared the world might end at any moment; humanity was destroying itself and he, Albert James, had done nothing to prevent it.

She placed the box with the ashes in a plastic bag and was pulling a shawl over her shoulders when the maid's daughter and teenage granddaughter arrived to take away the laundry. The older women chattered in Hindi, folding sheets with rapid, identical gestures. They wore bright saris and shared an obvious togetherness. But the girl sat quietly at the sitting-room table, her big eyes glancing around the room with troubled curiosity.

'Your son was not staying very long, Mrs James?' the girl said politely. She was small, darker skinned than her mother, her thick hair yanked back from high cheeks, a bright bindi on her forehead. As she spoke, the girl noticed the deep dent on the tabletop and reached across to touch the splintered wood with her fingertips.

'Yes, it's a shame you couldn't meet him,' Helen said. 'He had to go back for his work.'

The girl turned away and her mother came hurrying across the room with the small bundle of washing. There would be less now Albert was gone. 'Vimala is being so lucky,' she said. 'We have happy news to tell you Mrs James!'

A cloud of irritation passed over the girl's face.

'She is going to be married!' the laundry woman announced. 'Oh it is such a happy thing,' said the grandmother, following and clapping her hands. 'It is a good family. He is a good boy, and the family is also good. They are known to us – and from the same community. Also in the laundry business.'

The girl forced a smile, but a few moments later she turned abruptly from the door and looked straight into the Englishwoman's eyes. 'I am sorry about Mr Albert,' she said.

Before Helen could take in the intensity of the gaze, mother and daughter had gone, their sandalled footsteps slapping on the cement stairs. The grandmother was already turning back to the kitchen, humming some Hindi song.

'Is Vimala pleased with her man?' Helen asked.

'Why not?' grinned Lochana. 'Nothing is more beautiful for a girl than marriage.'

'Albert,' Helen muttered as she stepped out into the street. 'This is our last walk. Let's enjoy it.'

The sensible thing to do would have been to find a taxi. Nobody walks in Delhi. Instead, Helen set off, the bag swinging in her hand. It was a quiet day, and the air was warming. The cold season was over. She met Hoshir Singh Road, then crossed to Lodhi Road. Autorickshaws slowed beside her, but she shook her head. Vimala had gone to St Anne's, she remembered now, where Albert taught. Instead of paying Lochana, they had helped with the girl's fees. 'It was illogical of you to teach,' she muttered, 'irrational to help with a girl's education if you didn't believe in intervention.' She remembered the schoolgirl who had cried at the crematorium, a girl who had listened no doubt to Albert's strange lessons, the way he would hold up a dead starfish – 'If you had never seen one of these, children, how would you know *anyway* that it was once a living creature?' 'There are things you know that you don't know you know.' Albert loved to say that. People loved to hear him say it. He also said it would be far better if one could avoid growing up altogether.

Helen turned left before Humayun's Tomb. She had already been walking half an hour and more. 'I want to dissolve into the dirt,' he had told her. There were the inevitable tourist buses. He said he had begun to feel he was already part of Delhi's muddy red earth, the heavy sediment in the Yamuna. 'You don't invent ceremonies,' he insisted. 'They have to come naturally.'

'And it did,' she whispered now; 'it did, Albert, in the end.'

He didn't answer. She pictured him walking beside her, his tall, slightly shambling walk. She heard his footsteps.

'We made mistakes with John,' she muttered.

She didn't raise her eyes to India Gate. A boy was raking the sand by the pavement. If there was one part of Delhi Helen disliked more than others it was the Delhi of the Raj. Cooking smells from a string of kiosks on Mathura Road could not turn her head. You need to eat to work properly, she told herself severely. She would have liked to hear Albert tell her this. 'You need to eat, Helen!' But he was clattering against her knee.

Helen began to think about the biography. She was approaching the Mahatma Gandhi monument and half the morning was gone. Why did people travel so far to see what were no more than a few stone slabs when the man was best recalled by reading his work? It was curious, she remembered, that this American had written a biography of Gandhi. Albert had thought him a monster of manipulation.

She walked as far as the parapet and looked out across the river. She had planned a cheerful and orderly recall of their life together: do you remember when we met; the argument at

Timothy's dinner party; when we arrived in Kankanamun and the boat sank by the landing stage? But the mental effort seemed too great. She had never guessed it might be so hard to fill the world without him.

The meagre winter water of the Yamuna was some way off, sluggish and brown between mudbanks thick with litter. Two or three scavengers worked their way along, turning over anything promising.

'Where do you want me to sprinkle you, then?' she asked.

She started to head north, another half mile, beyond the ghats toward the Red Fort. She had to leave the river here. The city was enormous, the traffic exhausting. She stood aside to let a procession pass. She didn't recognise the images they were carrying. The dance steps and drumming were always the same: the clatter and motley. She saw these manifestations as a tiresome hangover from the past; she hated the pujas and Diwalis her colleagues invited her to. Albert loved them. He loved to be the non-participating guest. Helen stopped and took a deep breath.

There were the usual crowds around the fort: the hawkers, would-be guides and milling Americans. The hawkers knew at once that she was not there to buy. Only the rickshaw wallahs bothered her; they could see she was tired. How could her son have bought a stone elephant of all things? 'When he came into the bedroom, I thought it was you, Albert,' she said out loud.

She followed the road through a throng of cart wallahs and makeshift dwellings down to the river and then along to the old iron bridge. The press of trucks and ricks and taxis was frenetic. As she set out on the pedestrian walkway a train rumbled overhead. The structure shook. Looking up through the ironwork, she saw men and boys hanging out of open doors. Then a legless creature with a bright red cloth on his head was propelling himself toward her on a trolley. She turned back. She would not give to beggars.

Helen walked on. It was infuriating how hard it was to get

down to the river's edge. You were constantly forced back to the big road. I just need a quiet place, she thought, somewhere private. We were always private as a couple. A half mile on, she hesitated by the entrance to the Hindu cremation area. She had been here when patients she'd got to know had died. She had seen the pyres and the smoke and the mucky ordinariness of the body's destruction. 'I won't mix your ashes with theirs,' she whispered.

A little later she entered the compound of a small Sikh temple and beyond the parked cars found the river. A boy was bathing. Three or four women stood in the water scrubbing at clothes. Behind her, a haze of pollution hung over the city. My life is over, she thought. She had enjoyed wearing a veil at the funeral. Perhaps I could only really work when Albert was there to tell me it wasn't the right thing. 'It's the only thing I'm capable of,' she would answer. 'Do it,' he had whispered. 'Please, Helen, do it now, this evening!' She turned back to the road. This wasn't the place.

Just before the Wazi Bridge she found a path winding among mounds of earth and grasses and leaning trees. Here and there men squatted under tarpaulins; the women carried baskets and sacks. In a small clearing, a makeshift shrine had a cluttered tinsel look of reds and blues and bits of sugar and cake in gaudy offering to some god or other.

The river was a hundred yards away when she came across a small monument, a single flat sandstone slab, in memory, the inscription said, of a group of schoolchildren who had died in a bus accident. Helen vaguely remembered having read in the papers about the monument being broken and defaced. She stopped. Someone had shat on it. The grass round about was white and dry, waiting for rain. 'Twenty-eight schoolchildren,' she read in Hindi. Their bus had plunged through the railings on the bridge. Eight years ago.

She turned. The Wazirabad Bridge carried the inner circular

road across the Yamuna. It was booming with traffic. She sat on the broken memorial stone. Somewhere a drum was beating. The article, she remembered, in the *Times of India*, had deplored the fact that because the monument was so badly defiled the parents had been obliged to perform their annual *havan* by the water's edge under the bridge.

Helen shook her head: this madness of communicating with the dead, she thought, of keeping anniversaries. This madness of believing in souls and lighting little lights and burning incense and offering plates of fruit whilst walking waist-deep in filthy rivers supposedly holy. All at once the widow was angry with herself. 'You can't talk to Albert now,' she muttered. 'The dead are dead,' she said out loud. 'He's gone. Everything you are doing is false and stupid.'

In an action she had not imagined, she reached inside the plastic bag, pulled out the box and tugged at the lid.

It wouldn't open. She tried again, pushing her fingernails under. How silly. She prised at it. It wouldn't come. Is it vacuum-sealed? How bizarre. And she was reminded of *Three Men in a Boat* and the can of pineapples. 'Albert!' she cried. Perhaps it was peaches. Albert had loved *Three Men in a Boat*. Or apricots. He had loved *Alice in Wonderland* too. 'Albert, help me get you out!' There was a way in which her husband had always been very English.

Now she laughed rather wildly. Here I am talking to him again! A nail bent painfully. Perhaps I should just leave the box on the monument with the schoolchildren. He always said his greatest pleasure was teaching children, even if he never wanted a child. 'Children are beautifully unfinished,' he said, 'they are beautiful propositions.' But if she didn't actually scatter the ashes, someone might take possession of them. Someone could carry Albert away.

She studied the box. How had they sealed it? It was simple white plastic, a lid sunk into a tight rim. Again she placed it on the monument, half overgrown with grass and dead lichens. There was definitely a human turd. Albert would say that respect and vandalism called to each other, the monument and the turd were part of the same pattern. Then she put a foot on the box and shifted her weight onto it. It didn't give. Carefully, Helen lifted herself until she was actually standing on it, on Albert. Nothing. Why had they made it so strong? She bounced a little. The box gave a sharp crack. Stumbling, she had to put down a hand not to fall. The plastic had split open and there he was: grey grit.

Helen walked away. She felt extremely agitated. What am I doing here? For a moment she stood by the riverbank, looking up at the busy bridge from which the school bus had fallen. The water slid by. Then she came back and circled the monument in the deep dead grass, looking at the box. She walked round it two or three times. The air was windless so that the gritty ash had spilled a little and lay still on the stone slab. Helen crouched and looked. She lifted the box with both hands and shook it violently over the slab. Her husband's ash drifted into her face. She licked her lips. The taste was sour.

'Teach the children, Albert,' she muttered.

She took a taxi back. Even so it took forty minutes. Why had she disobeyed his orders? He had become fascinated by water. He had understood something, he said, about the relation of water to the question of patterning. He wanted to be washed away. The completion of a pattern is its dissolution, he said. He was glad the Yamuna was a dirty river. That was where he wanted to go. Then it occurred to her she no longer had the plastic bag or the broken box. She couldn't remember checking if it was properly empty. I've added to Delhi's litter, she thought. Some little boy gathering waste to sell would pick it up.

As soon as she was home Helen went to the phone and called the Ashoka.

'I'm afraid Mr Roberts is not answering, madam.'

'But is he in his room?'

'I'm afraid, I cannot know that, madam. Would you like me to leave a message?'

'No,' Helen said. 'Or yes. Yes. Please.' She hesitated. 'The message is from Helen James. Yes, J-a-m-e-s.' She waited while the man wrote. 'The message is: I will not give you my permission.'

'Not give,' the receptionist repeated.

'*Not* give my permission.'

CHAPTER NINE

'Dear John . . .'

He had found the letter on his return. Elaine had picked him up at Heathrow but she was in a hurry, she had a script-reading meeting. 'Come up for a kiss,' he insisted. He took her arm. It was late afternoon. We can make love, he thought. He could smell her perfume. His flatmates would be at work. On the table by his bed the airmail envelope with its Indian stamps distracted him. He tore it open.

'Dear John, for some time now . . .'

'No, I should run.' Elaine was saying. There were sheets of handwritten paper. 'It's Dad,' he said. He sat on the bed. The whole ride from Heathrow they had seemed further apart in the front seats of the car than sending messages at six thousand miles. 'It was so sweet of you to say that about us marrying,' she had twisted her elfish mouth and laughed. Perfume always excited him. Now she asked: 'Your father? How weird!'

'Dear John, for some time now I have been plagued, perhaps blessed, by dreams of rivers and seas, dreams of water.'

John shook his head. What was this about?

The girl stood over him in her tight white blouse, head cocked, a lopsided expression of enquiry on her face. 'What does he say?'

she asked. 'When did he send it? I should really rush,' she repeated. She had changed her hair; ringlets held up in a pink band. She seemed more confident, mischievous.

John checked quickly through the pages. There were eight, closely written on both sides. He had wanted to grab her, to overcome the awkwardness of the car journey by forcing their bodies together in pleasure. He wanted to return to his solid life. Father's letter confused him. It shouldn't be here, but he couldn't ignore it. 'Let's meet later,' she said. She was already at the door. 'I've got to go.'

'*Dear John, for some time now I have been plagued, perhaps blessed, by dreams of rivers and seas, dreams of water. There can be little doubt, even if I only recall three or four of these dreams, that they form, as it were, a sequence. If, for example, one came across them as a number of unrelated cinema scenarios one would nevertheless be obliged to notice that each has, as it were, a familiarity with the other, as people of the same race . . .*'

John threw the papers down. He stood up and walked through to the kitchen. Why on earth, on his deathbed, had his father chosen to write him this stuff? And in that weird lecturing tone he had. John put on the kettle and called the lab. It was 6 p.m.

'More news than you'd want really,' Martin said wryly. He was a graduate on work experience. 'Some Australian university has published something right up our street.'

John had meant to discuss how the project's various experiments were progressing. There was a protein they were trying to produce synthetically, genes they were seeking to isolate. Instead he had to hear that a team at the University of Adelaide had found an enzyme that tricked the tubercular bacterium's ribosome into making false copies of itself.

'Is Simon still there?' he asked.

The others were in a meeting at Glaxo, Martin said.

John put the phone down. The guy who actually rented this flat was a small-time sports journalist, Peter. The place was full of posters of sports stars and pretty models: girls complacent and alluring, young men gritting their teeth in action. Mug of tea in hand, John shuffled back to the bedroom and picked up his father's letter again. There was something from the bank too.

'*The first dream*,' he read, '*or rather the first I have managed to recall, since it was only when I became aware of what I have called a sequence in these dreams that I decided to go back and look for some controlling logic that . . .*'

Am I really going to read this guff? John wondered. He felt anxious. Perhaps he could phone Glaxo directly. His father's handwriting was dramatically but very regularly slanted, as if vigorous thrusts had been determinedly channelled and contained.

'*. . . begins at the seaside. A wide open beach. Perhaps it is Cromer. Perhaps it is Indonesia, or Goa. I am on holiday with some kind of group, a dozen people who are standing shivering on the water's edge. I am alone behind them. I decide to show off; I will run past them and plunge into the sea. I change out of my clothes and start to run. As I reach the others, I realise I haven't put my trunks on. I am completely naked. I race even faster toward the sea, only to find there is no water. The sand stretches away. Without my trunks, I can't turn back. I come to a small railing, as when workmen fence off a hole in the road. And there is a hole in the sand, full of black, brackish water. I tumble over the railing and into the hole.*'

John drank his tea. Father had always chosen to communicate in code. It was his charm and his downfall. If anyone else had written this, John would have chucked it in the bin without a second thought.

'*The second dream is full of mud rather than sand. I am walking . . .*'

He broke off to read the letter from Barclays. 'Your current overdraft is £1,487 . . .' An interview was required. Why hadn't his father written something practical about money? Had there really been no life insurance? Or about the past, about their being father and son? Who cared about his dreams?

'*I am walking with your mother in the heart of the old town by the river. I say the old town without knowing which. It could be Cambridge, it could be Delhi, or even Angoram. We are disturbed to find there is no water in the river, only mud. I spy a handsome young person sitting on the parapet and he, or perhaps she, tells me he/she is going away to the sea at the weekend. Things are too bad in town now the river has run dry. Turning aside, I see an old newspaper buried in the mud. I dig it out and see the date: 7 August 1945.*'

John drained his tea. Was 7 August a significant date? Dad had been born in 1945, but in January. John flicked through the pages to see if there might be anything more interesting. The regular slant of the very long tops and tails of the handwritten letters created a mesmeric effect, perhaps because they met the shadow writing on the other side of the page in so many right angles. It looked like a grid, or net, or as if one side of the page were cancelling the other out.

'*I hardly need to discuss with you, John*' – he found his name at last, just over halfway through – '*the possible interpretation of these dreams. Whenever patterns emerge in the material we are studying, there is always the temptation to read them as "standing for" this or that, discarding, as it were, the metaphorical aura for the cognitive husk. However . . .*'

'What a pretentious jerk! Dad! You're dying, for fuck's sake. Say something real!'

'*The third dream . . .*'

'Dreams are ridiculous!' John shouted out loud.

He stood up and kicked his suitcase. Father had gone off his head. How did Mum put up with him? Some metastasis in the brain, perhaps. It would have been like Dad to have left going to the doctor until it was far too late; or to have gone to some local healer. He loved that stuff. Probably to drive Mum crazy, to refuse her brand of medicine. Dad never took medicine. But now John remembered his own dream of the odd shoes they had sold him at the airport shop. He frowned. Why had it made such an impression?

'The third dream and the last I shall bother you with is not as sharp as the others. Once again I was with a group of people on holiday, but in particular with a younger person, an indistinct figure, friendly and subordinate, a graceful shadow by my side. We left the others to pitch a tent on a sandy cliff directly above the sea. It was a beautiful place but before we had finished the tide had saturated the sand and the tent was collapsing. We tried to move it, but had to give up. Then we went down to the sea, myself and this younger companion. The breakers were majestic and inviting, but we did not dive in.'

It was six-thirty. Outside, in Maida Vale, the winter night had fallen so that the black pane of the window gave back John's reflection. He glanced at his ghostly image and immediately looked away. I should unpack, he decided. There was a lot to do tomorrow. Skipping ahead, he found:

'However, the question I wanted to raise with you in this long and no doubt unexpected letter . . .'

Suddenly curious – for there had been no mention of illness, let alone of imminent death – John picked up the first page again. Was there a date? No, it just began, Dear John. Where did I put the envelope? In his haste he had thrown it aside. It was on the floor with dusty slippers and a tangle of computer cables. The postmark was easily legible. January 18th. He thought back. That was the day after his death. But now John realised the address was not written in his father's hand. It was printed rather childishly. Vale was spelt Veil. Maida Veil.

'. . . unexpected letter is that in our dealings with the world and each other it will be necessary to consider the whole system, everything, and above all to avoid becoming locked into the general process of polarisation at work in society, a process itself subordinated . . .'

John did not even try to make head nor tail of this. His eye slid down a couple of paragraphs.

'In New Guinea it is believed that character traits in families skip a generation: father and son have opposed traits, while grandfather and grandson are alike. Certainly you have more in common with your grandfather than I do. Like you (and your mother for that matter), he was very practical. And I and my brother were similar in differing from our father, yet opposed in the ways we differed. My brother's death, as you know, came very much out of an ugly triangle of incomprehension between himself, the girl he wanted to marry and your grandfather, a triangle in which each followed his own bias to the extreme.

'*What I would like to suggest about these dreams, then . . .*'

The phone rang. John was at once relieved and disappointed. In his weird way, perhaps Dad was at last getting close to saying something. There was one more page to go.

'Good evening, Mr Southwood, this is Neville Ingrams from Open Technologies, a software house specialising in databank management. As you may know—'

'I'm afraid Mr Southwood is out at the moment,' John said, 'I can't . . .' Then he asked, 'Elaine?'

'I beg your pardon? My name is Neville Ingrams.' There was a brief pause. 'I was hoping we might be able to interest you in a package of programs aimed at increasing . . .'

But Elaine burst out laughing. 'I did get you for a moment, though! I did!'

'God, for a moment, yes. I really thought it was a man.'

Her voice changed. 'Anyway, I'm just calling to say I can't make it later.'

'Oh.'

'There's a sort of cast get-together, you know, after the script reading. I'd better socialise.'

'What about later later?'

'It'll go on pretty late, I think. You should sleep. What was in the letter?'

'I don't care how late,' John said. 'Just come over when you're finished.'

'I'll see.' She seemed to hesitate: 'The package we are proposing, Mr Southwood, would allow you to coordinate all your manifold activities, business, social and family, in real time, introducing an intelligent and autonomous organising—'

'I have a present for you,' he interrupted.

'Mmm, in that case! What?'

'Come over and find out. Or better still pick me up and take me to your place. Or I'll walk over there.'

Putting the phone down, John again returned to the letter and found he was reading the last lines:

'. . . *about balance between basic elements, water and earth, or creation and dissolution, while the emotional tone is established by this shadow companion (is the young person setting off for the sea in the second dream the same as the companion in the third? And are both of those figures stand-ins perhaps for you, John, or my brother, or anyway some figure I desperately need to complement my nature, as he/she perhaps* . . .'

The letter ended in mid sentence, in mid parenthesis.

John stared. *Desperately*. The word was unexpected. *Desperately* was definitely not Dad. He went back and forth through the pages to see if he had misplaced one. No. They were in order. Anyway, this sentence broke off halfway down the page: some figure I desperately need. Dad hadn't finished the letter. So why had he sent it? Or maybe he had decided not to finish it and not to send it. Writing *desperately* had stopped him. Or remembering his brother, which made him think of his own death. But then who *had* mailed the thing? Not Mother.

John studied the envelope again. Perhaps it was a practical joke. In the years when Albert James still wrote to his son, at school, he would occasionally claim that he and Helen had discovered some bizarre, as yet unclassified animal, with seven legs perhaps, or two heads, or that they had 'collected' some curious ceremony that involved the chief men of this or that tribe dancing on stilts. He would make elaborate drawings. He would offer long analyses of the evolutionary history of the beast he had invented. 'I like to see if you know when I'm playing, John,' he would say if his son was disappointed.

Surely, John thought, staring at the last sentence of the letter – surely you don't *play* when you're dying. Elaine, for example, would hardly make a funny phone call like that, if she thought she was fatally ill.

Peter, the sports journalist, came home, then Jean-Pierre, John's French room-mate. There was small talk. Peter's young girlfriend was there with a bottle of vodka. She was Romanian. As usual they were arguing. Petra liked to flirt. She was pretty. Jean-Pierre played along and poured drinks. He was a big boy with a compulsive laugh. In the absence of mixers they stuck the electric whisk in a can of peeled tomatoes. John was glad he had an English girlfriend you could feel at home with. There were no barriers of language and culture. And she wasn't a flirt either.

'Did you 'ave any faan in India,' Petra asked, 'Mr 'andsome? Did you 'ave any nice dark spicy Indian girls?' She tried a belly-dancer's wriggle.

'The poor guy was going to his dad's funeral,' Peter protested.

Leaving the others in the kitchen, John went to unpack. The elephants were in a plastic bag with dirty socks and underwear. He put them on the bedside table. The largest had lost part of its trunk. The smallest now looked very crudely carved. Why did I buy them? he wondered. 'Three elephants, sir, not one.' John sat and studied the things. He could hardly give them as a gift until he had glued the trunk back on. How did it break? Elaine would ask.

'Phone for you Johnny!' Jean-Pierre called.

He hadn't heard. They brought him the cordless.

'How did it go?' Simon, the research team leader, was respectful. 'Your mother surviving?' Then the man explained that, yes, Glaxo seemed to be going a little cold. They were asking for concrete results before the funding renewal. It wasn't so much what the Australians had published as some forthcoming rationalisation of departments in different countries. 'We should get together tomorrow to see what we can offer in the way of work in progress.'

It was ten o'clock. Without putting his coat on, John walked out of the flat. 'I'll be at your place,' he texted Elaine.

A January wind had begun to nag. It was a long haul up the Edgware Road and into West Hampstead. The clothes he was wearing were too light. Suddenly, he saw his father, balding and lanky, shambling naked across empty sands. There came a sharp feeling of sadness, even shame. *My brother's death came out of an ugly triangle of incomprehension.* Why had Dad brought up that ancient story? John's grandfather had been famous for his work in genetics. John had never read the book he'd written. Was Dad trying to tell me something about my career: that while he needed Grandfather's qualities as a corrective, I needed his? *As he/she perhaps . . . needs me.* That was how he had meant to go on. Like a hole in the head! Then John realised his father must have broken off the letter precisely because he was unable to write that, unable to write the words *needs me.* The tears rose to his eyes. *Some figure I desperately need. A graceful shadow.* Why couldn't the man speak openly?

'I'll be very late,' Elaine's message came back. 'Stay home.'

John walked on. He rang one of four bells. A girl called Frances let him in and there was Elaine's other flatmate, Nancy, watching a debate on population migrations. The two girls argued with the television, legs tucked under them on the sofa. They were bulky, hostile presences. 'I'll wait for Elaine in her room,' he said.

All round her bed there were posters of actors and actresses. John didn't know their names, but it was obvious that they were dressed up to act. They were not the kind of people you could really mix with or talk to. 'Elaine is the one,' he muttered.

He took off his shoes and lay on the bed. The pillow had her smell. He buried his face in it. Vaguely he was aware of Frances and Nancy talking in low voices in their bedroom. His mind began to wander. Then, in the complete dark, he was suddenly on his feet and lurching to his mother's room, the heavy stone elephants in his hand. 'Albert!'

John sat up, disoriented.

A diesel was ticking over in the street. Feeling fragile and slightly sick, he went to the window. Elaine was standing by a car in yellow street light, her skirt blowing against her legs. She leaned into the car, laughed. He loved the way she was very conscious of herself, yet seemingly natural too. He loved the way she needed his encouragement, she needed him to tell her she was beautiful.

'I waited,' he said from the darkness.

'John!' The girl started and snapped on the light. 'Shit, you frightened me, I told you not to!'

'Just dying to see you,' he said. 'I did send a message.'

'I had my phone off,' she said sharply.

She seemed to spend an unnecessarily long time in the bathroom. John almost fell asleep again. Finally, she came to the side of the bed, but then turned away. 'Look at this. There's a bit of the play that goes into mime. There's a big explosion, then I have to move in a sort of trance. Only I can't get it right.'

She took off her skirt, and began to step around the small room in just her pants and tee-shirt. Her arms flowed from side to side, brushing the bookshelves. Her face was bright with concentration.

'You're beautiful,' he told her.

'Sshhh! I'm in the aftermath of this terrible explosion.'

She was looking for something, in the distance now, up in the air, down beneath her feet. She stretched, she crouched. She was very still, then very fluid. John ached. It was almost 2 a.m.

'You know my uncle wrote a play,' he said. 'Seems when no one wanted to put it on, he killed himself.'

'I beg your pardon?' Elaine stopped.

John laughed nervously. 'They wouldn't put his play on, my uncle's, and there was some bust-up with his girlfriend and my grandfather. He killed himself.'

'But John! God! When?'

'It was before I was born.'

'Oh, so why are you telling me now?'

'Ellie. I really want to marry you,' he said. 'I'm crazy about you.'

The girl frowned. 'You can't just say these mad things.'

'Why not? It's what I feel.'

'I've just got this part, John,' she said softly. 'I need to concentrate. There's a scene where everyone is blown up. I lose my child.'

'Well concentrate! I'll support you every way I can.'

'Jo, we're twenty-three!'

'Twenty-four,' he said. He propped himself on his elbow. 'We're adults, aren't we? It will help with our work, not hinder. We'll be a team.'

She stood by the bed lifting herself up and down on her toes. 'You didn't tell me what you thought about the mime. When I move fast like that I'm supposed to be being blown about. But also revisiting my past. Look.'

She repeated the movement, spinning round the room. Then one hand struck the wardrobe.

'Ow!' She examined her knuckles. 'Hanyaki says I'm too obvious. I look like an actor miming.'

'He's Japanese? The director?'

'Didn't I tell you?' She laughed. 'John relax, you're so wired up. If we stay together a year or two then maybe we could talk about getting serious. Who knows?'

'So let's live together.'

She gave him a puzzled smile and sat in the chair by her desk swivelling this way and that.

'Was he the guy who drove you home?' John asked. 'I thought you'd gone in your car.'

'It's on the way for him.' She smiled. 'And my present?'

'When I unpacked I found it was broken.'

'So you didn't bring it? Oh John! All promises and then nothing!'

Raising her nose in the air, Elaine swivelled the chair away from him in mock disappointment. John jumped from the bed and grabbed her. His hands went round to cover her breasts. His face pressed hard in her hair. The chair turned as he tried to pull her off it. She struggled.

'Hey!'

His hands gripped very hard. The smell had woken something animal. 'Come on Ellie.' He began to force her.

'John! Shit.'

'Come on!'

He had her standing and was tugging at her shirt. It tore.

'Stop it!' Her elbow caught his neck. 'Don't!'

'Ellie?' a girl's voice called. There were footsteps on the landing.

CHAPTER TEN

It was reading *Wau* that had enabled Paul Roberts to divorce. 'Your book was a catalyst for change and liberation in my life,' he had written in his initial letter to Albert James. 'I would like to pass on your therapeutic vision to a wider public.'

'Liberation from what into what?' James had replied.

In the luxury surroundings of the Ashoka, Paul Roberts scrolled up his notes on the screen of his laptop.

Albert (after Einstein) William (after Blake) James.

Born into one of England's foremost scientific families.

Brought up atheist. Rather: science a religion. Father involved in the field of genetics. Aggressive polemicist. Also highly cultured. Visits to plays, opera. Owned original paintings by major artists (Munch, Braque). In postscript to *Wau*, James quotes father as saying art a higher form of achievement unavailable to scientific James family.

Elder sister Amelia killed by drunk driver while celebrating double first in botany and chemistry.

James fourteen.

Elder brother, John, refuses to study sciences, drinks, gambles, womanises. Falls in love with Irish beauty, Bridget MacDowell, who lives with him three months before running off, apparently with older man.

Fierce quarrels with father about money. Writes poems, novels, plays. Without success. Father cuts off allowance. John cuts wrists in the bathroom of the National Theatre.

James seventeen.

Parental expectations all on third child, previously considered dull boy. First in biology. Fieldwork, amoebas. Tells tutor he is unhappy with impersonal nature of formal science. Meets highly politicised young doctor, Helen Sommers. Marriage and mission of medical help in Third World.

James twenty-seven.

Kenya. Laos. Borneo. Metamorphosis. James abandons biology and medical philanthropy for anthropology. Writes *Wau*. Birth of John James.

Paul frowned. He had read *Wau* by accident. Who would have dreamed of reading a work that spent 500 pages examining a bizarre ceremony played out between nephews and their maternal uncles in a remote tribe of headhunters? Paul had been into Gandhi at the time and was writing a series of articles for the *Globe* exploring opportunities for non-violent civil resistance in contemporary America. Meantime he was fighting with his second wife. He was fighting off a mistress. There was a pretty Chinese girl. 'Since you're on an exotic trip,' remarked the arts editor, 'how about checking this?' He handed Paul a review copy. Neither journalist had heard of the publisher.

'Why are literary descriptions of a culture more satisfying than scientific analyses,' *Wau* began, 'while scientific analyses are nevertheless felt to be more "useful"? Can the two be merged, or are they mutually exclusive, like contemplation and action?'

Albert James then proceeded to talk in seemingly random detail about a group of people who lived in huts perched on stilts in swamps, fishing, gathering sago, memorising long lists of ancestral names, competing to see who could carry out the most painful initiation ceremonies on their adolescent children, delighting in homicide whenever they could. 'It has never been clear to me,' James had written, 'why I should pursue one detail rather than another; there is a unity of ethos in the way the hunter prepares an arrow, the way his wife squats by the cooking pot, a child is invited to push a spear into the belly of a defenceless prisoner.' To demonstrate the fact, James had filled the pages with photos, though here the most obvious unifying factor was the poor quality of the images.

Paul Roberts had been unable to understand at first why this bizarre book had affected him so profoundly. There was no way in which the puritan obsessions of his mother and wife, the possessive aggression of his lover, could be compared to the weird behaviour patterns of a bunch of savages. But for the first time it occurred to him how far his own identity and behaviour was caught up in a pattern of disguised rituals. He was constantly transgressing a long list of dos and don'ts, but always in secret and always feeling sufficiently guilty to step back from any decision that would really offend the status quo. All your rebellion, the journalist told himself – and at this point he had discovered James's earlier work *Mythical Individuals* – is a theatre of rebellion, foreseen in the script your culture has been playing out for generations. You do nothing but play naughty boy. It was time to get real, Paul thought.

In a coda to *Wau*, James had described the devastating effect on the tribe when a group of young men who had gone to Australia to work in copper mines eventually returned and failed to observe the rules. They casually let slip the taboo names of family totems. They did not feel the need to keep their musical instruments perpetually hidden from their womenfolk. 'The whole complex structure of the tribe's life was brushed away,' James had written, 'like a spider's web in a puff of wind. Though, as we know, the spider is indefatigable in rebuilding his web.'

'The liberation your book brought me,' Paul had responded to his mentor's provocation, 'lay in its revelation of the mesh of relations that bound me in an unhappy and unproductive situation.'

'Strange,' James replied – he used a minuscule italic typeface which made reading his emails rather difficult – 'unhappy situations are usually the most productive.'

Seven years after *Wau*, in Chicago, James had come up with the theory that brought him brief notoriety: a schematic classification of family structures and type conflicts that could lead to corresponding neuroses: anorexia, compulsions, phobias. Seized on by therapists as a powerful tool, *Systems and Sanity* was pilloried by family associations and drug companies. James had been doing everything he could to distance himself from the controversy, declaring his book more a work of aesthetics than psychology – most of the examples he had given were from novels, not life – when two policemen arrived at his home to question him about claims made by a fifteen-year-old Puerto Rican girl.

Paul glanced again through the folder in which he had saved their correspondence. It had been tantalising. Albert James had a habit of replying at once, within minutes, or only after a lapse of three or four weeks. He could be telegraphic or tediously verbose. 'By all means take on my ideas, but please don't exhume my corpse,' was his first reaction to the proposed biography. Was he already ill? Paul wondered now. Asked what he was working on at present, James had answered: 'The Land of Faery'. Pressed, he had come back with a Word enclosure of some forty pages of highly technical considerations on the nature of spiders' webs. 'The determining difference between spiders and their victims,' he concluded, 'is that while the former move easily within the sticky pattern they have created – something science has yet fully to explain – the latter cannot, or not until they have become one, as it were, with the spider, or his innards.'

'Everything you tell me,' Paul had replied, 'makes me more eager to go ahead with this book.'

But the man remained elusive. Paul had rushed to Delhi when he received a message from Albert James's email account: 'MR ALBERT PASSED ON. CREMATION AT ENGLISH CEMETERY.' 'Could you let me know who sent this?' he replied from his BlackBerry, already at the airport. There had been no response. Paul had spoken at length to Sharmistha Puri and her companion Heinrich in their apartment in Saket, but Sharmistha explained she had only communicated with Albert by phone, or at the weekly meetings of the research team she was writing for. He had mentioned being ill and there had been two or three long absences, but she had had no idea where he was being treated or what was wrong with him.

'He was a man' – and here the handsome woman ran her tongue over gleaming teeth – 'who always wanted to know about you. About others. He never spoke of himself.'

'Wonderful listener,' Heinrich put in. 'Came along to my psychiatric ward a few times. He would just sit down with patients and listen for hours. He'd even listen when they spoke in Bengali or Gujarati, which he didn't know at all. He'd always tell me to stop giving them drugs and leave them alone.'

The German was tall, lean, earnest and polite, with a way of bursting into loud laughter. His greying eyebrows were formidable. Sitting on cushions beside him, her back resting on the wall, Sharmistha had a composed, somehow furtive beauty, her head always cocked to one side. 'When he asked you about your life,' she explained, 'you understood that he was feeling for patterns, trying out hypotheses. What was strange was how you couldn't help but cooperate. He'd say, "You must treat me as if I wasn't really here, Sharmistha."'

'You do know he used to ask if he could set up a video camera at dinner parties and things?' Heinrich shook his head 'Just set it up and let it run. Like a security camera.'

'Come to think of it,' Sharmistha chuckled: 'Albert was probably the only man aside from my father who never tried to seduce me.'

'Oh, but he seduced you *completely*!' Heinrich came back and slapped his leg enthusiastically. 'You were in love with him, Shasha! And he with you! And his son did the same right after the funeral! First meeting, you couldn't resist the boy.'

'Albert charmed everyone,' Sharmistha agreed.

Paul Roberts watched the couple. From time to time they exchanged knowing smiles. An age difference of about twenty years, he guessed. But they were unable to recount a single specific anecdote that he could put in his book, nothing Albert James had actually *done*. 'Was he a help in your work?' he asked the woman.

Sharmistha frowned. 'You know, my job is just to turn this spider project into an interesting book. A spin-off, if you'll excuse the pun. Talking to Albert, you felt he was giving you fantastic ideas. Was the spider exclusively interested in catching flies, or was there an aesthetic investment in the web per se, or even an aesthetic rivalry between spiders: who can make the neatest web, sort of thing? Or the most mesmerising web? Was there a comfort factor about being inside a web? What was the relationship between the world around the web and the web itself? Did they interact? How did the spider feel passing from one to the other? Did the spider gloat over his prey, or did he take free food for granted and perhaps not associate the trapped flies with the purpose of web-building at all? Did he eat them merely to stop them messing up his web? Was it possible to find individual traits within the species' common pattern of web construction, and if so, why? Does a spider differentiate himself from other spiders? How? Did different angles in the web create different patterns of vibrations when the whole was disturbed and how did the spider experience that?'

Sharmistha laughed. 'Albert could go on forever. I mean it. Perhaps sometimes he was just kidding. Anyway, when I got back to writing the book, I realised he'd only made everything more complicated. To get anything done I had to forget every word he said.'

The young woman smiled, hands perfectly still on the emerald green sari covering her legs. There was a fine silkiness to her skin where chin met neck beneath elaborately worked silver earrings. Paul couldn't decide whether to envy Heinrich or to pity him.

It became difficult now for the American to know how to use his time in Delhi. He had meant to come here and get Albert's life story out of him in a series of interviews. He had just applied for and procured his visa when the email arrived announcing the man's death. It was some days before Paul realised how profoundly this had altered his project. To have heard details and ideas from the man's lips was one thing; to reconstruct them through research was quite another. This could not be like the Gandhi biography where he had merely applied his skills as journalist and philosophy major to offer his own take on material that had already been written about a thousand times. On the contrary, no one really knew much about James. In the public domain there were only the books (remarkable), the articles (curious) and some conference papers (baffling). So now he was no longer there to be interviewed, it was obviously essential to get the cooperation of the woman he had spent his life with. But you mustn't hurry her, Paul told himself. You mustn't be ghoulish.

On the other hand, Paul Roberts wasn't the kind of man who wanted to spend too long on one project. James had become an object of veneration for him; he would love to turn the man into a cult figure; but a book remained a commercial enterprise. Paul was a doer. Staying in India, he was missing a girlfriend, missing visits to his children. If things went slowly, he would grow restless.

How to get going, then? Albert James's son had disappeared almost before the biographer had realised he was there. Talking to him would mean a trip to London. He could do that on the way back to the States perhaps. In the meantime, he made a preparatory phone call, then followed Sharmistha's directions to the home of the Theosophical Society, in a quiet street by Rosnahara Garden. The weather was warming. Beyond the low wall of the garden there were trees in orange blossom.

Dr Bhagwan Coomaraswamy had only ever spoken to Albert James, he said, at the society's monthly gatherings. 'Yes, here, in this very place.'

Dressed in a white tunic, the Indian flapped a limp arm at walls of bookshelves and dark wooden furniture. Paul was surprised by the size of the place, the number of people, old and young, bent over mahogany tables consulting old periodicals and making notes. There was a colonial feel to the marble busts of eminent men in dusty corners.

'Professor James's ambition,' Dr Coomaraswamy pronounced in a high-pitched, throaty voice, 'was to explore the territory of the shaman with the tools and thought processes of the scientist. You know?'

The doctor smiled queerly over his spectacles. Doctor of what? Paul wondered. The two were standing together in the middle of the room. The American hadn't been invited to sit down.

'Albert had a vocation for arduous paths, Mr Roberts. Admirable and fruitless.'

'Why do you think James came to Delhi?' Paul asked.

Dr Coomaraswamy pondered. There was an evasive benevolence to the man that was irksome and somehow at one with his neatly ironed tunic, the smell of freshly shaven skin, a certain unassailable complacency in blinking eyes behind rimless glasses.

'Perhaps the answer,' the Indian eventually said, 'lies in a comment Albert once made to me vis-à-vis our recent history here. Partition, you know, the massacre of so many Muslims. He said Delhi was a city where he was constantly reminded of violence, yet never felt personally threatened: he wasn't part of our quarrel.'

Paul Roberts was unimpressed. 'There are quarrels Albert James wasn't part of all over the world,' he remarked. The slim, ascetic Indian made him feel awkward and gauche.

With a condescending smile, Dr Coomaraswamy said he regretted that he knew no one who could really help the biographer, no one who was on intimate terms with Albert James, aside of course from Mrs James. 'Albert had many acquaintances,' he said, 'and one or two fervent disciples, but no friends, I don't think.' He began to move toward the door.

'What was his interest in theosophy?' Paul asked. 'I mean, was it academic or personal?'

'I very much doubt whether Albert would have distinguished between those categories.'

'But did he speak of it as being part of his research?'

'He never spoke of his research.'

Paul was determined not to be hurried out. 'I presume,' he said, 'since he came regularly to the Theosophical Society, you must have talked theosophy together. I mean, did he believe in reincarnation, did he believe in the Masters?'

Coomaraswamy sighed. 'Professor James would arrive a few minutes after proceedings had begun, listen to whichever speaker was presenting his work that evening, have a cup of tea afterwards and go home.'

'Do you think he aspired to be a Master himself,' Paul hazarded, 'a Mahatma, a Guardian, perhaps guiding mankind from beyond the grave?'

'One doesn't aspire to become a Guardian, does one, Mr Roberts?' The exasperating man coughed and cleared his throat. 'That would be vanity. One aspires to wisdom. A Master becomes a Master only by election.'

They were at the door now. Coomaraswamy opened it and made a little bow. The whole conversation had barely lasted five minutes. Paul stopped on the threshold. 'Theosophy teaches the need for unmediated personal experience of the divine. Am I right? That's the essence of the business.'

He used the word 'business' deliberately. The Indian raised an eyebrow.

'So, would you say that Albert James had achieved or was seeking such an experience?'

Coomaraswamy smiled wanly: 'That is really no concern of yours or mine, is it, Mr Roberts?'

The following afternoon Paul took a taxi to St Anne's. Again, he had had the name of the school from Sharmistha. Crossing the chaos of Connaught Place he remembered how much he disliked Delhi. It was a constant hubbub of bodies, smells, sounds, all of them alien and for the most part unattractive, with neither the efficiency of the modern nor the charm of tradition. I'll get what info I can, he thought, and then go back to Boston. Only the women held his eyes, the bright saris side-saddle on scooters, the swinging ankles. But there seemed to be no way of approaching them.

'Was there any particular reason,' he asked Sister Nirmala, 'why Albert James had wanted to teach here?'

The plump headmistress reflected: 'He sent in his curriculum like so many others, sir,' she said. 'I'm afraid, despite his many writings and very superior mind, poor Mr Albert still needed to sing for his supper. We were rather concerned, when he put himself forward, that a man of his remarkable calibre might not be taking such humble work as we could offer very seriously; you know how it is sometimes with intellectual men, they think teaching children is beneath them. But after all when it came down to the nitty-gritty Mr Albert was really most diligent. Most most diligent. He was really rather a saint, if such a thing is possible for a man who is not a Christian. We were always very happy to have him on our staff.'

Built in grubby parkland to the north of the city, St Anne's was a once ambitious project fallen into disrepair, a common category in India. Paul Roberts asked the headmistress if he might be allowed to talk to Mr James's last class. In the event, the girls were delighted to be let off a few minutes of mathematics and chattered away happily.

'Girls!' shouted the sister in a surprisingly stentorian voice. They wriggled on their thighs in their green and gold uniforms. It was a pleasantly old-fashioned classroom with desks straight from the fifties. 'Girls, this American visitor is writing a book about your wonderful old teacher, Mr James. He wishes to ask you some questions; since he is a man of some achievement, I hope you will want to show him the utmost respect.'

The girls looked at the bulky American and tittered.

Paul tried to smile. It hadn't occurred to him what a powerful experience it would be to stand in front of a class of alert adolescent girls. There was a strong animal odour in the room. Leaning against the teacher's desk, he tried to present himself as both vigorous and relaxed: 'Girls, I, er, just wanted to know if you young people had any stories you could tell me about the way Albert James taught you.'

Paul found it unsettling that Sister Nirmala had decided to stay in the room. There might be things they wouldn't say in the nun's presence. Some of the girls glanced at each other. There was whispering in Hindi. They all wore their hair in gleaming black pigtails.

'Come on now, girls,' said the sister briskly. 'Everyone knows you adored Mr Albert.'

'He was a lot of fun for us,' a voice eventually said.

'In what way?' Roberts asked.

'Nobody has ever failed his exams,' said a bright face.

There were giggles. It was curious to think of lanky, abstruse Albert James driving out here three times a week to stand up in front of these kids. There was something disquieting about their imprisoned liveliness, their massed femininity.

'He asked us to draw the weather,' one girl said.

'To draw the weather?'

'And invent new insects,' said another.

'Mr James liked to apply very experimental methods,' Sister Nirmala agreed.

'Then we had to think of ways to change the world to suit the new insect we had drawn.'

'Or the new weather we invented.'

'Sometimes he took a film of the lesson,' said a voice. 'We looked at it on the computer.'

'Why did he do that?' Paul Roberts asked. 'Did he tell you?'

Nobody answered. Whenever a girl spoke out she became individual and defined, but when they all shut their mouths they were one silent animal. In the front row a small girl was picking at the skin round her fingernails. She wouldn't look up.

'What do you think, casting your minds back now, was the main thing Mr James was trying to teach you? I mean, if you could sum it up in a few words?'

'He taught science,' said a voice.

'The man didn't *mean* that,' another girl protested and burst into giggles. Sporadic voices rose as if released from a hush expectation.

Finally a solemn, full-cheeked girl in the second row said: 'Mr James told us that even when a lesson is about spiders or snakes it is also about all of us in the classroom. He said: what you are drawing, that is who you are. And who your ancestors were. The way you draw an elephant is India.'

'The history of India,' someone said.

'And the future.'

Towards the back another girl covered her face with her hands. It seemed some emotion was stirring. As with Coomaraswamy, but in a completely different way, Paul again had the impression that vital information was being withheld. Had he come to Delhi just a few weeks before and met Albert James in the flesh, everything would have fallen into place. Instead, he had arrived only in time to see the smoke drifting up from the crematorium chimney. The man had escaped him.

Returning to his hotel room, Paul found a scrap of yellow paper under the door bearing the words: 'TELEPHONE MESSAGE. From: *Mrs James*. Message: *I will not give my permission*.'

CHAPTER ELEVEN

John emailed his mother, but received no reply. 'You can't force me to do what you want,' Elaine had said, 'any more than my father can.' 'I have no money, Mum,' John wrote again. He didn't want to phone. Elaine reminded him that he owed her £200. She wouldn't even talk about living together. 'If you hurt me again, it's the end,' she said.

John tried to bury himself in the lab ten or twelve hours a day, but his enthusiasm for mapping out the invisible world of tubercular gene expression was faltering. In Adelaide a group of Australians had done something very similar to what their own team had envisaged. They had tricked a ribosome into some bizarre behaviour precisely at the moment when the bacterium passed from dormant to active. Even at the other end of the world these ideas were in the air. It was an expression his father had often used. 'We don't possess our minds, John. These things are in the air.'

Gazing stupidly at the computer screen, John shook his head. I should have confronted Dad, I should have gone out to see him. About what? 'Mum,' he wrote, 'I am now in debt to the tune of £2,000.'

He typed his father's name into Google again. This time he

clicked for images. A dozen faces appeared. None were familiar. It was the first of twenty-three pages. You could write a history of photography, of portrait painting. There were hundreds. Someone was setting up a family tree with photos that went back to the 1860s. There was an Albert James with an eyepatch and handlebar moustache, a young black boy in a baseball cap, an able seaman who had died on HMS *Hood*. 'We shall not forget,' read the caption.

John's father appeared on the fourth page, his green eyes amused and pained. Bizarrely, he was standing arm in arm with a Zulu in full tribal dress holding a spear. On the tenth page there was a cartoon caricature of Albert James that had appeared in the *New York Review* shortly after the publication of *Postures*. The artist had been able to think of nothing better than to emphasise the anthropologist's sticky-out ears.

His mother didn't reply. It seemed impossible. Elaine assured John she had forgiven him, but she was very, very busy with rehearsals. 'Get some paid work,' she told him. 'Part time.' The girl seemed intrigued and scared by what had happened between them that night. They both had bruises. Neither wanted to talk about it.

'MOTHER,' John wrote, 'PLEASE LET ME KNOW IF YOU HAVE RECEIVED MY MAIL.'

'She is trying to force me to beg from Grandmother,' he told Elaine, 'to go and ask the old witch for money.' He wouldn't do it.

In an unplanned gesture John copied the email to his father's old address. How did Yahoo ever find out you had died? Maybe Mum checked Dad's mail to inform those who hadn't heard. At once, there came an out-of-office reply: 'Albert James regrets that he will not be able to respond to his email for some time.' There was a phone number. 'In case of emergency, phone . . .'

John stared at the number. It was not the home phone in Delhi. A mobile? The young man felt anxious. On three consecutive nights he dreamed his father was in the basement lab at St Mary's, simultaneously alive and dead. A conviction that dreams were meaningless didn't help. He was upset. The coffin must be opened, he dreamed, and something done. Some cells must be centrifuged. But the coffin was also the dissecting bench. John was taking bacteria from the lungs of a mouse. That was always a tricky business. In one dream the basement lab was knee-deep in stagnant water. Maybe it was sewage. The coffin was floating and bumping against the walls. How could he work on a surface that moved? Definitely a sequence of dreams, Dad had written. But what is the point, John demanded, of reflections that can lead to no useful action, that have no issue in the world? Ignore them.

In the real lab he and his colleagues must analyse the properties of hundreds upon hundreds of genes: those that continued to be expressed after the tubercular bacterium's contact with the immune system and those that did not. This was the passage from active to dormant state. Each gene must be examined with care, each complex experiment repeated at least three times. Glaxo were right that the only point of any research is to arrive at a product. It would take time. The third night John tackled the coffin but couldn't open it. There was no lid, no hinge, no lock. It seemed all of a piece. Yet, as if through frosted glass, he could see his father's face inside. The man was moving his lips. He was explaining.

Recounting these dreams to Elaine, John noticed, won him back some sympathy. Her boyfriend had become more interesting; he wasn't just a science nerd; he was going through a difficult patch.

'It shows you loved him,' she said earnestly. Sometimes, she held his hand as if he might be ill; she smoothed the blond hair on his forehead and planted a kiss by his ear; but again she reminded him of the £200: 'In the end it wasn't mine, Jo; it was Dad's.'

Days and weeks passed. John explained to his project organiser what the situation was. He was penniless. Sympathetic and avuncular, Simon was shocked to find how blindly his young collaborator had been counting on a contract once his thesis was complete. 'You haven't spoken to Personnel at all?' he asked. 'You haven't even applied to the grants commission?'

John said he had thought it was a sure thing. After all, he was constantly being complimented for the thoroughness of his work. People treated him as an essential part of the project.

'Research is easy compared with getting yourself paid for it,' Simon joked. He couldn't understand how the young man, who was also his best student, could have been so naïve. Everybody else seemed to know the score. 'I'll look around,' he said. 'We can't afford to lose you.'

John felt lost already. He cadged meals. He walked the three miles from home to the lab. 'Why aren't you on the dole?' friends asked. 'MUM!' He sent another mail. He blew the typeface up to thirty-six points and changed the colour to red. He wouldn't go on the dole. No. I am doing a highly complex job in a field where there is plenty of money, he told himself, yet none is coming my way. He felt humiliated. '***MOTHER***!' He used italic bold. She didn't reply. She is taking it out on me for smashing her table, he thought. He knew the table was irrelevant. It was the moment in the bedroom that mattered. She has washed her hands of me. 'Why don't you phone her?' Elaine asked. 'How can you expect others to help, if you won't help yourself?'

Elaine was kind to him, but busy. In the past, she had been the vulnerable one. Now she had her rehearsals, she had a place in the world. Practising her mime in the sitting room, she swayed round the sofa with staring eyes, arms waving languidly. 'After the explosion,' she said. 'I'm supposed to be looking for my baby. But how can I really know what it would be like after an explosion?'

John watched her, her arms and wrists in particular. They were the movements of a plant underwater, he thought.

Returning to Maida Vale, he sat on his bed, and tossed the three green elephants at the dartboard above Jean-Pierre's bed. They clattered and dropped on the coverlet. Sometimes one dropped on another and they knocked together. They chipped. He hadn't tried to repair them. Not one elephant, not two elephants, but three, three elephants! They were ruined. You couldn't even fit them inside each other.

Sleeping early, he dreamed he came ashore on an open boat among mudflats where severed heads had been thrust on poles. Why was he dreaming so much? His father's head was among them. 'It is not easy to do field research on headhunters,' his father had famously observed in the opening pages of *Wau*. It became a family joke. 'It is not easy to do field research on nuclear explosions,' his mother needled at dinner table. 'On the dress habits of ghosts,' Father came back. 'On a child's thoughts in the womb,' Mother capped him. 'Your father risked everything,' she had told John that evening, 'to take his study in unconventional directions.' 'Why on earth did you buy those ugly things?' she had demanded after he had smashed down the elephants on the tabletop. John couldn't get her voice out of his head. 'Those ugly things! They're horrible!'

Finally, his flatmate Peter warned him that if he couldn't pay the rent he would have to leave his room. He had talked to Jean-Pierre about it. 'Next month,' he said. 'I'm sorry.'

All the same, forty-eight hours after this conversation, when John found himself standing outside his grandmother's rather grand corner house in Richmond, he had the impression he had arrived there by accident; he had gone out for a walk in Maida Vale and stumbled across this place, eight miles away. He hadn't planned to be here at all.

Helen James's parents lived in a quiet street near the river. The house must be worth a fortune, John thought, pushing the garden gate. His jaw was aching with tension. He had never quite grasped the fact before. He had been so young when he came here for holidays; he arrived in a cab, played, was pampered, watched television, got bored and was put back in a cab again.

It was drizzling softly from a slow, turbulent sky. John turned back through the gate to the street and walked to and fro on the pavement behind the hedge. He kicked the wall. 'Why have you always been scared of people?' his mother had asked, 'scared of asking for things? Because you've always had everything on a plate,' she answered her own question. 'I asked Elaine,' he muttered. Elaine had refused him. Never in his life had John been violent. He hardly knew what violence was. I am being forced to beg, he told himself. He kicked a drainpipe. They send me to Winchester, then I'm forced to beg. They prepare me for a highly professional career, the James family career, in biology, then all at once I'm abandoned. I have to beg. Father had written to him frequently at school, far more than Mother, but the letters were experiments in explaining things, as if assessing whether a child could be made to understand such and such an idea in this or that idiosyncratic way. They came complete with anecdotes and drawings. They didn't answer the questions John always asked: Where shall we go next holiday? Isn't there a school in Chicago I can go to?

John walked away. He would find any old job and forget the lab. Let's see how Mum reacts. His parents had groomed him for this career. The James family had been scientists for generations. They went to good schools, took good degrees. Then a phone call, a funeral and he was destitute. Let's see how she reacts to her son washing dishes. Mother daily examines every kind of ugly illness, he told himself, touches infected skin, looks into ulcerated mouths, sews up anal fistulas, but she won't reply to my email.

John stood still in the quiet street. 'Your father is dead,' he whispered. He remembered the young Indian who had sold him the elephants. 'Hello, sir. You are wanting a bargain, sir?' That was the spirit. Sell yourself. John walked determinedly to his grandparents' front door.

In her early eighties, Granny Janet was everything her daughter Helen was not: flowery and frilly, talkative, seductive, perfumed, posh. 'Johnny!' she cried. 'My my my!' There were earrings and jewellery on her powdery skin, smart black stockings on her legs. 'Johnny come lately! Indeed! Don't we phone, John James, don't we announce our extremely rare visits, my dear little boy? Come in, come in! How long has it been? How many years?'

At four in the afternoon she insisted on pouring gin and tonics. She offered long cigarettes. She put the young man on a deep leather sofa. 'Tell me everything. Everything!' She seemed delighted when her grandson started blurting out his problems in the crudest fashion. John hadn't smoked for ages but now accepted one cigarette after another. His eyes smarted and he coughed. He needed money, he complained, to live. He was in a very difficult situation. He was about to be evicted. Granny Janet nodded and sighed. 'Of course,' she was saying, 'of course your mother couldn't come directly to me herself, could she? She couldn't write to me directly. Or phone. Too proud by half!'

John had already finished his gin. Vaguely, he recalled this stale, upholstered atmosphere from a dozen years ago. He felt exhausted, ashamed of himself, infantile. He had spoken too quickly. The smoke had gone to his head. Finally, he sat back and looked the woman in her rheumy eyes.

'But by God you've grown handsome!' his grandmother cried. She stood up to kiss him so that he was overcome by a cloud of perfume. Her wrinkled lips were rouged, the skin powdered. 'Heaven only knows where those looks came from! Jack!' she called, apparently delighted. 'Your grandson's here. Hey, Jack! For

God's sake!' She shouted at the top of her voice. John saw she was wearing high heels. No one came. 'He's such an old fogy,' she laughed, 'sleeps all afternoon. Never comes down. Deaf as a post.'

Laughing and shaking her head, she insisted that John tell her about his projects. 'Tell me everything, mind, my dear. If you're asking us to invest in you, we'll need to know where our finances are going, won't we? Everything now. You know the Sommers like a good return on their money.'

She poured another drink. John collected his thoughts and began to explain about cell structure, the immune system, tuberculosis. The old woman watched, nodding sagely. 'Yes,' she said, 'yes, yes, I've heard of that, yes, I know.' He knew she knew nothing. 'Jack!' she called from time to time, but half-heartedly. 'So, there are five metabolic cycles,' he explained. 'Are there, indeed?' she exclaimed. Her fingers played with an expensive necklace. 'Who would have thought?' 'Or another strategy,' he was saying later, 'is to interfere with the bacterium's reproductive mechanisms, to make it impotent if you like. It doesn't die, but it can't reproduce.'

'Impotent!' Granny Janet interrupted. It seemed to be the first word that had really made sense to her. She began to ask if he had a girlfriend. She stood up, smoothed down a rather tight flowery dress and again fussed with drinks.

'There's a girl I'm planning to marry,' John said.

'Marriage?' His grandmother grimaced. 'You're a bit young to marry, Johnny.' She shook her head. 'Your grandfather and I . . .' the old woman went on. 'It would be lovely to take a photo of you, you know, you're so good-looking, but I've no idea where the camera is. Jack!' Even with the heels, she was smaller than John's mother, but with a fussy, brittle energy. 'Jaa-ack!'

She went out of the room and stood at the bottom of the stairs calling. There were rugs on parquet. 'Where's the camera, Jack? He's such an old fogy!' She came back and sat down again. 'Where was I? Your grandfather and I, ah yes, we didn't claim to be saints.' She smiled. 'And we didn't expect our children to be saints either. Not at all. Cheers by the way,' she leaned across a coffee table to clink her glass. Inside the silk frills at the top of her dress he could see the slack of her breasts. 'Certainly,' she said, 'we turned a blind eye to some of your Uncle Nick's . . .' she laughed '. . . naughtiness. He could be a bit of a pig you know, your Uncle Nick.'

'Yes,' John said vaguely. He knew his mother and her brother hadn't spoken since she left home.

'Your mother, on the contrary, decided to punish us all with her goodness. Right from when she was, oh, sixteen, seventeen, she always had to prove this point, that she didn't need our money.'

Granny Janet waited a moment to see how the boy would react. John sipped his fresh drink.

'And to do that, of course, I mean, to spend her whole life doing good, she had to marry a man blind and malleable enough to follow her to all those godforsaken corners of the globe where good can so easily be done, can it not? God rest your poor father's soul of course, it was hardly his fault.

'Now,' she went on briskly, 'I will give you whatever you need to tide you over this difficult moment. Of course I will! I'd be a monster otherwise, don't you think? Family is family. A year or two is the maximum, isn't it, dear? Let's say two years, to cover the period till they employ you, I'm sure they will, you sound so intelligent, really, on the understanding, however, the one condition, mind, that you promise not to waste your talent as your parents did.'

Together with a rising wave of relief, John grasped the fact that financial support was to come at the price of accepting that Granny Janet had always been right in her everlasting argument with his mother.

'I don't want you throwing away a clever brain,' the old lady repeated.

'No,' John said.

'The point is this . . .' The old lady cocked her head, listened, eyes raised to the door. 'Oh, I give up on Jack,' she laughed. 'Sometimes I wonder if he mightn't be dead up there.' She shook her head. The neatly permed hair moved like a loose hat. 'The point is this, Johnny' – now she lowered her voice – 'the Third World is a bottomless pit. You can't disagree with that. You can only throw energy away there, you know? What has your mother achieved over a lifetime? She has helped ten thousand people, has she? She has seen the thankful smiles on their brown cheeks? She has helped *nobody*! The next day they fall ill again. The next day their brother dies, their children. Their wives. Or they live on in wretchedness. I *know* the Third World, John, and nothing can be done. You can be as proactive as you like, but something is nothing in the Third World. It's a drop in the ocean. Jack's business took us to the Gambia, Zimbabwe, Nigeria. I've seen what I've seen and I know what I know. Your mother threw away her life on this idea of saving the Third World and meantime denied herself a place in the only world that was natural to her. England, London. The only place where what she could do would have made real sense.'

John nodded.

'And she's not even Christian!' Granny Janet started again. 'It would have explained it if your mother were Christian, wouldn't it, darling? There would be a sort of sense in it if they had been trying to convert poor ignorant souls and have them go to heaven. But no one is really religious any more, are they? Or atheist for that matter. Are you atheist?' she demanded. 'Of course you're not, my dear. You're a scientist! Nobody *really* believes they're going to heaven, do they? Fiddlesticks. Or anywhere else. We're all scientists really, aren't we, even when we don't understand anything? Belief and unbelief have really ceased to exist. An obsolete word. You know something or you don't. So why go and give your life to a bunch of primitives? Just because dear Jack was a terrible old Tory in the sixties, railing against the unions and supporting white Rhodesia (and, in retrospect, you have to say he was right), your mother decided to become a knee-jerk socialist and she's been punishing us all ever since. You know? Your Uncle Nick in particular. You can't imagine how upset he was when she broke with him. Just because he made a drunken pass at one of Helen's friends. She never grew out of it. Whereas Jack did vote Labour in 1997. Did you know that? Junk-bond Jack they called him at the Exchange. He voted Labour!' She burst out laughing. 'I thought pigs would fly!'

Sitting in the deep leather sofa, watching his grandmother's performance, John was somehow reminded of the situation between himself and his mother that last evening in Delhi. He had been invaded then by an extraordinary tension, fingers, lips and ears tingling with unwanted energy. It was still there, he thought now, that tension. He was still back in his mother's sitting room. Why?

'Do you think your father would ever have spent his life in the Third World,' she was saying, 'if it hadn't been for your mother's enslavement to this ruinous idea of international charity?'

'They were in America three years,' John finally objected.

'Yes,' Granny Janet cried, 'yes, they were, and just when the poor fellow was beginning to make a big name for himself she drags him back to bongo land because there is nothing for her to do in an advanced country. Or nothing that would make her feel like a saint. Sainthood is a perversion!' Granny Janet declared. She rattled the ice in her empty glass. 'And if I give you this money, Johnny love, it must be on the firm condition that it does not get thrown away.'

John tried to smile. 'Granny Janet,' he promised, 'I solemnly swear that I'll be building a sensible career in biochemistry, here in England, or at most the USA, and as soon as I have an income I'll start paying back.'

'Though, of course' – his grandmother paused to blow out smoke through pursed lips – 'if your father had had any nous at all, he would have made Helen follow his career and not vice versa. The way Jack did with me. It was always crystal clear what my place was, though I was actually earning more than him when we met. Did you know that? Yes, your granny was earning more as a secretary than him as a bank clerk or whatever he was.'

John was silent. Under a tall glass case a clock ticked in the arms of a porcelain angel. The room was filled with expensive Victoriana.

'Dad needed something to help him focus his ideas,' John eventually said.

Granny Janet turned from the window and stared, as if the boy had inexplicably changed the subject.

'I mean, a group project,' John said. 'Something team driven. Dad tended to be all over the place, following whims, or drifting with the tide.'

'Because your mother kept him entirely to herself! That was another reason she took him to the ends of the earth. She wanted him exclusively for herself.' Then in a lower voice Granny Janet added: 'Helen was very beautiful, you know. What a waste!'

'I know,' John said appreciatively. 'She still is.' He felt a rush of emotion.

Granny Janet looked at him sharply. 'I don't want you to marry while I am supporting you. Is that clear? You are too young.'

'Fine.' John steeled himself. 'I'll need about £5,000 right away,' he told her boldly.

Standing at a writing table, the old woman scribbled a cheque. 'Jack,' she called, again. 'Jack! Do come and say goodbye.' She waited a moment, then shook her head. 'He probably wouldn't recognise you, I'm afraid.'

'I'll go upstairs,' John offered.

'No, no, no. I'm too tired now, Johnny. This has taken a lot out of me, you know. Heavens, your barging in on me like this without any warning. I'm in my eighties, my dear, I will have to rest.'

In the event, she almost pushed him out of the door.

So, in just an hour and a half John James had got what he wanted: money. And if the journey out to Richmond had been a long, confused stumbling toward a place he hadn't even admitted he was aiming for, the return to Elaine's to give her the good news was a smooth pleasure of easy Tube connections and wide-awake contentment.

'Oh God, I've got rehearsals,' his girlfriend exclaimed. She refused to share a bottle but pulled him to the bedroom for the most rapid and eager lovemaking of all their time together. 'It's good news we don't have to marry!' she cried. The sly grin on her face dissolved. 'Congratulations, Jo,' she whispered. 'Welcome back to sanity.'

'Truth is, Mum worshipped Dad,' John told her a little later, after recounting his grandmother's long rant. 'And Dad admired Mum immensely. They were very close.' He spoke with his head on the pillow while Elaine hurried to get dressed and go out.

'Often she was the only doctor who would do things without being paid. Sometimes she even bought patients' drugs herself. In emergencies she used Dad's research funds. He never objected. Dad never really objected to anything.'

'Because she had a real vocation,' Elaine sighed, wriggling on her tights. 'And he really loved her. I hope I can be as dedicated to the theatre. I hope I get the chance to be.'

John objected that that was rather different. 'You do the theatre because you like it, and you want to be famous. Mum does it entirely for other people.'

'Not true,' Elaine frowned. 'It's because I love the stage, the art of it. It's a passion. Why do you think we always stay so late rehearsing?'

Her boyfriend watched her, his head shaking. But he didn't want to contradict. They were happy for the first time since he had got the news of his father's death. Perhaps now they could get on with their lives. For a start, her father could have his £200 back.

But about half an hour after she had gone out, John began to pace the room. Why hadn't his mother answered his emails? It should have been his parents giving him this money, he thought, not a gaudy grandmother with an unpleasant axe to grind. What did she mean he wasn't old enough to marry? Nothing has been settled. In a moment of agitation, John put on his coat and began walking back to his flat, then stopped almost at once at a small Internet place.

'Dad,' he typed. The only new mail in his inbox was junk. 'Dad, I hate you for this.'

The machines were in the basement under a café. When the message-delivered sign came up, John hurried upstairs and ordered a coffee. The man behind the counter was Indian. How appropriate, John thought. He felt exhausted. But why was it appropriate? Half the world is Indian.

He carried the coffee down the stairs and wondered how to use the half an hour he had paid for. Behind the monitor was the rough brick wall of an old cellar. The place smelled dank. Clicking on the inbox he knew he would only find Dad's out-of-office reply. All the same he opened it. 'Albert James regrets . . . In case of emergency, phone . . .'

John pulled out his mobile and called the number at once. No signal, the phone told him. He would have to go out in the street.

Then by one of those curiosities of email timing, when he returned from message to inbox a new message had arrived. 'From Dr Helen James MD, re: MONEY.' John was aware of an intense trepidation as he moved the cursor to click the message open.

Dear John,

I'm sorry your situation is so acute. I've been trying to find out exactly what resources are available. Very very few, I'm afraid. Your father was always happy to live from hand to mouth. You know his favourite Bible verse was, 'Consider the lilies of the field, they sow not, neither do they reap . . .' In the circumstances, the only thing I can do is write to your grandmother to ask if she will kindly move some money into your account. However, if you will forgive my saying so, you are now twenty-four years old and have completed your doctoral thesis, something of which I'm very proud, as your dear father would have been too. Given this situation, you should be able to look after yourself and hence I really can't understand the tone of these emails you've been sending as if you were the victim of some kind of tsunami. If you insist, I will write to your grandmother, but please think it over first. I'm sure you will feel much better if you solve this problem on your own like a man and I'm sure that that would have been your father's wish.

Apart from which, all is well here. The weather is hotting up and the long summer will soon be beginning.

With love,

Mum

John hurried out of the café and began walking fast. Without thinking, he headed east across the Edgware Road and into town where Elaine would be finishing rehearsal. He needed her company. 'I need some kind of medicine,' he muttered out loud. 'A drug.' Vaguely, he thought of the chemistry of emotion, the shifting balance of genes expressed and suppressed, the subtle alterations in infinitely overlaid metabolic cycles. It had come on to rain again. If ever there was a quack's paradise it was psychiatry, he thought.

He walked past shops with computers, with clothes, with furniture. 'I have money now,' he muttered. 'I can spend.' He crossed to Gloucester Place. His hair was wet. The night was chill. Then at the next corner he saw the actors and actresses already leaving the school where the company rehearsed. They weren't staying late after all.

There were a dozen of them in overcoats, under umbrellas. They crossed the forecourt and came out through the school gate. Some were hurrying to cars, some laughing; then four or five broke off in a dark little knot and headed for the pub on the next corner, the Ploughshare. What a stupid name. It was a new pub. Now he saw Elaine slipping her arms into her jacket as she walked. She was chattering, moving very self-consciously, as if imitating someone else, mincing in her denim skirt, enjoying the performance of being herself. The small, stocky man behind her must be the director, John thought. He was definitely Asian. One of the younger men started to sing, showing off. A baritone. Elaine added her own voice, but she was hardly audible with a car swishing by. Elaine had a beautiful voice, but not strong enough. 'Dad is always telling me my voice isn't strong enough,' she complained. Now she shook her hair in the rain and sang. John saw she was happy.

He hurried to catch up. We can go home together, he thought. We can make love again. This is my woman. I've chosen.

Just as the group stopped to push through the pub door, the squat director slipped his arm round Elaine's waist and pulled her toward him. They were behind the others. The actors were waiting to go in as another group came filing out. There was a moment's confusion. The arm was definitely around her waist, John saw. And it definitely stayed there.

CHAPTER TWELVE

The waiting room at outpatients was suffocating. Paul Roberts had looked in, stepped over a body on the floor, felt the press of women holding babies, old men with bandages, the decidedly unpleasant smells, and retreated. Outside the gate half a dozen women were sitting under a truck to shelter from the sun. The asphalt was broken. Some had children with them. The truck itself seemed to have driven out of the forties without ever being cleaned.

Paul paced up and down. The clinic was marked by a white panel with a red cross. There was a dirty red wall, a wooden gate. He watched a woman at an upper window cleaning her teeth over the street, a boy flying a kite from the roof above, a pig rooting through filth in the gutter. It was Old Delhi, by the railway, and everything was filthy. The boy's kite tangled with power lines. Then a beggar was pestering. 'Hello, sir.' It was a girl, a child, tugging at his trousers. 'Please, sir.'

Paul's normal strategy was to walk briskly away, but this morning he was determined to be at the outpatients' door when Helen James arrived. He was growing increasingly frustrated. The girl clutched at his wrist now. 'Sir!' Paul found two rupees to shoo her off and at the same moment Helen stepped out of an autorickshaw.

'It makes no sense giving to beggars,' she told him and was already past and inside the clinic. At once there was a clamour of voices. 'Hello! Hello, madam!'

Paul tried to keep up with the crowd as she turned right down a long corridor. 'What is it you're afraid I will say in this book?' he called. 'Can't you think again?'

Standing with her back to him, Helen produced a key for the door to her surgery. She was wearing a light green dress. 'You have no right to harass me,' she told him.

'Please, one good talk,' he said, 'then I'm leaving Delhi. You can hardly call that harassment.'

Removing her shoes on the threshold, the widow looked up. Her face was severe, but weary too, and suddenly vulnerable. Beyond her, Paul could see into a bare room with a table, a washbasin, a metal cupboard, posters in Hindi. For one second she let him look in her eyes. 'Why are you insisting?'

'Mrs James, please, if we could just . . .'

She turned away and took a white coat from a hook. 'Come back tomorrow afternoon around five.' Her voice was brusque. Already people were jostling to be first through the door. 'And I'll explain why your project is a bad idea. Please, everybody!' she raised her voice. 'In order of arrival, please. Except in cases of emergency.'

As it turned out there was an emergency that morning, but the child's mother was not aware of it and as a result Helen didn't see the girl until after twelve: a four-year-old with violent earache, her face dramatically swollen, skin burning and dry.

'How long has this been going on?' Helen spoke in basic Hindi.

'Two weeks.' The woman seemed doubtful. 'Maybe three. I work a great deal, Doctor.' She had five children, she said. Her husband was away. She lived out of town to the south.

The little girl screamed when she was touched. Her name was Shruti. A local doctor had given her some pills, but she hadn't got better. No, the mother didn't know what kind of pills. They were white, so big they had to be cut in half to swallow. Helen went to the phone and spoke to the ward supervisor. 'Then you'll have to put her on a mat somewhere,' she told the man firmly. 'I'd say three or four days, if it isn't meningitis already.'

The mother was anxious about leaving the girl alone, anxious about losing her job if she stayed. Helen was firm. 'The medicine must be given constantly, in the hospital, with a drip. You must take this paper to the supervisor.' It was pointless trying to explain the idea of a drip. 'Along the corridor and to the right. Ask for Shobha Devi.'

The mother's head was wobbling with perplexity. The girl whimpered in a daze of fever. Helen smiled. 'Shruti can get better, Mrs Ram, but only if you leave her here. Do you understand? You must leave Shruti with us. She is very ill. She could die.'

By two o'clock Helen had seen more than fifty patients. When the last was gone, she sat for a few minutes on her own. It was a relief to have recovered a little concentration and energy after those impossible days in January. Yet the more the time passed the more it was clear that things were not as they had been before Albert's death. One must accept, she had always thought, that work of this kind will be tiring and routine, even when dealing at every moment with life and death. And often discouraging. One must accept that there is little time for pleasantry or self-congratulation. You get on with it. She had always been dogged. Why did Albert's absence make it so much harder?

In truth, in the past, Helen had rarely been discouraged. As a rule, the patients responded rapidly to drugs and recovered quickly, which was gratifying; or alternatively they were soon dead. You forgot about them. You got used to it. Some left their beds without being discharged. You would never know what had happened to them. Many of the outpatients went off with their medicines and didn't come back to be checked up. 'What you've done,' Albert had once suggested, 'is turn the competitive spirit you learned at home against an opponent who will never relent: sickness. And in the Third World at that.' It was like fighting the ocean, he protested, or a river in flood. 'Always an easier enemy than my mum and dad,' Helen had laughed. 'Or my dreadful brother.'

Washing her hands now, she looked in the mirror. 'Albert,' she mouthed. 'Albert.' Perhaps she had chosen him as a husband because she knew he would never compete; Albert would never hurt her, and he always refused to be hurt on the many occasions when she had hurt him. He was my spectator, she said to herself rather unexpectedly. Now I've only got the mirror.

Looking into the grey-green of her irises, the enigma of the pupils, Helen experienced a moment of vertigo. She was so intensely present to herself she almost fainted. She had to turn away and put a hand over her eyes.

Helen ate in the clinic's small canteen with a young Dutch doctor who had come on voluntary service. She explained the options here for dealing with a long-term cancer patient.

'You mean, I accept that I can do nothing?' he asked gravely.

He was a handsome young man, the kind who until five or ten years ago would invariably have made a pass at her.

'I look at it in a more positive way,' Helen smiled. 'We never throw resources at a lost cause.'

Late afternoon, she visited the hospitalised patients assigned to her. Two drips feeding the limp stick of her arm, little Shruti lay on a pile of mats fast asleep. Her temperature was down somewhat but the skin still burned. Tomorrow they would know if her mother had brought her in time.

Helen returned to her surgery to pick up her outdoor shoes. Then it was as she was locking the door to go home that she saw the boy. He came stumbling round the corner of the corridor from the right, followed by the ward sister.

'I found this rascal, he was skulking by the kitchen door!' the woman complained. 'The little thief.' She was trying to shoo the boy out of the building. 'He cannot speak a word of Hindi, or English!'

Helen recognised the comically protruding ears at once, the exhausted, calculating eyes. 'He's been here before,' she told the sister.

The boy began a fit of coughing. It seemed he could barely stand up. 'Cover your mouth!' The ward sister shook her head. 'I think he's acting, Dr James. He was trying to steal food and now he's pretending to be ill. Outpatients is closed,' she scolded. 'You will have to wait till tomorrow, if that's what you want.'

'I'll see him, Meena.' Helen said. 'He's been here before.' Helen went to the boy, put a hand on his shoulder and led him to her surgery door.

Perhaps sixteen years old, the boy had appeared some time the previous autumn. October, or early November. He'd come alone. Helen remembered because it had been quite impossible to communicate with him. He knew not a word of any language she tried. She had called a nurse, then the supervisor. They could get no change out of him. He coughed, wiped a hand across his forehead, put his fingers on his chest and panted, opening his eyes wide. But they had already understood he was suffering from TB. Helen could smell it.

By chance it was one of the days when Albert had stopped by the clinic. Albert was always attracted by the people there and nothing interested him more than a communication challenge. He had sat with the boy for hours while he was waiting to do his various tests.

'He is Burmese,' Albert informed the ward supervisor. 'His name is Than-Htay, or Maung Than-Htay, he has a father and two sisters. His father was a teacher in his village. His mother was killed by soldiers and they came to Delhi as refugees. He was living and working in a silk factory, but when he started coughing they told him to leave. He couldn't find his father. He is alone now, begging and eating at the Sikh temples.'

It was standard procedure with a case like this to phone a specialised TB clinic, but after some toing and froing it turned out there were problems with the boy being Burmese. State money allocated to indigent patients could not go to foreigners, even if they did have refugee status, which in the boy's case wasn't certain. So they had kept him in the clinic to get his treatment started, then let him out when he was no longer infectious.

Unimpressed by his illness, Albert had been fascinated with the boy's unusual gestures and facial expressions, in particular a strange way he had of turning his head when he spoke. It was partly to do with his being Burmese and partly, Albert thought, because he was slightly deaf. Every movement, every smile, frown, grimace, was theatrically exaggerated. No doubt that was why he was not picking up Hindi, he concluded. Helen remembered that Albert had made a video of the boy. Then when he left the hospital she promptly forgot about him. He was no longer her responsibility.

Without a word, she sat him on a chair leaning forward, pulled up a dirty tee-shirt and pressed her stethoscope against his back. There was a wheezing as of bubbles through sludge. Probably he had stopped taking the antibiotics the moment he was discharged. Now something more powerful would be required.

She went to sit opposite him. The boy looked patiently into space from between his huge ears. She couldn't remember his name. Exotic names always escaped her. There was an unhappy curl to his upper lip, his nose was slightly flattened, the eyes were shrewd beneath drooping lids. It was the clinic's policy not to readmit those who had failed to follow through an initial period of treatment. This was a rule they made clear to every patient on discharge. And Helen knew that there were already more than thirty in the 25-bed ward. She sighed. The boy smiled wanly and said something. Helen didn't understand. His voice was full of catarrh. 'A-bet?' It was a question. There followed a few incomprehensible syllables and then again on this sick boy's lips the familiar name was repeated. 'A-bet?'

CHAPTER THIRTEEN

The following afternoon she and Paul Roberts sat in a coffee house in Khan Market. The air conditioning was working hard and Paul actually felt cold. To compensate, he ordered cheesecake and ate with an appetite that Helen James thought infantile.

'No one wants a book about someone who was entirely good,' she told him.

Enjoying the food gave Paul confidence. 'And so?' Now she had agreed to talk again he felt sure she would change her mind.

'So there's no point in a biography of Albert. It would be a flop.'

'Gandhi was widely supposed to be entirely good, but I'm only one of a score and more who have written about him. Sales are more than healthy.'

'Gandhi's life was politics,' she said. 'His non-violence was interesting *because* he was in the fray. And now his face is on every Indian banknote. But Albert kept outside every struggle. His face will never be anywhere.' For a moment her lip trembled. She had arrived at the clinic this morning to find the four-year-old Shruti dead. 'The only thing you might do is put together a synthesis of his thinking. That would be useful and I would give you all the help I can.'

'I'm not an academic,' Paul objected. 'I want to bring Albert before the public eye. I want to give him the visibility he deserved.'

Helen sipped her coffee. 'You want to make money out of him.'

'No,' Paul protested. 'I want to get people interested in his way of understanding the world.'

'I won't let you.'

Paul Roberts lit a cigarette. Inhaling, he found his most engaging smile. 'With respect, you can't prevent me writing the book. Or *a* book. The problem is that without your help it won't be as good.'

Holding his cigarette down by his knee, he leaned forward across the table. His ruddy face and blue eyes seemed sincere, even urgent, and his thick curly hair and solid bulk gave an impression of confident masculine energy.

'Mrs James.' He had a rather throaty voice. 'I have a proposal to make. Why don't you share in the project? Your husband's memory is a kind of inheritance, don't you think? You hold all his papers. It's a unique possession. Let's work together. We can sort out a share of royalties and you can view everything before publication.'

'I don't need money,' Helen came back.

Paul raised an eyebrow. 'The clinic?'

'The clinic doesn't pay me anything.'

'That's what I imagined. So . . .'

'That's my business. I survive.'

'Of course.' He hesitated. 'You are planning to go on working there then?'

'Is there any reason why I shouldn't?'

Paul hadn't expected to be sidetracked like this. 'Well,' he hazarded, 'I thought you might choose to leave because something important has changed in your life. One change prompts another.'

'Albert had no role in my working life,' Helen James said flatly, 'or not for the past twenty years. So his death hardly affects my job.'

Paul tapped the ash from his cigarette. 'I was thinking more in terms of . . .' – he inhaled again – 'well, of possible company. Not the job as such. Here in Delhi . . .'

'Please,' she said abruptly. 'I am old and my life is over. Albert was my life. I don't need company.'

He shrugged. 'I didn't mean to offend.'

Helen's face was flushed with repressed emotion. Paul felt sympathetic; he hesitated: 'Forgive me if I'm about to put my foot in it again, but I'm really struck by what you just said. You implied that you are going to go on working at the clinic, facing that tidal wave of sickness every day, at least in part because you feel your life is *over*. At what? Fifty-two? Fifty-three? You see, I just—'

'For God's sake!'

Helen shook her head in disbelief. She turned away to the window and looked down into the narrow street. A press of barrows and scooters were pushing past each other, weaving their way around women cross-legged on the ground beside baskets of bright fruit and children barefoot looking for amusement. It was all strangely soundless through the café window's thick glass.

She turned back to him. 'I don't want to help with your book and that's that.' She reached for her bag. 'And on this occasion, Mr Roberts, if it doesn't offend your pride, I'll get the bill.'

'Fine by me.'

Paul sat tight, his full cheeks creased in a smile of polite resignation. She stood up awkwardly between bench and table and began to slide out. He knew she was reluctant to leave; she had dressed carefully for their meeting in a nicely cut skirt and jacket. She is slightly taller than me, he realised. At the last moment, he asked: 'So what is it you're afraid I might write?'

'Don't start that nonsense again.'

But she had stopped moving.

'Don't you see,' he told her, 'what an extraordinary love story it has been: you and Albert together thirty years, your courage in all these medical missions, his remarkable mind?' Paul stopped. 'By the way, weren't we on first-name terms at the end of our first meeting?'

'That was after two vodkas.' She twisted her lips. 'There's a presumption about you that I don't like. Perhaps it's something American. In the end, you just want what you want what you want.'

'Guess I'm hustling for my job,' Paul said. 'Like anyone.'

After a short silence he shook his head and started again: 'Really though, there's something I don't understand in all this.'

She was still on her feet, one slim, sinewy hand resting on the table.

'And I suppose that intrigues me and maybe makes me a bit pushy. I get the feeling you're . . . kind of denying yourself the pleasure of talking about Albert. I'm sure it would be a pleasure for you to talk about him. So I start to think that you're not talking because there is something that mustn't be said.'

She sat down again.

'God, you're impertinent.' She frowned. 'And as it happens quite wrong.'

'Convince me.' Paul sat back but left his heavy forearms spread on the table. 'Convince me that Albert James was only a good man who never did anything worthy of a book. Really, you owe it to him. It—'

'Please,' Helen cut in. 'I can hardly owe him what he never wanted himself.'

She looked at the American with unusual directness. 'Doesn't it occur to you that I might be happy to chat to you, or any number of people for that matter, if only you weren't chiefly interested in making money out of Albert?'

'I'm sorry if it feels like that,' Paul said evenly.

She consulted her watch, twisted the strap back and forth on her wrist, appeared to reflect. 'All right, I'll give you two hours. Two hours. In which time I'll tell you everything there is to know. Does that sound fair? Then you can despair and give up the project and leave me alone.'

Paul grinned. 'I accept. Waiter!' he called. He asked the young man if they served alcoholic drinks.

'Of course, sir.'

'Excellent!' He turned to Helen. 'What will you have?'

She gave in: 'A gin and tonic.'

'But we only serve the alcohol with Sunday brunch, sir,' the waiter said. 'We are only having a licence for Sunday brunch.'

'Well serve us Sunday brunch!'

'But it is not Sunday, sir.'

Paul laughed. 'Okay, I'll have another coffee.'

But Helen James said no, she knew where they could get a drink. 'And you can call me Helen,' she told him.

'We met at a dinner organised by friends in North London. Finsbury Park. I remember the walk from the Tube. I was working in Casualty, in the Royal Free. Hampstead. It was my first job.'

Helen had taken the American to the garden of the India International Centre. Paul had stayed here once himself. She was drinking vodka, he Scotch. 'Two hours,' she repeated. The place was pleasantly flowery, quietly busy. Two or three acquaintances had nodded to her. It was now more than six weeks since Albert had died.

'I was very political in those days. I still am. Access to medicine has always been as important to me as medicine itself. Everybody was arguing public against private, it was the big question then, either or, nobody thought of a mix, and Albert was sitting quietly, saying nothing. You only noticed him really because he was so tall and trying to hide it, stooping, sitting on his hands and so on.

Then quite suddenly he said something like: If the charming young lady is truly anxious about people who get no treatment, logically she should be in Botswana, not Hampstead. And if the young gentlemen are truly convinced of the perversity of state medicine, they might want to take the first flight to Dallas.'

Paul smiled. 'As if he were some kind of referee?'

'Albert always stayed outside a discussion then suddenly commented on it. He'd just define positions, usually making them sound a bit naïve, then step back again. It could be quite offensive.'

'So, he wasn't just pure and good.'

'He was out of it.' She shrugged: 'Being good is often an offence in itself.'

'Surely, the person being good was you. He just had no personal interest in either side of the argument.'

'As you like.'

'But he was interested in you.'

'It took a little while . . .' Helen stopped. 'But to go back to that conversation: I told him that actually yes, I was looking into the possibility of voluntary service.'

'You had already planned to go abroad, then?'

Her eyes clouded. 'Yes, yes I had. I wanted to. But let's say it became more real after I had said it to Albert. So, a year later we married and, as you probably know, left at once for Kenya . . .'

'Hang on!' Paul raised a hand. 'You can't just jump ahead like that. How did you become lovers, how did you get married, how was it you decided to go to Kenya?'

'We married in a registry office.'

'I know that. Please, can't you give me just some idea of this courtship. Were there love letters? Did you have to break off other, er, engagements?'

Helen looked at the man. Paul returned her gaze. Her face was oval, attentive, and the eyes, catching the evening light, glinted. He couldn't make her out. Meanwhile, white-liveried waiters moved with slow Indian formality between the tables where the Delhi well-to-do sat in their colourful saris, sipped their cocktails and spoke with complacent animation.

'The first time we went out,' she eventually said, 'he asked me to some classical concert, Albert loved classical music, but I had a political meeting to go to. In the end he picked me up from home, drove me to my meeting, then went on to the concert himself, and we met again afterwards so he could take me home. I remember my mother was most impressed when he came to pick me up because she thought this man was taking me to hear serious music, and of course Albert had a sort of lanky academic look.' Helen laughed. 'We did that a lot. It saved me saying where I was really going. My parents used to give me a lot of stick about my politics.'

Paul shook his head. 'And then?'

'We married and went to Kenya.'

'Before exchanging kisses?'

Helen sighed. 'Albert was a wonderful man. That is all I will say.'

Paul bit the inside of his lip and narrowed his eyes.

'As I was saying, we were in touch with a local organisation that was eager to extend medical treatment beyond the urban area. Infectious diseases were the main concern. The idea was that we would establish a treatment and vaccination centre a couple of hundred miles east of Nairobi with a van to take medicines to the villages. Albert would run lab tests on the main diseases. I would be doing the direct work with the people.'

'But of the two of you, who was it who really decided to go?'

'I wouldn't have gone without him.'

'I'm not sure I understand.'

She seemed to reflect. 'Albert was the tenderest of men. Actually, I sometimes thought he was unnaturally tender. But he seemed to like the fact that I was brusque and practical.'

'Perhaps unnaturally brusque and practical.'

Helen laughed. 'Some people have said that. Anyway, what I'm saying is that he encouraged me, but he liked to stay in the background. He was enthusiastic about going, but maybe more to be away from England, or from his family, or just to watch me doing what I was determined to do. I don't know. Sometimes you thought a decision was yours, then months later you felt Albert had coaxed you to it, just by being there watching you.'

Again her eyes caught the light. She reached up and fiddled with the tie holding her hair. It was honey hair streaked with grey. The tie was green. When she'd got it right, she said in a completely changed voice, 'Order another drink.'

The American obeyed at once.

'And how was the work in Kenya?'

'There's nothing to say except that there was an extraordinary amount of it; an endless stream of people with every kind of complaint, and, as always in these places, every kind of political problem, every kind of obstacle, incomprehension, cussedness: gangs trying to get a cut and to control how we allocated the few beds we had, trying to tell us who we could work with and who we couldn't. It was always uphill. We were always exhausted.'

'And how did Albert feel about it? I mean, his background was scientific research, not medical work.'

The drinks arrived. Helen swallowed half of hers at once. 'I hate the crows in this country,' she announced. The birds were settling on the lawn as darkness fell. 'Albert had an intellectual approach. He worked out of curiosity, not for the work itself. The side he enjoyed most was learning the language. I never knew anyone who could pick up so much speaking so little. He was a sponge. He even wanted us to use Swahili at home, when I could barely say, Where does it hurt? He always loved to use local languages, even when he was guessing most of the time. And he always spoke everything with a strong English accent.'

'So it was learning languages that he began to shift away from aid work to anthropology.'

'Could be.' Helen looked away across the centre's garden. Her chin dipped. 'The truth was' – she turned back and picked up her drink – 'the truth was Albert always mocked me. In a way. He admired me . . . and he mocked me.'

Helen James burst into nervous laughter. 'There, I've said something you didn't expect, Mr Biographer. I loved him deeply and he mocked me, he encouraged me and mocked me. Now. Enough. I don't want you to write this book. You couldn't capture Albert. On the other hand,' and now she smiled more sanely, 'it would be very nice if you would take me out to dinner . . . sir.'

'I'll call a cab,' Paul said.

They talked about India now. If the caste system was far less rigid, the underlying mentality was intact, she thought, and sanctioned every form of inequality. Likewise the mad idea that you were reincarnated in the form you deserved.

'Albert loved the caste complications; which group eats what and wears what clothes on which occasions. I just can't be bothered. I've tried to learn the stories of their gods, but it never sinks in: Parvati, Shiva cutting off Ganesh's head, Garuda, Shesa. I don't know how anyone can take such a ragbag seriously. You can see where Bollywood came from. Albert adored it, all the myths and stupid fanfare. But he never submitted his mind to it. He mocked that too in the end.'

She had taken the American to a place in Vasant Vihar where they climbed three flights of stairs to a bare room with tables too close together and food simple and spicy. Paul was struck by her appetite. She had ordered mutton and beer. It was as if she had suddenly remembered how to eat and drink. She was a handsome woman, he thought. The hair was still thick. She held her shoulders well back, the breasts were full. And she seemed to do everything with so much purpose: eating, drinking. It was clinical, almost brutal.

'I always found India exhilarating and brutal,' he suddenly said. 'I'm always glad I've come, you know, but gladder still to go home. When I get out of the plane stateside I feel a fantastic sense of relief.'

'You get over that,' she told him, 'after a few years.'

'And you don't think of home at all?'

'You mean England? From time to time. But there would be no point in going back.'

'There would be your son.'

She hardly seemed to notice he had said this. 'Why don't you tell me about your next wife?' she asked. 'I presume there's another on the way.'

Paul laughed. 'Now who's impertinent?'

'I don't plan to write a book about it, do I? Anyway, you make it fairly obvious you're a sensual man.'

'I do?'

'You do.'

'There isn't anyone,' he said.

Helen looked at him sidelong. 'How old is she?' she asked with a wry smile. 'Or are you afraid of telling?'

'Okay,' he laughed. 'She's twenty-six. Amy.'

'Hah! An age difference of what, fifteen years?'

'You're flattering. Seventeen.'

'And you don't miss her?'

'We exchange emails every day.'

'So it's serious.'

He shrugged. 'We have a good time.'

'Which to your mind is a serious thing.'

Paul reflected. 'One thing that's always struck me about India is that despite all the vitality here it's not a very sexy country, is it? The women are pretty, but they don't shout sex at you, they're so covered up and contained.' He hesitated. 'Maybe that's why I love getting back.'

'To your frenetic love life.'

'I wouldn't want to exaggerate.'

'You said yourself you were a compulsive.'

'I did?'

Helen frowned. 'Albert thought one of the problems in the West was that people didn't so much have a life as a sex life. You know? Just blindly meeting and mating. He admired the way relationships are more under control here.'

'Admired and mocked?'

'That's right. Mocking and admiring were the same thing for Albert.'

'But how can you do that?'

'I've no idea.'

'But . . .'

'He did it,' Helen said. 'The more Albert loved something, the less he felt part of it. Life itself even. Maybe it was like watching children. You love them and laugh at them. That's how he felt about the headhunters in New Guinea. Alternatively, you could say he was like a child watching adults. You know how children find us ridiculous, superfluous.'

'Certainly true of my kids,' Paul agreed, 'whenever I get to spend five minutes with them.'

But Helen had turned away. 'Albert always said he would have liked to be a child forever.' The thought seemed to put her in a pensive mood.

She didn't want any sweet or coffee but asked directly for the bill. She has taken over the evening, Paul thought. He let it happen and realised that although she had changed approach completely he nevertheless sensed a strong continuity, even an intensification of who the woman truly was: a fighter, he decided.

'I'll pay this one,' he offered.

'Thank you,' she said. At the bottom of the stairs she smiled and took his arm. 'Come with me.'

The estate was lively with honking traffic and every variety of roadside cooking, men calling their wares, groups eating cross-legged on the ground out of dishes of tinfoil. Helen patted a cow tied to a water pump. 'Hello Daisy darling! Isn't it lunatic,' she turned and laughed in Paul's face, 'that people touch their genitals to be purified! Could you think of anything less pure than a cow's cunt?'

Helen James was striding along almost coltishly now, pulling the American behind her. She claims not to like India, he thought, but obviously she is at home here. At home not liking it perhaps. Without warning, she started across the street. Paul found himself being steered through four and more lanes of moving honking swerving cars scooters autorickshaws buses trucks. Every encounter with every vehicle was a brazen challenge. It was mayhem. Helen laughed out loud as headlights flashed and veered.

On the other side, squeezing between parked vehicles, he discovered that her goal was the counter of a liquor store open to the street. 'A half pint of Royal Challenge and a bag of water,' she told the man. The shopkeeper had a scarf round his neck despite the warm evening. 'Come in,' she beckoned to Paul.

The liquor store was a tiny space of grubby shelves with a big fridge for beer. Helen walked behind the counter and through a door to the back. Paul followed her into a room whose walls were piled with beer crates. There were just a few plastic stools scattered between. A man in his early sixties was sitting alone, drinking whisky from a plastic glass. He nodded to them, but without smiling.

'Sit down,' Helen said, taking a stool.

'We could have found a nice bar,' Paul protested. 'We could have gone to the Ashoka.'

'This is more my style,' she told him. 'And cheaper.'

The owner stood at the doorway grinning. He was plump, paunchy, pockmarked. 'Hello madam, yes madam.' He obviously knew her. The room was lit by a naked bulb. Helen divided the whisky into two glasses, tore the corner of the water bag with strong teeth and, holding it carefully in both hands, poured. Paul sat on a box watching. Her wrists and fingers were rapid and purposeful. 'I had no idea there were these places,' he said.

'So' – she handed him his glass – 'what is it you imagine I'm hiding from you about my genius husband? The most intelligent man of the twentieth century. Some reviewer actually wrote that once.'

Paul drank. The whisky was rough. 'How can I know?'

'I'm sure you think you know.'

Helen said something now in Hindi to the man at the door and he laughed showing filthy teeth; the man drinking alone nodded gloomily.

'Really I don't know,' Paul said. 'An affair, I suppose. Or affairs. It's hard to get through thirty years of marriage without an accident.'

She was already laughing. 'That's what a post-puritan New Englander with his divorces and young wenches would think.'

Paul decided to take her on. 'Well, there was that business in Chicago with the—'

'Albert was acquitted.'

Paul sipped the whisky. 'Despite the fact that a dozen or so other men whom the girl accused all confessed?'

'Yes, despite that fact. I always knew he hadn't done it.'

'But how could you be sure? A guy selling insurance house to house brings a girl with him and offers her as a prostitute. That was the story, right? Later when the police catch up with them she blows the whistle on everyone who had her. How can you be sure that of all of them Albert alone was innocent?'

'I'm sure,' Helen James said coolly. 'I knew Albert to the core. And he was acquitted.'

'For lack of evidence.'

'What evidence could either side produce?' Helen paused. 'You think I'd be worried about your writing the book because of that, when it's been in the public domain for years? That's got nothing to do with it.'

'Well . . .'

A young man hurried into the back room, clutching his quarter bottle of whisky and bag of water. He sat on a stool only a couple of feet from Helen and unscrewed the cap. Before pouring the drink, he rested the mouth of the bottle against the wall and tipped it a little so that a few drops of whisky dribbled down the bare bricks. Paul raised an eyebrow.

'For the gods,' Helen laughed.

The Indian smiled, as if this were a joke. He poured out half of the bottle into his glass and drank it off at once, then did the same with the rest. In less than five minutes he had finished and was gone.

'Impressive,' Paul said.

'They treat it as a little ceremony,' Helen told him. 'Albert used to love watching how people drink.'

'So what is the reason?' Paul asked.

She shrugged. With her long legs crossed on the small stool, he was very aware he was dealing with a woman who still knew how to play a woman's cards.

'Don't you want people to know about Albert, to read his work?'

She threw back her head and laughed. 'Maybe it's just that I don't want *you* to write the book.'

Suddenly, she leaned right forward from her stool, swayed a moment and almost fell in his direction. He smiled and caught an arm.

'But why not?'

She looked hard into his eyes. 'Because I don't like you, Paul.' She was struggling to her feet. 'I don't like you one little bit. You remind me of my brother: another slobby man who has to get what he wants.'

She swayed, pushed past him and stumbled out onto the street.

PART THREE

IN THE WEB

CHAPTER FOURTEEN

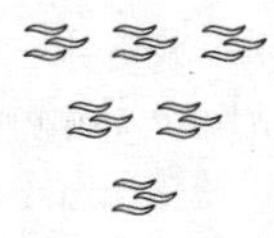

'I'm here,' he texted while still in the line for immigration. There was the usual jostling for position. John let them push. Already the heat was oppressive. The fluorescent lighting was oppressive. When the queue switched back in its snake of ropes, people sneaked to cut corners. They got a shoulder in front of you. This place is a battle, he thought. His mind was elsewhere. His mind was on the phone, but there was no reply.

'Where are you staying?' the immigration official asked when he stepped up to the desk. John stared. 'Where are you staying, sir? You haven't written an address on your landing card.'

John was blank. 'With my parents. Near the Lodhi Gardens.' He gave the address.

'You were here only three months ago, sir.' The official examined his passport. 'What is the purpose of your visit, please?'

'My father is ill,' John said. 'He's dying.'

The official looked him in the eye. John shifted from one foot to another.

'I'm very sorry to hear that, sir,' the man said and handed him his passport.

Now John headed for the exit. He had no baggage to collect. Already people were grabbing his arm, offering taxis, hotels, sightseeing tours. 'Sir!' It was a man in brown trousers, blue shirt. 'You are looking for a driver, sir?' 'Hello, hello! Hotel, sir, you are looking for a hotel?' They all wore plain trousers, plain shirts, grey or brown. They all said 'sir'. Suddenly, there was a woman whose skin was peeling from her cheeks in milky patches. She rose up in front of him. Her slack lips too might peel off, it seemed. She was pleading in Hindi, hands stretched out. John struggled across the concourse and out into the forecourt where he was met by a tremendous blast of heat and klaxons. How can I take a cab, he wondered, if I don't know where I'm going?

He was already sweating. He must wait for an answer to his message. He texted again, 'Where can we meet and when?' There was nowhere to wait. No shade. It was only 7 a.m. Perhaps the phone was off. Men constantly approached him. 'Water, sir?' 'Snacks?' 'Juice, sir? Hello!' Someone was blowing a whistle. I could call to find out, he thought. He didn't want to call. He didn't want to explain himself to a stranger on the phone.

The brown cabs inched and pushed across the forecourt, they piled into the space like animals squeezing through a gate. A voice yelled 'Pa-tai-yei, ma-ti-alli-yei!' Something like that. Then again. 'Pa-tai-yei!' It was a bellow. 'Ma-ti-alli-yei!' The man was selling something. John stood with his back to the wall, waving away all comers. A tall man had three crates on his head. 'No thank you. No, no thank you.' The size of people's suitcases was extraordinary. A man in a bright red turban laboured behind a heavy cart while an old woman with plump bejewelled belly kept up a harangue beside. A dog came to sniff John's leg, an unprepossessing mongrel. He must wait.

Then the phone vibrated and there was a message.

'JO! WHERE ARE YOU? YOU CAN'T REALLY HAVE GONE TO INDIA. WHY?'

It was the wrong message. He read the words twice but didn't reply. I'm not ready to reply. He hadn't felt ready to tell Simon either. He hadn't even called in sick. The trip had imposed itself. I must go back to India. He must confront this turbulence that had seized his mind and made life impossible. It was not something you could say to an immigration officer. I must get well, he thought. He must punish Elaine. 'Traditional scientific research can only be carried out from a position of stasis, from a level plane, in short in the most artificial of conditions.' That was something his father had written. John had found the piece on the Net. 'With sterilised gloves in sterilised spaces,' his father had written. 'With a clear and clinical mind.' John's mind was a pitching sea, a river that had burst its banks.

During the flight, a series of dreams had left only an impression of hard labour. No images or stories. When he awoke his muscles were tired, his back ached. He had been pushing trolleys, carrying crates on his head all night as the Airbus crossed Europe, the Middle East, Iran, Pakistan. I was working to get comfortable, he told himself, working like a dog to find a comfortable position. Now there was a dog at his feet again. Another mongrel. All the dogs in Delhi seem to be the same dog, he thought, gaunt and nervy and mongrel. He watched a woman with a baby slung at her breast, an older child on her back. She walked through the honking, thrusting taxis without concern. A driver rolled down his window to spit.

By eight o'clock John had begun to feel aggressive. He didn't want nuts. He wouldn't buy fresh molasses. There was a man grinding sugar cane. In a moment I'm going to hit someone, he muttered. I will. Then he was struck himself by the thought that Elaine must have texted her message in the middle of the night. It is 3.30 a.m. now in the UK. He watched the Europeans get themselves handed into limousines, or snatched into cabs. An elderly man fainted and had to be sat on his suitcase. Elaine was awake when she shouldn't be. A Sikh held up a card saying MR TINOTY.

The day was growing hotter; the sky was smudged and smeared with heat. MR TINOTY didn't arrive. The Sikh waited patiently. Then a line of women came carrying sand on their heads in broad shallow bowls. There was some scaffolding John saw now, to his left. The women went back and forth with their bowls of sand set on towels on their heads, their gaudy saris grimed with dirt. What if I receive no reply to my message?

An air compressor started up, then a drill. What would Granny Janet say if she knew this was how he was spending her money? The drill ate into the cement paving. It was Father's boast, John remembered, that he never did exactly the research he had described in his grant applications. Always something off at a tangent. What a stupid, stupid letter he had written! *Plagued, perhaps blessed, by dreams of rivers and seas.* 'They would never understand what I was really planning to do,' his father had laughed. 'But he always gives value for money,' Mother would add. Did she believe that? What value? When I'm ready, I'll surprise her, John thought. I'll turn up without warning and we'll have it out. At nine-thirty he went to fight at the prepaid taxi window.

'Connaught Place,' he told them.

John James had himself set down in the inner circle of the city's central plaza. He wandered for a few minutes along the luxury shop fronts, but his clothes were too heavy for this heat. And hotels will be expensive here, he realised. He turned at random into a radial road and wandered along for perhaps a quarter of an hour, checking into the streets right and left for hotel signs, avoiding beggars under a railway bridge, waving away rickshaw drivers.

Why am I walking so far? he asked himself. He had passed hotels, but not gone in. Why not? He had the impression he must be approaching Old Delhi and was struck by the thought that he knew nothing really about the town, or about India. His shoulder bag seemed impossibly cumbersome now. The crotch of his jeans chafed. I shouldn't have come, he decided. Real sanity would have meant hanging on at the lab, forcing his mind back into accustomed channels. But he had been trying to do that for months. He had tried to confront Elaine. She must have written that message in the middle of the night because that was when she had got home and found his note. Then John realised he hadn't tried the hotels because he didn't really want to be here. He was still hoping the whole thing could be avoided. Find a room now, he told himself, or you'll faint.

'Hello, sir. How can I help you, sir?'

John had climbed the stairs from the street. The Govind Hotel was on the fourth floor. A woman was pulling petals from a pile of flowers and floating them in patterns on a wide bowl of water on the reception desk. '900 rupees a night,' she said.

John watched her put a yellow petal on her fingertip. The pattern was a series of concentric circles. A bellboy took him along a long corridor, then round a stairwell, down some steps. There was a bolt on the door and a padlock. The room was narrow and brown with a small window opening onto a side street of broken stone, motorbikes and barrows. There was no loo paper but a hose to clean yourself as you sat. John showered, stretched on the bed and closed his eyes.

'You are obsessed by having your life organised and sorted,' Elaine had told him. 'So that you can bury yourself in your stupid lab with your precious research.' 'You're sick,' she shouted, when he tried to talk about Hanyaki. 'If you start coming to rehearsals to check on me, I won't be able to relax, I won't be able to move.' Far from being sweet on her, she moaned, the director was constantly complaining that she didn't put in enough effort. She didn't think hard enough about the part. That's why she stayed so late. He was constantly humiliating her.

Elaine made love eagerly now, but John had begun to wonder if it wasn't all false. It was a mimed lust, like her voices on the phone. Sex was a cause for irony. Elaine mimed sex. She pulled him to the bed, but she didn't really want to make love at all. So he sensed now. He couldn't understand if she really had orgasms or not. It troubled him. She came theatrically, he thought. Perhaps she couldn't do things if she didn't act them.

John was lost. Something unfathomable had happened between them. It started when he went to India, or when she had got the part in the play. It was about a terrorist attack in an airport. Or perhaps when I asked her to marry me. They made love, then she cuddled him and smothered him in baby talk. He didn't want baby talk. He was an adult. She had been acting her dismay when his father died, he thought. That was the first time he noticed it. She acted to prove she could act. Her family wanted her in an insurance office, or behind the counter of a bank. The real world, her father said. She acted her ability to act. Walking home one evening, John pulled his mobile from his pocket and called the number on his father's out-of-office emails. He was on the Edgware Road. The code for India was 0091 he remembered. At once there was a ringing tone. A recorded voice spoke first in Hindi then English. 'The person you have dialled is unavailable.'

He had sent a text message. 'Who is that? I am Albert James's son.' Perhaps if he returned to India he could undo whatever had gone wrong last time. Then he could come back and really be here. There was no reply. Reading a research paper on the use of radioactive beacons to trace gene expression in cancer cells he found himself writing in the margin: 'It is enigma that traps the mind.' He looked at his uneven handwriting beside the neat column of the printed article. It wasn't something he normally did. 'Please be in touch,' he texted to the number he had found on his father's email. Only then did he realise that Simon was standing in the doorway watching him. 'We'd like you to put together a presentation for the guys from Glaxo,' the director told him. 'The usual PowerPoint stuff. But we need to impress.'

John was efficient at the lab through April and May, but he was going through the motions. People supposed the fall-off of energy was due to his difficulty getting a grant. It was understandable. He put together the presentation for Simon. It said the obvious: there were thousands and thousands of permutations to go through before they could reconstruct the way a bacterium passes from active to dormant, then years later from dormant to active. He knew Simon couldn't object – it was lucid and well documented, the rhythm of delivery was fine, John was good at that – but he wouldn't be satisfied either. Something was missing, the excitement of a deeper engagement, an imaginative idea. As they sat down to show the slides to the Glaxo team, a message arrived on his mobile: 'I am a friend of your father. My name is Ananya.'

Was it a woman's name or a man's? John had made that mistake before. He checked as soon as the presentation was over. Google's first entry was a fashion shop, then a charity. He clicked on a site: *Ananya Discovering India*. 'Ananya means "no other" in Sanskrit,' he read. 'And India is like no other country, extraordinary, unalloying.' Unalloying was a strange word for a tourist site, John thought. What did it really mean? That it doesn't mix. It doesn't spoil. But India was all mixing. He selected Images and found photographs of Indian women. Ananya Chatterjee, Ananya Roy, Ananya Das. 'A friend of your father.' What kind of friend?

John had been distracted during that presentation to the team from Glaxo. He hadn't impressed. But he couldn't bring himself to worry. 'I feel taken for a ride,' he had said to Mother that evening after the trip to the Taj. How is it possible, John wondered, to say things without having planned to say them, to make complaints that make no sense, even to yourself? In what way taken for a ride? But that is how ideas come, of course, when you least expect them. They are in the air.

Not in the air of the lab though. He was having no ideas at work. 'You are seeing this Hanyaki or whatever he's called,' he accused Elaine, 'aren't you?' He started the conversation right after they made love. 'I can sense it, Ellie. I know there's something happening.'

Elaine was silent. 'If you don't believe me when I deny it,' she said, 'what's the point of my saying anything?' She added dryly: 'Actually I'm screwing all the guys on the cast. And the girls too. Hmmm, darling, will it be a threesome or a foursome tonight?'

Deep down, all John wanted to do was work. He couldn't. Perhaps deep down was not deep at all. Now that he had some money he took to drinking while Elaine was at rehearsals. He kept a few bottles of beer in the flat, then some whisky. It had begun with Father's funeral, he thought. There were the girls, the yellow petals, the short speeches, but the ceremony was over before it began. *Some figure I desperately need*, Dad had written. *As he/she perhaps* . . . The funeral wasn't proper somehow, John thought. And I needed nothing till this happened. 'Albert was my life,' Mother said, 'and I his,' and she had pressed the button at once. Dad had disappeared between the gold and the purple. 'Were you there when my father died?' he texted Ananya. Three days later she replied: 'I would like to meet you.'

As the days passed, John realised it was only a question of time. They were empty days. He was frightened. He still worked twelve hours at the lab, but in his mind he was no longer part of the team. He still saw Elaine most days and they made love, but he wasn't with her. You have become a loner, he thought. This Japanese bloke was twenty years older than Elaine if he was a day.

At the lab Simon asked if something was the matter; he had put in a request, the supervisor said, for an extra research grant: 'I'll do whatever I can to keep you, John.'

Elaine asked why he was so distant. She did little favours. She brought him sweets and cakes. John had a young man's sweet tooth. He wolfed them with whisky. She tried to get him involved in bitches about her father who was now offering to buy her a flat on condition that she find the proverbial proper job.

'They're scared of anyone who has a *vocation*,' she said. 'Maybe I'll have to run away to the Third World before they'll take me seriously.'

John listened but couldn't muster the indignation with which he had wooed her in the past. 'I'd like to know what Dad was working on when he died,' he said experimentally. 'I'd like to know why he was interested in spiders of all things.' He laughed. 'Maybe he didn't die of cancer at all. Maybe he was bitten by a tarantula.'

Elaine asked if he was still having those strange dreams about the coffin in the flooded lab. He wasn't. 'You know, Dad never owned a car,' he told her, 'he never learned to drive.' 'So what?' she asked. 'He used to say drivers were locked into a logic of killers and victims, chasing each other through a grid of streets.' 'Your father was nuts,' she told him. 'No doubt he got your mum to drive him around.' 'They always lived in the sort of place where you can afford a taxi,' John explained. 'Assuming there were any roads.'

'Can I email you?' he texted Ananya. As always the reply came some days later. She didn't have email. 'I'd like to meet you,' she wrote again. 'Are you in Delhi?' He kept her messages on the phone and reread them. 'I am a friend of your father. My name is Ananya.' 'I would like to meet you.' 'I don't have email.' It wasn't much. John wrote an email to his mother: he had seen Granny Janet, he said, and she had given him some money. 'She spent most of the time bad-mouthing you of course. By the way, Mum, do you know of anyone living in Delhi called Ananya?'

He read what he had written: 'living in Delhi' was very vague. He remembered how Mother had finally given way to emotion on his last night in the flat. 'I can't believe he's gone, John. I just can't believe it happened.' She had said the words as if literally she could not believe it. There was no acting there. 'I don't know what to do, or who I am,' she had said.

He didn't send the email. But it seemed scandalous to John that his mother hadn't written again to find out what had happened to him, whether he had got some money or was sleeping on the street. Vaguely, he wondered what would become of her. She would grow old and die in a foreign land. What would happen if she fell ill? She wouldn't ask for help. Perhaps there won't be anyone to inform me when she dies. Do these things matter? Elaine told him she would love to go to Delhi to meet John's mother. He couldn't see when she was ever going to get the time, he said sourly, with first the rehearsals then the play's run in the theatre.

'Suit yourself,' she said.

The moment came when he could resist no longer. It was a physical thing, or it felt physical. Towards the end of May. But there is no difference, John realised now, between physical things and mental. In the space of a few hours he was at Heathrow, he had his ticket, he was in the air. There was still £600 of Granny Janet's money to spend.

CHAPTER FIFTEEN

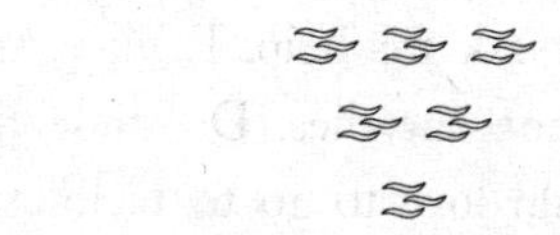

In the Hotel Govind John woke shortly after midday. His mouth was dry from the air conditioning and there was a mosquito on the loose. He scratched an ankle. It was strange, he thought, to find himself in the same city as his mother but without her knowing. Then he remembered and reached quickly for the phone. There was another message from Elaine. 'One day you ask to marry me, the next you run away. What am I supposed to think? I haven't slept all night.'

John needed to eat. He went out, found a place open to the street and sat down. He felt nervous being the only white person and seeing groups of young men looking at him. There were only men in the place, their heads bowed over bowls made of tinfoil. 'Some dhal,' he said. 'Please. A chapatti. Some lamb. A bottle of water.' It is madness to be here, he decided. The heat was suffocating. Granny Janet had been right that it was madness to spend your life away from home. There is a place that has meaning and there is everywhere else. Fans pushed air at him through a grill. But John had no home. He never had. Unless the lab. 'I am staying at the Govind Hotel off Bhavbhuti Marg,' he texted. 'Please be in touch.'

He felt simultaneously listless and tense. It was strange that he had visited so many countries in his childhood but never learned much about them. He had been enthusiastic about Chicago but his parents had left before he had had a chance to discover the place. Was it possible, John wondered now, that there was something shady in his father's relationship with this Ananya? His parents' perfect marriage had been the basis of the James family myth, it was the fixed point in all their moving. They were an exemplary couple, a partnership. 'Partners in shipping,' mother laughed. How could John ever form a relationship to compete with that?

The food was good. Afterwards, he wandered around the streets. It was too hot. He was wearing shorts and sandals now; it seemed amazing that the Indians could wear socks and shoes and long trousers in this heat. He needed water. At a crossroads he watched a little girl picking fleas out of her mother's hair while the woman sat in the dirt beating her hands on a drum. The girl squatted shifting from haunch to haunch, her fingers lifting strands of her mother's hair, plucking away the fleas. Meanwhile, the woman kept up a listless rhythm on the skin of her conga. John bent down and put a coin on the piece of sacking beside her.

It was not until the third morning that a message arrived. It was on his phone when he woke up. 'Come to bridge near Red Fort. 6 p.m. I have bicycle.'

But now John had diarrhoea. Perhaps it was cleaning his teeth with the tap water. He called reception and they brought him pills, bananas, bottles of water. He spent most of the day on the loo, washing and washing himself. 'Chaos,' he muttered.

More and more John felt angry that he had come. He had been drawn against his will by an invisible thread. It was thousands of miles long. His spidery father had strung it out, drawing him to a place that made no sense. I was never attached to my parents, he thought, and here I am throwing away everything I've worked for to find out about a man who never produced anything. Why not wait for the biography? he laughed sourly. At five he left the hotel.

He had planned to walk. It was less than a mile, he thought. After a hundred yards he faltered. He was entering Old Delhi. The crowded pavements and busy traffic were hard work. His stomach seemed to give. Things were shifting.

'You need help, sir?'

At once a man was at his elbow.

'Hello, sir! Where you are going?'

The Indian was in his forties perhaps, with dark toffee cheeks under a mop of hair. One eye was still and dead, but the other brilliantly alive. He was constantly smiling, his head wobbling under the thick black hair.

'You please come with me, sir!'

John tried to resist but a few moments later found himself high off the ground on a bicycle rickshaw.

He had never taken a real rickshaw before. He had never meant to take one. There was something obscene about the little man's thin calves straining to pull him along. John clenched his bowels looking at the ferment of the streets.

Because the driver imagined he was a sightseer, he went out of his way to take him via Chandni Chowk. The rickshaw slowed to walking pace in the market throng. Peddlers were shouting their wares. Beads and fans were waved under his nose.

John felt dazed. When the Red Fort appeared, forbidding and solid at the end of the street, he instantly understood the attraction of a severe Islamic order. I need a walled place, he thought, a quiet place, where you can think and work. The Muslims had once been great scientists, he remembered. Had they? They created artificial spaces. With – what were they called – jawabs? For symmetry. Why on earth had Dad sent him off to the Taj? Now I am going to see a woman who knew Dad, he reminded himself. And I am seeing her behind my mother's back. Behind my girlfriend's back. This aspect hadn't struck him before. As if I were to have a child with Elaine and in twenty years' time that child were to visit a woman who knew me without discussing the fact with Elaine. Or as if the son of the Japanese director came to visit Elaine without telling his mother, the director's wife. John smiled. 'Even paranoids can be betrayed,' he remembered. It was something Dad once said. He would never have imagined he remembered so much his father had said.

The rickshaw man took him to the left of the fort down a steep hill with fruit stalls, pigs and filthy gutters. It was actually a rather pleasant way to get about. The vehicle's wheels were nicely sprung and the cushion beneath him thick. He was comfortable. Others on the street were labouring. The driver had to resist the momentum of the pedals as the slope dipped and the vehicle accelerated. They passed beneath a road bridge where bodies slept among rubbish and flies, then down to the grubby riverside and eventually to the bridge.

John realised now that he had seen it before in photographs: a long, rickety Meccano structure of two parallel one-way bridges, each with two tiers, the road traffic running back and forth on the lower levels and trains rumbling above.

'You can leave me here,' John said.

The driver didn't want to leave him. 'Where you are trying to go, sir?'

'This is fine. Thank you so much.'

It was ten to six.

'You would like to cross the bridge, sir? Or you are wanting to go to the ghats? Very beautiful. Vijay Ghat. Raj Ghat.'

John took out his wallet and gave the driver a hundred rupees. It was way over the top. He climbed off the seat. 'I have to meet somebody,' he said.

'I am waiting, sir. Perhaps I am taking two people sir. Yourself and your friend, sir.'

Instead of encouraging him to go, the money had made the man more determined.

'I don't want you to wait. My friend will have a bicycle.'

The driver wouldn't go. He pulled his rickshaw off the road onto the muddy riverbank. John's bowels were rumbling again. Leaving the man on the bank, he went to stand at the point where pedestrians and cyclists were crossing the bridge on a walkway separated from the road by iron railings. Everything was old black iron. He gritted his teeth and clenched his stomach. Twenty feet below, the river was brown and sluggish, speckled with trash. Boys swam like rats in a yellowish foam. Broad and melancholy, the further shore seemed disconnected from the noisy back and forth on the bridge. What kind of woman will it be? he wondered. Europeanised? In her fifties? Her thirties? A fat Sikh trundled a broken scooter. Two Muslim girls passed in burkhas. Who had Father given his mobile to?

'Are you Mr John?'

He turned and found a nervous, pouting smile, bright, uneven teeth. A girl in her teens, wearing loose trousers and smock, stopped her bicycle and put down her foot. 'I am Ananya. Come, you must walk beside me.'

She climbed off her bike and began to push it onto the bridge. 'I don't want people to see us,' she said.

He didn't ask why, but fell into step beside her along the wooden boards. She was much smaller than himself, gracefully quick. Out of the corner of his eye he noticed the rickshaw driver was following.

'I thought you would be older,' John said.

The girl turned. She wore her hair in a single heavy braid of satin black. Her cheeks were round and dark.

'Mr Albert had many young friends,' she laughed.

The bicycle was between them. It was an old-fashioned lady's bicycle. Her trousers and smock were pea green, with a maroon scarf tied round the neck. Her hands on the handlebar were tiny. The traffic thundered and the bridge rattled and shuddered.

'Mr Albert was very kind.' She had to raise her voice. 'We were trying to help him with his research.'

'What research was that?' John asked.

'Research,' she said vaguely. She smiled, leaning forward to push the bike. 'There were a lot of us. Ten, twelve. Acting things.'

'And did my mother know about you?'

The girl looked puzzled.

'But how did you meet him?' John asked. 'Why did he give you his phone?'

She seemed pleased to tell the story. 'I was dancing at a wedding. I work for my father; he has a sari shop. It was a wedding. Mr Albert asked me and the other dancers to help him. He knew one of the other girls. Vimala. We had to act things. It was a theatre. It was very beautiful. He wanted girls who were not actors. We must stop catastrophes.'

'I beg your pardon?'

There was a storm of klaxons now. About halfway across the bridge an autorickshaw had broken down and its driver was changing a wheel. Between the iron rails each side there was only just room for other vehicles to pass. John was struck by the urgency of the klaxons and the contrasting calm on the drivers' faces. As if these people were simultaneously in a frenzy and at peace. Changing his wheel, the autorickshaw man remained quite unperturbed by the clamour he had caused. John's rickshaw driver held his position a few paces behind them. When John turned, he smiled extravagantly from stained lips.

'What do you mean, stop catastrophes? And the phone?'

'Oh,' she laughed, 'you have so many questions!'

As they talked, they were constantly having to step aside for pedestrians coming the other way. Beyond the river, day suddenly dissolved into night and smoke rose in luminous smudges from the sandbanks.

'Albert wanted us to tell these stories,' the girl said, 'and also to make dances and act things.'

'But why?'

She shrugged her shoulders, then stopped the bicycle a moment. Her forehead wrinkled. 'There was an expression he used. I've forgotten. We were having fun with him. I got some new friends. We must prepare a performance. Everybody was very excited. Then Mr Albert died.'

The bridge was a good 400 yards long. They walked on, stepping aside for a man with a goat. It was just another of Father's anthropological projects, John thought. I have thrown away hundreds of pounds to meet a dumb girl Dad had roped into one of his zany projects.

'People are rabid dogs,' the girl announced. Her face brightened. Again she stopped her bike. 'People are rabid dogs. That was something Mr Albert said.'

'Rabid dogs? And?'

'We must stop them biting.'

'But how?'

She shook her head. 'It was his research.'

When John caught her eyes he saw she didn't understand herself why she had been involved. Quite probably his father hadn't wanted them to understand.

'It was fun for us.'

They were nearing the end of the bridge. John could see a policeman directing the traffic at the junction where the vehicles crossing the river met the embankment.

'But why did he give you his phone?'

'I don't know. He said he was going away. Your other friends' numbers are on the phone, he said, if you want to meet when I am not there, if you want to go on with the performance.'

The girl looked at John rather defensively.

'So he gave you his phone when he knew he would die.'

'The battery is no good,' she said. 'It only works when I can use the charger. In my father's shop. And I am not going there every day.'

They stepped off the walkway onto the bank. 'We must say goodbye,' she told him. 'My father will pass soon on his scooter.'

'But . . .' John cast about.

She watched him, catching a lip under protruding teeth. 'Also I wanted to say . . . you are his son?'

'Yes.'

'You don't look like him.'

'Of course I'm his son.'

'Your father did not seem so ill, Mr John. It was strange he gave me the phone. He said he was just passing my father's shop and he came in. He said we must go on even without him, I must use the phone, but the others were all arguing and we stopped.'

'Look, did you post a letter to me from him?'

'I am sorry?'

'From my father. Did you find a letter he had written and post it to me?'

'I don't understand,' she said.

John returned to the hotel with the rickshaw driver who was waiting nearby, grinning and signalling and sure of his prey. They plunged into the overheated chaos of the traffic going back into the city. Beneath a balcony a goat stood on a large block of wood, its neck chained in such a way that if it stepped off the block it would be choked. From the towers of the Jama Masjid a wail to prayer tensed the darkness. A crowd surged up the steps through smoky lamplight. John felt that all power and purpose had been sapped out of him.

CHAPTER SIXTEEN

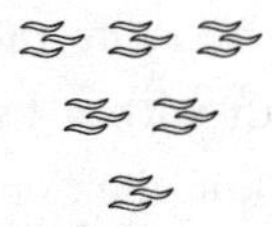

Dear Helen (if I may),

I will shortly be returning to Boston, but before I leave I wanted to show you the opening pages of this biography in the hope that you might change your mind about assisting me.

As you will see, the introduction offers a brief overview of your husband's life, suggesting the scope and ambition of his work. To whet the reader's appetite I have dared to surmise that his ultimate goal was to find a new state of mind, or pattern of behaviour, that would provide the departure point for a solution to many contemporary crises: political, environmental and existential.

In the second chapter I have outlined the major formative incidents in Albert's childhood, and here I would be very grateful if you could correct anything I have gotten wrong.

It goes without saying that your decision not to give my work your backing is not only a major setback but a source of considerable personal regret. It would have been a great pleasure to work with you.

Sincerely,

Paul Roberts.

Paul had taken this letter together with fifty pages of typescript in person to Helen James's clinic, receiving, less than forty-eight hours later, a phone message inviting him to dinner at her flat. He was hugely encouraged. His work had convinced her, he thought, and he would now be rewarded with a view of Albert James's home. Preparing to go out in the evening's stifling heat, Paul shaved carefully and dressed to charm in a light linen suit and maroon-coloured shirt.

But on arrival at the James's apartment, the American found he was not the only guest. 'Meet Kulwant Singh,' Helen James said in a bright voice as she led him into the main room. It was some kind of party. A burly Sikh with a handsome blue turban and thick beard sat cross-legged on the floor in loose old trousers, his back against home-made bookshelves, while a middle-aged lady with sizeable midriff was kneeling forward on a cushion in the centre of the room, holding forth most earnestly to a gaunt Englishman and his younger Chinese partner.

Removing his shoes, Paul apologised for not joining the others on the floor – 'I'm just not a flexible guy,' he confessed – and took a place on the sofa where he was at once served some kind of cocktail by a tall girl who hurried back and forth prettily barefoot with drinks and snacks. No sooner had Helen sat down beside him to make the necessary introductions than she was on her feet again to welcome another couple, this time two elderly and jovial Indians. In a simple white cotton dress she seemed rather girlish for a woman of her age. Heading for the door, she called, 'Oh by the way, Aradhna, Mr Roberts is an expert on Gandhi,' and coming back, among a flurry of handshaking, she announced of the woman speaking intently from her cushion: 'Aradhna Verma is president of the Delhi Gandhi Society.'

So even before he could take a proper look around the apartment, Paul found himself embroiled in a polemic about the way India's media would only pay attention to the plight of the rural poor if some celebrity or other happened to say a word on their behalf. 'And even then,' Mrs Verma complained, radiant with disgust, 'the journalists are always more interested in the celebrity than the poor! They want to know what are Arundhati Roy's holiday plans or where is her husband shooting his next film when she is trying to tell them about a rescue package for small debtors. Have you any idea,' the woman demanded of the gathering group, 'how many poor farmers have committed suicide over their debt problems just in the last year? It is quite disgraceful. Thousands! Many of their wives have also killed themselves. And in almost every case a life could have been spared by the gift of just 1,000 rupees. 1,000 rupees! Or of course by the arrest of the moneylenders who are all miscreants of the worst calibre. The police should nab them at once, but of course they take backhanders. And these journalists want to know if Arundhati is going to the Cannes film festival!'

Elegantly dressed in a silver grey sari and orange blouse, beringed fingers twined over her knees, Aradhna Verma swayed persuasively back and forth as she spoke. The decision to kneel had put her in a position of command over those who sat cross-legged and whenever there was a hint of interruption she raised a voice that seemed to resound from deep in her solid belly. It was only when she accepted another gin and tonic that Paul was able to remark: 'Of course Gandhi himself was very much a celebrity.'

The woman turned on him. 'What I am saying is that the Mahatma's lesson has been quite forgotten by today's media men and so we have to find more aggressive and creative ways to bring his agenda to their attention.'

'Aggressive?' Paul asked. The young girl offered a tray of snacks on sticks. 'Thank you,' he said. He loved to eat.

'Non-violence doesn't mean we must be passive,' the woman told him. 'That is a confusion you Europeans are constantly making. Either you are colonising the world with your assault weapons or sitting back doing nothing but whine and talk of peace and love.'

'I'm American,' Paul laughed. 'Which is worse, I guess.' Raising his eyes to draw in the rest of the company, he said: 'Perhaps the problem is that celebrities really are more interesting to readers than the rural poor. Gandhi was certainly more interesting than the people he was trying to help.'

'But is news for you only a question of what is *interesting*?' Aradhna Verma came back. 'A man kills himself for lack of 1,000 rupees and you are worried about entertainment!'

Regretting he had joined in, Paul recalled how seriously Indians took their political debates and how many aperitifs they could put away before getting to table. The Sikh man, however, was smiling beneath heavy eyelids.

'I'm afraid I forgot your name,' Paul told him.

'Kulwant Singh.' He reached across to offer a large hand. His voice was pleasantly deep, his small eyes playful.

'And how is your daughter, Kulwant?' Helen stepped in. The ice in her drink tinkled as she sat on the sofa. 'The poor girl hurt her leg in a road accident,' she explained to Paul, simply talking over the drone of the Gandhi woman, who was thus obliged to address herself more directly to the Englishman and his Chinese girl.

'I'm afraid the marriage is off,' Kulwant said. He grimaced. 'Not because of the groom's family in the end, but because Jasmeet was so upset that they had hummed and ha'd when she was needing surgery. She says she will not marry somebody for whom she is no more than goods and chattels. She wants equality.'

'Good for her!' Helen clapped, and added with a wink: 'Kulwant's daughter sometimes helped Albert with his research.'

'How interesting, in what way?' Paul asked.

Kulwant shrugged his shoulders. 'Don't ask me! But actually' – he turned back to Helen – 'it was very stupid of Jasmeet to object because of this hesitation on the groom's side. Nobody would want to marry their boy to a girl with one leg, would they? If it had come to that, which praise God it didn't. To my thinking, his family was in the right to wait.' Teasingly, he said: 'Would Albert have married you in the end, if you had had only one leg?'

Paul was surprised at the indelicacy of the question given the man's recent death, but Helen seemed amused.

'I'm sure he would, yes,' she said. 'But perhaps legs were not Albert's main concern.'

The Sikh man burst into crude laughter, as though privy to some information that made the remark hilarious. He spluttered and pulled out a handkerchief.

'Bless you,' Helen smiled, and went on: 'What about you, though, Paul? Would you marry your little Boston beauty – forgive me, I forgot her name – if she lost one of her slinky legs?' To the Sikh she expanded: 'Our Mr Roberts is about to marry for the third time.'

'Oh, my warmest congratulations, sir,' Kulwant bowed his turban. There was something mischievous about the way his moist lips moved in the dark beard. 'You Americans are so enterprising! I'm afraid in the Sikh religion marriage is forever, as my dear wife never ceases to remind me.'

'Would you marry her,' Helen repeated, 'if the girl had some accident?'

'I wasn't actually planning to marry next week,' Paul stalled. He noticed that Helen James was forever putting him on trial, as if he wasn't quite serious. 'Thinking about it, though,' he said, 'no, I wouldn't. You are right,' he told Kulwant, 'a man likes to marry a girl with two good pins.'

'Something to be wrapping round his backside!' the Sikh laughed too loudly.

'What are you people talking about now?' enquired Mrs Verma.

Helen smoothed the dress on her lap: 'Our American friend here has just said that if his young girlfriend loses her leg, he will not after all make her the third Mrs Roberts.'

'Oh dear, is she ill?' asked the Chinese girl.

Paul laughed. 'It's a purely hypothetical situation. I was being provoked into saying something politically incorrect.'

'And how much younger is she, may I ask?' enquired Aradhna Verma.

'Seventeen years.'

'But that is so sad!' The Gandhi woman clapped her hands in shock. 'So sad!' The silvery material of her sari slithered. 'I mean, what kind of *company* can a grown man have with a little chit like that? And what can she see in you, poor thing, when she should be wriggling her tiny bottom in the discotheque?'

'No doubt she sees about thirty pounds too many in me,' Paul admitted. 'But I can assure you we get on marvellously.'

'Like a house on fire,' the Sikh laughed and had to wipe his nose again.

The women pretended to protest.

Paul added: 'Actually, of all his teaching, you know, I always thought Gandhi's position on celibacy was the one that made least sense. Did he really have to be celibate?'

'Celibacy is the hallmark of the saint,' Aradhna Verma responded severely. 'The renunciation of sexual matters can have a very great influence on your disciples. It is the guarantee of purity.' But now she too broke into a smile. 'Still, I don't suppose any of us would be very pleased if our husbands *forced* it on us, like the Mahatma did with Kasturbai. Can you imagine? Listen, Wife, no more sex!'

'The problem is not celibacy with one's wife,' Kulwant observed, 'but elsewhere!'

'That's for sure,' Helen said. She jumped to her feet and hurried off to the kitchen.

More guests arrived. More drinks were passed around. Keeping out of an argument between the mild Englishman and the Gandhi woman as to whether the British Raj had deliberately exacerbated caste divisions, Paul was finally able to look around. At once it was clear that the apartment was smaller than he had imagined and shabbier. The sofa was threadbare, probably second-hand when bought, or perhaps the place was rented furnished. The floor cushions were no more than dusty old pillows and not at all the lavishly coloured fabrics that Indian families loved to sport. The air conditioning was noisy and gave the room a sour, damp smell. There were no ornaments of any kind, nor any pictures on the wall, which was strange surely. No photographs, Paul realised, of Albert and Helen, or even of their son. They would be in the bedroom, perhaps. His book would need photos.

Meantime, angular and brisk as ever, Helen seemed to be in an uncertain mood. She joined the group round the sofa, was witty and worldly, but remained somehow fragile, unsettled. The party atmosphere actually underlined a brittleness about her, as when she had hurried off to the kitchen just as the Gandhi woman at last loosened up. Watching her begin another round of introductions – 'Hakim Azad,' she was saying, 'yes *the* prize-winning director' – Paul had the impression his hostess was going through the motions. Her mind was elsewhere.

'Ladies and gentleman,' Helen announced with a touch of irony when finally they took their places at table, 'as you've probably guessed, this is the first dinner party I have organised for a very long time.' She laughed. 'Normally I'm in bed by nine, I admit. Albert loved parties, but only, alas, in other people's houses. So I suppose if there is any meagre advantage in being alone, it is that I can now return your generosity over the last five years. It is a wonderful thing to see this miserable old flat so full.'

It was a rather odd allusion, Paul thought, to Albert's departure and for a moment there was silence. Then with much head-wobbling the elderly couple began to congratulate Helen on a lovely evening and remembered how there used to be many more pleasant dinner parties twenty years ago. Now partying seemed to be the exclusive reserve of the affluent young computer folk. 'I just felt that without Albert I was in danger of falling into a black hole,' Helen confided more privately to the Chinese girl as they settled down on their chairs. But she had allowed Paul to overhear, deliberately, he thought. And she had sat him beside her. She must be planning to tell him what she thought of the pages he had sent. Why else would he have been invited?

At table the Gandhi woman monopolised the conversation. She had no qualms about speaking with her mouth full. Next to her, wearing a long white kurta, the handsome Hakim Azad complained that environmental causes were being starved of funds. He directed wildlife documentaries. He spoke about tigers in Madhya Pradesh. Paul ate and listened. What kind of relationship had Albert James had with these people? The only concessions to the environment, Aradhna Verma said, were the ones made at the expense of the poor, when they were told that they mustn't use a certain pesticide or cultivate some bit of land where a rare snake lived.

Suddenly Helen protested: 'Aradhna, what matters is not tackling the media or blaming the rich but just doing the right things ourselves and then shutting up about it. If I began to list all the outrages I see every day, it would be endless. Find a small problem and solve it.'

The head of the Gandhi Society was not put out. 'Helen, dear, it is a question of how best we are impacting on the world, isn't it? If you save a life at the clinic, that is very positive, but if I persuade a hundred or a thousand others to save lives, that is more so. That is what the Mahatma did.'

Helen turned to Paul. 'Our American guest has written a book on Gandhi and has just begun a biography of Albert. Yes,' she responded to the expressions of surprise, 'he wants to write up Albert's life. So what's your line on this, Paul?'

There were a dozen people round the table now, eating with their fingers, served by the silent young Indian girl and an elderly lady who had been presiding over pots and pans in the kitchen. Scattered across the table were dishes and sauces and spices of every kind. Upon Helen's unexpected announcement, the guests all turned their eyes to the thickset American in his maroon shirt and linen suit.

Paul demurred. 'There's nothing I can tell an Indian audience about the Mahatma.'

'Try,' Aradhna Verma said threateningly.

'Do you see any similarities in Albert?' someone asked. 'I mean, they were both men of extraordinary ideas. And of peace too.'

Paul set down his fork. He looked round at his audience. Helen was putting him on the spot again.

'It's evident,' he said carefully, 'that the Mahatma was a very remarkable strategist and propagandist. He saw life as a moral task and believed in the absolute value of personal intervention in public affairs. What's more, he believed that you could act decisively and still remain pure through passive disobedience.'

He paused. 'Albert on the other hand . . . gee . . .' Paul pushed a hand across his bristling hairline. 'I guess I started this project without really understanding why. Albert didn't believe you could act and stay pure. Or maybe purity wasn't the issue for him. Maybe he didn't believe in *purposeful* action at all. He . . .'

Paul stopped. There was a certain embarrassment around the table. Even the serving girl stood still by the table, the tray hanging from her slim arm, listening, watching. When Paul raised his eyes she dropped hers. He was struck by a curious submission in her posture. She was very attractive.

Limp and polite, the Englishman said, 'I'm afraid I have to confess I know very little about Albert's work. We only met when he dropped by the council to suggest some project or other. I'm afraid his ideas never really fitted with what London was after. Perhaps you could tell me what I should read first.'

'Graham runs Delhi's British Council,' Helen explained.

'The main titles are obvious enough,' Paul said. He mentioned two or three and drank from his wine. 'They had a huge influence on me,' he added.

'In what way?' the film director enquired.

Paul couldn't understand if they were genuinely ignorant of James's work or if there was some kind of conspiracy of silence.

'Anyhow, it's Albert's *story* I'm interested in,' he ducked the question. 'Not just his thinking. It's a different kind of story. A harder one to tell, maybe.'

The serving girl was still motionless by the table. Her hair was fiercely parted in the centre like a schoolgirl's, the scalp almost white. A heavy black tress gleamed behind her head.

'Please, do go on,' Hakim Azad insisted. 'What every artist dreams of is influencing people's lives.'

'Albert was a scientist surely,' the lady of the elderly couple objected. 'Not an artist.'

'There is art in all presentation,' her husband remarked.

'Okay.' Paul dipped a stick of celery in some red sauce and looked around the table. 'Let's summarise like this: believing in action, Gandhi set himself at the centre of one of the century's most extraordinary stories, Indian independence, and sacrificed everything to it, appetite, wealth, sex, he . . .'

'Not exactly sacrifice, and not exactly to independence,' Mrs Verma objected. 'Gandhi's point was—'

'Please!' Helen said sharply.

'Let the man say his say,' the elderly lady chipped in. 'Albert was such a charming fellow, wasn't he,' she said warmly.

'That was Gandhi,' Paul said. 'But Albert stayed outside every story, or he got into them briefly, but only to dissolve them, or complicate them. You always come away from his work feeling . . .'

'Yes?' Every face was watching him.

'Well, I think the underlying idea was, embarrassing as it may sound . . .' But now he stopped again. He leaned back, grinned: 'Why not just wait for the book, folks? A man's influence isn't over the day we bury him. Maybe one day I'll be sitting at dinner with the president of the Delhi James Society.'

The film director laughed. 'Well said,' he announced. 'We will all be on the very edge of our chairs until your book is published.'

Amid a general sense of relief that the difficult moment was over, Helen remarked: 'Albert wouldn't have wanted that, though.'

'What?'

'A society, or even a biography.' She frowned. 'You know,' she hesitated. She seemed undecided whether to speak. 'Actually . . .' but again she wavered a moment. She drew a deep breath: 'Albert's greatest ambition was to be a ghost.'

'A ghost?' Kulwant raised an eyebrow.

'How do you mean?'

Helen now made a determined effort to smile. 'Albert wanted to be present and not present. Like a ghost. Or like the guy who holds the camera for the movie.'

'Interesting,' said Hakim. 'It would certainly be easier to film tigers if I was a ghost.'

'Perhaps he's here now then,' the Chinese girl offered. 'I am sure we all see the dead from time to time. My mother saw my father's ghost many times.' She stopped. 'How do you know, for example, when there's a big crowd, that some of the people are not dead?'

The serving girl turned on her heel and hurried away, banging her tray on the door frame.

A few minutes later, when he went to the bathroom, Paul was convinced he could hear crying somewhere. Looking in the mirror as he dried his hands, he saw a shelf on the wall behind and, turning, pulled down an annual report of the Royal Anthropological Institute. Every margin was crammed to bursting with tiny, slanted, spidery writing. Paul had to turn the book round and hold it right under the light: '*It may prove*,' he read, '*that what I have spent my life seeking to map out is nothing more than a vast tautology: If P, then P.*'

They ate sweets and drank lassis. The Gandhi woman had once again taken over the evening. Despite Helen's apparent endorsement of his role as biographer, Paul found himself unsettled. He must talk to her directly and bluntly and then tomorrow he would book a ticket home. Otherwise he would lose touch. He would lose Amy, if he hadn't already.

'Twenty years ago,' Mrs Verma was saying, 'people talked a great deal about socialism and equality of opportunity, but not any more. Today we are all resigned to the slums and the child beggars and the traffic of organs. All we talk about is Bollywood and statues of Ganesh accepting milk from devotees.'

'Oh, I read that story,' the British Council man remarked.

At this point the elderly lady reminded everybody that toward the end of the last monsoon season, people north of Bombay had started drinking the seawater because they said that Ganesh had performed a miracle making it turn sweet, 'when obviously it was just the monsoon rain washing fresh water into the ocean!'

'You see, even we are digressing now!' the Gandhi woman complained.

'The poor you have always with you,' Paul threw in provocatively. He would be the last guest to leave, he decided. He would have it out with Helen.

But the American had reckoned without Kulwant Singh. Her food barely finished, the Gandhi lady remembered another appointment. The Englishman wiped his mouth and stood up with his girlfriend: he had to be at the office early tomorrow. The director of documentary films became concerned about drinking too much before driving. The elderly couple, who it turned out were neighbours from the flat above, protested tiredness. All these people made their excuses and left before midnight, thanking

Helen profusely. The serving girl too and the elderly maid had washed the dishes and gone. But the Sikh hung on. A bottle of whisky had been found and the man was drinking hard. Helen too began to drink. She seemed excited.

The Sikh started to tell scabrous tales about the hospital where he worked. A young fellow doctor, another Sikh, had got himself invited to the States by an elderly American patient who had paid him for sex. 'Yes, it was a *man*,' Kulwant confirmed, 'he wanted to be buggered by this young doctor. He asked just like that. Will you bugger me!' Kulwant savoured the word. 'What a rascal! So the colleague went, *with his wife and family*, and is now settling down in Los Angeles. The American is even giving him a house. For being buggered! This is the sort of globalisation that will save India perhaps.'

Helen smiled. Paul was struck that she had no problems with such talk.

'Kulwant works in a private hospital offering high-quality minor surgery to foreigners,' she explained. 'All paid for in dollars, euros or pounds. Then he does a few hours at our clinic to save his soul.'

The Sikh banged his glass on the table. 'It is because I would rather work free for the poor people than go to the temple and pray. I say to my wife, Guru Nanak will forgive me for not going to temple because I am charitable to the poor people. My wife is in the temple every day all the day.' He poured another drink. 'Drink and be happy, Mr American! When you are happy, God is happy! We are all happy.'

It was one o'clock and the man wouldn't go. Helen had fallen into a meditative mood. Like many who usually go to bed early, once she had abandoned her routine she seemed to lose all sense of time.

'You did the right thing to organise a little party,' Kulwant was telling her. 'You need to have friends. You cannot spend your life mourning your departed husband, God rest his noble spirit. Let us drink to Mr Gandhi,' he suddenly announced, and picked up the bottle again.

In desperation, Paul said: 'Helen, can we talk about the book? Have you read the pages I sent?'

She looked at him. For a moment she seemed not to remember who he was or what he was talking about. Then she said, 'All right, yes.' And to the Sikh: 'Kulwant, I'm afraid you'll have to go now. I need to talk business to Paul.'

'You can talk in front of me,' Kulwant declared brightly. 'I am a silent man on these matters. I am silent as the tomb. As two tombs!' He laughed.

'Please, Kulwant,' Helen said.

The Sikh looked very hard, then got to his feet, hitched up his loose grey trousers, sighed, smiled. 'A very good evening,' he said in an unnecessarily loud voice. 'And thank you very much, madam.'

'Oh don't be such a clown,' Helen laughed.

As soon as she had shown him out of the door, she came back and said: 'Stay the night here, will you? Please, Paul.'

CHAPTER SEVENTEEN

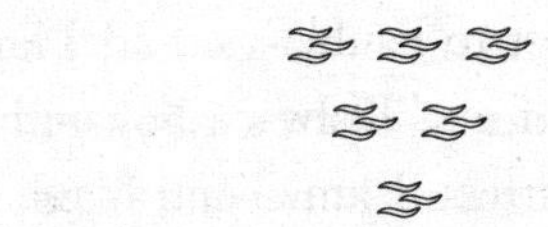

'I just fear I won't be able to sleep now,' Helen told him. 'Then I'll spend the night talking to Albert.'

She sat at the table and laid her hands on the wooden surface. The American irritated her, yet she had asked him to stay.

'This place is so empty,' she added. She was shaking her head. 'To think I threw the party to force my mind elsewhere!'

Paul was embarrassed. When he had decided to write about Albert James it was because he wanted to take his work in a new direction, to free himself from the coercive mechanisms of publishing and grow up as a writer. On the other hand, he had never had plans to become part of the Jameses' story.

'I'm sorry,' he said quietly.

'I'm afraid drink keeps me awake. It happened the evening we had dinner together too.'

'It can have that effect,' Paul said.

'Then I fall into an endless monologue, talking to Albert. Or dialogue. When you've been married as long as we were you can imagine the responses.'

'I suppose so.' Paul felt sympathetic but cautious. Her mixture of austerity with an edge of wildness unsettled him; and Helen was a good-looking woman. She must have been seriously beautiful when Albert carried her off to Kenya. Or she him.

'As soon as I close my eyes, he is there.'

The air conditioning seemed louder now; the room was very still.

'So what do you say to him?' Paul asked. It seemed there was no way he could just start talking about the book.

'I ask if he is happy, if he is calm, if he thinks we did the right thing . . . things, that is. Oh I know that's stupid. I know he's dead. Or I talk to him about patients. There's a boy with TB now, for example, a kid Albert had got to know and liked. He's very ill.' She shook her head. 'Albert had this theory that when a person is close to death, beyond the reach of this world, his mind enters into a special state that brings a superior wisdom. The Celts used to call it faery. I think there's a word in Hindi too. He'd hoped he'd enter that state himself and stay there a while, perhaps even convey what he discovered.' She shrugged her shoulders. 'In the end all his ideas had something contradictory about them.'

'Didn't he say something about that in the conclusion to *Postures*?'

'"An idea isn't worth considering unless it contains a contradiction",' she quoted. 'Want another drink?'

'I've had enough,' Paul said.

She poured for herself. 'It's strange but I've talked to him more since he died than in the five or six years before.'

Paul watched her; she tended not to let their eyes meet. Weakly, he said, 'I guess one day it will pass.'

'Sometimes it feels the less Albert actually did the more effect he had on people and the more he drew them to him.'

Then with a brusque change of tone, Helen said: 'But of course, what you want to know is whether I'll let you look at his papers, right, and these videos?' She waved at the shelves.

'That's what I came to India for.'

She frowned. 'I still don't want you to write this book. It's not that I'm protecting a secret. I just wouldn't like you to expose the extent. . . well,' she took a breath, 'the extent of Albert's failure, his sense of defeat.'

'You didn't like the pages I gave you?'

'I didn't look at them.'

Disappointed, Paul watched her in silence. 'So why invite me tonight, why announce in front of everybody that I am writing this book?'

'Too much to drink,' she said flatly.

He couldn't fathom it. 'But what if I *don't* think Albert was a failure? The books alone constitute a major contribution. As I said, I'd be more than happy for you to see—'

'You just won't let go, will you?' she interrupted. There was a note of anger in her voice. 'You *are* like my brother. You can't imagine not doing something that you, Paul Roberts, have decided to do, not getting what you want. You're trapped by it, by that determination.'

Paul began to object but found Helen looking straight into his eyes. 'Listen, Albert was obsessed by achievement, in a way, or by the issue of achievement. He came from a family of achievers. It was expected of him. His father expected it. His mother expected it. *I* expected it. He expected it of himself. But the ideas he had blocked his path. They were all ideas that said don't do this, don't do that, you'll only do damage. Whenever he published something, he felt guilty. Did you know that? He thought it would be misunderstood. It would affect people. Why do you think he wrote in that difficult way, switched areas of study so often? He'd have a great idea, people started acting on it, and then he'd step back at once saying they hadn't understood, he'd never meant them to *act* on it. Albert didn't want a biography. He never read a single review of his work. He hated to see his name in print, his photograph, to see himself discussed. The moment you pay him any attention he'll disappear. That was achievement for him. He'll melt away. You're wasting your time.'

Helen stopped and pushed her chair back from the table. Fleetingly, she thought of the Burmese boy. He too wanted to disappear, she sensed. Than-Htay and Albert were kindred spirits.

'That's it,' she announced. 'I'm off to bed.' She stood up. 'I'll call you a taxi.'

Paul was taken aback. But precisely these rapid changes of mood made it hard to leave. Coolly, he said: 'If you won't be able to sleep, why don't we watch one of Albert's videos?'

She had gone to pick up the phone from a low table by the window. She held it a moment and he heard a recorded message. Then she put it down. She appeared to consider, sighed. 'All right.'

'Great.' He reached over for the bottle and poured himself another half glass after all. At the same moment, the lights went out.

'Blackout!' Helen cried. 'Dear old Delhi. Hang on. There are candles in the kitchen somewhere.' She seemed pleased.

Paul sat in the dark, listening to her move round the table. Her dress brushed him as she passed, then she had gone towards the kitchen. She doesn't wear perfume, he realised. Without the air conditioning the room was silent. He heard a small laugh. 'It must be Albert,' she called. 'He doesn't want us to watch his old videos!'

A flame appeared and flickered as she came back towards the table. When it guttered she had to cover it with her hand so that the light was thrown up on her face. She looked young and lively.

Then as she set the candle down and sat opposite him she leaned across the table and placed a hand on his. It was a very natural gesture, as though between old friends, or sister and younger brother. Her hand lay on his. 'I'm sorry about this, Paul,' she said. 'I'm behaving oddly. And Albert and I were such scientific people.'

Without thinking, Paul turned his wrist so that the palm was uppermost and the two hands clasped. At once he was startled by the intimacy of the touch; an eager energy was being transmitted directly into him. He looked up for her eyes but Helen was looking at their hands, hers sinewy and cool above, his heavy and fleshy beneath. 'So no video, I suppose,' she sighed and withdrew.

They sat in silence. Then, perhaps because the flame was too much between them, Helen slid the saucer with the candle to one side, across the table. Sliding, it tilted and almost toppled. Paul grabbed it.

'Ow!'

A drop of hot wax had fallen on his hand. He pressed it to his mouth.

'Damn, damn and hot damn!'

'I'm so sorry! Are you all right?'

'Just a small burn, it's okay.'

'It's that stupid dent,' she said. 'Come to the kitchen and put it under the tap.'

'No, it's okay.' He was blowing on the back of his hand.

'You're sure?' She watched him as he swelled his chest and blew. After a moment she said: 'Can you believe, John did that, my son. The dent there.'

She recounted what had happened, how she and her son had gone to sleep on his last evening in Delhi. He had been rather belligerent. 'Then I woke up and there was someone in the bedroom! He actually had his arm raised over me. For a second I was sure it was Albert. It's so irrational, I know. Anyway, John ran in here and bashed this silly ornament he was holding on the table, right where I always work. It was quite a heavy thing.'

'Very weird,' Paul agreed.

Matter-of-factly, she asked: 'Do you think he meant to kill me?'

'For God's sake! Why?'

'There's something resentful about him. He was holding that heavy stone thing over me, after all. What else would he have meant?'

Paul reflected. 'In what sense resentful?'

'He's like a grown man with a little boy's resentment. I don't know why. I suppose Albert wasn't cut out for being a father.'

'Didn't he want children?'

With a pop and a hum the electricity came back on. Helen jumped up and went over to the shelves across the room. 'So, what movie do you want to watch, Mr Biographer?'

Paul shrugged. 'Whatever you think might be interesting.'

'I lost track of how he catalogued things.' Helen pulled out three of the less dusty cassettes and found the remote on the sofa. As she sat down, the television came on showing an advertisement for some out-of-town nightclub. 'You put it in,' she said. 'I'm almost afraid to watch.'

'If it bothers you, let's leave it.'

'No, not really afraid,' she said. Her voice dropped slightly. 'I just can't believe he's gone. I don't seem to be able to function without him.'

Paul left the table, took the video from her hands, slotted it in the television and stepped back to the sofa.

'Get the light,' she said.

He stood up again and turned off the light.

After thirty seconds of darkness, the tape started abruptly with an image of a man kneeling in the road, his right hand working back and forth with a brush in the gutter. There were big uneven paving stones, a telegraph pole with a battered plastic bag beside. It must have been the monsoon season because everything was wet and the light had that odd monsoon glare of humidity and veiled sunshine.

The man's forearm moved rhythmically pushing mud along the gutter with a short stiff brush. People walked by, a long barrow with two men pushing, a donkey. The soundtrack was all street noises, motorbikes, the cries of a vendor. The camera must have been on a tripod because the picture was steady. Then a dog came, and sniffed in the gutter, a thin, hungry dog, and the man looked up and grinned broadly. His few teeth were brown, his eyes bloodshot, and he wore a loose orange turban with one end that dangled on his shoulder.

'He's cleaning the drains,' Paul said.

'I don't think so.'

They were sitting about a foot apart. There was a pleasant tension between them, Helen thought. She would never have watched one of Albert's videos on her own.

From the plastic bag the man pulled out a shallow bowl and began to scoop mud into it. Now they saw that he was missing the top of one forefinger. His wrists were scarred. The dog barked and the man looked intently into his bowl of mud. He poked in it, stirred it, lifted it and let it dribble back. He must have been aware of the camera because now he looked up at it, shook his head and said something, just audible over the noise of a motor.

'What did he say?'

'No idea,' Helen said.

They sat on the sofa watching. It must have been two in the morning now. The camera remained fixed on the man kneeling in the gutter, again brushing the mud, gathering up scoops of sludge, examining, pouting, shaking his head so that the tassel of his turban swayed from side to side.

'Ah,' Helen sighed. 'I know.' She touched Paul's sleeve. 'It's a guy in one of the streets off Chawri Bazar. I've seen him there.'

'So what's he doing?' Paul too found himself at ease. This mystery of the video was much easier than the conversation earlier.

'Watch.'

The man was staring into his dirty plastic bowl. But this time he looked up and smiled. He set the bowl down, reached in his bag and pulled out an old tobacco tin. The camera made no attempt to zoom but shifted slightly as the man moved to squat on the broken pavement. He took a pair of tweezers from the tin box then bent over the bowl and very carefully picked something out. There was a tiny glint as he placed whatever it was in the tin, closed it and went back to brushing the mud along the gutter.

'What was that about?'

'It's the area where the jewellers and goldsmiths are. There are guys who pan the gutters for gold, there must be stray grains and tiny crumbs that finish up in the drains.'

'That's crazy.'

'I suppose they sell it back to the shops. Waste not want not.'

The camera was still fixed on the man who had returned to work with renewed care. The minutes passed. Paul turned a moment and saw Helen was watching the screen intently.

'What are you thinking?' he asked.

'Of Albert being behind the camera.'

The man stopped to light a cigarette, sitting on his haunches. He grinned and shouted something at the camera, apparently offering a smoke. There was no sound of a reply. Then, as abruptly as it started, the long take ended. There were a few seconds of fuzz and another image appeared. This time a boy was squatting on beaten earth, one hand behind his back.

'Marbles,' Paul smiled. 'I haven't seen marbles in ages.'

The boy was rolling them towards a hole about ten feet away. He had a supply in a plastic tub. The glass with its twist of colour moved erratically on the bumpy earth. The boy shouted, willing it on. He used his hand to smooth out a bump, breaking up the soil, then stamping it down. In the background people were flowing in and out of a wide entrance at the top of a flight of steps.

'It's a similar movement to the guy brushing the mud,' Paul remarked. 'That swing of the arm when he tosses the marble. And this attention to the ground, the earth.'

'Could be.'

When finally a marble hovered on the edge of the hole and dropped in, the boy turned to the camera, laughing and pointing.

'Images of success?'

'I'll fast forward,' Helen said.

There must have been fifteen minutes of this stringy boy with his marbles. Then another sequence began: this time a young woman was on her knees at the ghats, rubbing a sheet spread out on stone. She rubbed with a stick of soap. Again there was the same outward thrusting movement of the arm. She stopped and poured water on it from a bucket; the Yamuna flowed muddily across the top of the frame. The girl began rubbing again. There was a rhythmic elegance to her slim arm moving back and forth across the sheet in a lather of soap.

'No gold or hole to aim for this time.'

'Whiteness,' Helen said. 'Purity.'

The camera stayed focused on the girl's body swaying in her dark sari. Then she too turned to the camera and smiled. Paul recognised the girl who had served them their food earlier that evening. She wore the same green bindi.

'It's your girl who was serving.'

'Vimala. Her father runs a laundry.' Helen stopped the video. Let's find another. 'This is dull.'

'I was enjoying it,' Paul said. 'I don't know why. It's relaxing.'

'Watching other people work?' Helen said wryly. 'That was Albert's life.'

'Kind of hypnotic. You get a feeling of their presence.' He took another cassette from her and went to put it in the player.

'Didn't he have a DVD?'

'He switched to some computerised thing just a few months ago, but I never saw the results.'

Now there was dancing. But this video was different. No image or subject lasted more than a few seconds, but every gesture was picked up and continued by another movement in a different situation: a dancer's extended arm became a man reaching to shake hands, then a woman stretching her hand to turn a tap on, now a barber moving to scissor hair in the courtyard outside the central station. When the dancer moved her arm around, so did a guide outside the Red Fort, a woman saying her puja in the water of the Yamuna, a cook swinging a tray of small cakes from oven to table. Flashing in between, were stills of Hindu deities from statues or paintings, always filmed to occupy the same space on the screen, always continuing the gesture of the other subjects. It was as if the same person were constantly transformed while always going through familiar, compulsive motions: crouching, swinging, waving.

'Intriguing,' Paul said.

Helen touched his sleeve. 'That's Jasmeet, Kulwant's daughter.'

'The dancer?' The image had already changed.

'Yes.'

'Lovely girl.'

'Isn't she?'

The dancer came back and back every ten images or so, her bright yellow tunic and purple blouse offering a rhythmic punctuation to the rest. She was dancing on a low stage at some kind of party, hair glistening with oil, hands hennaed, face smooth and expressionless. Then her pirouette became a soldier swinging round with his rifle at the Red Fort, a fisherman turning to cast his rod.

'It's really too bad she damaged her leg,' Paul said.

For just a second Helen recognised the Burmese boy. He skimmed a stone across the river and was gone. The wrist flicked, the body turned, the face was framed. Helen stopped the video. She was surprised, disconcerted. Albert must have seen Than-Htay after he had left the clinic, after he had stopped taking the drugs. He hadn't told her.

'What is it?'

She shook her head. 'Oh it's all much of a muchness when you've seen what he's up to, don't you think? One more?'

'I can't believe there are so many of them,' Paul said. 'Why didn't he sell something to the TV?'

'He had them catalogued and cross-referenced in some way. There was a logic to these edits. He was always planning the definitive version. A compendium of all gestures, all patterns of gestures.'

Paul took another. This cassette had the title *Webwork* scribbled on a sticker. Paul slotted it in and sat back. A spider was making its web.

'The university grounds,' Helen said. 'Up on the Ridge. Where the student canteen is.'

Paul watched the rapid back and forth of a huge yellow spider moving across a space defined by two branches, one five or six feet above the other, but displaced, so that the web was skewed, symmetrical in its main concentric circles but complex in its adaptation to each twig and leaf. There was no sound. Each of the spider's legs trembled as it felt its way across the threads, intense and delicate. Then a moth collided with the silk.

'I don't like this,' Helen said.

'I guess if my book is going to say anything, I'll have to make sense of the zoological aspect.'

They watched as the moth was wrapped in silk, then pulled upwards towards the top of the web.

'Don't write anything, Paul.'

Suddenly and deliberately Helen leaned against him. After a few moments, she muttered: 'Nobody admired Albert's work more than I did, but he was sick at the end. He knew he'd failed. He only studied spiders because no one could imagine he was prescribing ways to change their behaviour. He'd got scared of humans.'

Paul felt the weight of the woman leaning on him. The article Albert James had emailed, he remembered, described a species of spiders where the female spun the web and the smaller males risked being mistaken for prey when they approached her. 'The anchor lines that pin the web are stronger than Kevlar,' Albert had written. 'So far attempts to produce the silk synthetically have failed.'

'Helen,' Paul said quietly. At the same time he was struck by the sheer size of the web this spider was weaving; it must be at least ten feet across, but the way the camera was set up it seemed that the creature was moving across the whole expanse of an old brick façade located about fifteen yards beyond the trees where the web was hung. Slightly blurred by the filaments of silk and the shift of focus, a constant trickle of young men and women hurried in and out of a swing door. Paul tilted his head and saw Helen had closed her eyes.

'Please,' she muttered, 'turn it off, now. Albert wasn't well at the end. I think the cancer had got to his head. He just wanted to die.'

'How long was he ill?' Paul asked.

The spider was lying still in a fuzzy area just off centre of the web.

'I don't want to think about it.'

Helen pushed her head into his shoulder as if she might burrow in there. She liked the man's solidity, his straight-forwardness and insistence, and these were also the qualities she found irksome. Then she had the odd idea that Paul had been *sent*. He had arrived the very day of the funeral, hadn't he? Albert had sent him. He had sent the biographer. And Than-Htay too. They were emissaries.

Still with her eyes closed, she said, 'You know one wonderful thing about Albert was what a great mimic he was. When you went out with him he was always listening to people and copying them. After an evening like this he would have had so much fun mimicking Aradhna: Do you have any idea, Helen, how many untouchables have castrated themselves in East Bengal in the last month? Do you know how many widows have jumped on their husband's pyres in Tamil Nadu?'

'I can't mimic to save my life,' Paul said.

'Me neither, as you just heard.'

'Oh, I don't know.' He pointed the remote and turned off the television. They were in the dark again.

'Did you like Kulwant?' she enquired.

'Very much. A funny guy. And nice too.'

She didn't move but he found he had put an arm round her shoulders. Perhaps she wanted comfort. All the same, without thinking, he said: 'Actually, if it had been any other situation, you know, I might have imagined he was a lover.'

The air conditioning laboured on. Why had he said that?

Eventually she replied, 'Might you indeed?'

'I said, in any other situation.'

Helen sighed. 'And aren't you worried that being here in the middle of the night with Helen James might compromise your relationship with little Miss Massachusetts?'

'Why?'

'Well, I wouldn't want to spoil anything important for you.' She still had her head against his shoulder.

'Why the heavy irony all the time?' he objected.

'Maybe defence.'

She dug her fingers viciously hard into his thigh and jumped to her feet in the dark.

'Ow!' Paul started.

'I'll make up the spare bed for you,' she said in quite another voice.

She was gone. The light came on in a room behind him. His leg still hurt. After a moment he stood and went to watch her as she tucked in a sheet round a narrow single bed. It was all very brisk, very feminine.

'This is really kind of you,' he told her lamely. 'I could still get a taxi if you want.'

'Please stay.'

She didn't look up as she spoke. Her voice was neutral. Leaving the room a few moments later, she added: 'You dream of your little girl now. I'll talk to my ghost.'

CHAPTER EIGHTEEN

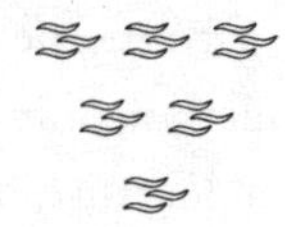

John had never been alone for so long. It made him anxious, but he was unable to break the spell. 'Just a word,' Elaine texted. 'You can't disappear like this.' Exhausted by another day of stomach pains, he dreamed of exams. Signs and numbers appeared under his pen, but dictated by an alien will. He didn't rightly know what equation he was supposed to be solving. Panicking, he woke up.

In the morning, he took a shower and had breakfast on the roof. His clothes felt damp. The first day, when the receptionist had pointed him to the roof, he had imagined pretty tablecloths and a buffet under bamboo awnings. At the top of steep narrow stairs he found two plastic chairs and one battered table that wobbled on the uneven tarring of the empty rooftop. Everybody else had breakfast in their rooms, with their air conditioners.

John walked to the parapet. To one side were the glass façades of Delhi's business centre, but on the other you could look across laundry lines and antennas toward India Gate. The sun was pale in a haze of heat. The warm air was alive with birds and bird cries, with honking and street vendors, smells of fuel and burning. When the waiter brought his scrambled eggs the man had to wave off the crows. He shouted cheerfully: 'They are very hungry, sir!'

The birds gathered while John ate; he could hear their claws scraping on the corrugated iron over the stairs.

The waiter had laid a copy of the *Times of India* on his tray and he read an article about compulsory Aids tests for railway workers. A laboratory in Bombay claimed it had discovered a cocktail of proteins that extended life by up to twenty years. John didn't check the details. Although Father had always been a maverick, it occurred to him, he never claimed dramatic successes. Rather the contrary. The patterns he wrote about were never susceptible to useful manipulation, only liable to destruction. John stopped chewing. Dad was a defeatist, he thought. He didn't help me because he didn't think help was possible.

Spreading jam, John watched the crows. It was hot hot hot. He was breathing heat. Today I will go and see Mother, he decided. A constant tension was drawing him to her. Equally constantly, he resisted. He didn't want to see her. He needed to solve something before going to Mum. Solve what? Something that would force her to see reason.

Finishing his food, he felt frustration turning to anger. I'm marooned here. My career is ruined before it began. The lab would never want him now. Elaine will not want me. Nobody would give him money again. He sat at the table surrounded by the crows, which strutted on the parapet, the stair housing. His father had crow's feet round his eyes. 'If you want to study patterns, just look in a mirror,' Mother laughed. The corners of Dad's eyes were river deltas. He was always so tense, so concentrated. Concentrated on what, though? On dreams, dreams of young companions. *And are both of those figures stand-ins perhaps for you, John?* he had written: a young friend who put up a tent with the sick and ageing Albert James, who walked with him along the beach beside the surf. Dad's forehead was always deeply furrowed. Elaine must be just such a companion for the Japanese director, John thought. A child. It was obscene with such a difference in age. 'Don't you see,' she had texted, 'that disappearing like this you'll actually cause the thing you're afraid of.' I'll go to Mum and demand an explanation, John decided. He pushed his chair back. Before he reached the stairs the crows' beaks were clattering on his tin plate.

No sooner was he on the street than his intestine struck. He had to hurry back to the hotel. How can you do anything with your gut in this condition? Part of him was glad of it. Then he was angrier still. He was furious. Bananas were the solution. He went back down to the street and found a woman squatting on her heels between baskets of fruit. There were limes, pears, apples, things he didn't recognise in heaps of bright colour. She was serving an elderly lady. On a barrow beside her a young man lay asleep.

'Three bananas,' John said.

Motorbikes were pushing their way through the crowd. The street was narrow. The vendor didn't understand. She had set up an umbrella to shade her wares. The young man woke and said something. Then she picked up a large bunch of dwarf bananas and offered them.

'Just three,' John repeated. It crossed his mind that this paraphernalia of India was getting dreadfully in the way. He showed the woman three fingers, but she shook her head. He needed to act, to go straight to Mother's, and instead here he was struggling to buy bananas to settle a stomach poisoned by the endless bacteria in this filthy country. How could you solve anything in India?

Yet there was something fascinating too: the baskets, the heaps of fruit, the blotch of crimson on the woman's forehead, her thin wrists poking from the shadows of her sari. It was all so much richer and rawer than life in Maida Vale. It is beautiful, John suddenly thought.

Sitting up, the young man on the barrow spoke aggressively to the woman. He seemed upset. There was a gold thread round his neck. John pulled out a hundred-rupee bill and got fifty-five change. Now he had a dozen green bananas. It was stupid, but he was smiling. I'm glad to be distracted, he thought.

He stood with his back to a wall and was at once surrounded by children stretching out their hands. He shook his head, but they clamoured. It was hard to peel his banana, eat it and hang onto the bunch with all these small hands reaching out to him, touching his clothes. He tore off a couple of bananas for them, but now it was they who shook their heads. Not bananas! They wanted money. One banana broke in half. John pushed past the children and headed for the square and the autorickshaws.

Instead of giving his mother's address he asked to be taken to the university. Mother would be in the clinic, he remembered, and he didn't know where that was. He was relieved. I can go to the flat this evening. A message arrived on the phone. 'I love you, John. Why are you punishing me?' He paid the driver and asked a passer-by where the department of zoology was. People sent him this way and that. The streets were leafy and might have been pleasant if it wasn't for the heat. Then he recognised the building where they had eaten after Father's funeral.

Still with his bunch of bananas, he found the canteen and, leaning against a tree, watched through glass doors as students went back and forth with their trays. How quickly, he thought, remembering the conversation that day, he had lost interest in his work, in microphages and granulomas, glycolysis and pentose phosphates. He felt no desire to find out if there were people working in his field here, maybe right in this building. He didn't want to know what equipment their labs had. As if I were born yesterday, he told himself rather strangely.

John went back to the entrance, sat on a step, ate a banana and watched. Kids arranged themselves in drifting circles, one hand on a companion's wrist, the other holding a phone. Girls and boys laughed. It was so familiar. What really mattered to me, then, about the work I was doing? he wondered. The position it gave me in a team, perhaps. He loved working with other people, he shone, but on matters that were quite impersonal: the microchemistry of the cell, the battle between infection and immune system. You worked together with people to understand something else, not each other. There was a clearly defined collective goal: a new drug. But away from the team he wasn't interested in mycobacterial tuberculosis at all. He didn't care about people who suffered from it. He was hardly interested in Elaine. My life has been one institution after another, he thought. He felt at home on the steps of a university. There had been the house cricket team, the college boat, the group lab projects. I always pulled my weight. If I went back to the lab I would be interested again, he thought. At once. Like a light going on when you enter a room. He knew he would. He would enjoy bending his mind to metabolic pathways, to hydrocarburic chains, in a team with the others, showing them what he could do. But Father had *always* been passionate about his research; he didn't need to be in a lab or anywhere particular. And he studied *alone*. If there was a team, Dad left it. Yet what he studied always had to do with people, not impersonal things. With a woman who sold you bananas. Father would have made a video. A girl picking nits from her mother's hair. Vaguely, wordlessly, John felt a glimmer of comprehension.

'Excuse me? Is it Mr James?'

He looked up and saw the earnest, bespectacled young lecturer who had sat across the table from him months ago.

'Hello,' John said. His mouth was full. Embarrassed by the bananas, he scrambled to his feet. 'I'm afraid I've forgotten your name. But how did you remember me?'

'There aren't many Europeans around, are there?' the man laughed. 'I'm Dinesh. But I don't think I told you my name.'

Dinesh took him into the canteen for tea and John remembered why he had come to the university. 'I was looking for Sharmistha,' he said, 'do you remember, the woman sitting beside me at lunch that day? I don't know her second name.'

'Puri,' he said. 'Sharmistha Puri.' He began to say how interesting he had found John's comments that day: that any vital phenomenon was too complex for a single mind to grasp, so minds had to connect together in a structure. He himself worked in communication theory, where of course most people just wanted to know how best to get a message across to someone else so as to have them behave in a certain way, to buy something or to vote for this or that party, forgetting that all communication was bidirectional.

The Indian laughed and lit a cigarette. 'Businessmen and politicians are so naïve! They imagine they're calling the tune, but their behaviour is more determined by the public than vice versa. This was your father's field, of course. He came to talk to the students a couple of times a year. I remember he said: Only a dead man can communicate without being altered himself. Or God of course. No feedback to the stars!'

John stared at the man. 'Do you know where I can find her?' he asked. 'Sharmistha, I mean.'

Dinesh led him across the campus to the zoology department where they eventually found an office that would have Sharmistha's phone number. A fan turned idly, stirring a muddle of papers. A middle-aged woman fussed about privacy rules. The upholstery was shabby and the ancient phones had locks on their dialling discs. 'Please, madam, this is the son of Professor James,' Dinesh protested. 'Dr Puri will be delighted to hear from him.'

'Call her from my mobile,' he offered in the corridor. He seemed to have understood that the young Englishman was going through some kind of crisis. Perhaps he thinks I have a crush on her, John thought.

A man answered the call. Although John guessed from the

accent it must be the German who had accompanied them to the Sufi tombs, he didn't say hello, just asked for Sharmistha.

'I'm John James,' he told her.

'Oh but that's wonderful!'

At once he understood that he had called at an embarrassing moment.

'I'm back in India for a few days. I wondered if we could meet.'

She covered the receiver to talk to the German. Then her voice was full of enthusiasm: 'Come tonight, John, there's a farmhouse party, out of town.'

John could hear the German's voice in the background.

'I'll pick you up at your mother's. Around nine.'

'I'm not staying at Mother's.' He gave her the address of the hotel. Just off Bhavbhuti Marg.

'But why's that?'

'I'm not here for my mother,' he said flatly.

'How interesting. Why are you here?'

John hesitated. 'It's complicated.'

Dinesh was watching him. 'You want a cigarette,' he asked.

John accepted. 'What's a farmhouse party?' he asked.

'A sort of late-night garden party for the rich and chic,' Dinesh said. 'I hate the things.'

John spent the afternoon wandering. He must decide what to do. When the heat became unbearable he went a stop or two in the metro, which was air-conditioned. He didn't care where he was, but explored streets as if they might hold the answer to his questions. The tangled wires sagging from telegraph poles, the motley of shop signs, the schoolgirls piling into autorickshaws, held his gaze in a way street scenes never had in the past.

Near the main station in Old Delhi, he received another message from Elaine: 'Am thinking of the time we went skinny-dipping in the Cam. I keep crying.' John went into a fabrics shop and in the space of five minutes paid almost 3,000 rupees for a pure pashmina shawl. He didn't reply to her. She was right not to marry me, he decided. The shawl was a pale purple with gold embroidery. Perhaps he had paid too much. It would go wonderfully with her frizzy black hair and camellia skin. He couldn't afford it. He didn't understand what a girl like Elaine could see in a man as old as Hanyaki. Perhaps it was just for the part in the play. Perhaps she was being smart. Only now did he realise he no longer had the bananas.

After another trip in the metro, another slow, stifling walk, he found he was by the river, in the grounds of a temple. 'Sir!' A lanky boy wanted to be his guide. 'Sir, sir!' John kept turning away. He climbed down the muddy bank and watched men diving from a low wall near the sluice gate of a barrage. It was a big dam. The boy followed him. The water boiled and swirled. There were three or four divers. They walked barefoot along protruding stonework between sluice gates, then plunged.

'People throw things in water for good luck,' the boy told him, 'when relatives die, you know, maybe it is dead person's ring or jewellery, they throw it there, from bridge' – he pointed – 'These men dive in the river to find it.'

'Don't the people who throw the things get upset?' John asked. The moment he spoke, he knew he had accepted a contract and would have to pay.

'Upset?'

'Angry.'

'Why angry?' the boy guide asked. 'If thing is in river, it is in river. You can get.'

John watched. Wearing shorts, the men dived into the churning water to emerge some twenty yards further down, dragged along by the current. He imagined their fingers grabbing at the muddy riverbed in the swirling dark. 'It's mad,' he said. The boy was earnest: 'Swimming here is very dangerous, sir. Sometimes they are killed. But they are cool in hot weather!'

John remembered the night skinny-dipping in the Cam after a party. Elaine's skin was goose-pimpled but she looked beautiful when she dived. She stretched on tiptoe on the bank, her breasts high. It had been one of their best moments. I was walking with your mother by the river, he remembered his father's letter. But there was no water, only mud. I have nothing of Father's to toss in the water, John thought. 'Get me a rickshaw,' he told the guide. 'Take me to the railway bridge.'

From five-thirty to seven, he waited for Ananya, at the same place where they had met before. He texted her and told her he would be there. She didn't appear and didn't reply. He was dizzy with the day's long heat and paid fifty rupees for a bottle of water. At least his stomach had held out. At seven-thirty he arrived back at the hotel.

'Somebody came to see you, sir.'

Behind the reception desk, the same rather efficient woman was sitting beside the bowl of water and the floating petals; when people walked by the water trembled in wide spirals of brilliant colour.

'It was a young lady, sir. She waited a long time, then she went away.'

'Did she leave a message?'

The woman smiled at his eagerness. 'No message, sir. She waited, but when you did not come, she went away.'

In his room, after showering, John sat at the tiny table under the TV screen projecting from the wall. He found a pen in his bag and, after some searching around, a piece of paper: the hotel laundry list. He began to jot things down. He wrote a few lines about the dogs he had seen. 'It is as if they were all the same dog,' he wrote, 'thin, brown, sniffing and shitting and begging.' He wrote the name Dinesh. Why would people throw a valuable object in a river, knowing that other men would fish it out? All Dad's dreams had been about meeting people beside water. *The surf was majestic*, he had written, *but we did not dive in.*

Then John started to sketch. It was a girl's face. He tried to remember Elaine's lopsided grin. The grin and its lopsidedness *were* Elaine. He couldn't draw. The hair came out frightening. Then he was drawing an elephant. He chuckled, and turned the trunk into a fat snake. Link it all up with a complicated doodle, he decided. He began to hang lines between girl and elephant, snake and words. It was odd to look at the words as part of the drawings. Towards ten the phone rang. 'There is someone for you in reception, sir.'

CHAPTER NINETEEN

In the car John found Sharmistha, Heinrich and another couple, Priya and Rajit. They were following friends in a white government Ambassador that was going too fast and kept disappearing. There were frequent phone calls to find out where they had got to. Rajit was driving, a slow, sad, cautious man with a thin moustache. John was in the back beside Sharmistha who was so small that he had a plain view of the scrubbed and bony Heinrich across her head. The older man smoked and laughed sardonically. Everyone was merry, everyone had been drinking. It was the party of a famous German architect who was going back to Europe. Nobody knew him personally, though someone in the car in front did. The venue was to the south of the city. The roads were unlit, chaotic. 'It's Friday night,' Sharmistha exclaimed, 'and my stupid book is almost written. God, am I fed up with spiders! I want out of those cobwebs!'

As soon as they were at the party, John wished he hadn't come. On the edge of a slum of shacks the car turned into a gateway in a long, high wall. Completely segregated within, were a wide open lawn, trees, a low, extensive, white-stuccoed house. At a line of tables food and drinks were being served by a dozen servants all in white jackets while a disc jockey had set up strobe lights at the top of a low rise and was inviting people to dance to a crashing muddle of disco rhythms and oriental themes.

Sharmistha disappeared. An assorted crowd of Indians and Europeans milled and danced. John found a plate and helped himself to various foods. The tastes seemed at war with each other and with his stomach. At the drinks table he got himself a gin and tonic, then another. The night was warm. There wasn't enough ice. I might as well get drunk, he thought. He tried to respond to a middle-aged Indian man who asked him something, but it was impossible to communicate over the boom of the music. The man would have continued to talk, he put his hand on John's shoulder, but John gave up and moved away. He sat on the grass and watched the dancers. There was no great enthusiasm. The women's bodies were graceful but not exciting. He wanted to be back at the hotel. It must have been Ananya who had come. He should have gone and seen Mum. That had been the plan. Then lights came on around the swimming pool.

The pool was beyond the tables, near the house. John walked over there. Half a dozen people were already in the water which was lit from above and beneath. Others sat on the side, drinking and pouring drinks into the mouths of the swimmers. You could talk here; the music was further away. Suddenly, Sharmistha was beside him, in her costume. 'Jump in!' She had a pleasantly sing-song voice. He hadn't brought swimming things, he said. 'The hell,' she laughed. 'Get in in your pants. Or with nothing! Who cares?'

Petite and shapely, she climbed down the ladder and launched herself across the luminous water. Her hair was tied above her head in a bun. Her costume was tight and black. She swam the short length, turned, and swam back. Her dark eyes sparkled with invitation. 'Get in! Stupid!'

An older man pushed a woman into the water with her clothes

on. There was commotion. Someone had broken a glass; two or three men were trying to find the fragments on the floor of the pool. John took off trousers and shirt and left them by some bushes. His pants were decent enough, he thought. When he got in the water Sharmistha was immediately beside him. She splashed him. She seemed madly playful. 'Oh I've had a hard couple of months,' she laughed. 'Working working working. On those creepy spiders and their ugly sticky yucky webs. But how are you? How's your research going?'

'Nothing special,' he said. The drink hadn't loosened him up at all.

'You were so excited about it last time we met.' She stood with her back to the side of the pool, her head just out of the water. Then she took his arm and pulled him to stand beside her.

'So, why have you come back to Delhi?'

'I don't know.'

Turning, he looked down into her face and found it unspeakably beautiful. The eyes were so large and soft, the lips so full of promise, the cheeks sharp and high. She was beaming, mocking. She raised an eyebrow and before he could understand what had happened he was kissing her. She turned so that she was pressing against him and kissed warmly and deeply. John was bewildered, unsure even which of them had started. Now she was nudging a knee against his legs beneath the water. He kissed quite violently and all around there was the noise of the music, of laughter and shouting, and someone swam back and forth close to them.

'What about Heinrich?' he asked, breathless.

'That's not a problem, sweetie,' she whispered. She began to kiss again. John felt excited and anxious. She was touching him under the water and he put a hand on her breasts.

'I need another drink,' she said abruptly and swam to the ladder. John got out of the water, hurried to his clothes, pulled out his phone and checked it. Sure enough, there was a message. But not from Elaine. 'I am giving your hotel address to a person who knew your father very much more than me.' It was Ananya.

'Perhaps you came to Delhi to see me again,' Sharmistha laughed. She had reappeared with two glasses. 'It's vodka. Come and meet some people.'

They sat in the warm evening with their feet in the water and talked to an Australian and his Indian girlfriend. Living in Delhi allowed him to write because life cost so little, the Australian explained at once. He was in his early forties, a novelist. 'In Sydney I'd be fighting just to pay the rent,' he insisted. His girlfriend was smoking quietly. John saw Heinrich standing in the shadows, a plate in his hand. I have lost all sense of time, he thought.

'Let's swim again,' Sharmistha grabbed his hand. She seemed to have no problem showing the others that they were on intimate terms. Getting to his feet, John asked: 'Do you think my father was in India because it was cheap?'

'Maybe!' She accepted a cigarette from someone then climbed down into the water, tapping the ash into a glass by the side of the pool. In a moment John was beside her and smoking too. The night had taken on a velvety atmosphere, blurred and greenish. He inhaled deeply. He had always thought smoking the most stupid of habits. Two or three people were swimming and they had to hold their cigarettes high out of the water.

'It's funny how like him you are,' Sharmistha said. 'The way you talk, I mean.'

'I don't feel like him,' John said. 'Actually I'm feeling rather dizzy. By the way, did you know that Dad had put together a group of people to get them to act out their lives or something? So someone told me.'

'There was a young show-off from the drama school at the funeral,' she said. 'Remember?' She stood right beside him, brown skin lit by the underwater light. 'Albert was a fantastic man,' she added.

'And at the same time he was studying spiders! You know it gets me angry sometimes,' John's voice became urgent. 'I mean how Dad just wasted his talent. Doing weirdo stuff. It drives me crazy.'

Sharmistha watched the boy. She seemed to find his intensity attractive. 'All I understood,' she said, 'was that he liked to spend a long time observing the most different things, different people, and then seeing if he could map them onto each other. That was a favourite expression of his. Mapping something onto something else. He always told us we'd never have any new ideas about spiders' webs unless we mapped them onto something quite different: subway systems, leaf patterns, choreography.'

John shook his head, but all at once she had her mouth against his ear. 'Why don't you map onto me tonight, sweetie? Do you want to?' She was kissing his neck. She spoke breathily. John looked up and saw that others were seeing. One fat old Indian woman smiled as she shambled by in a dressing gown.

In the car going back, Sharmistha again had Heinrich on one side, John on the other. Again they could look at each other over her thick hair. The man seemed quite relaxed. She had undone her bun. Up front, Priya was driving now, while Rajit, who had drunk a lot, kept turning and frowning and scolding Heinrich. 'You should be watching out for your woman,' he told him quite audibly. His moustache stretched and bristled. 'What's wrong with you?'

Sharmistha kept giggling. She leaned heavily against John and stroked his legs. 'We'll drive you back to your hotel,' Rajit told the English boy, but Sharmistha insisted John would sleep at her place. 'The hotel will be locked at three in the morning, Rajit! Isn't that right Heiny?' 'I don't know,' Heinrich said.

John hadn't properly understood until they were all taking their shoes off in the entrance that Heinrich and Sharmistha actually lived together. I've drunk too much and smoked too much, he thought.

'Make some coffee,' Sharmistha told the German and she led John by the hand down a corridor to the bedroom. Her bare feet scampered. She was almost running. John followed. The proximity of the woman had overwhelmed him, the smell of her skin, the willingness of her kisses, the soft, certain touch of her hand on his body.

'Your clothes are damp,' she said. He'd put his trousers on over wet underwear. She was already pulling off her tunic. He was in a daze, rather proud of himself, relieved that he had stopped thinking about his father and mother. In a moment he was beside her on the bed. He was telling her how beautiful her skin was, how lovely her voice. He didn't know what he was saying. Vaguely, he mumbled some formula about protection. Her lips were at his neck; she seemed to be covering him with her saliva. 'You don't need anything,' she murmured. 'Honestly, sweetie.' Their bodies wrapped together. I'm living, he decided. It was good. And he thought, maybe this was just the thing that would free him back into his own life. Back to Elaine even. Sharmistha was pulling him hard against her. She wanted him. Then he felt cold fingers on his foot.

At once John was electrified by a terrible, negative alertness. A hand had settled on the top of his foot. It was stroking his ankle. Yet Sharmistha's hands were both at his shoulders. He struggled to get his head off the pillow. Over the girl's shoulder, Heinrich raised bushy eyebrows and smiled. In an instant John's body was limp.

'Oh God. Don't worry yourself about him,' Sharmistha whispered. She tried to make her voice reassuring. 'Don't touch,' she hissed to Heinrich. 'Shit!'

John had closed his eyes. He was flat on his back.

'What's wrong, sweetie?' Sharmistha asked. 'Just ignore him.'

'I don't want to be here,' John murmured.

'Please.' She was whispering with her mouth pressed against his ear. 'Please, sweetie.'

Heinrich said calmly. 'Sorry, Shasha. I'll leave you young guys to it. Don't go, John. Enjoy. She's drunk.' And he left the room.

When John opened his eyes he found Sharmistha's looking into them. He let her kiss him, but a gelid soberness had taken possession of his body. 'I really can't,' he said. 'I shouldn't be here. I should have gone back to the hotel.'

'Oh fuck,' Sharmistha sighed. 'Or rather,' she smiled, 'no fuck.'

They lay together for some minutes. 'Fuck fuck fuck fuck.' She was shaking her head.

'I'm sorry.'

She laughed harshly. 'Don't be, why should you be sorry?'

'I just wish . . .'

'What?'

'Nothing,' he said.

She was stroking his hair. 'You remind me so much of your father when you talk. You know? Though you don't look like him at all.'

John was lying on his back, his head on his hands. Without thinking, he said, 'Do you think Dad had other women? I mean, he and my mother had the perfect marriage, they were such a *team*.'

'It hardly matters, does it?' she asked.

'I feel angry with him,' John said.

'So you said.'

'I feel I want to hit him. Really hit him. I *need* to.'

She propped herself on an elbow. 'He's dead. How can you hit someone who's dead?'

'I just feel like that,' John said weakly.

She chuckled to herself. 'If you want to know the truth, I would have loved to go to bed with Albert. I adored him. And he liked me. We spent some afternoons together, we took walks. He said some beautiful things to me, but he would never do anything. Not even a kiss.'

'So he was faithful to Mum?'

Sharmistha sighed. 'When I told him about our problems, me and Heinrich, he said it was normal: for couples not to make love.'

John tried to imagine his father saying these words. Eventually he asked: 'But why would a woman like you be interested in a guy like my father, so much older? You are fantastically beautiful and Dad wasn't even handsome.'

'I like you too,' she said. 'Heinrich is much older than me if it comes to that.'

John said nothing.

'Albert was so knowing. I think he understood me completely. He didn't have to say anything. And without ever criticising either. He just knew you and you felt it. It made him very sexy. I thought it would be such a victory to make love to him. Like a big achievement, if I could draw him in. But I never came close. He had very strong defences. Or inhibitions.' She laughed rather sourly. 'The only thing he ever said . . .'

Sharmistha stopped.

'Tell me.' John half sat up.

'Well, when I told him that we, me and Heinrich, had done what . . . well, what we almost did with you this evening, you understand, don't you?, he said he envied Heinrich, he envied him watching me make love to someone else.'

Towards seven, as the others slept, John let himself out of the flat and took an autorickshaw back to the hotel. In reception a young woman stood up from the sofa and came towards him with a marked limp.

'You are Mr John James?' she said. 'My name is Jasmeet Singh.'

She held out her hand. As soon as he took it, she began to cry.

John looked round. The receptionist was laying flowers on a piece of paper. 'I'm sorry,' he said. He felt exhausted.

'Mr John,' the girl gripped his hand. 'Mr John, I am afraid I am the one responsible for your father's death.'

PART FOUR

AN ACT OF LOVE

CHAPTER TWENTY

Helen started to tell Paul about the goings-on at the clinic. More than forty people had been brought from a wedding with food poisoning. The director was convinced that the chief administrator was taking a cut on supply contracts: drugs, dressings, laundry. Their biggest problems really were lack of medicines, lack of beds. There was a TB sufferer now, for example, that Burmese boy she had mentioned, who was spending his nights on a mat in the yard. She mainly handled outpatients. Of course if the public hospitals worked properly there would be no need. Or maybe there is always need, everywhere. Helen chuckled. 'Especially when you use the cheapest caterers at a wedding.'

'And Kulwant?' Paul wanted to know.

'He holds a surgery for urological problems. A couple of hours a week. It's not nearly enough. At his private clinic he just does prostate surgery for those who can pay. A lot of them Americans.'

'So he understood Albert's problem, I guess?'

'Kulwant wanted to operate. Albert wouldn't hear of it.'

'And he and Kulwant got on?'

'Albert got on with everybody.' She shot the American a glance. 'It isn't such an unusual thing to refuse therapy.'

Paul watched her. Each morning she left the flat before he

woke up, came home in the evening, washed, changed, put out the food her maid had prepared. While she was out, for five consecutive days, Paul had looked through Albert James's books, sampled scores of videos, failed to find anything indicating a major work in progress.

'He must have had a laptop,' he eventually remarked one evening. 'Didn't you say he'd got a camcorder?'

Helen hadn't given him permission to look through Albert's papers, but she hadn't told him not to. She hadn't asked him to stay in the flat, but she had shown no surprise and made no objection when she returned that first day and found him still there.

'Have you any idea where it is?' Paul asked. 'There might be a whole new book in it.'

'I did look,' she said. 'He had a laptop, but I can't find it.'

'At the university?'

'He didn't have an office there. He just went to discuss things with people in various research teams. That was always his way.'

'He might have left it in a friend's office.'

Helen shrugged. 'I haven't really enquired.' She added: 'The last six months were very stressful. He was in a lot of pain.'

They ate together. Dhal, vegetables, a chapatti. She kept her eyes on her food. 'Albert was mad about living,' she said. 'He had such an appetite, like a child almost, particularly for seeing things, and at the same time he was eager to die. He said it would be exciting. Sometimes I think he mixed the two up, as if dying would be the most vital thing he could do.'

Helen spoke with a hint of bitterness, glancing at Paul from time to time to assess how much he had understood. Physically, the American was a reassuring presence. Later, alone in bed, she spoke her husband's name out loud.

'Albert? So?'

She lay on her back, waiting.

'Did you finally get to the pattern of patterns?' How had he put it once: the weft on which all waters are woven? 'You should have been a poet,' she told the darkness. 'Did you?' Just before the end, there had been a moment when he had looked at her very intensely but couldn't speak. Well into the early hours her mind went back and forth between anger and tenderness.

Retiring to the small bedroom, Paul had never felt closer to a subject nor further from being able to start writing. The more notes he took, the more difficult it all became. Perhaps Helen was right and Albert James had lost direction after they left the USA. That was when his interest in insects and spiders began. The court case, the accusations of an underage prostitute, had unsettled the man, it was understandable, likewise the controversy surrounding his speculations on mental illness. He had always been happy to let others steal his ideas and grab the limelight.

Paul had brought a dozen books from the sitting room and stacked them on the bedside table. '*Where the flow of information is necessarily interrupted*,' he read a scrawl on the flyleaf of the first, '*there we can be sure we are approaching the sacred*.'

It was a university text on communications theory, published by McGraw-Hill. Paul tried to make sense of the words. He had soon realised, on rapid examination of the publications in the flat, that the first thing to do would be to establish the order in which James had read them; then he might make more sense of the comments in the margins. But how to do that? And what did he mean: '*Where the flow of information is necessarily interrupted*'? What information? Why '*necessarily*'? What did he mean by '*sacred*'?

Albert's books were shelved in alphabetical order with works on electronics sitting beside tomes of anthropology, novels, history, philosophy, physics, math. You had the impression that he read widely but indiscriminately; he was following a thread that remained obscure; or he was deliberately dispersing himself, distracting himself, not following a thread, disappearing, as it were, into other people's thoughts so as to weave connections between them, spread his mind across them, perhaps precisely to avoid reaching any conclusion of his own, as if such a thing would be some kind of transgression.

Many of the works were illustrated: art books, Hindu iconography, hand-weaving in Kashmir, photographs of Delhi, Bombay, Calcutta. With each author Albert James seemed to strike up a different relationship, a particular tone of excitement or complicity or dismay. Even the handwriting changed. Ancient school editions of *Alice's Adventures in Wonderland* and *Through the Looking-Glass* were especially densely annotated. '*The terror that is of the nymphs!*' he had scribbled. It was clear that he had come back to some books at different times and written notes beside notes, upon notes, between notes. On a copy of the *New York Review*, between the columns of an alarmist piece about global warming, he had written: '*The snake, the pool, the liquid eye!*'

On the fifth day Paul found a stack of letters. There was no filing cabinet in the Jameses' flat. He had lifted down a box from the top of the large wardrobe in the main bedroom. It was serious snooping, but Helen had left him on his own here. She must know this could happen.

It was a large box that had once held twelve bottles of Kingfisher beer. He put it on the table. Lochana was at work in the kitchen and he wondered if the elderly maid referred these liberties to Helen, or again if he could ask her about the girl who had been there the night of the dinner, the charming girl washing sheets on the video.

There were letters from Coomaraswamy of the Theosophical Society, a dozen of them. So much for the man's candour saying he only knew James from occasional meetings. '*You ask me if I think religious experience is a middle ground between consciousness and unconsciousness,*' Paul read. The man had a rather girlish handwriting: '*You tell me that you see our language-driven, hyper-aware, purposeful and predatory mode of being as an evolutionary dead end that can only lead to the cancellation of mankind from the planet. For myself, I wonder about the tormented eschatology of your anxieties.*' '*It is not for me to say,*' one of Coomaraswamy's letters ended, '*but for you to know, whether you have been chosen.*'

There were scores of letters from sponsors and potential sponsors. These had been packeted together with an elastic band. '*Dear Professor James, our agency is in broad agreement with your concerns and aims. Nevertheless, we feel that the project you have put forward is too theoretical and speculative to satisfy our parameters for funding, however modest your requests.*' The embossed letterhead was: The Federal Agency for Urban Planning, Washington DC. '*However,*' the letter continued, '*if you could give practical examples of how the collective psychology of a particular urban environment might be shifted toward the more benevolent attitudes you refer to, we would be willing to reconsider our decision.*'

A note from the Arachnid Society asked Albert James where he was up to in his research: '*We are particularly eager to hear about your considerations on male and female web structures.*'

A London publisher reminded James that his delivery of a typescript of approx 80,000 words, provisionally entitled *Mapping the Unknowable*, was now more than eighteen months overdue, and that according to the terms of the contract the initial advance of £5,000 (paid into your account in March 2001) should now be returned. '*Could you reassure us,*' the letter concluded, '*that the book is approaching completion, in which case we shall not press for return of the advance?*'

Paul went to the window, opened it and lit a cigarette. The day was a blast of heat and fumes. It did not seem that James had kept copies of the letters he had sent, unless on his computer of course. Perhaps if Paul were to make a note of all the addresses here he could ask correspondents if they would allow him to consult what

James had written. It seemed like hard work for little profit. Coomaraswamy for one would not cooperate, otherwise he would have mentioned these letters at their meeting. 'Either I just get on and write the goddamned book,' Paul muttered, 'or I drop the whole thing and cut my losses.'

He was feeling restive. Dying when he did, Albert James had escaped him, and at the same time had drawn him away from his ordinary life, was still drawing him away. Paul hadn't checked his email for days. He was losing any sense of his Boston self. Yet the fascination Albert aroused didn't seem to be getting him anywhere. His ideas were more confused now than when he arrived. It would have been wiser, Paul caught himself thinking, to have taken on a simpler project, something more obviously marketable, an idea he could have researched back home. 'One Hundred American Heroes' was a project he knew would be easy to sell. On the other hand, he had staked a large part of himself on this biography. You deliberately chose someone difficult, he thought, a task that would force you to grow up. Now deal with it.

He went to the kitchen table and turned the box upside down, sorting through the papers very quickly. More than half were invitations to conferences. He barely glanced at them. On world peace. On communication among reptiles. On language and psycho-pathogenesis. Exploring primary and secondary thought processes. Learning to learn how to learn. Towards a Behavioural Response to Global Warming.

Then he came across a handwritten letter. It was from someone who had heard Albert James speak as recently as 2005 at a conference in Calcutta: Models for the Development of India. Quite probably this was the last conference James ever attended.

Esteemed Professor James,

I was among the many regional delegates who listened to your very learned paper on the importance of maintaining flexibility in all variables of human activity. I confess that during your long speech I fell asleep on two occasions (you will remember how many very taxing speeches there were that afternoon and, alas, I am well advanced in years). Only afterwards, remembering the diagrams you showed, did I realise the extreme importance of what you were telling us: every time we impose rigid forms of behaviour we limit our chance to respond to changing circumstance.

I have thought a great deal about this, Professor James. It is a gloriously simple idea, at first it seems innocuous, but the consequences are most dire and some people will find them repugnant. For what you deeply mean, I think, is that such sacred principles as freedom of individuals, democracy, marriage, monogamy, respect for all religions, supreme importance of human life, these are all behaviour forms that have been 'fixed' and that we need to question before they lead us to calamity.

This is extremely polemical. These are very important principles that our troubled and multicultural society has attained only over many centuries and with the greatest effort and discipline. If ordinary people shed such principles what will become of them? What will become of all of us?

But of course you understand that. You strike me as a man of profound wisdom, Professor James (a wisdom, if you will permit me this licence, that radiates from yourself, and not from your words). Yet you are saying we must remember we can organise in different ways; you are saying nothing must be sacred if we are to survive.

Esteemed Professor James, I wish very much that you had chosen to spell out this conundrum more clearly for the conference delegates and regional politicians of India. Your ideas are very challenging, but you present them so that it is easy for your audience to turn a deaf ear or even nod off. The delegates listen to you, indeed they are captivated by your charisma, yet at once they start to feel sleepy. You do not galvanise.

I would very much like to invite you to our ashram (see enclosure), but only if you are willing to furnish clear replies to our members (about 300) about how you think future development should best be undertaken in the world that is fast coming. At the end of your speech you said a possible way is to 'heal the aesthetic from the virus of purpose'. Do I remember rightly? This is not at all clear to me; as I said, I am old and perhaps growing stupid. Surely you do not believe that we must spend our lives looking at works of art?

Esteemed Professor, you are speaking in code. It does not bode well. You have enemies, perhaps? Please come and explain to us in Uttar Pradesh what you mean. I have an intuition that it may be important.

I remain, sir, your admirer and, potentially, your pupil,

Dr Radha Ladiwale

Paul took the box to the main bedroom, climbed on a chair and put it back on top of the wardrobe with the dust and cobwebs. Getting down, he looked round the room. Again he was struck by the fact that there were no photographs, just the bed, a chest of drawers, the wardrobe. He looked inside. The floor of a wardrobe is always a likely place for storing things. There was nothing. Only Helen's clothes hanging neatly. Paul went through them: plain dresses and tunics for work. This is the first woman's wardrobe I ever saw, he thought, that isn't full to overflowing.

Still, there were two or three elegant things: a long robe in a turquoise satiny material, a black minidress. Paul pulled it out, smelled it. Something she must have worn when younger. He found it strange that she would keep such a thing, though she still had a good body. Some women were lucky. He breathed deeply. In the chest of drawers, among heaps of plain things – pants and undervests laundered a thousand times – there were half a dozen pieces of silky underwear. Of Albert's clothes, not a trace.

When Helen came back that evening he asked if he could take her out to eat. 'Lochana has prepared some food,' Helen said. 'It will go to waste.'

'For a drink then,' he proposed. 'I've been in all day.'

'That's hardly my fault,' she objected. She was tired. Then she pursed her lips, looked around: 'Okay. Just let me shower.'

As they walked down the stairs and out into the hot evening, exchanging greetings with the condominium sweeper in the forecourt, Paul was struck by how much they must seem a couple. Helen had put on her white cotton dress, the same she wore for her dinner party, and walked at an easy pace, apparently immune to the heat. Dark glasses lent her a certain glamour. He was sweating in his linen jacket. A chipmunk ran along the pink wall of Lodhi Gardens. The air had a sullen, pre-monsoon feel.

'I've run into trouble with my project,' he told her.

They sat down in the cool of an air-conditioned café. The waiter brought drinks.

'I really need to have a better sense of how it ended, for Albert. Otherwise I can't get a grip on the thing. I'm losing it.'

Helen showed no sign of helping. She loosened her hair from its tie, shook it out, gathered it again.

'Basically' – Paul tried to sound matter-of-fact – 'I need to know about Albert's death, whether he thought he had brought his work to a conclusion and what that conclusion was. At the moment it's as if his life were leading to something really major that isn't there. It stops short.'

She granted him a glance as she slid the tie up her ponytail. He knew she knew things. For her part, Helen wondered why she hadn't just told him to go away. Finally she said: 'You could talk to his Ayurvedic doctor. I have the address somewhere.'

Paul was riled. 'So why didn't you tell me before?'

'I never said I would help with your book.'

'Then why are you letting me stay with you? Why give me the address now?'

She smiled. 'Your company is not unwelcome. You know that.'

Paul hesitated. 'Today I read some letters, the ones in the box on top of the wardrobe, in your bedroom.'

She raised an eyebrow. 'I didn't know you had a search warrant.'

'You must have guessed I would look at things.'

'Must I? Albert would never have done that.' Before he could resume, she said: 'You know, I think you should ask yourself why you became so determined to write about Albert.'

'I told you. It began with reading *Wau*. And a feeling there was some affinity . . .'

She shook her head. 'It's to do with your family, Paul,' she said. 'Your women above all.'

'How so?' He was surprised.

'Perhaps you are looking for some sort of authority for living the life you have chosen, for being apart from your wives and children, for having serial romantic relationships with young girls. You need a kind of secular saint or religion to substitute the ones you grew up with, to overcome your feelings of guilt. Albert was always attracting people like you.' Helen paused: 'I think it would be dangerous, though, for you to follow him too far.'

There was a brief silence. In a sharply frank voice, Paul said: 'Helen, why don't you help me a bit? Then I'll leave you alone.'

She sipped her drink. 'You did say a few days ago that you were in a hurry to get back to Massachusetts; the bliss of little Miss.'

'And I am.'

'It doesn't feel like that, Paul. It feels like you're changing.' She hesitated. 'You remember I said that you were like my brother.'

Paul nodded.

'My brother was, probably is, single-minded to the point of cruelty. He rode roughshod over everyone. He treated my mother like a doormat and she loved him for it. I hated him. He encouraged my opposition because he saw it would push me out of the family and give him complete control of my parents' money. Which he soon got. In his early twenties, he destroyed a close friend of mine. He used her in all kinds of ways, left her pregnant, almost crazy.'

Helen smiled wryly. 'Well, forgive me, but I had got the impression that you were a little like that and that Albert was just a smart project for you, a sort of New Age stepping stone to celebrity. But now I see I was wrong. I see Albert is undermining your confidence in every way. Which is what he did to everybody. You are getting confused. If I were you, I'd drop the book now and go straight home.'

Paul collected himself. 'Helen, let's leave my motives out of it, okay, and concentrate on the business in hand. Reading those letters, I had the impression that some sort of conflict in Albert's mind was reaching a climax: on the one hand he wanted to retreat into a backwater, on the other he felt he was under some awesome imperative, I don't know, to save the planet or something.' Paul stopped. 'I thought he might have been frightened by himself somehow. I can't explain.'

'I told you,' she said, 'Albert wasn't unhappy to be ill. In a way it thrilled him. I also told you that the place to start your book was his family.'

'But you were his family.'

Helen didn't reply.

'And did he go and talk at that man's ashram, the one who wrote the long, handwritten letter?'

'Which man?'

'Dr Radha Ladi-something?'

'That's a woman's name!' Helen laughed. 'Albert loved ashrams. Probably he did go. He was away for a few days in December as I recall. You could go yourself and find out.'

'After I've seen the Ayurvedic doctor?'

'Remind me to give you his address. A charlatan no doubt.'

They were both aware of a powerful tension now, of playing the decisive moves in some undeclared game. But while Paul sensed that Helen could read him like a book – and he had nothing to hide – she remained completely enigmatic. The pale lips and grey-green eyes concentrated more wilfulness than any woman's he had known.

As always Helen looked away. Knowing he was puzzling over her, she let her eyes wander over the familiar café. There were adolescents in European clothes, eating snacks and drinking Coke. Three well-to-do women in lush saris had their heads together over ice cream. It was an expensive place. Then, abruptly, the door was flung open and a small child ran in. Naked, thin as a rake, hair tousled, feet filthy, the boy dashed between the tables laughing and snapping his fingers at the customers. He came to a stop in front of Paul and shouted, 'Yah! Yah! Yah!' He seemed possessed, teeth flashing. 'Woo, woo, woo!' The boy's head wagged madly from side to side inches from the eyes of the American. His infant ribcage heaved. The owner of the café appeared and yelled; the boy turned and, shrieking with laughter, ran out into the heat.

'What the hell was that about?' Paul asked. He was shaken.

'I suppose he just wanted to see this side of the window for a moment.' Helen chuckled: 'You should have seen your face!'

The moment seemed to have cheered her up. 'Listen, Paul,' she said. 'Darling,' she added ironically. She looked him straight in the eye for once. 'Why don't you leave Albert be and stay in India to work with me? What about it? We could go out to the villages where these kids are. Like this boy. There is so much to do. I know of any number of projects. There's a tam-tam with these things. I'm tired of Delhi. You could write about aid work, if you have to write. There's a market. And it would do some real good.'

She laughed at the surprise on his face. 'Then if you really care so much, about the Boston babe, I mean, if she's not just a roué's amusement, get her to come over here too and work along with us. The more the merrier. What does it matter to you what Albert was doing in the end? He had a good life, he enjoyed his torments and contradictions. I can see writing about his ideas, but not a biography. Leave be.'

She took a breath. She was speaking persuasively. 'Come on Paul.' She reached a hand across the table and placed it on his. 'Come out to the villages with me, see the real world. Some place where we *know* what needs doing and we do it. That's living. It would be a revelation for you.'

Paul felt it harder and harder to be sure of himself; he had left Boston, now she was asking him to leave his work, himself really. Lighting a cigarette, he raised a hand for more drinks while she went on talking.

'You'll see things you never imagined. And you'll know you're doing something positive. I'm sure deep down you want that. Don't you? You're from a religious family. Then when you see someone recover from TB, when you see someone able to live and love because of something you did, you'll feel fantastic. Later, like I said, you can even make money writing about it. Why not? People will be far more interested in that than they ever would be about an old eccentric like Albert.'

Paul blew out smoke. Resistance was on automatic now. He sighed. 'Helen,' he said finally, 'Helen, a man doesn't just suddenly die in his bed of prostate cancer. Does he? It doesn't happen that way.'

She withdrew her hand and sat back.

'I mean, I've been thinking about this, there would have been a long period when a sufferer like that was bedridden, when he needed help and nursing.'

'Let me enjoy my drink,' she said dryly. 'I had a tough day.'

Paul watched her. He felt pleased with himself for turning a difficult conversation round, yet cruel too. Then he wondered if he wasn't moved more by a desire to break this woman down than a wish for information. He had got drawn into something, something unusual. They were silent for a while so that he became aware of the chattering all around him. There were a couple of pretty girls enjoying a tête-à-tête. Discussing men, Paul thought at once.

'I had two patients die today,' she told him.

'I'm sorry.'

'One was a girl with a haemorrhage; she was on the floor of the waiting room when I arrived. She must have given birth during the night. She bled to death. There was nothing we could do but clean up.'

Paul waited a moment. 'Is that kind of thing common?'

'It's not unheard of.'

'You think she hid the pregnancy and killed the baby?'

'I don't think anything,' Helen said acidly.

'And the other?'

'The other was an old man with cancer of the bowel. He wanted to die at home but his relatives brought him in because it was too much for them. Which in India is saying something.'

She looked at him.

'Paul, that was the kind of scene Albert very much wanted to avoid: the terminal situation. He didn't want to get anywhere near it. The pains he was dealing with were already enough for him: the endless trips to the bathroom, the constant sense of blockage. Do you understand? Or do I need to tell you exactly what dosage we give patients when the moment comes?'

CHAPTER TWENTY-ONE

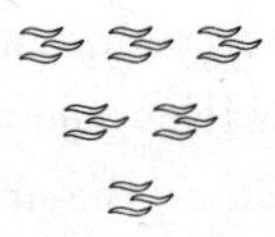

Helen and Paul walked slowly through the warm evening towards India Gate. At a certain point arms were linked. A strange mixture of solemnity and light-heartedness had descended. They smiled when accosted by the autorickshaw drivers. 'Sir, madam, hello! Climb in!' They laughed at the antics of some boys kicking a can. But they did not break the silence between them. When they reached the open space around the floodlit gate, they ignored the inevitable snake charmer, a girl with a monkey and a drum, and sat in the shadows on the dry grass amid couples and families and children running with balls.

Eventually, Helen lay on her back and closed her eyes. 'Why didn't I just tell you to leave me alone?' she sighed. 'That would have been much more sensible.'

Paul said nothing. Despite the clamour of traffic and peddlers, the evening had taken on a peculiarly still feel, but drawing them somewhere, like a quiet river. He let it drift.

'Now you know enough to put me in gaol.'

He looked at the woman, lying with arms outspread, eyelids trembling in a tired face. He liked her tiredness. The cheekbones were smooth and high. The knees, just beneath the hem of her dress, were nicely turned. The inside of the wrist was ivory white.

'Whatever would I want to do that for?' He waved away a fly that was trying to settle on her hair.

After a short silence, she said, 'So tell me about your girlfriend.' She wriggled to make herself comfortable. 'You don't talk about her much. For a man in love.'

A vendor was pushing a refrigerated trolley, calling out the price of ices. Another man had a basket with flower garlands that he tried to drape over every young girl who passed. The evening simmered with abrupt cries and bright lights in a broth of warm, liquid colour.

When Paul still didn't reply, Helen said dryly, 'You know I'm beginning to wonder whether the inquisitive biographer isn't trying to start something with the widow so as to find out all he can about his subject.'

Paul laughed. Her arm on the grass seemed to be beckoning. Without thinking, he reached over until the tip of his forefinger touched her pulse. She started, then frowned behind closed eyes.

'The biographer has considered that possibility, I presume?'

'It did half cross his mind at some point, yes.'

'You try it with every woman, don't you, Paul?'

'What? To get information about their dead husbands?'

She smiled. 'Sex.'

'Oh that!'

Sitting with his knees gathered to his chin, Paul let his fingertip trace the vein from open hand to elbow.

'Kulwant's like you,' Helen said. 'And Sikhs are supposed to be so dignified and chaste!' Her voice had a hint of indignation.

'Everybody's supposed to be chaste.'

'That's right,' she agreed.

Once more they were quiet. Paul watched the flow of traffic, the girl with the monkey on a lead walking away. Helen lay still, eyes closed, feeling the ground against shoulders and head, listening to disembodied sounds.

'So why hasn't Mr Biographer tried with me?'

'Mrs James,' he said in mock exclamation. 'Please!'

'I mean, all this time here in India without a woman. It must be quite a trial.'

'How do you know I haven't had a woman?'

'You're right. How do I know?'

'I haven't.'

'I still don't know,' she told him evenly.

'No,' he agreed. 'Still, as far as the lady in question is concerned, the widow I mean, and aside from the biographer's respect for her bereavement, she did make it abundantly clear at one point that she didn't like him and even told him on two or three occasions that she felt her life was over, something that would appear to preclude adventures.'

'You're flattering,' Helen said. 'It's my age. No, please don't stop.' He had taken his finger from her wrist.

Paul thought about the situation. 'You look fine to me,' he eventually said in a matter-of-fact voice. 'Guess I'm not in the habit of mixing work and pleasure.'

'Liar! I bet you've mixed everything with everything a dozen times.'

'Maybe not a dozen.'

She didn't answer, enjoying the darkness of closed eyes, the slightly acid smell of the dry earth, the light touch of the finger on her arm. At last she said: 'Actually you should write a book about Albert.'

'Oh, I *should* now?'

'Not a biography. A sort of profile. Ideas and character. The main achievements. You could get over what a delicate, spiritual man he was. Unlike yourself.' And she added tonelessly: 'Then you'll understand what I meant when I said my life was over.'

Paul patted his jacket pockets, found his cigarettes, tipped the lighter out of the box. The smoke tasted good in the warm evening with so much busy life going on around.

'So,' he said briskly, 'once again, my Boston lady's name is Amy, right? Amy Henderson, and she is about five-seven. She's slim, blondish, moody, sings in a band that plays sort of jazzy rock, one CD that got nice notices and no sales, works part time in the governor's office. Passionately liberal. Smokes heavily. Lives with two other girls the same age. Young women on the move. Says she doesn't want children but no doubt will if and when she moves in with a man. Maybe me, maybe not.'

As he spoke, Paul watched Helen's face.

'Go on.'

'That's about it, I think.'

'You haven't said why you like her.'

One hand on her arm, one slipping his lighter away, Paul spoke with the cigarette between clenched lips: 'Easy to be with. Sparkling eyes. We have fun. It's effortless.'

Helen frowned. 'But it could be like that with any number of 26-year-olds!'

'Hey, where's the dotted line?' he laughed. 'Let me sign up!'

'And you would marry someone on that basis? Fun, lack of effort?'

'I'm not marrying next week. Actually, I haven't seen her for some months now. Perhaps when I get back she'll have found someone else.'

'But why marry anyway? You said she doesn't want children. You can have your fun without marrying.'

'True.' Paul reflected. 'I guess marriage is something I haven't got right yet. I have children whom I hardly see because my ex-wives have new husbands who want to play dad. They want to forget I exist.' He stopped for a few moments, then added: 'One thing that attracted me to Albert, to writing a biography, was your long marriage. I wanted to write about that.'

'Why? Why does that impress you? Your parents must have been together just as long, if not longer.'

He pulled hard on his cigarette. 'My parents are ankle-deep in conventional glue. No, up to their eyes in it. They are middle-class America. The pressure around them holds them together: the mortgage, the golf club, the Church; above all the Church. With you and Albert it's the mixture of the marriage *and* your complete independence. It's you two against the world, all over the world, out there in the flux, a story completely detached from any real background, no support. That's what everyone dreams of in a marriage, I think. Actually, that aspect is as important to me for the book as Albert's ideas. Especially now . . .' – Paul hesitated, eyes following his finger as it ran along the blue vein of her forearm – 'especially now that you've told me about the way he died.' He paused again: 'That must have been an act of love.'

Helen closed lids beneath lids. How had he known to say those words? She let herself sink into a deeper dark, the dark of their bedroom when it was decided and done, the warmth of that last embrace. Beneath her hips and shoulders the hard ground of the park melted away. Only this American's finger touching her arm kept a part of her present and afloat. Sinking, she would have liked to explain all kinds of things. In truth, she had told him very little. But then he would write those things down. She would have liked to tell him how beautiful it had been. But then she would have had to explain the wretchedness that came before.

In a distant voice, she muttered, 'A long marriage can become a burden.'

'Ditto a brief one,' he quipped at once.

'When you move around all the time, living in the places we lived in, you rely exclusively on each other for everything. Everything's invested there, in that one person. It's unbearable sometimes. Especially when that person changes, when you change.'

Paul said nothing. He had sensed how their conversations swung and circled. Perhaps he should just stop talking.

'Things weren't always easy,' she said.

Submerged in the dark behind her eyelids, she waited for his question. The biographer would want details. When Paul said nothing, she went on: 'Sometimes, in a marriage of thirty years, you find yourself asking: can it really go on, *as long as life*? It becomes a sort of eternity. And a question mark.'

Still he didn't respond. His finger continued its slow back and forth on the skin inside the elbow. He is keeping me here, she thought, when I could be sinking into Albert's embrace, rubbing my cheek against Albert's stubble. Vaguely, Helen heard the sounds of traffic and people laughing: the vendors, the faint fluting of the snake charmer. The creature would be uncoiling from the bottom of his basket, mindlessly rising to the seductive dirge as she was sinking into her dying husband's arms. She had such a powerful sense of his presence. I'll open my eyes and he'll be here, she thought.

But the finger insisted, wandering gently up and down her arm. She wouldn't be allowed to sink. The sounds grew louder again.

Helen shook her head a little and said more firmly: 'Then, you know, Albert always saw everything in terms of patterns, and trajectories.'

She hesitated. 'He loved the word trajectory.'

Paul wouldn't speak. Without a question to fence against, Helen was uncertain; it was as if she were feeling her way through dark rooms. 'How something ended, how anything ends,' she murmured, 'showed you what the trajectory had been, who a person was. Albert always said that. It's the shape survives when the thing is gone. That's what form was for him, the shape of something gone.'

Still Paul didn't respond. He was very aware now of having found a new card to play. Silence. He felt strong and at the same time more powerfully drawn than ever.

'They're odd things to talk about, aren't they?' she said. Her tone changed. 'Actually that was where his fascination with Shiva came in.' For a moment she was presenting her husband's work at conferences again, she was condescending. 'Creator, destroyer. People see it as a contradiction but for Albert destruction was the completion of the act of creation: like cutting a string to the right length.'

Again Helen sighed. In her head the sounds around rose and fell like water lapping. She didn't want to open her eyes. The man's touch on her arm was holding her here, preventing her from sinking. But she wouldn't look at him. In a way she had drowned months ago in the deep silence when Albert's breathing stopped, when the embrace cooled. And beautiful though it had seemed when he seduced her to it, as soon as she was alone, as soon as the arms grew heavy and lifeless, she knew it had been a terrible mistake, a terrible, terrible mockery. It was the greatest mistake Helen James had ever made, the greatest mockery she ever suffered. Hurrying to take himself out of the world, Albert had invaded everything; he was in the smell of the grass, the thickening air of the summer evening, the feel of her body against the hard earth. She would never get beyond him.

But perhaps the American has understood, she thought now. Why not just tell, then? Helen held her breath. 'When we left America,' she began, 'the idea was . . .'

There came a siren. The approaching wail drowned out the smaller noises. Paul turned to the road. The first siren was joined by another. A police car pushed through the traffic light and sped away shrieking along the Amber Road. There was a storm of honking.

'Yes?' He turned back to her.

Helen was relieved to hear his voice, but the moment had passed.

'Speaking of the States,' she said, 'if you're flying back via

London, perhaps you could talk to John and tell me how he's getting on. I think I should keep away from him for a while myself. I got the feeling he wanted to use Albert's death as a reason for attaching himself to me. You know? It's better if he becomes independent now. He's old enough.'

Paul stubbed his cigarette on the dry earth. 'No problem,' he said. 'When are you going back, by the way?'

'I'm not sure. It depends.'

'On what?'

'It just depends.'

Helen took a deep breath, braced herself and opened her eyes. The floodlights pointed at India Gate were painful. She squinted. There seemed to be smoke in the air and birds stirring the darkness. Still touching her arm, Paul had his eyes elsewhere. She saw his strong jaw in the bullish head, his curly hair matted by the heat. Something had caught his attention.

She raised her head. Perhaps twenty yards away a flower vendor had put a garland of white jasmine over a pretty girl's neck. Her young man pulled out his wallet. Sitting in a circle, their friends were laughing. The girl dipped and swayed in a couple of celebratory dance steps, shaking the flowers from side to side.

Helen lowered her head and closed her eyes again.

'Touch me,' she said.

He turned back to her. Despite the crowds and the bustle and the incessant traffic, there was something languid and suspended about this Delhi evening after the day's torrid heat. They were suspended together in the long tepid evening, floating he thought. He let the back of his hand drift above her elbow, up the rounded inside of her arm. All this will prevent me from writing the book, he realised. Now it rested on her bare shoulder beside the strap of her dress where there was a small scar. Or perhaps it would be a different book.

'Touch me,' she whispered again.

His fingers moved round the blemish. They slipped into the sinewy hollow of her neck. Helen sighed. He saw her breast rise and fall. In a moment she will withdraw, he thought. She was smiling as if through pain. He opened the palm of his hand to move it firmly up the smooth skin below her hair. She will start talking about Albert again. He was sure. She will retreat.

Helen tensed her neck against his hand so that his fingers were forced into her hair. She liked the strong feel of his fingers meeting her resistance, sliding into her thick hair. Paul felt the strangeness of it; the woman wanted to annul herself, pushing against him. It wasn't, he realised, a change of mind in his regard. It was something different and, for the first time he guessed, desperate. Helen was desperate. He would have liked to speak, to defuse the tension. But now it was she who didn't want it. She was thrusting her face blindly against his bare hand. The strangeness of it excited him and he looked up and around to see if they were being observed.

Helen burst out laughing. Abruptly, she sat up, jumped to her feet, brushed down her dress. She moved so quickly she felt giddy and had to clutch at his hair to steady herself.

'Ow!'

'I just remembered something, something Kulwant said about Prince Charles and Camilla.'

'Is that right?' he asked drily. 'And what was that?'

'Doesn't matter.'

She had left him, she was walking quickly through the people sitting and playing on the dry grass. Bewildered, irritated, Paul followed. She walked coltishly, he noticed, as she had the evening she got drunk. He followed without hurrying, lighting another cigarette. As he did so, stopping to touch the flame to the tip, he realised that he felt at home in India tonight. He felt good. He liked this scene of vendors and families on scooters, this mixture of repose and frenzy, the smell of burned dust.

'Paul!'

She had stopped by a man with a tray. She was calling him.

'Come here!'

He had to step round a boy and girl eating out of paper.

The vendor was in a pool of light beneath an old-fashioned lamp. She was paying him and as Paul arrived the man tried to drop a long trail of white flowers over her head.

'No no no,' she laughed.

Helen took the flowers and turned to Paul. She came abruptly face to face, lifted the garland and let it fall over him. Before he knew it, her pale lips pressed against his.

Then she stepped back.

Paul took the string of flowers in his hands. Her face had a wry questioning look. He sensed at once that it was false.

'Is this some kind of ritual?' he enquired.

'Let's get a taxi,' she said.

CHAPTER TWENTY-TWO

On 15 February 2005, at 10:32, Jasmeet Singh wrote

Dear Mr Albert

Sudeep is very nice but I will have to marry a Sikh. A Jat or nothing Father says! Hope I will be able to come very often.

Jasmeet

On 15 February 2005, at 09:46, Albert James wrote

Dear Jasmeet,

I'm glad you enjoyed yesterday evening. It was very promising. You ask what lies behind it. It's simple. Each person takes a part – suitor/princess – robber/victim – Muslim/Hindu – employer/worker – guru/disciple – man/wife – spider/fly – then, as the drama approaches its crisis there is a dance and you reverse roles. Don't worry why. It's an experiment! Just enjoy the fun.

Everybody will start with an easy part from their own family or caste then switch. We'll look at videos of people to help us. And animals too. Animals are useful because they don't disguise their feelings. They just are. You and Ananya and Vimala can help a lot with the dancing. The reversal moment has to have a graceful, ceremonial feel, a kind of enchantment. It has to be beautiful. I hope you like the others. Sudeep is a nice boy, don't you think? He's studying drama at the university.

Thanks for coming along and do say hello to your father.

Albert

On 15 February 2005, at 09:07, Jasmeet Singh wrote

Dear Mr Albert

Thank you for a nice evening. I hope it is helpful to have me even if I don't understand really what we were doing. Can you explain? Thank you also for dinner.

Yours sincerely

Jasmeet Singh

'But there are hundreds of messages!' John mutters. He hasn't slept. He feels confused and his head is heavy. Clearly, this is the revelation he came to India for: this girl, this computer. Equally clearly, he isn't ready. He doesn't want to read his father's emails. Suddenly, he doesn't want to know about his father at all. The night with Sharmistha and Heinrich has unsettled him. John needs to shower. He wishes this girl was Elaine. He doesn't want to meet strangers. He wishes he was here on holiday with Elaine. Or with Mum. He will send her a message: 'Thinking of you, bought you a present.'

But right now he has this girl in his room. She is pretty enough with a full round pouting mouth and jet-black hair under a yellow headscarf, but she keeps crying. John feels inadequate. He hasn't slept. I should have stayed in London, he thinks. In the end it would have worked out at the lab. It is his mother's fault. Every turn this trip takes makes him angrier with his mother.

'I was going to cancel everything,' the girl murmurs. 'But I couldn't. I couldn't destroy everything we wrote.'

She has followed him to his room. She has a strong accent. Not like Sharmistha. Sharmistha sounded almost American. John was surprised the receptionist didn't object. He imagined some rule in Indian hotels that would keep girls from coming to your room, especially a single room. The place is a den, a burrow; it smells stale. He needs to sleep. There are his socks and underwear on the floor, grubby clothes on the table. It's funny this mix of India and John: a bric-a-brac Ganesh beside his Imperial College tee-shirt. The girl is sitting on the only chair, by the TV, in loose trousers and smock, her strong chin pushing forward a little, slim hands clasped between her legs. He can see she has slim legs. The light comes from a greasy window where the room narrows beside the bathroom. It's the reflected glare of the early day. The air conditioner is rattling. I need to shower and sleep, John tells himself. I'm ill. He knows he isn't.

He sits on the bed with the laptop that the girl has put in his hands. The screen is glowing.

On 20 March 2005, at 13:56, Jasmeet Singh wrote

Dear Mr Albert . . .

John wants to be unconscious. 'This is your father's computer, Mr John,' the girl had said. 'The password is JohnJames.' But he can't sleep now. He can't even lie down. His own name the password! Or his uncle's name. The email account is swamped with messages from Jasmeet Singh.

On 20 March 2005, at 14:07, Jasmeet Singh wrote

You are so kind to answer so soon, Mr Albert!

'And you are Jasmeet?' John asks stupidly. His eye scans down the inbox. Every message is from the same address

Re: Sudeep

Re: Re: Sudeep

Re: Re: Re: Sudeep

Re: Caste and marriage

Re: Bandi Chhorh Divas

Re: Ananya and Vimala

Re: Spider webs

Re: Death

Re: freedom!

Re: my father

Re: Re: my father

Re: Love!

Re: Re: Love!

Re: Re: Re: Love!

Re: Re: Re: Re: Love!

Re: Re: Re: Re: Re: Love!

Re: Re: Re: Re: Re: Re: Love!

Re: Re: Re: Re: Re: Re: Re: Love!

'Yes, I told you,' she says. 'That is me.'

'I'm sorry. I had a rough night.'

The girl looks around at the hotel room, distracted and curious, wiping tears with the back of her forearm. Bracelets tinkle. One of her knees has started to jerk rhythmically. She's a strong physical presence in such a small room, animal and girlish. Quite tall. She has a tall neck. John wonders what he is supposed to do. Is he supposed to read these messages? In front of her? There are too many. There is a book and more. He wants to know what's in them, but he doesn't want to read them. He wants to have known all along. I'll have to confront Mother, he decides. He wants it all to be in the past, like an exam studied, passed and forgotten. Now he notices a smell; the girl has a perfume, something musky and different.

'Was it you who sent me that letter?'

'I'm sorry, Mr John?'

'I got a letter from my father. Did you post it? It arrived in London after he died.'

'Ah,' she smiles and sniffs. 'He wrote that letter at the Neemrana.'

'The what?'

'You don't know?' She seems genuinely surprised. 'The Neemrana! It's an old fort. A hotel. Very famous. On the road to Jaipur. It ended in my bag.'

'It wasn't finished.'

'I found the letter in my bag. I don't know how it came there. He was thinking a lot about you. He wrote the letter at the Neemrana.'

The girl is looking at him as she speaks. 'Everything went wrong, Mr John. I posted the letter when he died. The address was in the computer.'

John is at a loss. He has come back after a miserable, drunken night and now there is this drama that he must face. He cannot avoid facing it. Things are going to come out. Like it or not. Father is coming out of his coffin. The awkward box has been bumping about too long in the flooded basement. John wants to go to his mother and demand to know who this girl is. He wants to send Mother down to sort out the basement. Explain this girl, Mum! His parents' marriage was perfect, it was mythical. What other justification could there have been for their always ignoring him, their always disappearing together to one godforsaken destination after the next? John wants to be beside Elaine the night they swam in the river. If Elaine is fucking the Jap he'll go crazy. He knows she is fucking him. John sits staring at the screen.

The Indian girl stands up and limps to the door. 'I will leave, Mr John. You can read the things Albert wrote.'

'No, stay,' John says. He very much wants to be alone, but not with these emails. They will choke him. He will sink and stick in them. He can't let her get away. 'What's wrong with your leg?' he asks.

'An accident.'

She is standing at the door. It isn't properly closed. There are sounds of other doors banging, cleaners calling to each other down the corridor.

'Stay,' John repeats. Now he decides he must get the truth out of her. He would much rather hear the story from her than read all these messages. They will exhaust him. Then he'll have the facts he needs to go to Mother. 'What did you mean,' he asks slowly, 'that you're responsible for Dad dying?'

She looks at him, wiping her cheeks with her fingers. 'Mr John, I've brought you the computer. You can read it.'

'Please, sit down.'

She sits on the edge of the chair. 'I never cry,' she says. 'I didn't think I would cry.'

'What was my father doing?' he asked. 'This research you were in.'

She shakes her head. 'Please, take me away. Could you take me away, Mr John? Could I travel to England with you?'

John is out of his depth. 'Let's eat,' he says. 'I'm hungry.'

At reception, when John asks if they can have breakfast served on the roof, Jasmeet changes. She speaks confidently in Hindi, ordering things, trading brisk remarks, treating the receptionist as a servant. She asks for a tissue. In the water bowl the day's petal arrangement is intersecting triangles of mauve and blue.

On the stairs, the girl limps heavily. It's her right knee. She can't lift it to the stair above. The left leg always has to lead and the right is pulled up to join it. But the ankles beneath loose trousers are slim. Her white sandals are pretty. John tries to gauge what size they are. Elaine has very small feet. Girlish feet. His own are huge. Pushing open the iron door onto the roof she seems untroubled by the glare and the crows, unsurprised by the bare asphalt, the lone plastic table.

There's a warm breeze blowing. The waiter arrives. 'These crows, sir, they are beastly!' The man is hamming. He waves the birds away. 'Beastly, shoo!' It's a way of showing his amusement that John has found himself a girl. It's theatre. He imagines we slept together. Meanwhile, John can consider the girl more carefully. She's in her early twenties, he decides, older than Ananya, my own age probably. Jasmeet is looking rather shrewdly round the rooftop view.

'I think you have met my father,' she says sitting down. 'You had dinner with him the day before Albert's funeral. His name is Kulwant Singh. He is a friend of your mother.'

'Of course! God. I didn't realise. That was your father?'

'Yes.' She didn't smile.

'He was talking about the royal family. A doctor, right?'

'I've left home now,' the girl says. 'I'm not going back.'

'You've left home. I don't understand. When?'

'Now.'

John's head throbs. There must have been three or four gins, four or five vodkas. He sits looking across the table at the strong young woman in her pyjama outfit and lemon yellow headscarf that flutters in the hot breeze. Never having lived at home, John never had a chance to leave. 'Don't come out this summer,' Mother wrote from Chicago, 'your father isn't well.' John wants to bang on his father's coffin, with a stone maybe, a stone elephant, and he wants to make sure it stays shut too. He doesn't want to read those emails. He needs an argument.

Jasmeet is looking straight in his eyes. 'I am going to go to London, Mr John, I have decided to leave India. I have some money. I have a visa.'

In his room she had been crying. Now in the glare of the rooftop she is hard and resolute. 'I am not tolerating my father any more,' she says. Her voice has an attractive lilt. At first he thought she didn't speak very well. Now he realises it's a way of speaking.

'You don't know the hours and years he spent telling me how a Sikh girl must behave: Guru Granth Sahib this and Papa Ji that. My brother does what he wants. He studies law. He went to a better school. He has better English. I must be a secretary, a wife. They want me to marry a Jat doctor. But when I hurt my leg, his family got cold feet.'

She stopped. 'That is too funny? I hurt my leg and they got cold feet.' She laughed loudly. 'Your father, Mr John, said I was a crazy girl. Jasmeet, you are a crazy crazy girl!'

John can't keep up. It seems impossible this young woman could have had anything to do with his father, with a man who never remembered to pull up his fly, who wore shoes without socks, or sandals with socks. Not a woman's man. Distracted, self-absorbed. A saint without a religion. And ill in the end. An older man with prostate cancer, sick in his most intimate parts. John looks at the girl. Still, it is more possible with Jasmeet than with Ananya. Her manner tells him that she knows things. Her eyes and a sly twist of the lips. And her body.

'How did you hurt your leg?' he asks. He will grasp anything but the nettle. When he does he will take it straight to Mother.

'I was getting off a bus, in a hurry, it wasn't the stop, and a motorbike, zoom, crashes into me.'

She looks away to the parapet and India Gate. 'I was in a hurry, to meet Albert.'

Before John has time to comment, the waiter is back. The crows rise to greet the food. The man tries to slip napkins under the teapot but the wind snatches them. Two paper rectangles blow across the asphalt.

'Very strong wind, sir. Perhaps a dust storm is coming, sir. You must be warned, when the wind is from this direction, sir.'

He sets their trays down: scrambled eggs for John; for Jasmeet, some kind of fried potato with yoghurt and pickle. She eats rapidly with her fingers, dipping her head sideways almost to the plate. She is hungry. John can see the strong jaws, the elastic lips. He pours tea. He likes the madness of hot tea on hot mornings. His head will clear.

'You got up early?' he says. 'It's not even nine.' He doesn't understand if she really meant that she left home today.

She speaks with her mouthful. 'Do you think you can take me to England, Mr John? Can we just go to the airport and get a plane to London? I have a visa. Albert helped me. I have some money. I am twenty-four. With office experience. I can work.'

John can't respond. Making an enormous effort, he says: 'Tell me about you and my father.' He pushes the fork in his mouth. He isn't tasting the food at all. Mum will be forced to take him seriously when he goes to her about this, when he says, who is Jasmeet Singh? What was she to Father? Then she will have to tell him things. Then she will come back to England with him.

Jasmeet has her head over the plate, filling her mouth. He's struck how red her tongue is. The colour is very intense. Like the inside of a wound. 'Read the messages, Mr John,' she says. 'It's too complicated.'

'I'm not going to get upset,' he protests.

'Please. You will understand, if you read the messages.'

John doesn't need to understand. He needs to *know*.

'Read the messages,' she repeats, pulling a napkin from under the sugar bowl. 'I'm a bit afraid of travelling to London alone.'

'What about this research, then?' John asks. 'This experiment with acting?' Actually he isn't interested in this at all. He couldn't care less about Father's so-called research. It was time-wasting. The man was burned out.

Jasmeet wipes her mouth. The breeze is blowing loose hairs across her lips. 'We were meeting at the Delhi Drama School. Sudeep studies there. In the evening. We were learning to act things. We had to make catastrophes, he said, and then,' she hesitated, 'to dance. To unravel them, he said.' She shook her head. 'He wanted everybody to learn this, he called it a new way of behaving. There were five girls. Five boys. Sudeep could explain. You have to recognise a bad moment coming and then dance it, dance it away.'

'I don't understand,' John says flatly.

'Oh me neither really!' Jasmeet smiles with her mouth full. 'Everyone had to bring a story.' She swallows, frowns. 'Let me remember.' She brushes thin fingers over her lips. 'Okay. This was something Sudeep told: there are two Muslim people on the ground floor of a block – they are married many years, but not blessed with children, and upstairs there is a Muslim girl who is married to a Hindu man of a low caste with many relatives who are making a lot of noise all the time, always celebrating, always festivals late at night, and they have a baby too, he is very noisy, and the two families are insulting each other, also because this used to be a building only with Muslims and the Muslim woman downstairs thinks the girl upstairs shouldn't have been marrying a Hindu, and then because she hasn't had children herself she is angry about this noisy child, she is cleaning all the time, and hating the noise, she has bad headaches, and so the two Muslims plan to kill the Hindu baby and the mother when the father is away. This is a real story that happened in Sudeep's building. I was acting the young Muslim girl who married the Hindu.'

John stared at her. What was this about?

'We had to feel all the feelings very strongly, then learn the moment to dance. We must find a . . . trigger, that was Albert's word. Before the catastrophe. There is a dance where you become the opposite of what you were in the story. It is a ceremony. You do your opposite. Your father was experimenting a lot. He said we must make it beautiful or it wouldn't work. It had to be beautiful.'

'Dad was crazy.'

'Or for example' – Jasmeet was getting excited, she was happy to remember this – 'there is a family where the son is fighting his father because he wants to be a poet, you know, and on the contrary the father wants him to be a professor of science and they have arguments and the son's girl, his fiancée, who is very beautiful but she is a snob and she is afraid of being poor, she agrees with the father, her boyfriend's father – maybe she even likes the father and he likes her, you know, she's very sexy and he's a very powerful man – and the son starts drinking a lot, he is angry, really angry, and everybody argues and he is going to kill himself to punish them. I was the girlfriend and Sudeep the son and your father the father.'

'That is my uncle's story.'

Jasmeet looked at him coolly. 'I know. It was your Uncle John.' She hesitated. 'Albert said it was a method that must be making a rabid dog a poodle, or teach a spider to undo his web.' She laughed. 'Your father worried very much. Then he was excited like a child. Then he drank a lot. You know he wanted to make a play of *Alice in Wonderland*, is that how you call it? He said . . .'

John doesn't want to hear any more of this drivel. It pains him. He pushes away his plate. 'So why did you say it was your fault he died?'

Jasmeet shakes her head. 'Maybe I learned the lesson he was teaching. I wanted to stop the catastrophe.'

CHAPTER TWENTY-THREE

Paul took the elevator to the third floor, leafed through a Hindi magazine in the waiting room and saw the previous patient leave on the stroke of ten. The young man didn't look ill at all.

Paul waited to be called in. The magazine was glossy and appeared to be about astrology; it was one of the few subjects on which Paul and his religious parents had always agreed; which is to say that they had thought every form of divination was of the devil, while Paul just found the notion that his destiny was in the stars idiotic.

He went to the window. A dry wind was blowing, piling up litter, shaking the leaves off dusty trees. Were there circumstances, he wondered, or a state of mind perhaps, that prompted a person to consult a system of science, or pseudoscience, in which he had no faith whatsoever? If so, what was that state of mind?

'Mr Roberts?'

Dr Bhagat was a trim fellow in his late thirties, wearing a smart suit and tie. He emanated a brisk confidence. 'Mr Roberts, this is my wife, Bala.' A small woman offered her hand with a smile at once kind and shrewd. 'We work together,' he explained.

Paul took a seat opposite the doctor who sat behind an impressive desk. His suit was light grey and his tie yellow. The wife arranged herself to one side, pen in hand and notepad in her lap. Everything was clean and very neat.

'As I said on the phone,' Paul began, 'I haven't come for myself, but to talk about a patient of yours who died some months ago. Albert James.'

'And as my wife no doubt explained, our consultations with patients are strictly confidential.'

'I understand that,' Paul told him, 'and of course I'm very grateful you agreed to see me at all at such short notice.'

He paused. With its lowered blinds and quiet air conditioning the room conveyed a mood of sensible modernity. Paul had expected something more fancifully charlatan: drapes, lamps, iconic knick-knacks.

'I am writing a biography of Professor James,' he said. 'His wife thought you might be able to tell me something.'

'You are a writer?' the doctor enquired. He had the bland deference of one professional man showing interest in another.

'That's right.' Paul hesitated. 'I'm curious about your branch of medicine and about why Professor James chose to come to you.'

The doctor appeared to think about this. 'Bala,' he asked, 'get Mr James's file, will you?'

There were separate shelves for blue, green and red files. Albert's was green. Paul was aware that he might ask about these colours; instead he enquired: 'Were you surprised by Albert's death?'

The doctor opened the file and began leafing through notes and receipts. He had two small moles above the left corner of his mouth. 'We didn't actually know Mr James was deceased until your phone call. The last time he visited us was' – he glanced at the uppermost sheet of paper – '15 November. Many months ago.' Dr Bhagat looked up. 'But no, I am not surprised. Saddened, but not surprised.'

'He was very ill, then?'

'Ill?' The doctor raised an eyebrow.

'He had prostate cancer.'

The Indian's small wife leaned forward: 'We wouldn't actually be thinking or talking about a patient in quite those limiting terms, Mr Roberts. A man is not just a cancer.'

'I have spoken to his urologist at the Sir Ganga Ram hospital,' Paul told them.

'He had a urologist at Ganga Ram?' Dr Bhagat asked. 'Now you do surprise me.'

'He had consulted one, yes.'

'Ah. *Consulted.*' The doctor pursed his lips. 'What was written on the death certificate?' he enquired.

Paul was taken aback. 'I've no idea,' he said.

'Ha!' the doctor came back. 'I would be very interested to know.'

Paul reflected. 'Perhaps you could talk about him more generally. I mean, your impression, things he said, without betraying a doctor's trust, naturally. Though, of course, Professor James is dead now and I am a great admirer of his work. I can assure you that this will be a very positive biography.'

'I have treated quite a number of Westerners over the years.' Dr Bhagat sat back, fingertips on the edge of the desk, legs stretched beneath. 'Of course they grew up in a culture that relies almost exclusively on scientific instruments, on measurements of determined chemical substances, on photographic images of a foreign body or an area of alteration in the muscles or organs.' The doctor made a show of reflecting on this. 'A culture at once technically sophisticated, sometimes marvellously efficient, for certain conditions, but spiritually primitive.' He scratched at the corner of his mouth. 'Many come to India to flee that; they go to the opposite extreme, the mystics, gurus, meditation centres, to the exact opposite of what they are used to. This is rather naïve. From the frying pan to the fire as it were.'

Paul waited.

'Those who come to an Ayurvedic doctor . . .'

When he hesitated, his wife chipped in: 'It is because they are aware of the need for a more integrated approach. Allopathic and homeopathic.'

Dr Bhagat sat up. 'Mr James was not *ill*, Mr Roberts. Not *just* ill. Not in my professional opinion. He was full of *vata*. He was bursting with it. Blocked *vata*.'

'I beg your pardon?'

'It is ether,' said the wife. The high collar of her blouse gave her a rather prim look.

'*Vata*, Mr Roberts, is an energy that runs in our body and needs to be kept in constant circulation. One of the five key elements. It needs to be balanced and to balance other elements. In Mr James the *vata* did not flow. That is not so unusual. It gathered and poisoned. What was unusual was the intensity of this condition in Mr James's case. He came to see me and began speaking of the symptoms of what you call prostate cancer. Certainly, he did have these symptoms. I am sure that is no secret and his wife will no doubt have confirmed this for you: the very frequent and difficult urination; certain pains, some quite strong, yes, in the belly, the abdomen, and a general and sometimes very intense discomfort, in the bladder area. In fact, his problem was *vata*. It couldn't flow because of the tussle in his mind. A very fierce tussle. I told him that within five minutes of his walking into this room. Or even sooner. Even before he was telling me his problems I told him.'

'I remember,' his wife said.

'Because of the tussle in his mind,' Paul repeated.

'You would have needed to be blind not to see it. And then if you have my experience . . .'

'And what was this tussle about?' Paul enquired.

'Ha!' Dr Bhagat cried.

'A tussle like this is not really *about* anything,' his wife explained. 'It is part of his *prakruti*.'

'The personality, Mr Roberts. Or if we want to put it in a finer fashion, we might say: the collision between the inherited personality and its acquired traits. Yes. A grave tussle can manifest itself in this or that dilemma, but the tussle does not go when the dilemma is resolved. No. The tussle is simply looking for the dilemma so it can appear in the world. When one dilemma goes it finds another.'

Paul was sceptical. 'So, how do you treat a condition like this?'

'There are many ways of treating an accumulation of *vata*.' The doctor's tone became more practical. He turned a pen back and forth between his fingers. 'There are massages using oil mixed with certain herbs. When the *vata* has gathered in the bladder and groin areas as in this case one can also prescribe an enema of oil: one hundred centilitres of sesame oil with appropriate herbs to be held in the colon as long as the patient finds possible. Certainly not less than forty minutes.'

'Enemas? And Professor James did that?'

'I certainly prescribed it. Whether he did it or not is another matter. Your Mr James was like a man looking in from outside. Perhaps he was just curious.'

'Westerners put a high value on curiosity,' the wife said.

'In any event,' the doctor concluded, 'I warned him that these treatments would only be palliatives. He must address the tussle in his mind.'

'You have no cure for that?'

Dr Bhagat reflected. 'It is not easy to cure the *prakruti*. In a way you are asking a doctor to undo someone's life. Do you see? There are approaches rather than cures. Astrology is very useful in these cases.'

'Astrology?'

'You are surprised, but I have a great deal of experience, Mr Roberts, in using astrology both for diagnoses and cures.'

'For tussles in the mind?'

'This is part of Ayurvedic medicine, Mr Roberts. The body's balance of elements is very much determined by the position of the planets. We must understand who we are dealing with before trying to help. However, Mr James did not allow me to make a birth chart and pursue this line.'

'He didn't believe in astrology?'

The wife smiled: 'Your professor said he was afraid he would start believing in it if my husband did it successfully.'

'This is the typical contradictory response coming from a man with a tussle in his mind,' laughed Dr Bhagat. 'I have helped many such patients with astrology,' he repeated, 'though I never came across such a severe case. I am sorry he died. He was an interesting man.'

Paul watched the doctor. 'Sorry, but not surprised?'

'No.'

Paul tried to make his perplexity apparent. 'Can I ask why not, if you didn't even think he was ill? I don't understand. I mean, do you die of this . . . *vata*?'

Leafing through his notes, the doctor again appeared to reflect. 'Mr James told me nothing about his private life. He was very reserved. To be honest I did not know he was a professor. He gave his name only as Mr Albert James. He seemed a modest man.'

The doctor frowned, scratched lightly beside his moles. 'Of course I cannot disclose all the symptoms he presented; no, some of them were rather unusual for the illness he believed he had. I feel it would be wrong for me to reveal those things; they were presented to me in confidence and of a rather intimate nature. Let's say' – he hesitated – 'yes, let's say I had the impression that Mr James's situation was not *sustainable*, without really understanding what that situation was. He appeared to be – how can I put it? – running out of time.'

The man relaxed and his voice altered. 'But now Albert James's problems have been resolved, have they not, one way or the other, or at least taken to another life?'

The doctor's wife said: 'Often there are deep feelings that prevent us from wanting to be healthy.'

Her husband added: 'Maybe the easiest thing we can say is that some way of living this patient had developed was becoming impossible for him. That can happen. A man can stand on one leg for so long.' He smiled. 'Although, in my experience, it is remarkable how very long some people can stand on one leg, and even run sometimes.'

Paul's exasperation peaked. He stood up and reached for his wallet.

Dr Bhagat didn't move. 'You are in a hurry, Mr Roberts?'

They had agreed on a fee of 400 rupees. Paul counted it out.

'Perhaps you could tell us why you are writing a biography of Mr James. What is it that attracts you to this man?'

'You yourself also seem a little fretful,' the wife said.

Paul stayed on his feet but lifted his eyes from his wallet. Okay, he thought, and sat down. He would stay for his money's worth.

'It had seemed to me,' Paul said, 'reading Professor James's considerable body of anthropological and scientific writings, that he had gone further than anyone else in understanding how people behave in relation to each other. Also, he had a fascinating life and marriage.'

There was a long silence, as if the doctor and his wife were waiting for more. Paul thought he had said quite enough. Eventually, almost as though speaking to himself, Dr Bhagat murmured: 'Yet there is a problem, I sense.'

'A problem?'

The doctor looked up, and spoke more confidently. 'There is a problem with what you are saying. You do not sound so convinced. You say, it had *seemed* to me, not, I am sure.'

'Well,' Paul acknowledged, 'the truth is that Albert James died before I could meet him and now that I have come to Delhi he seems to have led me into a sort of maze. I can't find him.'

'*Seems* again.'

'I mean, it feels like that.'

'You feel your dead man is hiding from you?'

Paul shrugged. The Indian was amused. He began to run his tie through his fingers.

'I believe the dead are dead, Doctor.'

'But you said he was leading you into a maze.'

'Metaphorically speaking.'

'Ah,' the doctor said.

'Metaphors,' the wife smiled.

For a few moments none of them spoke. Dr Bhagat and his wife were a clever double act, Paul thought. They had imposed a strong mood. As always when he met a real couple, he tried to imagine the two of them making love. It was a habit he had never shaken off since his adolescent wonderment on discovering that his puritan parents actually got down to it between the sheets. For the first time, it occurred to Paul that, rather than meeting Albert James, the important thing would have been to have met Albert and Helen *together*, to have seen how they were *together*, to have seen them make love, he thought. The idea distracted him. Something twitched in his neck.

'We feel there is something else, Mr Roberts,' the doctor said.

'In what sense?'

'There is something that is troubling you.'

Paul hesitated, then thought, why not? 'In the last few days,' he said, 'I have begun a relationship with Professor James's widow.'

'Ha!' The doctor shook his head and rubbed the moles at the corner of his mouth. He seemed almost gleeful. 'That is most interesting!' He went on shaking his glossy head. 'So you know what to expect,' he chuckled rather merrily to his wife, 'when a writer arrives to write a biography of me, Bala! Or no? Beware! Beware!'

The lady remained expressionless.

'Perhaps, Mr Roberts,' the doctor resumed his more professional manner, but he was still smiling, 'perhaps you would like me to draw up a birth chart for you? We could examine some of the decisions you have to make. Steer you out of this maze.'

Paul looked at him. Nothing could have been further from the ethos he had been brought up in. Nothing would be more convenient than to know how to deal with the future.

'I'll think it over,' he said dryly.

'Looking through my notes here,' the doctor said now, 'I find I have written down one thing that Mr James said which perhaps I could share with you. I do not think it would be a breach of trust.'

'Yes?'

'Here. Let me see . . . when I asked him – this was at our first encounter – why he had come to me, he said he thought Ayurvedic medicine was, and I quote, "absolutely charming".' The doctor frowned, stroking his yellow tie again. 'A strange expression, don't you think, to describe a learned practice that goes back many centuries: absolutely charming.'

Closing the door behind him a few minutes later, Paul decided to take the stairs. There were only three floors. But between the second and the first, as he hurried down the steps, he heard a voice call his name. 'Paul?'

Paul stopped and walked back to the landing. It was a man's voice, he thought. There was no one there.

Paul looked up the stairs towards Dr Bhagat's office. But now he realised that the doctor didn't know his first name. No one knows my name here, he thought.

He stood on the landing, his breath a little short, wishing he could wind time back a moment. Paul. Paul. He turned and went back down the stairs. Outside, he found the street was a cloud of swirling dust.

CHAPTER TWENTY-FOUR

John wants to go to his mother now. He can see an end: an encounter, a crisis, then home. He wants to hurry it along and be on the plane back. Very soon he will go to some Internet point and send an email to Simon. He'll think of an excuse: 'Mother very ill.' This interlude won't destroy my life, he decides. He'll text Elaine: 'Coming back. Love you.' But he doesn't text her. Elaine has written: 'If you knew how that shit Hanyaki is treating me you'd be ashamed of your accusations.' And in another message: 'I doubt if I'll make it to the first night, never mind the last.' Every time she writes, it seems harder for John to write back. 'I HATE YOU,' she tells him. She should stop.

He unpacks the pashmina shawl. The material running through his hands is marvellously soft, liquid-feeling; the gold embroideries are intricately symmetrical on their lilac base. They are tiny elephants, he sees now. He hadn't noticed. Tiny liquidy snakes. 3,000 rupees. Elephants in sets of three with their trunks raised and coiled like snakes round lilac borders that ripple with gold. Handwoven and embroidered by the girls of Kashmir. There is a hotel bill to pay too. John should be keeping track, but he isn't. Smelling the cloth's clean smell, he imagines wrapping it round Elaine's frizzy, perfumed hair, the elephants and snakes framing her elfish and very English face. Do I love Elaine, or don't I? Do I know what that question means? First he must peep inside his father's coffin. The screen glows. 'johnjames', he types. 'Forgotten your password?' 'JohnJames'. Case sensitive.

On 10 May 2005, at 08:35, Jasmeet Singh wrote

Can you believe Sudeep tried to kiss me last night after you left us!

On 11 May 2005, at 12:40, Albert James wrote

To solve this or that practical problem makes no difference, Jasmeet. Honestly. What matters is learning to be different. Better still, *learning to learn* to be different!

On 11 May 2005, at 17:20, Jasmeet Singh wrote

I must hurry now; we have to go to the temple to knead the bread. (Can I say Gurdwara? Do you know that word?)

John tries to read the emails in chronological order. He's impatient. He only wants the facts, an outline of the facts, but something prevents him clicking on the last messages first. Elaine always reads the last pages of novels first. You get more out of a book, she says, when you feel relaxed about how it ends. You don't hurry. John finds it hard to believe that the Sikh girl left home this morning. She had no bag with her. She walked off after breakfast as if she knew exactly where she was going. Limped off. 'Very certainly a dust storm, sir,' the waiter insisted. 'I was going to meet your father when it happened,' she said.

Actually, John doesn't want the facts at all. He doesn't care what the girl's doing. He wants to go to his mother and persuade her to come back to London with him. She will be very upset by this Jasmeet story. She will need comforting. They will be together. Elaine and Mum will get on well. Elaine admires his mother. Mum will see the sense of going back to England now. She will tell Elaine how crazy it is to waste time with the Japanese director. John is beginning to feel confident.

On 16 June 2005, at 10:17, Albert James wrote

Jasmeet, I know you were all angry! But distractions are important. They unlock the trap. The automatisms get uncoupled. I never imagined Sudeep would get *so* mad, though.

John has to go back and forward to other messages to find out what all this is about. It's confusing because each email contains many old ones and whereas his father's computer is fixed so that the most recent message is always at the bottom, the girl's is set the other way round with the new message added at the top. There's no reliable sequence. He has to look at the dates, go back and forth between mail received and mail sent.

Is there any point? He has understood that Jasmeet works in a call centre replying worldwide to customer queries about software problems. Sometimes she pastes these queries into her mails, asking Albert James to explain things she doesn't understand: queries from Hong Kong, Iceland, Portugal. She asks for his help:

The bios is snagged in prov mod. Utility tools function me not enter in menu drop.

His father's answers are pathetic. The man knew nothing about computers. She must have sensed this. So she was only asking for the sake of writing to him. His father pontificates about the development of an international community that will ultimately communicate in computer code rather than language.

The difference between language and code is the difference between survival and destruction.

God knows what he meant by that or why he bothered writing it to this young girl.

Jasmeet says she is frustrated with her job. She wants to do something more creative. But the family has only paid for her brother to go to university and her brother does nothing. Her brother is the laziest creature in Delhi, in all of India.

He doesn't study and he doesn't go to Gurdwara. My father is always praising my brother but Gobind does nothing nothing nothing and then sometimes Father gives him a mad clout round the ear. He beats him hard. Gobind never hits back, he takes a thrashing. But he doesn't change his life. It drives my father mad. You know Sikhs are proud of working very hard.

All this before John finally discovers that Albert James had arranged for a boy to come into the rehearsal room where the group were acting one of their stories and to make fun of them. The boy, who usually shone shoes at the railway station, had a whistle he kept blowing and strutted about making faces, then bursting into fits of coughing. He obviously wasn't well and he didn't seem to know a word of Hindi. He had a Mongol-looking face. A foreigner. Trying to concentrate on his acting, Sudeep had lost his temper. He came running down from the stage and wanted to throw the boy bodily out of the rehearsal room. There were insults. The boy crouched down in a tremendous fit of coughing. Albert James had to intervene and explain that the distraction had been planned. The boy was paid to do it. Meantime he had videoed the scene.

On 19 June 2005, at 12:15, Albert James wrote

Sudeep showed he's missed the point of what we're doing, I'm afraid.

On 19 June 2005, at 13:56, Jasmeet Singh wrote

Sometimes I think it's you making fun of us, Albert. Of all of us.

There were scores of these mails. The older man and the girl had been writing for months. John feels superior but weary, lying in the poky room with its noisy air conditioning. He's still hungover, his stomach is rumbling again. For some reason he has laid the laptop on the pashmina shawl. The black keyboard lies in a lilac lake with golden snakes and elephants. Oddly, he imagines taking the shawl into his old lab and draping it over the centrifuge. He imagines the snakes coming alive in a lake of lilac, the elephants swimming with their trunks held high. Where do these thoughts come from? John misses the calm organisation of the lab, the clarity of the given task shared with a team of sensible colleagues. Breaking off, he moves to the desk and begins to sketch quickly on the back of another laundry form. His father's voice is coming through these emails much more clearly than it does through his articles and conference papers. John begins to draw him.

He has trouble getting his biro to flow. He licks the tip. For a moment he has that fretful feeling of trying to recover a dream that refuses to surface, as though the mind were pressing against a dark wall. Then all at once, with a dozen strokes, he has the lips, the nose, the drooping eyes, the amused, retiring look. He has Dad! Dad's sticky-out ears, Dad's wispy hair. He can't believe it. He was never any good at drawing. He never even liked it. Father used to include drawings in all his letters when John was at school: drawings of insects and animals and natives in traditional costume, often invented. John hardly looked at them. He never drew in his replies, just asked what they would do on holiday, would there be anyone at the airport; that was always an anxious moment, when you got off the plane and there was no one there. Now his father's face is mocking him from this piece of paper. It's uncanny. John stares at his father on the back of a hotel laundry list. Albert James: that knowing, endearing, mocking smile. He scores six straight black lines to frame the man, in his coffin. Then he is tracing snaky ripples across it all. The image starts to drown.

On 3 August 2005, at 08:42, Jasmeet Singh wrote

My parents want me to marry a man from Jaipur, a Jat Sikh, a Khalsa. He is a representative for a pharmaceutical company in Ahmedabad. He's quite nice, I suppose, very tall, a little bit stooped. Like you, Albert! He obeys the five K's, oh-Kay! The big snag is I don't really like him.

On 10 August 2005, at 10:07, Jasmeet Singh wrote

Sudeep is a bastard!

On 14 August 2005, at 09:10, Jasmeet Singh wrote

Albert, I'm sorry I didn't come last night. I don't want to come any more. You have Ananya and Vimala and Bibi. Sudeep can put his filthy pig paws on them.

On 14 August 2005, at 11:35, Albert James wrote

You are a very special person, Jasmeet. It would make me very sad if you left the group. You have a special and beautiful energy and you are the only Sikh. It is good for us all to have you with us. We all feel that. You are a wonderful dancer. I will talk to Sudeep. I'm sure he didn't mean to be disrespectful.

On 27 August 2005, at 18:43, Jasmeet Singh wrote

Avinash does business with my father and his pharmaceutical company will pay for my dad to go to London soon. Everybody is keen for me to marry him. Avinash says his prayers, even the Sandhana, and never cuts his hair (never never never, not even the most split split-end!) and when he travels he takes parautha and pakoras that his mother bakes for him. I will be preparing his lunch box all my life. They don't want me to work after marriage. I will be *buried alive*, watching television and going to Gurdwara like my mother.

On 27 August 2005, at 18:52, Jasmeet Singh wrote

Ps. His beard will suffocate me!

On 29 August 2005, at 14:01, Albert James wrote

Imagine evolution as a path through a maze of obstacles, like those computer games where you have to keep growing and rearming and looking for secret doors while all kinds of dangers are coming at you so you can never stay still. There are dead ends and you have to double back and start again and some dead ends are longer than others. Well, imagine that we have all been going down a dead end for more than 2,000 years! Imagine that the dead end is leading to a monster we can never overcome, not even with all the fruit we've found. The catastrophe is very close now. Question: can we still turn round and double back to a better path?

John wonders what the girl made of this. She was still after Sudeep it seemed, for all her supposed aversion to his wandering hands. Jasmeet is a live wire, John senses, a flirt, a drama queen. She has a high opinion of herself. She is excited by men's interest in her.

I love my family, Albert, but it's all such a bore sometimes, you know,

Sikh virtues. Men and women are supposed to be equal, but they're not. My mother prays at the temple and bakes the bread and saves for the poor and my father looks at pornography on the Net and spends his spare money on whisky!

Sandhana is when you get up two and a half hours before dawn, take a cold shower (very cold) and then spend an hour and more chanting the name of God or the name of all the gurus. All eleven! For hours! Dad praises Avinash for doing his Sandhana before going out and selling medicines to doctors by promising them free trips to London or New York and meantime he has his computer full of real filth (my Dad not Avinash!) He doesn't even bother changing his password!

There was an anxious message from Albert James:

Dearest Jasmeet, I really can't see the point of your telling your mother. You will only upset her. I'm sure deep down she knows the man she married, if you understand me. You risk destroying your family.

My father is a villain! What do you mean she knows him? My mum doesn't even know how to turn on a computer!

Some barrier has come down between the Sikh girl and the older anthropologist now. As he reads, John feels a growing alertness and revulsion. They are talking more freely. The girl tells him that she was always molested by her uncle, her father's brother, but her father pretended to ignore it. He wouldn't believe her when she complained. Albert James's responses are alarmed, but cautious. It's not clear what he really thinks about Jasmeet, but he answers five, even ten emails a day. Looking away from the screen, John is distracted by the window. The sky has dimmed. Dust is swirling through the street. When it gets serious he will go and take a look. He has never been in a dust storm.

In the story we are doing now, I can't see really why Indira would stay with such a man. Does she *want* poverty? Is it because they are very physical together???!!! You know what I mean. I don't think Vimala understands her part. She doesn't get angry enough. But I'm sure Jamal likes insulting her! If you don't give us a pukka script, Albert, something serious will happen one day because it will be like real people! We will make it up so well we will start hitting each other! Then we will have a real catastrophe!

Is it true Vimala is sometimes the maid in your house? That you paid for her school? She's very pretty. More than Ananya. Doesn't Mrs James mind? I think Vimala is in love with you.

Sudeep says you only bring pretty girls! He thinks you romance with us all! Sudeep is one-track minded. I told him you are always the most correct gentleman. Unlike him! Mr Paws!

What's it like being married, Albert? I'd like to meet your wife. I need to understand. I need to decide if I am going to obey and marry Avinash. Vimala is the kind of girl who always obeys. They say I must decide *now*. But I can't. My father will kill me. Sudeep says marriage is crazy. He's a modern kind of person. If my father knew about Sudeep he would kill YOU! He thinks I'm safe in your care preparing a performance for the theatre, and instead . . . In the new world there will be no marriage, Sudeep says, if there is still a world. He thinks the world will end and we must enjoy now. He says a time is coming when no one will be able to breathe and there's nothing we can do about it so we may as well have fun now. Sudeep wants me to join the DDS but my parents would never give me money for that even if I wanted. I don't want to be an actress. I don't want to marry Avinash. I want to travel, like you, Albert. Your life is the ideal life for me. You have lived everywhere and you are a good man, always with the same woman, not running after every girl. I envy your wife too! You have always let her do the work she wants. She doesn't sit at home and she doesn't go to Gurdwara. My father says Mrs James is crazy because she works for free all hours of the day, but I think she is doing it from a real love of poor people.

Sudeep says I should cut my hair, THERE, IN THAT PLACE. HA HA HA! A Sikh girl can never do that. By the way, did you know my dad rinses colour in his beard to look more sexy.

They've decided the dowry. A small apartment in Indira Vikas Colony. An apartment! For Jasmeet! I can't believe it. I didn't know we had so much money. Gobind is furious. Father told me I am his favourite now. My brother is a disgrace to the family name.

Oh I am too silly! The dowry is only the DOWN PAYMENT on the apartment. Avinash must pay the mortgage from his salary FOR THIRTY YEARS! The parents are all agreed. They are writing a contract. Today an Australian customer asked if I would send him a photo. I sent him this. Do you think it was wrong?

John clicks the attachment and a photo appears. It shows a round-cheeked Jasmeet smiling from under very long, thick beautifully brushed hair. There is a flirtatious twist to the corner of the mouth, a wild warmth in the eyes, a small blemish along the line of the upper lip. Since the photo has opened in Windows Picture and Fax Viewer, John clicks on the arrows right and left to see what else is stored here: Jasmeet at some kind of ceremony in lavish red; various close-ups of a yellow spider on a web sparkling with dew; diagrams of a steady-state, thermostatic feedback system; Jasmeet dancing at night in garish purple and green on a low stage outside with two other girls; Jasmeet standing beside an older woman against a backdrop of mountain peaks; Jasmeet as a schoolgirl sitting in a rickshaw beside a fat boy; Jasmeet side by side with a conceited young man wearing European clothes, neatly groomed and clean-shaven. John recognises the face from the crematorium, the speaker who nearly fell off the podium. Sudeep.

Dearest Jasmeet, mightn't it be that happiness lies in going the way your parents want you to go? I will always give you what help I can, if you decide differently, but experience tells me there is a wisdom in these traditional arrangements. I would be very happy, for example, if my parents had chosen a person like you for me.

What strange things you say, Albert! How could your parents ever have chosen me?

What is beautiful is the idea of coming together with a partner without having to act to take her, without calculating or grabbing. That is a great gift.

My father looks at pornography of boys too! I hate him. And you're wrong. Vimala is NOT happy with the man her parents have chosen. She told me she thinks he is gay! There are lots of gays but everyone pretends there aren't. She is definitely in love with you, Albert, you know. She is always talking about you.

I chose Alice's Adventures in Wonderland, Jasmeet, because it's the story nearest to what we've been doing, where nothing happens, everything dissolves into beautiful equivocations. Do you see? Perhaps that's the only way some stories can go on for a long time without coming to grief. What I want to do is introduce the five pieces we've been practising into a sort of Alice frame, like so many dreams. So one of the characters in our stories is always Alice, or an Alice-like person. Do you see? And it is always she who begins the dance, at the right moments, to stop things happening. Then all the other characters dance around her.

What a mess! Today a man tried to touch my breasts on the bus! They should have buses only women can use, like the train carriages. I stamped on his foot. He was ancient! There was a real hullabaloo!

I think you made a bad choice making Ananya play Alice and Sudeep thinks so too. She's so ignorant! She doesn't really understand your ideas. Do you like her most? I'm sure I could do it better.

The Australian sent me his photo! He's called Sean. He's really gorgeous. What do you think? Maybe too old for me!

John clicked on an attachment and opened a JPEG showing a sporty type, in his late thirties, with white shirt open on a solid chest, square, complacent face, a determined sincerity about the eyes.

Maybe we should play a play about me and Sudeep and Vimala. Except that might be dangerous! It could end with me killing him! Really!

Jasmeet, what do you want me to tell you about marriage? I can't help you. It's something people do impulsively in Western culture because no one offers a clear path for us and we wouldn't follow it if they did. Helen and I met when she was your age and I was a bit older. She wanted to be a doctor in poor countries and I admired her very much. We had many fascinating years travelling around and dealing with all kinds of situations. You imagine there are just people who are ill and need help and instead you find complicated political and cultural tangles. You have to negotiate with gangs who want to protect your clinic or control who works there. There's always a local doctor who spreads bad rumours about you. In Kenya they tried to burn our clinic down.

Reading this, John reflects that his father never said any of this stuff to him. He knew nothing about an attempt to burn their clinic. All the same, Jasmeet isn't satisfied.

You're not telling me very much, Mr Albert! You know I want to know more. What about sex? Did you ever betray your wife? Please tell me. Wouldn't you like to have sex with Vimala when she comes to your house? It must be soooooooo tempting. I know my father would. My mother would never let a maid like Vimala anywhere near our apartment. She is too beautiful. I told Sudeep, one day a woman will castrate him! He is an animal!

Would you like to come and see me dance, Albert? There is an evening of bhangra to celebrate an anniversary. I'm quite wild when I dance to bhangra. You won't believe it. You could bring your wife.

Sex is beautiful, Jasmeet, but difficult, and sex between people over many years is a thing that comes and goes.

I'd get bored. Perhaps I'm a rascal like my father! Maybe that's why I hate him sometimes. Because I am like him. Anyway, I don't want to be like my mother. She is a doormat! You know Jamal stopped me outside the toilet and told me he fancies me like mad! It's too crazy. Surely, I'll never kiss a Muslim!

Albert, I just read your message about sex again. I think it is very sad. My dad told me you had talked to him about a serious problem. Are you ill, Albert? I wish I could make you better.

Yes, Jasmeet, yes, it seems I am ill.

John stands and goes to the window. The air is swirling with smut and ripples of sand are running like water along the uneven road. He doesn't like reading these messages. Heading for the door, he hesitates, stops, turns and, scrolling up the endless list, clicks at random.

Re: Re: Re: Update

On 25 October 2005, at 17:55, Jasmeet Singh wrote

Albert! You know you're too funny when you mimic Sudeep. Really, you're as sexy as he is!

Re: Re: Re: Re: Update

On 25 October 2005, at 18:43, Albert James wrote

I love your slim hands, Jasmeet. And how nice to have tea together!

John shakes his head, clicks again.

Re: Re: Re: Re: Re: Update

On 25 October 2005, at 19:15, Jasmeet Singh wrote

And I love your eyes, Albert, when you are always looking at me. There is something mad about them.

John is on the edge of a precipice. He doesn't want to click again, but he does; it's a message from early November. His eyes flicker reluctantly over a full screen of type.

. . . as if I were dissolving into beauty, Jasmeet. Jasmeet! Sweet flower. When . . .

John forces himself to his feet and stumbles away along the corridor. He leaves in such haste he doesn't even stop to snap the padlock.

CHAPTER TWENTY-FIVE

'Mr John!'

Only as he pushed open the door to the stairs did he realise the girl was sitting in the lobby. She was struggling to her feet.

'You have read it all?'

'I thought you'd gone to work,' he says.

'I lost my job when I was in hospital, Mr John. You have read the messages? I was waiting for you.'

'Some,' he says. 'I'm going to my mother's now.'

The girl's eyes open wide. The head wobbles slightly. 'Why? Why are you doing that?'

'Is that Mr James?'

From a dark corridor behind him, the older of the hotel's receptionists appeared. The owner quite probably. 'Excuse me, Mr James.'

John turned. Fingering a necklace, the woman squeezed behind the desk and opened the big register. 'You are being with us a week now, sir, I think. We ask payment by the week. How long are you planning to stay now?'

'I don't know.' John hesitated. 'A couple more days?'

The woman showed him a bill with 6,800 scribbled at the bottom. Rupees. John can't calculate how much that is. His mind is not functioning. 'There is also the breakfast,' she says. 'We have to insist on payment at the end of each week, sir. You understand.' Beside her a phone began to ring. She picked it up. 'Govind Hotel. Good afternoon.'

The Sikh girl has limped up behind John and touches his elbow. 'Why are you going to your mother?'

'I'll pay this evening,' John tells the receptionist as she puts a hand over the receiver. It has crossed his mind he must take cash out before giving them his credit card. He mustn't be left without cash.

Jasmeet seems on the edge of hysteria. 'You can't go out in that dust. Haven't you seen the storm, Mr John? You can't.'

'I have to see my mother.'

As he walked towards the door, she hobbled after him. 'Mr John, don't you like me?' The stairwell is stifling. 'Do stop, please! For the sake of your father!'

John turned and drew a deep breath. Jasmeet is standing a flight of steps above.

'It's not a question of liking,' he said.

Seeing him undecided, she turned on a truly radiant smile and was hopping down towards him like a wounded bird, one hand pressed against the wall to keep her balance. There is no handrail. 'You talk just like Albert,' she said brightly, hopping and swaying. 'You have the same voice.'

When she was beside him she stood and smiled; her teeth were brilliant; then reached out and straightened his tee-shirt. It had got hitched up on one side. Her wrists were slim in the glitter of a dozen coloured bracelets. Her fingers rested a moment on his chest.

'I want to go to England. I have a passport and a visa. I have all my money. Let me travel with you.'

John turned away again and began to hurry down the stairs, but at once he slowed and let her catch up. 'How come you had my father's computer?' he asked abruptly. Then it occurred to him he hadn't even looked to see if there was any work in progress on the thing.

'You have not read the last message?' She held his arm to steady herself. 'He told me to take it. He told me where he would leave it. He was dying. He didn't want other people to see.'

'So why did you bring it to me?'

She hesitated. 'I need help, Mr John. Albert was always saying he would help me if I decided to leave. You are his son. I thought you would help.'

John shook his head. The girl is a distraction. The whole of India has been a terrible distraction from the work he should be doing. He must have it out with his mother and get back to London and to work.

Again John started down the stairs. She was hurrying after him. There are four stale, stifling floors, the stairway turning and turning past old brown doors, their feet clattering in the heat. At the bottom, at the end of a long corridor, a man in uniform was leaning against the wall. Seeing them hurry to the door, he said something to the girl in Hindi and she replied with a note of exasperation.

'He says it is a bad storm.'

John pulled open the big door. As he stepped out into a gale of dust, he realised he had left his mobile in the room. He'll miss Elaine's messages. It doesn't matter. Elaine too is a distraction. Only essentials matter. Only the coming collision. Behind him Jasmeet grabbed his shirt. 'Mr John! Wait!'

In the street the dust came thickly in sharp dry gusts, then swirled and sifted like dark snow. He walked fast. There were moments when everything was brown and impenetrable, then the road reappeared with moving shadows of cycles and cars and rickshaws. John had almost reached the taxi stand when he remembered he needed cash. He needs a cash dispenser. He turned a corner and walked. Where did he get money last time? There was the usual cacophony of horns. A cow had sheltered behind a parked truck. Jasmeet was still limping behind, covering her face with her scarf. John can't decide what to do about her. He cannot decide. Then a gust brought so much grit he found his mouth full of it and turned for shelter to a doorway. The wind was furious. He was grinding sand between his teeth. Jasmeet came, bent double, loose clothes flapping.

'Come in here,' she said. 'Come in here, Mr John.'

It is some kind of eating place. A ceiling fan turned. There was a small old wooden counter and high shelves with tins and jars behind greasy glass: on every surface there are adverts that seem to have come out of the fifties for cigarettes and soft drinks. The tables were wooden and an elderly man was sitting reading a book.

'Let's stay here,' Jasmeet said.

Trying to wipe the dust from his lips, John sat down. There was a crustiness round his nostrils and in the corners of his eyes. All in a minute's walking. Beyond the tables, the floor rose a couple of steps and there were men sitting on the ground eating from the same large dish, talking quietly.

Jasmeet shook the dust from her scarf. The room was hot. The old wooden chairs are rickety. 'It's an Iranian place,' she says in a low voice. 'They will have nice cakes.'

John's frustration is mounting. What on earth am I doing here? He wants resolution. Automatically, his hand moves for his phone and finds once again it isn't there.

'How can I help? Please?' The old man scraped his chair and looked up over spectacles from his book. As he spoke, a dark shape whisked across the floor. It shot from beneath the counter and disappeared under shelves in the far corner.

'We would like tea and cakes,' Jasmeet says.

'I have no money,' John protests. He would rather have a Coke. He hasn't had a Coke for weeks.

'I can pay,' Jasmeet smiles. 'Don't worry!'

Now the girl seems prim and pleased with herself. These shifts from anxiety to confidence are confusing John. Did the others see the rat or not? It was definitely a rat. He tries to focus on the girl as she folds her scarf around her hair again. They both have sand on their lips, round their nostrils.

'Have you really left home?' he asks.

The waiter, or perhaps proprietor, was getting to his feet. One of the men at the far end of the room came down towards the door, said a few words, looked out at the storm, grimaced and went back.

'Yes. I told you.'

'When?'

'Yesterday.'

'So where are you going to sleep?'

'Last night I slept in the lobby of your hotel. I arrived very late.'

'But why did you leave?'

'You have read the messages. You will understand.'

John found it hard to match the girl in front of him with the writer of the emails. Jasmeet is looking at him eagerly, her mouth nervously alive, eyes bright.

'I want to choose my life,' she says. 'You must understand that.'

'You could go to Sudeep.'

She sat up dramatically. 'Sudeep tried to kill me after what happened with Albert!'

'He knows? Sudeep?'

'Everybody knows! They were all jealous.' Jasmeet giggles. 'I could marry you, Mr John, and stay in London!' She hesitates. 'If I close my eyes when you speak it could be Albert.'

'But Sudeep came to the funeral. He said nice things about my father.'

'Sudeep said it was me killed him. It was my fault. I had destroyed a very great man. He loved Albert. He called me a bitch.'

John can't think what to say. When the proprietor sets a tray on the table he feels ill. His bowels. Suddenly, he needs to go to the bathroom. The man smiled at Jasmeet who smiled prettily back and began to pour the tea into cracked cups from an elaborate china pot.

The girl drank and nibbled a rather dry cake, looking at him. Again she lowered her face to the food rather than bringing it up to her mouth. She dipped the cake in her tea and sucked it. She looks squirrelish. And she has an odd way of swaying slightly while she sits, as if moving to music that he can't hear.

John needs the bathroom.

'Albert was in love with me,' Jasmeet eventually said. She still has food in her mouth. 'But he kept saying it was a catastrophe. He kept drinking so much whisky. There was a big fight with me and Sudeep. He said he would kill me. The play was ruined. Everything cancelled. Maybe it *is* my fault. While my father was in London we went to the Neemrana. Albert took me. It was very exciting. Neemrana is a palace fort, on the road to Jaipur. I told you. There are pretty green birds and a swimming pool. The food is really too nice. And beautiful rooms with beautiful old furniture. Very old. Albert was so happy, he ate a lot, but also he kept saying it was a catastrophe. He kept drinking. He was ill.'

The girl sighed deeply. 'I wanted Albert to take me to England. Nobody has ever been so nice to me. His voice was exactly like yours, Mr John. It was very beautiful to be with him. He talked about all the places we were going to go, then he said it was a catastrophe. It was a word he used so much.'

She paused.

'Albert said he was sure we were going away, to live away together. He was happy. He was writing a letter to tell you about us. That we were going away. Then he could never finish this letter. He told me perhaps the letter was not for you. I was upset. He kept writing other things too. There was an old desk in our room. Albert couldn't sleep. He was having strange dreams. He kept waking up. He was happy, he said, but he couldn't sleep because of his dreams. He was trying to write them down.'

She stopped and reached a hand across the table. 'Are you listening, Mr John?'

John looked up. The girl had a crumb at the corner of her lips. He was clenching his bowels.

'So what else did you do? At this fortress place?'

'There is a swimming pool there. We went for walks. Nearby there is an old step well. You know? It is very famous. It is like a big building upside down going down deep into the ground.'

John didn't understand, but he was struck by the mistiness in her eyes. You couldn't disbelieve her.

'We walked down down down every flight of steps, it is a very deep well, holding hands. There are nine floors going down into the ground. Have you ever seen one? It is like a temple upside down. Very very ancient. You climb down. Nine floors. But at the bottom there is no water now. It's an ancient well. Albert said it was like paradise.' She hesitated, remembering. 'He liked to hold my hand. He said he liked it very much.'

'And?' John was suffering. He needed bananas again. Not cake.

'He liked to see me dance. I danced for him at the bottom of all the steps. By the well. There was no one. He said even if there was no water my body was liquid. Liquid like a snake.' She laughed. 'It was beautiful to feel him watching. He said beautiful things. He said he could hear the water in my dancing. It was like a dream.'

John really didn't want to hear this. His father should have known better. 'Wasn't he ill? He must have been quite ill in November.'

She was picking up crumbs. 'Not so much. Not so ill. He just had some pains.'

'But, if . . .'

'Albert was very happy and very . . .' She sighed. 'Maybe he thought of your mother. He had a sad destiny, I think. I don't know how to say it.'

'So why did you say you were responsible for his death?'

Jasmeet's eyes clouded. 'I left him, Mr John. I thought: this man cannot decide, he will never decide, he cannot even finish a letter. Soon my father will return from London. There will be hell to pay. One day there was a Sikh driver who was returning to Delhi and I asked him to take me back. I was avoiding the catastrophe.

'Then after I came home and my father returned and Avinash was coming to eat with us, everything was horrible. It was horrible. They were telling me I must marry. I started to wish I had stayed with Albert. I thought, maybe after I had been away from him for so long, he would decide. He would understand now what he was losing. He had started to send me emails again. I thought it was a sign. He said he loved me. But you have read that on the computer.

'So one day I decided to go to him and surprise him. I just wanted to see him too much. I couldn't resist. I took the bus to the university. It was raining hard and I was in so much of a hurry to get off and run for some cover I didn't see the motorbike. You know. Zoom. Bang. Then I was waking up in the hospital and I couldn't see anyone for days. Now I will never dance again.'

Jasmeet paused and bit her lip. Speaking in a lower voice, she said, 'I think Albert died of love for me.'

Only the acute discomfort in his midriff prevented John from bursting out laughing. 'People don't die of love, Jasmeet,' he said. It's the first time he has used her name. The absurdity of it cheered him up. 'Particularly not a bumbling intellectual like my dad!'

The girl's face darkened.

John leaned across the table through his pain. 'You know Dad wrote that love was just a loaded word in a communication game. He didn't believe in it.'

Jasmeet turned her chair away and sat very still. Then she looked at him over her shoulder. 'Albert said I had changed *everything* in his life. He told me he would die of love. He wrote it in his last message. You will see it on the computer.'

'More like he thought he would die of shame if my mother found out,' John said brutally. He got to his feet. 'I need the bathroom.'

Pushing aside the chair, John found it hard to stand up straight. The girl was upset. As he turned to ask the proprietor where the bathroom was, she just repeated: 'Albert *promised* he would help me.'

'I'm afraid there is no light in the toilet, sir,' the proprietor said. His English was surprisingly superior. 'I wouldn't advise that you use it, sir. We have a little problem with the light.'

'I really need to go,' John said.

The man put his book down and smiled. 'Well, at your own risk, sir. I'm afraid it is not a very gentlemanly bathroom and we have no light. I am waiting for the electrician to come and repair it. It is very old wiring, you know, in this part of Delhi.'

John's stomach was groaning. It was a matter of seconds, he thought, and at the same moment he realised what a farce this was: his father's ideas, this scene in the café. It was complete farce. And I left a serious job for this! Instead of working out how to trick a ribosome into sterility he himself had been tricked into a situation that was quite grotesque, and certainly sterile. His gut was screaming.

'It is up the steps on the right,' the proprietor said, still with a note of warning.

Forcing his bowels to hold fast, John walked stiffly to the back of the room. Up the two steps beyond the restaurant area everything was filthy and much hotter. The four men sitting on the floor appeared to be workers of some kind, unshaven, loosely turbaned. Perhaps they too had come in from the storm. They had finished eating and were talking quietly, drinking from bottles of orange soda. Beyond them the space split into dark corridors.

'The toilet?' John muttered, embarrassed.

'Toilet?' The men started to talk to each other in Hindi.

'Not toilet,' one of them shakes his head. He nods towards the blackness to John's right. 'Not use toilet.' He pouts and makes discouraging signs with his arm. One of the other men is laughing.

'There is a toilet, isn't there?'

The man's head wobbles apologetically as if to say, there is, but then again there isn't. John can't hold on. He heads to his right where the man pointed and after a few yards of deep shadow finds a door.

'Sir!'

John turns. With absurdly grim faces all four men are shaking their heads.

The door is greasy, of black splintered wood with a hook latch that drops into a ring. John has no choice but to lift it and wrench the door open. As he does so he releases the most fetid stink imaginable. It seems impossible he didn't notice it the moment he entered the café.

His bowels won't hold. They had accepted to wait on the understanding that it was a matter of minutes, then of seconds. They have convinced themselves release is imminent. As he opens the door he feels a rush of pressure beyond resistance. The men behind are laughing. The smell is coming from pitch blackness. There is not the faintest glimmer. Automatically, his hand reaches to the wall for a switch and amazingly finds it at once. But clicking brings no change. What if the blackness is simply a hole? Some kind of pit? It might be vast or tiny. He will fall into filth. Talk about catastrophe. But he has to shit *now*! There's no going back. He takes one step, gets behind the door and pulls it to. If there's a latch this side he doesn't bother with it.

There's no time. The stench is overwhelming. Likewise the heat. There's a scuttling noise. His right hand feels at knee level for a seat. There's nothing. Don't breathe. Now he's leaning with his forehead pressed against the door. Otherwise he might lose all sense of orientation. He unbuckles his jeans, thrusts them down, crouches, craps violently, liquidly, Christ, hoping he has got his arse beyond his jeans, beyond his feet. He gasps for breath. There's more. He's crouching, one hand on the door, shivering, bowels burning, cold sweat starting out on his neck and temples.

And there's no paper. John feels so angry. Why was he tricked into coming here? First the storm, then this awful place. Perhaps there is a hose and tap somewhere, or a bucket. He can wash. But how, when he can't see? He can't just pull up his jeans. He's filthy.

The smell makes him want to vomit. Again he's aware of a scuttling sound. If I fainted, I could be devoured by rats. He's panicking. It's a nightmare. This is something to wake up from. Blessed or cursed with dreams of water. Hand in hand down to a dry well. I could die here! John says through clenched teeth. He wants to scream. There had been shit floating in the water with his father's coffin. He remembers the scene vividly now. The coffin was bumping about in water and shit. In a place like this, then. He crouches in the pitch dark, waiting to wake up, waiting for it all to dissolve. At least his bowels are relaxing.

Then he has the solution. Yes. I'm not stupid. Not for nothing the PhD. Now. He stands, slips one foot out of a sandal, balances precariously on the other leg – hard in complete darkness – slips jeans and underpants off the leg, then the jeans back on, then the sandal. There's something slimy on the sandal. He's breathing deeply now, however horrible the air. Now there's definitely the sound of a creature. It doesn't matter. This is the only solution. He repeats the rigmarole with the other leg. Jeans leg and underpants off, jeans back on. Symmetry. Balance! God knows what his jeans may have picked up touching the floor but now he has his underpants free and clean in his hand. Where's the sandal gone? For a moment his toe touches the damp floor. Please, the sandal! There. He can wipe himself with his underpants.

John works out that if he folds them carefully, he can have three attempts. He's regained some composure. He works quickly but carefully, trying not to touch the shit. Never again. When he's done as much as he can, he tosses the pants away into the blackness – God knows what's there, he hates India – and pulls up his jeans. As he does so, something runs over his foot, over the top of his sandalled foot, which automatically kicks out, stubbing his toe into the door. Oh Christ! There so much pain in the body just waiting to be unleashed. He almost falls, clutching at the door, picking up a splinter on the old wood. Definitely a splinter. But he's done it now. He's done it, he's okay, and he's going to his mother's and then straight back to England. Straight back.

A moment later, when John emerges from the door and confronts the four men, he has a determined smile on his face, albeit grim. The men smile back. The proprietor looks up with curiosity from his book. Jasmeet asks: 'Are you all right, Mr John? You are pale.'

'We need a taxi,' John says.

CHAPTER TWENTY-SIX

Helen had known that Albert was not telling the whole truth about his torment. But this knowledge was not available for reflection or elaboration. It was locked away. There was a knowledge of Albert, of their marriage, their entire life, which had always been locked away, from day one, from that first evening when he had driven her to her political meeting and then disappeared to his concert. That obscure part of themselves and her awareness of it had to be there to make the marriage they had possible; equally, it had to remain locked away. It was one of the conditions of life that one did not question. 'One does not question,' Albert had written for one of the conference papers she had presented for him, 'the mental processes of visual-image perception that moment by moment construct the world around us, even though experiments have shown how fallible those processes can be. One does not question them because to do so would mean chaos.'

Helen had wondered, standing at a microphone to read this out to a respectful academic audience, whether Albert hadn't simply found another of his indirect ways of telling her something. She had always felt that he was speaking to her in riddles through his work, that his work in fact was primarily addressed to her. Or rather: it was the need to tell her things without speaking to her directly that made his work possible. And because the method was indirect she was also invited not to understand, or to lock away her knowledge in some file that could never be opened: in any event to go on unquestioning, even to speak his words for him at prestigious conferences *as if they had been meant for others*. The important thing was that the two of them must never really speak. To do that they must know what they mustn't speak about. Helen was good at this. If she hadn't been, their marriage would not have lasted. 'Every behavioural stability' – she had read out Albert's conclusion to those New York professors – 'indeed all functioning interrelationships, are thus predicated on falsifying systems of perception, interpretation and communication, of which the language in which this paper is written is but one.'

Albert loved, Helen had sensed during the ensuing applause, to leave an audience with a conjuring trick that saw both himself and the arguments he had just advanced vanish in a puff of smoke, the moment of maximum intellectual brilliance coinciding with the most drastic self-effacement. Only she was left behind, at the podium, ready to take questions with an embarrassed smile, as she had been taking questions for months now from this irritating American. 'You are doing this for me, Helen,' Albert had whispered in the dark of their last night. 'You don't know how grateful I am.' They were arm in arm. The familiar tension had reached its climax. The web they had woven was at its tightest and most fragile. His voice was tormented, seductive. He was leaving her behind. The syringe was ready for his effacement. To have her do it was an act of brilliance. It would be the first injection he had ever let her give him. 'Helen, Helen, Helen,' he whispered, 'what a beautiful completion.'

For *you*, she muttered through the long nights that followed; for you, dear Albert, but not for me. Her husband's death had not been a completion for Helen. It was pure loss. It had seemed beautiful, but only as it happened, only as fulfilment of his wish, to die in her arms, at her hand, in the fortress of their marriage, to complete and end his own story as he wanted. And he had wanted it urgently. But afterwards she knew it was a terrible mistake. Albert's torment was not the torment of the cancer sufferer, she forced herself to realise. It was not the ordinary fear of a slow agony. There were years of life in Albert. I knew that, and I still did as he said. I pretended not to know. I didn't ask him to explain. I didn't demand to know what he was afraid of.

Why?

While Albert was alive Helen had been able to pretend. Or rather, she hadn't been able to do otherwise. But now he was gone, the mechanism was breaking down. Day by day the old complicity was decaying. There are moments, now, when Helen seems unable to put one foot in front of another, at the clinic, on the street; some crucial lubricant has dried up, she can't move. She remembers his embrace slackening, she feels his cheek against hers, turning chill. Why had he wanted to die? Why by my hand? With Albert's death, a buried knowledge began to moulder. This is something you can't just cremate and scatter. She must go back over things. Why else would she have started talking to Paul?

Yet out of habit Helen could not finally arrive at the place that she and Albert had learned to avoid so well. 'The strongest complicity,' Albert had written apropos of climate change, 'is the complicity of shared denial.' There were things Helen undoubtedly knew, things she physically felt – why she and Albert had come together in the first place, why they had lived their whole lives abroad – and she would circle around those things; it was impossible not to, given the gravitational pull they exercised; but she would not plunge and explore, she would not dig them out and name them. So she had chosen, in effect, to discuss Albert with the one man whom she could not really speak to, not openly, because of course he would write down whatever she told him. Then her life would lose its secret sense, the uniqueness their strange marriage had conferred on it; then she would stand naked before her son, whom neither she nor Albert had spoken of at all in the days when his death was decided.

So rather than tell everything with candour, she had insisted that Paul give up his writing project, that he pay attention to her not to Albert, that he see the excitement and superiority of a life of service: her life, not Albert's. If nothing else, she would win that old debate at last. She had teased the biographer with intriguing details and simultaneously discouraged him; she had made him curious and told him his biography was pointless. She had fostered mystery without giving him the key to understand. What were Albert's abstract and tortured considerations, she had hinted, beside the smile of a destitute boy returning from death's door, a girl with hepatitis recovering her bright cheeks? And she had used her body too, what charms remained. Why fret over the dead man when there is still some mileage in the widow?

She had definitely done all that, even if it wasn't planned. She wasn't a calculating woman. The man's ingenuousness encouraged it. And his blundering. Paul had absolutely no idea. He was a naïf. But she had never expected the American to agree, to *capitulate* even; she hadn't expected she would have to hear his drawling, gravelly Yankee voice say: 'Hey, by the way, Helen, I want to accept your invitation. You know? I'd like to go and work with you somewhere remote, if it's really a prospect.'

'I beg your pardon?'

They were eating lunch. Helen had gone to the clinic that morning but the dust storm had deterred the sick. There were few patients. Helen was at a loss when the flow of suffering was interrupted. She had wandered around the clinic for a couple of hours, visiting the bed cases assigned to her, trying once again to talk to Than-Htay. The boy was not recovering. The infection had responded somewhat to the drugs she had found for him, but his vitality had not returned. Not quite sick enough to be given a bed, he drifted around the clinic like a ghost, hovering in doorways, sleeping in the shade in the courtyard, nibbling a chapatti in the canteen.

Normally such a case would have been discharged to his family, but Than-Htay had none. He was still not speaking Hindi. He didn't try. If told to sweep, he held the broom between limp fingers as if he had no idea what it was for. His eyes were luminous, but vacant. Asked to help unpack a van and sort some boxes, he simply stared. He too was locked away somewhere, Helen thought, in the realm of some trauma she would never fathom. Albert would have got in there and found out. Sufferers knew at once that Albert could be told things. They understood he would not try to heal them or wake them from their trance; so they told him things, they let him film them. They understood he was just looking; he wouldn't take their precious pain away. It was curious that he never filmed me, Helen thought. He made no videos of the way his wife bandaged an ankle, or swabbed clean a sore. But his eyes were always on me. It was Albert's gaze made everything possible, Helen thought; even when the eyes mocked.

Towards midday she had come home in a taxi through the swirling grit. The wind was rising. 'I'll be on night duty later,' she explained. 'I'll take the afternoon off.'

Paul kissed her cheek at the doorway and smiled. The man was more chivalrous than she had imagined, more ordinary. They sat down to eat the food Lochana had prepared and he said: 'Helen, I accept your proposal, if you really meant it. I'd like to get involved with your work for a while. I've decided to drop the book. I want action.'

Helen was wiping her mouth and her hand folded tight around the paper napkin. 'You've changed your plans?' She wasn't used to men who came round. 'Just because you spent a night in the widow's bed?' She smiled sardonically. 'It was hardly a mythical experience.'

'Nothing to do with the night,' Paul said. Frowning, he poured sauce on his rice, dug in his fork, ate. With his mouth full, he said: 'I went to see Dr Bhagat this morning. Maybe that decided me.'

'Ah.' Helen raised an eyebrow. 'Interesting?'

Paul swallowed, wiped his mouth, looked at her. 'He said he hadn't thought Albert was really ill but all the same he wasn't surprised by his death.'

'Oh.' Helen looked away at her food. 'How . . . paradoxical.'

'Quite. In fact, he asked me what was written on the death certificate. As cause.'

'To be honest I wouldn't know.' She pushed her plate away, stood up and went to open a cupboard. Casually she added: 'I had Kulwant write it.'

'Ah. Kulwant.'

'So you could ask him. If you're interested.'

Paul knew it was a provocation and let it pass. He hesitated: 'Anyway, as I was leaving . . . well, I decided, enough is enough. You know? I need to do something different, as you suggested. I need action, real living, not abstruse ideas.'

As she turned back to face him, a rush of emotion tensed Helen's throat. This she hadn't expected: a man who agreed with her. She came to sit down, picked up her fork again, tried to smile. 'Actually, I had been thinking it was probably a mistake to have invited you. You're too used to the easy life, in the end.' She looked straight at him now. 'Aren't you, Paul?'

That made him laugh. 'Very probably!' He dug in his fork again. 'But now I need to get my hands dirty.'

'Doctors do their best to keep their hands clean,' she murmured.

'I'm not expecting to do open heart surgery, Helen.'

'And Albert?' Suddenly, her voice took on a little-girl's squeal of scandal. 'You want to abandon Albert! After all the fuss you've made, bothering me all these months? His ideas were not abstruse.'

Paul was perplexed. Again he had to wait till he had swallowed before speaking. 'Listen, Helen, I'm not getting anywhere with the book. It's time to put it aside. For the moment I need air.'

Helen seemed almost contemptuous. 'You won't find much of that in Bihar in the monsoon season.'

'Bihar?'

'There's a kala-azar epidemic. If you read the papers you'd have seen. They're calling for trained aid workers. I was thinking of volunteering.' She shook her head. 'You don't even know what kala-azar is, do you?'

'I'm eager to hear.'

'It's ugly. A mosquito-transmitted infection. Fever, lethargy, swollen spleen, the lips and eyes bleed. It's truly horrible to look at, smells atrocious, and kills.'

'I'll come,' Paul said.

She kept her face over her food. 'Because you need air?'

'That's right.'

Helen was completely thrown. 'And your little lady? I'm afraid her name always escapes me. I can't be as exciting as her, can I?' When Paul smiled wryly, she cried: 'You're far too narcissistic ever to stop writing!'

'Hey, Helen!' Paul complained. 'Don't try to dissuade me now I've made up my mind. I want to change. I'm excited about that. Let's leave the woman question out of it.'

She stood to boil water for coffee. Did the man suppose she would tell him everything about Albert as soon as he claimed to have given up the book, perhaps after he had worked beside her for a month or two to 'prove' it? Was it a ploy? But she knew Paul was not that kind. He is pushy, she thought, but he's not a creep. Helen has known creeps.

The teaspoon trembled as she transferred coffee powder from jar to cup. Has Albert's death bound her or freed her? Can she really be bothered with this man? Or any man. Albert had never been pushy; but he was awfully seductive. Day after day Albert drew you in, until something quite grotesque seemed reasonable. 'Let's go and lie down, love,' he had said that evening. He had been drawing her to the bed. He had been agitated for months. He had been anxious, excited, distracted, distant. She had never asked why. Then, suddenly, he was calm. He was hers again. He was decided. And he had known she wouldn't insist on knowing why he wanted this. 'I just want it to be you,' he repeated. 'I want to be yours. To finish. I'm finished, Helen, done. It's what I want. Please.' He had showered carefully so he needn't be washed. He had dressed properly so she needn't dress him. 'This will bind us forever, and free us both,' he whispered. She made no comment. 'Let's go to bed,' he said. He had led her by the wrist.

'Let's go and lie down, Paul,' Helen muttered when they had finished coffee. 'There's nothing else to do in a dust storm.'

Paul had spent the previous night in her bed, in the James's marriage bed. The two had made love rapidly and wordlessly. She seemed to take a purely physical and perfunctory pleasure in it all. For Paul it was unusual to feel that his libido was not centre stage driving the performance; it was as if he were being pulled, prompted, not exactly against his will, but in response to something beyond it. Helen made all the moves, showed him what she needed. He was almost obliged to be passive, a passive actor. Afterwards, it seemed nothing had really happened, everything was still to be decided between them.

Now, as yesterday, Helen didn't want the light. She drew heavy curtains over the drama of the churning dust in the street. Yet she wasn't shy or ashamed. It was her face showed her age, not her body. Naked, she pushed herself blindly against the younger man, pressed her nose into his neck, her breasts against his chest. He tried to calm and caress her, to have the woman relax and respond; but today every contact, every sound and smell, was turning her back towards Albert. The tension built. Paul couldn't understand it. The woman was frantic.

'I can't!' Helen eventually cried. 'I want to, but I can't!'

She turned away. After a long silence, she said quietly: 'So now I suppose you can get up and go, Mr Journalist.'

'My name's Paul,' he said. He kept a hand on the small of her back.

'For a busy man like you, this must be so much wasted time.'

'I'm moved,' he said quietly. 'And curious.'

'About Albert.'

'About Helen.'

'Liar.'

'Okay. About Albert and Helen. And about us.'

She let him stroke her. Occasionally a limb twitched. She was tense beyond control.

'How can you betray your pretty girlfriend just like that?' Helen suddenly demanded.

Paul didn't reply. It was a non-question.

'Not that I don't know all there is to know about betrayal,' she added.

After another silence, he asked: 'So when do we set off to Bihar?'

'You're too fat,' she muttered.

He laughed. She was lying with her back towards him and he pinched her softly at the waist. She didn't respond.

After a few minutes, Paul withdrew his hand, lay on his back. He found himself calm and not at all worried about the future. It was unusual. He was giving up a big source of income. He would follow Helen and watch how she went about her work in Bihar. He would learn and change. I've finally escaped my life, he thought. Lying quietly, he heard the wind banging a door. Someone was shouting in the street.

She turned brusquely. 'I betrayed Albert a dozen times,' she said harshly. 'More. Don't imagine that's the problem. As if I'd never made love to anyone else.'

'Helen,' he said.

Their eyes met.

'I didn't hide it either. There's nothing exclusive about sex. Our marriage went much deeper than that.'

'You're an unusual woman,' Paul told her.

She stopped. 'So, now you can change your mind again and write your book.'

'Betrayal is always a good selling point.'

'Ahhhhhhhhh!' Helen shrieked. She turned away from him and let her voice yell from the bottom of her belly: 'Ahhhhhhhhh!' Then again and again: a powerful, inarticulate howl. Then it became a moan, lower and sadder. Face to the wall, she pulled her knees to her chest and hugged them and moaned. Eventually, after a couple of minutes' quiet, she told him, 'Go away. Just go.'

There was no question of Paul's going.

'Go!'

He knew she didn't want him to.

In a coquettish voice, she eventually said: 'You'll get bored with me. I'm too old.'

He said nothing.

'I can't add to your brood of abandoned children, you know.'

'Surely a point in your favour.'

'You'll get bored!' she shouted. 'You'll be fed up with miserable villages and dull ignorant peasants and fetid smells and filth and people dying dying dying all the time, helpless people with nothing to hope for buzzing round you like flies, always wanting something, always with their hands out, begging begging begging. Always always always.'

She had exhausted herself.

'If you haven't got bored all these years,' Paul asked quietly, 'why should I?'

'You'll start studying spiders!'

'Ha. I don't think so.'

'Or arranging theatricals for lush little girls.'

'That's a little more tempting.'

'So you can smell their spicy young bodies and feed off their blind young energy.'

She lay rigid, disoriented. Why had she said such an ugly thing? She clutched herself fiercely, dug her nails into her sides.

Paul saw and yet felt perfectly calm. It was uncanny; usually a woman's unhappiness would make him anxious and guilty. But not today.

Then once again she whirled round and now a fist came down on his chest. 'Damn you!' she shouted. She punched him hard. 'You're making me say things I never even thought before. Damn you. Go! Get out!'

He pulled himself into a sitting position and grabbed her wrists. She was screaming. 'Albert is here beside me! Always! There's no room for you! No room!' Her face was thrust towards his, eyes and mouth straining. He was enthralled by the intensity of it, excited by his own calmness.

And now the phone rang.

They were both still. Helen's body relaxed. He felt the tension go out of her. She was pleased the phone was ringing. She got up and hurried round the bed and out of the door. He watched her move, tall and pale in the shadow. Even naked she had a sort of mature reserve.

'Hello?' she answered. She was in the sitting room, out of sight. Paul reached for his trousers and, without thinking of asking permission, lit a cigarette. He felt pretty good. Who would have thought this when he came to India, when he took the taxi to the crematorium, planning his book? He was going to change his life.

'No,' he heard her saying. 'I'm sorry. God. No, I don't know. I wish I could help.' Helen went on and on repeating these formulas. She had no idea. No, it wasn't a good time to come round. No. She was on night duty tonight. Soon she'd be going back to the clinic.

'Kulwant,' she announced, returning. 'Jasmeet has run away from home. His daughter. Apparently she took a lot of money.'

'The dancing girl?'

'Ex-dancing girl.'

She looked at him. Paul saw she was herself again.

'Sorry about the hysteria,' Helen said.

'No problem. I'm paying you back by smoking in your bed.' Paul smiled. He tapped the ash out into the top of the cigarette packet. 'Surely the girl is old enough to leave home if she wants to.'

'He's a protective father,' Helen said. 'They're Sikhs.'

She went to look out between the curtains. The dust storm was blowing hard. The silhouettes of the buildings opposite came and went. 'He wanted me to give him the phone numbers of some other people Albert had got her doing things with. His theatre thing, whatever it was. He's afraid she's run off with one of the boys. But I don't have any numbers.'

'They'll be on his phone,' Paul said.

'I don't have it.'

'No laptop and no phone? He must have left them somewhere.'

'I couldn't care less. Let her run off with the boy. She's a flirty, empty-headed little thing and they want to marry her to some dull, devout fellow in pharmaceutical sales. Obviously she runs away.'

Helen came back to the bed and sat down with her back against the bedstead, her arms folded. After a moment or two she told him in an even voice: 'You made a mistake, by the way, how you were going about the book.'

'Oh yes?'

'You'd have been fine if you'd started where I told you. With his brother's death.'

Paul lifted his eyes.

'I'll tell you a story,' she said.

'Go ahead.'

She looked at him. What was she trying to achieve? She frowned: 'Just before we went to Kenya, right at the beginning, Albert took me to see his parents. It was the only time I met them. We'd married without telling people, in a registry office. Albert said the only way to do something his father might object to was to present the man with a fait accompli. He was rather scared of him, I think. Anyway, they lived in a big house on Headington Hill, wealthy outskirts of Oxford, and as it turned out his father was charming, rather gallant, not at all worried about us marrying or moving to Africa, not at all interested actually. He talked about his research the whole time. He was an expert in dominants and recessives and terribly concerned that I understand exactly what was at stake. We talked for hours. But his wife, Albert's mother, fussed, interrupting all the time. She was a tiny woman, really very pretty for her age. Albert kept ruffling her hair – he was much taller than she was – he kept saying, "Don't worry Flower, Helen will look after me. Kenya's okay." She was older than his father, I think, by quite a few years. He called her Flower and she called him Bumble. I found it sickening. Albert and I never called each other anything but Albert and Helen.'

Paul closed his eyes. He enjoyed listening to her very English accent. It had a hard, exciting edge.

'Anyway, in the afternoon, when his parents were both out, Albert showed me his brother's and sister's old rooms. He had to search for the keys, because they were kept locked. He'd obviously waited for the parents to be away on purpose. Well, Amelia's room was bright with fresh flowers on the dresser beside a portrait photo. She wasn't very pretty, nothing like the mother. More like a female version of Albert. There were her books, an old stereo system, a hockey stick. That sort of thing. She was a lot older than

Albert and he hadn't been close to her. She died when he was only about, what . . .?'

'Fourteen,' Paul said.

'Right.' Helen paused. 'But John's room was a shock. When we opened it dust sifted off the top of the door and swirled up from the floor. The curtains were pulled to, it was dark and stale and there were clothes spilling out of drawers, books open on the floor, cobwebs everywhere. It must have been shut ever since he died, seven or eight years before. Even the bed was unmade and thick with dust; I touched it and there was spidery fluff on my fingers. Then Albert showed me a photo on the bedside table; it was the only thing in the room that had been wiped. It was Bridget, the girl John had gone mad about. A real looker. Albert said: "There, I've shown you," and closed the door again.'

'Strange.'

There, I've shown you. No sooner had Helen spoken the words than she heard Albert's quiet voice saying them again. Despite the heat, she shivered.

'Still,' Paul said, 'all this hardly matters now I've decided not to write the book. Does it?'

Helen looked at his thick chest on the sheets. Who was this man to her, if not Albert's biographer?

'About what just happened,' she began.

'Forget it.'

'No, I'm not apologising.' She hesitated. 'I just want to explain. Because there's something that . . . that has been driving me mad, to be honest, and that makes all this . . . with you . . . so difficult.'

'Spit it out,' he smiled.

With unexpected promptness, Helen said: 'Albert and I didn't make love for the last . . . maybe, five years.'

'Ah.'

'That side of our life stopped. Or rather, he stopped. We never made love in this bed, for example. Never.'

She sat with her arms folded, rocking slightly against the pillow.

Eventually Paul asked: 'But isn't that normal, maybe, in a long marriage? I can imagine there's a moment when you just lose interest. I mean, in sex.'

She didn't answer.

'I stopped making love to my second wife right after the honeymoon. I can never understand how we managed to have a child.'

Helen shook her head. 'It was important for us.'

'His illness?' Paul suggested. 'I don't suppose prostate cancer encourages sex.'

Now she laughed bitterly. 'Kulwant says the first thing most men do when they're diagnosed is grab a new woman. To prove they're still alive. For some men it actually jump-starts a stalled libido.'

'How interesting. So maybe he did that and felt guilty.'

'Albert never felt guilty, because he never did anything. If anything, it was that that tormented him. Not doing anything.' She faltered. 'He became more and more tormented towards the end. His work sort of broke up into a dozen odd projects. He rushed off to ashrams and came back frustrated and angry. There were all kinds of ailments. There were nights and nights when he didn't sleep, always in the bathroom, days he wandered about aimlessly.'

Paul was perplexed. 'What did he say when you asked him about it? The sex. Lack of.'

'I didn't ask him. At first, I wondered if it wasn't some kind of experiment, to see how I'd react. Albert was capable of that.'

'So how did you react?'

'I waited. I concentrated on my work. I tried to read what he was writing, hoping to understand. But he had almost stopped writing these last years. Aside from notes in other people's books.

Once he said that to complete a whole sentence from initial capital to final full stop seemed a form of violence, a trap to catch flies.'

'Where would that leave Proust?' Paul joked.

She shook her head. 'God knows how he was supposed to teach in school if he didn't believe in writing whole sentences.'

'Could it be, like Gandhi, he'd started thinking celibacy was necessary, for his task?'

'Albert hated Gandhi, he hated the idea of the crusade, of being good for a purpose.'

After a while Paul tried: 'Perhaps he'd got wind of these betrayals you mentioned.'

'But he'd always known!' She shook her head back and forth as if to fight off an unpleasant idea, then said: 'I *told* him. Maybe I even did it to excite him. Partly.'

'Out of my repertoire, I'm afraid,' Paul acknowledged. 'I thought I was coming here to write about a genius anthropologist and his angel, aid-worker partner.'

'Don't be an idiot!' Helen said sharply. Then she went on: 'Albert wanted me to be larger than life. He said since I was around death all day, it was understandable I had lovers.'

'Kulwant was one of them?'

'Now and then. But Albert *knew*. He knew it was *nothing*. God, he knew Kulwant was an idiot. You can see that for yourself. A nice idiot, but an idiot.' Helen banged her head back lightly against the wall. 'I wondered if it could be to do with the trial. It began right after that. It stopped, I mean. Sex. We should have been celebrating. He was acquitted, his reputation was saved. For what that's worth. We were travelling again. Albert loved travelling. Oh *why*?' Helen suddenly raised her voice and shouted the word. 'Why? Why did he do that to me? *Why?*'

Paul said nothing.

'I defended him to the hilt in Chicago.'

'Perhaps he didn't want help.'

'No, he was grateful. I could see he was.'

'Perhaps he wished he had fucked the girl.'

'You would say that. But he would never have done it.'

'You had lovers. He might have . . .'

'*Other people* did things,' she said sharply, 'but not Albert. He lived to be near me living.'

'Admiring and mocking your busy life.'

'That's right.' She nodded, paused. 'In a way he sucked blood from me.'

'And you got upset when he stopped.'

Helen was shaking her head slowly from side to side. In a low voice, she murmured: 'Albert took himself away from me. In his mind. I don't know where. The last six months were awful. Just at the very end he came back, and I was happy. He had been so tormented. I think it was his sense of failure. His father had been such a success, with work, with women, with family; his brother had had the courage to slash his wrists. That's how Albert saw it. He was capable of seeing suicide as a positive thing, a victory, a ceremony. He was obsessed by ceremony. At the very end, he began to talk of love again, of being fused together. Us two. Our marriage was his masterpiece, his destiny. It was art, a story, a trajectory. And I was so happy he'd turned back to me.'

Helen groaned. 'He died in my arms. Our faces were together. I could feel his breath on my face. In the end, I lay all night beside him. I remember the exact moment when the breath stopped coming, when his arms went limp. I felt him go. I saw it. I *saw* it. Like someone leaving the room. I got up and laid him out. If I could, I would have cremated him right here with our own furniture, I would. I would have done it. I would have gone with him if I could. Believe me. Like some stupid suttee. Sometimes I wish I had. God, I wish I had.'

'Helen.' Paul opened his mouth to say more, but she fell

sideways onto him and across him. She deliberately lay across him. All at once he found his face pressed against her stomach. 'Bite me,' she was saying. 'Bite me till I bleed. Please.'

Paul recognised the same wildness as when she had tossed the flowers over him the previous evening, the same falseness. Obediently, he opened his mouth and felt her skin sink into his mouth.

At the same moment there was a ring at the door.

PART FIVE

THE STORM

CHAPTER TWENTY-SEVEN

Old Delhi flew apart. Its sandstone walls had dissolved and were howling their release. Vision came and went with every breath, with every gust. A minaret a phone shop a tea kiosk swirled away in torments of dust and litter. John's gut had dissolved too. He ached. Jasmeet had him by the hand, or he her. And his mind whirled. Thoughts appeared careered disappeared with debris in the murky air. His eyes were screwed to slits. He fought the wind, the sour air in his throat, on his tongue. Grit, leaves, petals: again and again the world made up and swept away. On the first corner they reached, a telegraph pole was down in a tangle of wire. The dusty wind seethed around a goat trapped and bleating in the broken cables.

'We must go back to the hotel,' the girl begged.

In the midst of the tumult John was intensely alert. Sirens shrilled. Crossing the road, he pressed his arm against his mouth to block the dust, breathing his skin. Start and end with breathing, he remembered. The other hand grasped Jasmeet's. Why had Dad written that? Why do I keep remembering it? They were bent low. Then a curtain of dust dissolved to reveal half a dozen black and yellow autorickshaws sheltering between a low wall and acacia trees. He pulled the girl that way and she limped and hopped after. There were quite large objects in the air: a newspaper, a Coke can. This is the opposite of my laboratory; the idea blew through John's mind, the opposite of my teamwork and controlled conditions. He felt elated. How volatile my emotions are. Surviving the toilet experience had done it. Or I'm in the centrifuge myself. He smiled. Over their heads, the acacia branches waved frantically. He didn't feel afraid. This was Father's world, he suddenly thought. All phenomena stormed about his senses. Yes, this was it. He honestly didn't care if he ran out of money. Let them do what they wanted. Stumbling, John pulled aside a tarpaulin to get in the first rick. The small vehicle rocked as they slid across the seat.

'Where's the driver?'

'The drivers are waiting for the wind to stop,' Jasmeet said. She was clutching her knee. 'No one is driving now. The motors will choke in the dust.'

John wanted to see his mother *this minute*, in this moment of clarity, of volatility. Now he would know the right thing to say; or rather, what he said would become the right thing. He wouldn't be inhibited, he wouldn't let his embarrassment get the better of him, or her severity. I will stay in Delhi with you, he would tell her. Why not? He might say anything. Communication would be immediate and total. He would tell her about Dad and Jasmeet. Yes. That was necessary. But it had suddenly come to him: perhaps Father *had* been onto something. Being here in India, in this storm. Onto, as it were, *everything*.

John's mind took a sudden jolt: Father deliberately lost control, submerged himself in everything. Was that the experiment? It was ridiculous. As a scientist, Dad was ridiculous. He'd have done better to write plays like his brother, the way he always mimicked people. I will stay in India and continue Father's work, he could tell Mother. But how could such an idea come into his head? That is the opposite of you, the opposite of what you want to say!

John wanted to take his mother back to London. He must check, he thought, what had been left on Dad's computer. An explanation somewhere. It had been a waste of time reading those emails. Who cared about Dad's feelings for this girl? Perhaps he was right to fuck her. Perhaps that too was an experiment. Jasmeet was beautiful. Perhaps I will fuck her myself. At the same time he knew his mind might switch back any moment to where it had been only seconds before. It was disgraceful. It was absurd. You love Elaine. He fretted. He wouldn't know what he felt or who he was until he opened his mouth to speak to Mother.

'When will the driver come?' he demanded. 'Where is he?'

'We must wait, Mr John. You should be patient. They won't drive in such a storm. They will stay in shelter.'

He tried to sit still but he wanted to be moving along with his thoughts, moving fast. 'What are those?' he asked. From twisted threads of red and gold an assortment of painted trinkets hung from above the steering bar. The garish things swayed when the rickshaw trembled in the gale. Jasmeet looked up from her knee. 'Religious knick-knacks,' she said. She wasn't interested. 'All the drivers have them.' Her knee was obviously causing pain.

John leaned forward. A tiny red and gold figure had snakes round his neck. The face smiled inanely. He reached out and took the next one in his hand. A miniature Ganesh was riding a rat. It was lacquered wood. The colours were bright. 'It's a miracle the guy can see through all this rubbish to drive,' John remarked. 'Everybody has trinkets,' Jasmeet said again. 'To bring good luck.' John examined a female figure sitting on . . . what? An owl? How did they think of these combinations? Here was a woman with too many arms riding on a tiger's back! How could that bring good luck? But it was a stupid distraction. 'I'll go and find the driver,' he told her.

As he spoke the autorickshaw shuddered in a wild gust and the girl reached her arms round his waist to hold him. 'Don't go.' She pressed her head against him. 'You mustn't tell your mum about me. She will think the worst things. My father will kill me. Seriously. He will kill me. He gets too angry. Remember, your mum and my dad are friends. They are close friends.'

When John didn't reply, the girl pleaded. 'Please take me to London.' And then almost angrily: 'You will never find anyone better than me, you know that, Mr John? Where will you find someone like Jasmeet?'

John didn't answer. Lifting the rick's tarpaulin on the scene outside, he saw a world so fragile it could be swept away in an instant; it would dissolve like a dream that seizes your mind one moment and is gone the next. A wind like this must brush away a million cobwebs, John thought. The girl held him tight.

'I've got to go,' he said.

'Your father and I never had real sex,' Jasmeet whispered. 'I hope you were not thinking that, Mr John.'

He could have throttled her. Just because he was set on going to Mother, she was backtracking. First she boasted, she showed him his Dad's love letters, then she denied. Still, John let her hold him and even cuddle against him as they sat waiting for the rick driver. His body was tense and numb. He did not know what would happen when he saw his mother. He did not know what he might say, who he would become, how she would react. It would be decisive. She would be upset. He would shout perhaps. He would go down on his knees. Jasmeet pressed her softness and smell against him. He was aware of her smell now, the sweet tang of her skin, but it had no power over him. His head was locked up elsewhere.

'Albert said he could not make love to me because he thought of me as his daughter, or his son's girlfriend.'

'What?'

There was a sound of glass crashing.

'He kept saying it was like a dream, him and me. It was real and it wasn't real. At the same time.'

She's lying, John thought. She's inventing. He was hardly paying attention.

'He said he thought of me as your girl, Mr John. He liked to think of me like that. So he couldn't make love to me. It started when we were playing the story of his brother, John. Sudeep was too jealous! Albert mimicked him really well. He wanted to help me the way a father helps his children, taking me to England.'

'Dad never helped me at all!' John snapped. Again he pulled back the rick's tarpaulin and saw the wind had blown a rag against the pole of a signpost and was simply holding it there, flapping.

After a few moments' silence, Jasmeet said, 'I like you, John. I like you a lot.'

He felt the violence intensifying.

'Let me stay in the hotel tonight,' she whispered. 'I can sleep on the floor, then we can go to London.' She lifted her smock and showed a pouch fixed to her belt. It was a glossy plastic red against the flat smoothness of her belly. She unzipped it and pulled out a passport. He saw a wad of notes. 'We only have to buy the ticket,' she said.

They sat on. There was no sign of a lull, no sign of a driver. Occasionally there were horns, sirens, cries. John imagines a man lifting the tarpaulin. 'Lodhi Gardens,' he tells him. The man climbs in and the rick begins to trundle through the flying dust. But he had only imagined it. The rick was only shuddering in the wind. He sees the tarpaulin lift again. A brown face appears, a man with stained lips, crooked teeth, a dead eye. It is his rick driver the day he went to meet Ananya. 'Lodhi Gardens,' he says. 'Quick!'

'What?' Jasmeet asked. The girl had her arm round him, her face against his chest. She had been speaking. She was still saying things about herself and his father. About Sudeep, about going to England. 'Maybe I will marry you, like he imagined.' John hadn't been listening. 'Before it is too late, your dad said.' 'To Lodhi Gardens,' John muttered. The brown face was grinning through the tarpaulin.

'What?'

'Nothing,' he said.

John grinned, embarrassed. He knew there was no one there. The girl held him. The rick's tarpaulin has turned purple; it is the curtain in the crematorium. John stared at it, waiting for the Indian's face to appear again. Or his dad's face. He remembers the undertaker with the yellow woolly hat. I should have asked him to open the coffin. Instead, he had sat still in the back of the car with Mother. 'I kept up decorum,' John mutters. He remembers very powerfully his mother's elegant detachment behind her black veil. Immediate and intense, the memory passes over him in a wave. 'I am not here,' he announces. He remembers the strangely brooding, theatrical atmosphere of the cemetery with its Victorian angels, its hooded figures lying on the tombstones. 'Perhaps I could live in the graveyard,' he murmurs. 'With the other destitutes.'

'John!' Jasmeet cried. 'What is it?'

He had squeezed her tightly. Had he? He is vaguely aware of having squeezed the girl rather fiercely. The wind rocked the rickshaw. He was conscious of an ominous uneasiness in his head. His headache is a weather front. The storm edges closer. His thoughts are tangling in the acacia branches. They are thoughts the wind lifts from the dusty earth as the rain approaches. It wraps them round a pole and pins them flapping. He felt sick with expectation. The wind blows away the mind's cobwebs, he thought. He must take shelter.

'Where, where can we shelter?'

'What's the matter?' the girl asked.

'I was remembering his funeral,' John shook his head. His voice is distant and mechanical. His jaw feels stiff. He mustn't let her understand.

'Whose funeral?'

Now he recalled the schoolgirls. Their little feet trooped past him. Green and gold uniforms. He was reliving the funeral. What pretty young girls. What pretty yellow petals they sprinkled on his coffin. Why is there so much yellow in India? he wondered. He saw faces painted saffron. 'Why are you wearing a yellow scarf?' he demanded. Jasmeet looked up and smiled. 'I like yellow. I always wear yellow.'

The flowers meant something, John is sure. He knew now he should have kissed the coffin. At the very least. That was the solution. If he had kissed it, it would have ceased to plague him. If I had kissed the polished wood it wouldn't have festered in the basement with the sewage and the stagnant water. The water was in his mind. Can't the girl smell it? And even better if I had seen the body. Why had his mother prevented him? 'Albert was all my life,' she had said. She deliberately prevented him seeing his father's body. 'And I his.' John is nothing, she meant. Instead of seeing his father, John can go and see the Sufi tombs, John can go to the Taj Mahal with its jawab and its mosque. John can see other graves, not his father's. His father has been dispersed in the river. Disappeared. Dad has escaped forever, into water. My parents' perfect marriage excluded me, John thought. The more they excluded him the more impossible it was to leave them alone. He shivered, though the air was warm, the wind was warm, the dust is warm and sour. He shivered uncontrollably.

'Mr John!' Jasmeet cried. She had been calling him for some moments. She was sitting up now and shaking him. John tried to focus on the driver's trinkets swaying in front of the rick. Why does that tiny woman have so many arms? She is a spider on an owl.

'John! Mr John!'

It went against the grain, but John made a massive effort to be himself, to get back into himself. 'Jasmeet,' he said. His voice was forced. 'I can't go back to England with you.' It made him tired to speak. He breathed deeply. 'I have a girlfriend in England. We are going to get married. My mother is coming to England for our wedding.'

'Let's go back to the hotel,' Jasmeet said. 'Please.'

Then it came to John quite suddenly that his mother would be at her clinic, not at home. Why do I keep thinking of Mum at home when Mum was never at home? She was always away with the sick and dying. Cunningly, he asked, 'Jasmeet? Where is the clinic where my mother works?'

'Off Shadhanad Marg,' she said.

'And where's that?'

'The road from the station to Chandni Chowk. By the railway line.'

John knew where the railway station was. It wasn't far from the Govind. He could walk there in fifteen minutes.

He sat rigid, calculating. Outside there was a crack of thunder.

Jasmeet was nervous. Timidly she asked, 'Are you really getting married, Mr John? What is your fiancée called?' She seemed genuinely disappointed.

John felt clarity coming and going. It is pointless saying anything, a voice told him. The words were spoken quietly and convincingly, as if across a table in a quiet room where everything is calm and reasonable. It is pointless *saying* anything. John listened and saw at once how true that was. It was a wise voice. Talking is pointless. He hadn't really been listening to the girl, after all, had he? And she hasn't been listening to him. Why say anything? She just wants to take advantage of you. She's been telling you lies. Elaine had certainly lied. All the messages Elaine sends are lies. Text messages were invented for lying. John soon realised that. It's too easy. Then he was overwhelmed by an image of Sharmistha's body, her golden nakedness swam into his mind. She is right beside him. Her lips covered his. Her hair is on his face. And he started at the touch of Heinrich's hand.

'No!'

'John! Mr John!'

John looked at Jasmeet's yellow scarf. How had Father managed to escape through the gap between the yellow and the purple?

'Okay, we'll go back to the hotel,' he said quickly.

'Oh yes!'

He would leave her there. He would say he was going down to reception a moment and he would walk to Mum's clinic. By the time she realises he's gone, it will be too late.

Jasmeet was already sliding off the seat. She pushed back the tarpaulin and hopped out.

As they moved beyond the relative shelter of the wall, he saw that the wide expanse of Connaught Circus was now a lake of sand flowing in fast waves, and swimming through them, head held high, body undulating in liquid ripples was a snake, a long snake. Four feet. Perhaps five. It slid effortlessly through the orangey dust, its head swaying rhythmically back and forth, sending a fluid yellowish wave rippling down the length of its body.

John was fascinated. The creature seemed one with the dust, but streaking across it. Jasmeet hadn't noticed. She pulled his arm. He was standing still. He recalled the drawings in the book Dad had scribbled in: snakes as lightning bolts. That was the night I asked Elaine to marry me. That was when he picked up the three elephants and went into his mother's bedroom.

Pulled along by Jasmeet, his eye still searching the point where the snake had disappeared, John marvelled at this astonishing flux, violent and fluid, dark and bright, and he recognised in the awful tension in his head, in this feeling of pressure and sickness but also of vistas opening, forming, dissolving, an intensification of his feeling that morning when the boy had sold him those three elephants. He must buy another set as soon as he had money in his wallet.

In less than ten minutes they were back at the hotel. 'You're not well, Mr John.' Slipping into the hallway, she smiled with puzzlement and tenderness. 'You remind me of Albert so much. He also had bad moments.'

John was impatient. On the stairs he thought: The girl is dragging her foot on purpose, she isn't lame at all. It was a ploy she had thought up to get sympathy. She invented that daughter-in-law story too. It was a trap.

'Room seventeen,' he said at reception.

There was a young man on duty. Someone he hadn't seen before.

'I'll come down in a few moments to settle last week's bill,' John told the man in a loud voice. That would be his excuse for going out. Then, approaching his room, he saw that the padlock hadn't been closed, the door was ajar. He pushed it open and knew at once that the computer was gone, yes, and his phone was gone. The pashmina shawl is gone.

Jasmeet didn't understand. All she saw was that her blond Englishman was shouting. He rushed to the window. The sky was black. It's pointless saying anything, the calm voice repeats. Don't say anything, John. It's his father's voice. Lightning flashed. Everything has been taken from me, he thought. Things are given to John only to tease him. Beauty is sent only to be taken from him. How Mother mocked when his girlfriends left him! How she chuckled. 'Let's hope it goes better this time,' she had smiled that evening. She was mocking.

John turned to Jasmeet, shouting, waving an arm. All over the walls are drawings of strange animals. There are drawings of figures with elephants' ears, with snakes on their heads, with too many arms. There are rats and strange birds. Dad. Dad has been in here, drawing on the walls. Dad has taken his computer back. It's his revenge because I drew him. God. Where is his drawing of Dad? Where is it?

Jasmeet is on the bed sobbing. 'Mr John. Mr John. Stop it!'

When she lifts her face he sees her nose and mouth are bleeding. He backs away alarmed, then rushes to the bathroom to be sick.

CHAPTER TWENTY-EIGHT

'I was so sure he would be here,' the young woman repeated. Standing at the window, she was in a state of shock. 'I thought I'd surprise him. And now . . . it never occurred to me . . . What shall I do? I don't know what to do.'

She stopped. The wind had fallen and it was raining hard. Beside her, Paul saw the taxi pull up in the street three floors below and Helen move quickly from the door to climb in, closing her umbrella as she did so.

'I feel so stupid!' the young woman said. 'I was so excited about coming.'

They had tried calling John's phone but it was turned off. She had sent him any number of messages to say she was here. He would see them as soon as he turned on.

She sat down. 'I thought it would prove to him I cared. I thought he'd be so happy.'

'That's a big step,' Paul agreed, 'getting on a plane to India.'

The American looked at her. She was a curious creature, almost too slim and with an odd abruptness to her movements, as if shifting quickly from one pose to the next. Then she was still, but with the tension of a cat about to spring. Above tight jeans and a few inches of bare waist, her breasts were incongruously large, more than filling a tight tee-shirt. She seemed painfully self-conscious. Paul smiled.

'I hope I haven't frightened Mrs James,' she said.

'I think it would take a bit more than that,' he assured her. 'She's a tough lady.'

It was now more than an hour since the doorbell had rung. In a matter of seconds Helen had switched from extreme mental ferment to the coolest practicality. Paul liked that.

'It will be Kulwant,' she had said, pushing her arms into a bathrobe. 'Tell him not to do something and you can be sure he'll do it.'

'Want me to disappear?' Twice divorced, Paul was used to the farce of adulterous affairs. He had pushed girls under beds and once been caught himself, hiding in a wardrobe.

'Whatever for?' Helen asked, already tightening the cord round her waist. She couldn't care less what people thought.

Then, opening the front door she found a young woman with a backpack and a Boots plastic bag.

'Are you Mrs James?' the girl asked. 'I'm Elaine Harley, John's girlfriend.'

Paul had stopped at the passage door to watch the scene. There was something gently skewed about the girl's face, as if she were speaking from one side of her mouth. She had light freckles on milky skin and a thin nose that wasn't quite straight. Helen was polite and warm. 'Oh, how wonderful! Yes, Elaine! Do come in!'

She made the girl sit down. She brought her water from the fridge. She told her she must be tired. 'What a marvellous surprise! Heavens. John spoke so much about you when he came in January. I had no idea you would be visiting.'

Elaine's smiles froze: 'But isn't he here?' She looked around the apartment.

Helen had just sat down: 'Who? John?' She saw the girl's face. 'No. Should he be?'

Elaine trembled. 'He isn't here? Has he gone travelling somewhere?'

'John is in London, isn't he?' Helen asked. 'That's the last I heard.'

'Oh.' The girl's voice faltered. 'Oh God . . .' It was a few moments before she could bring herself to explain. One hand came up and tugged an ear lobe. John had gone off ten days ago, she eventually said. 'Quite suddenly. He left a note saying he was going to India. I was sure he meant here.'

'No, not at all.'

Helen didn't seem thrown, Paul noticed, by the younger woman's anxiety, nor by her son's odd behaviour. Her mood hardly changed at all. She was welcoming, but detached. 'I haven't heard from John for weeks.' She paused. 'Obviously there's been some misunderstanding. Are you sure you don't want to lie down? You must be exhausted.'

'But he left his flat, and his place at the lab!' The girl was frightened. 'That's everything he had. You *must* be in touch with him.'

She stared at Helen as if the older woman might have simply forgotten that her son was in Delhi, or even in another part of the building.

'I'm afraid not, John never tells me anything. This really is a muddle. Are you really telling me you came out here on purpose to find him?' But now Helen was looking at her watch. 'Oh dear, and I'm afraid I'll have to be going to the clinic soon. I'm on night duty.'

Elaine was baffled. Helen made tea. She was clearly finding it difficult to give the girl the proper attention.

'Perhaps it's just a question of a young man's haring off,' she suggested vaguely returning from kitchen to sitting room, 'feeling he needed experience, you know?' Men did that kind of thing, she said, and John was notoriously short of experience. 'All he's ever done is study.'

Elaine sat in silence, unable to take it in.

'John never actually worked for money in his life,' Helen went on, pouring tea. She spoke automatically, evidently repeating things thought and said a thousand times. 'I hope he doesn't owe you anything, does he, dear? Perhaps saying he was going to India was just . . . I don't know . . . an excuse.' Helen frowned. 'After all, why would John come to India? He has no reason to be here.' She got up and bustled about packing her work bag. Without looking at Elaine, she asked: 'Had you been arguing perhaps?'

The girl admitted they had a bit. 'He was upset that I was so busy. With rehearsals, you know. I'm in a play. It's opening in a couple of weeks. He wanted me to be there every evening, but this was my first chance to really do anything.'

'John was always a demanding child,' Helen agreed. 'By the way, this is Paul,' she finally remembered to introduce him. Paul was still on his feet at the doorway to the bedrooms.

'Paul is staying here with me at the moment. He's researching a book about my husband, who as you know . . .'

Helen stopped and smiled as if the sentence was already complete.

'I'm so sorry,' Elaine said. 'Pleased to meet you,' she told the bulky man who now came towards her with a gallant little bow. After a pause, the girl said 'John was very upset. Especially that he hadn't had time to see him before it happened.'

'See who?' Helen frowned.

'Sorry, his dad, before he died, I mean. He was very . . . that's why when I saw this note, about him coming to India, I thought he must want to spend some time with you. He said you hadn't had much time to talk when he came over.'

'He was only able to get away for two or three days,' Helen said.

Paul watched her.

'Oh heavens,' she hurried on, 'I'll have to be getting dressed. I'm afraid we're very short-staffed these days. I'll be late.'

For a moment it crossed Paul's mind that Helen must know where her son was but didn't want to tell the girl for some reason. Otherwise how could she be so unconcerned about his disappearance? Unless she was still locked up in the desperate mood of half an hour before? Either way, he admired her for the decision to go to work anyway. Helen doesn't allow things to overwhelm her, he thought. Other women he knew would have been frantic.

'If I call him with my phone,' Elaine was saying, 'perhaps he won't answer. He hasn't been answering my messages. But maybe if someone else tried . . .'

'Give me the number,' Paul offered.

'Yes, have a go,' Helen said, buckling on a belt. 'He's probably just off on his own somewhere.' She picked up her shoes by the door.

Paul keyed the UK number into his own phone and called it. He waited through a crackle of radio beacons searching for connections, then got a recorded voice.

'He's switched off.'

Helen seemed neither surprised nor disappointed, perhaps not even interested. She picked up the house phone and called a cab. Evidently eager to be alone, she stood smiling falsely at them while she spoke in Hindi, then closed the call, moved to the sofa and perched on a cushion opposite the girl.

'Elaine, dear . . .'

Unexpectedly, she reached across the space between them, took the younger woman's hands and smiled more warmly. 'Elaine, I'm sure this is just some kind of misunderstanding or communication breakdown. You know?' It was the voice she used for reassuring patients as she left the ward at the end of the day.

'John really was *so* enthusiastic about you when he was here. He was telling me what a wonderful actress you are and how happy he was to be with you and I was happy for him, of course. Now, do you have anywhere to stay the night? We're rather tight for space in the flat here, I'm afraid.'

Elaine hadn't arranged anything. The plane had been delayed for hours, circling and circling because of the weather. She had been so sure John would be here.

'Never mind. So, let's see, for tonight Paul will sort you out and find you a hotel, won't you Paul?'

'No problem,' Paul said promptly.

'And then tomorrow we'll have a big think what's to be done and how we can find out where John is for you.' Now Helen sounded as though she were speaking to a young child.

'Thanks,' Elaine muttered.

Upright in a white dress, Helen glanced around to see if she had forgotten anything. Yes, her umbrella. 'The taxis only have to come from round the corner,' she said, 'I'd better rush.'

Paul and Elaine were left with a half a pot of tea to drink. They stood at the window watching the car pull away.

'I know she's very committed to her work,' Elaine eventually said. She sat at the table and stared at her fingers. 'John admires her really a lot. He's always telling me stories about her.'

'She's a very remarkable woman,' Paul agreed. 'And Albert James was a remarkable man.' He felt for a moment that he had become a sort of acolyte. The Jameses were a religion.

'I did try to read a book of his. John gave me something. But it seemed rather difficult.'

'Depends which,' Paul said. 'The early ones are easier. As with most authors.'

He found it strange now that Helen had mentioned his researching Albert's biography when in fact he had told her three or four times that he wasn't. 'Actually,' he suddenly felt the need to say, 'I've given up the idea of writing about him. I'm going to do a year or two of aid work. Helen's finding something for me.' He hesitated, wondering why he was explaining this. 'Maybe India has that effect on people.' He half laughed. 'Beware.'

Elaine hadn't listened. 'Can you try his number again?' she asked. 'Perhaps he's switched on.'

Paul took his phone out and pressed to repeat the last call. There was still no response.

'Oh I can't understand it!' she bounced to her feet again. 'He always keeps his phone on, *always*, even when he's asleep. He loves getting messages. Unless maybe he's lost it.' One hand clutched in her hair, she hurried to the window, as if to catch sight of her boyfriend in the street. 'I was so sure he'd be here. How can he disappear like this?'

'You thought he'd come to see his mother?'

'He's been a bit weird since his dad died. I don't know. I was sure he'd come back here. He kept talking about his mother.'

Paul didn't know what to say. He was aware that he must be coming across to her as a friendly avuncular figure and at the same time he wondered if he really fitted that description. The more distracted the girl was, the more animal and attractive she became.

Elaine turned, hesitated, then went back to the window. But the drama of the situation released her from ordinary inhibition. Quietly she said: 'Actually, he'd got it into his head I was seeing someone else. I mean, that was part of it. It was all muddled.'

'Ah,' Paul said.

'It was stupid. I thought he'd come out here, sort of to punish me. Like a test. That's why I came.'

'We'd better find you a hotel. Don't you think?'

As he was speaking, a phone struck up the Marseillaise. It was Elaine's. Since it was lying on the sofa, Paul picked it up and handed it to her as she hurried across the room. She looked at the screen. A frown puckered her lips; she went back to the window and answered in a low voice, her face averted: 'No, I'm sorry, I can't speak now.' It was a different voice from the one Paul had heard so far, efficient and defensive.

Elaine closed the call and stood looking out at the rain. 'Is this the monsoon, then?'

'Too early,' Paul said. 'You get these little rehearsals, but the heat will be back, I'm afraid. Let's see if we can get you in at the India International Centre. It's close by and there should be rooms. This isn't a tourist month.'

All the same they needed a cab. Paul phoned. Elaine stood, texting a message. She looked up. 'Is it expensive?' she asked. Speaking to the taxi company, he smiled and shook his head.

They ate in the dining room of the International Centre. Paul had waited a half-hour and more in reception while Elaine checked in and went to her room. He had felt very sure of himself earlier in the afternoon, sure of a major change in his life. Now he was on edge, he needed to think, but the girl was alone and it would be unkind to leave her to her own devices. Helen wouldn't want that, he decided.

Paul studied his heavy form in the reflection of the glass door. There was the familiar unfamiliarity of the mirrored face: that strange, plump, rather debonair man! His hair was greying just a little at the temples but still thick, still virile. It will be good to try this different life in Helen's company, he muttered. He liked the way the older woman's constant irony challenged him. He would enjoy proving to her that he could handle harsh conditions. I will lose weight. Perhaps at some unconscious level, it suddenly occurred to Paul, what had most drawn him to Albert James's ideas was the implicit invitation to professional suicide: convinced, as James clearly was, that journalism's interminable assertiveness was ugly, that it was futile seeking to sway people's minds, to convince them of this and that, you could relax and give up. Paul was aware that he always tried very hard to persuade people, in professional matters and private. He was aware, too, of trying to seduce readers when he wrote. He needed them to succumb to his way of seeing things. And he was ambitious. In the end, his whole life had been an attempt to put himself forward by convincing people of things. It didn't really matter what things. That was what had so impressed him about Gandhi, the man's ability to convince people. And that was what James no doubt hated about him. If you free yourself from that compulsion, Paul suddenly thought, if you escape from that need to cajole and convince and seduce, what is left afterwards will be you, your true self.

The lobby of the International Centre was quiet this evening and the PC under the stairs was free. Paul remembered it from years before when he'd been working for the *Globe*; the connection was slow and the keyboard sticky. He remembered having to wait while others hogged the thing. The elderly receptionist watched politely while the American paced and hovered in his damp jacket.

'No problem if you want to get online, sir,' she eventually suggested. She was clipping bits of paper together.

'I'm not actually staying at the Centre,' Paul told her.

'That's no problem, sir, if you are waiting for a guest.'

Paul went to the machine but hesitated. Amy would have written of course. He had always had a great time with Amy, but there was no question of asking her to come and join him in Bihar.

Still hesitating, Paul found his cigarettes and lit up. Albert James had thought every action determining and potentially fatal: every step a person took was irreversible, every experience was carved in stone. In my case, relationships are just water off a duck's back, Paul thought. He inhaled deeply. Compulsive though it might be, no one would ever persuade him to stop smoking.

There was an ashtray on a fancy iron stand beside the typing stool. Paul turned the cigarette round gently to free the burning tip. He liked doing that. You could always write to your mother, he chuckled, tell your mum that her bad boy is going to do some charity work. That would cheer the old girl up! But why was it still important what his parents thought? At my age! Or was everyone, he wondered, just waiting for a chance to reverse roles and shout how good they'd been?

Very conscious of being the older man waiting for a pretty younger woman in a hotel lobby, Paul smiled with half of his mouth. For a moment, standing at the bottom of the stairs by the computer screen, he had an impression of himself as exactly poised between his old, confident, hard-working, womanising self and someone entirely cut loose and ascetic: a slimmer, calmer, quieter, no doubt better Paul, in a muddy village, dutifully doing what Helen James told him to do, taking this remarkable woman as his model, learning from her vast experience. He would wash people who were sick. He would smell their vomit and shit. Later you can write about it, he told himself more candidly; then your work will have an authenticity it has never really had perhaps. Then they will have to take you seriously. He had always been thought of as a journeyman, an opportunist. After an experience like this he would be more convincing.

Paul looked at his watch and wondered if Elaine was showering or changing into nicer clothes. He rather liked the childish way she tugged at an ear, and that intense twist on her lips when she had jabbed out a text message. Deciding at last to sit down at the computer, he tried to imagine the economic consequences if he earned no money for a whole year.

The screen was the old cathode variety. Paul called up Gmail and had just typed in his address and password when there came a squeak of rubber soles hurrying down the cement stairs.

'Sorry to be so long.'

'No problem.'

It was clear at a glance that much of Elaine's time must have been spent trying to freshen her face after tears. She was wearing a knee-length skirt, but with trainers.

'Feeling better?' Paul asked encouragingly, then shouted, 'Aaaagh, forty-three messages, not possible!'

'If you want to finish your work, I'll read something,' she offered.

Scrolling down, Paul saw Amy's name a half-dozen times.

'We'd be here till tomorrow,' he said. He logged off. 'Let's eat.'

As can happen in India, the Centre's dining room was so fiercely air-conditioned they both feared they would freeze. So while they waited for the food they'd ordered Elaine went back to her room for a jacket. When she returned, not only the jacket was new, but she was wearing perfume too. A sweet, girly perfume, Paul noticed. 'And I brought a scarf for you,' she said smiling. She handed him a square of pink silk. The determination to be cheerful only made her anxiety more obvious.

'I'm not sure this will be good for my reputation,' Paul laughed, gamely wrapping the scarf round his neck. The air was definitely chilly.

'And what is your reputation?'

'Hmm, probably best if I don't tell.'

'The pink goes pretty well with the brown shirt,' Elaine told him. 'They suit.'

'Pretty's the word, I'm afraid,' he said tying a knot. He grimaced. 'Still, I suppose the effeminate look is in these days.'

She narrowed her eyes. 'You don't look effeminate at all,' she said. Then a message beeped on her phone. She read it and again hastened to answer with small quick fingers. Paul saw that the nails were bitten right down. She held the phone up to her face with two hands.

After the food arrived, chewing the first mouthful, she asked: 'Tell me about being a writer, then, Paul.' She used his name rather determinedly, as if she was afraid she might forget it. 'I've never met a writer before. Tell me about this book about John's dad.'

‘I thought I’d said, I’ve decided not to do it,’ Paul said.

‘Oh, right.’ She was pensive again. ‘John will be disappointed.’

‘Anyway, there’s precious little one can say about being a writer. In the end one form of megalomania is much like another.’

‘What’s that supposed to mean?’ She frowned, apparently eager for a serious debate.

‘Oh, people looking for celebrity,’ he shrugged. ‘Writers, actors, we’re all the same.’

‘I don’t think so at all,’ she protested. ‘The actors I know—’

Suddenly she looked down at her plate and her cheeks stiffened as if her tongue had found something unpleasant in her mouth. ‘Actually, I’ve just given up a project too.’

Paul waited while she ate another mouthful. He was not unfamiliar with the picture of a young woman going through a crisis. In the past such girls had been easy prey; they grabbed at anyone who would bolster their self-esteem.

‘I walked out of rehearsals two days ago.’ Elaine’s voice was steady but brittle. ‘It was going to be my first play. My big ambition.’

He watched her. ‘So why did you do that?’

Again Elaine tugged at an ear, head cocked to one side. She seemed unaware how childish the gesture was. ‘We’d been rehearsing for months and I still couldn’t do anything right. At least as the director saw it. I suppose it got to the point where I couldn’t take any more criticism.’ She gave a forced smile. ‘So, I lost my boyfriend and my job in the same week. How about that?’

‘Double whammy,’ Paul agreed.

‘He said I was never really *the part*, I was just *playing* it. Just mimicking. He thought people wouldn’t be able to identify, as if I was making fun of the play.’ She managed half a smile: ‘Actually it is a pretty stupid story.’

‘“He” meaning this director fellow?’

‘Hanyaki. He’s Japanese. He says I decided to be an actress just so people could see how good I was at mimicking characters I was superior to.'

'And that isn't how you feel about it, obviously.'

'You don't go to drama school,' Elaine said, 'for two years spending hours and hours in classes to show off that you can mimic.'

The girl was on the brink of tears again. Paul poured some wine for her. 'And now you're in India,' he said brightly.

'I walked out in the middle of rehearsal. Three days ago. Next morning I went straight to the Indian Embassy to queue for a visa.'

'Well, walking out takes courage. Not to mention getting on a long-haul flight.'

'More like desperation,' she said. She laughed nervously. The girl had shown no particular interest, Paul thought, in the Indian menu, no surprise at the arrangements in the large low dining hall, the characteristic Indian sounds and smells. He felt sorry for her. She couldn't have been more out of place.

'Well, sometimes you have to act on impulse,' he said philosophically. 'Actually, that's pretty much what it felt like when I decided to give up the book. It was a decision I *had* to take, even though I'd been so excited about writing the thing.'

She pushed her plate aside. 'I'm sorry, to be honest, all I'm thinking about is where John is.' In a rush, she added: 'Actually, he'd asked me to marry him. I know, it's crazy, isn't it? It really freaked me out. A few months ago. When he was here for the funeral actually. Now I was coming to say yes, I mean I've gradually got used to the idea, I wanted to appear at his mum's door and tell him yes, when he least expected it, and then when I arrive he's not even here! And he lied to me about where he was.'

Paul saw the confusion in her eyes. He sighed. 'That's really too bad, because it would have made a lovely story.' He waited a moment. He must get the girl thinking rather than just suffering.

'So why exactly would he have come out here?' he eventually asked. 'I mean, his mother wasn't ill or anything. You say he had a research position that was important for him. I don't get it. But then, frankly, I don't get why he'd have said he was coming if he wasn't.'

Elaine looked down at her fingers. 'He'd turned moody.' She said, 'I don't know.'

She shook her head. 'Want to hear something strange? I can mimic almost anyone, honestly, I've always been able to, but I can't mimic John. I never could. It's as if I can't really . . . grasp him. You know? Perhaps that means I love him. Do you think?' She smiled sadly. 'And I've seen his mother, what, ten minutes, and I could imitate her forever.'

Paul watched the girl. When their eyes met he raised an eyebrow. 'Go on, then.'

'What? Imitate her?'

'Why not? Might be more fun than crying.'

'Right.'

Elaine thought for a moment. She closed her eyes and sat very still. Then her face smoothed a little and somehow ceased to be lopsided. The lips straightened and thinned, the eyes opened a little wider, the nose was sterner, more pointed, the shoulders rose above the table and spread. In a completely changed voice, brusquer, deeper, more upper class, she said: 'There is really a lot of work to do, I'm afraid, at the clinic, heavens, I'm late!, we are *so* short-staffed, but Elaine dear, not to worry, I'm sure this is all just a little communication glitch. Let me phone for a cab, shall I? Hello? Helen James here. Yes. That's right. Opposite Lodhi Gardens.' She said a few words of fluent gobbledegook, vaguely Hindi. 'Now, yes, if you don't mind, as soon as possible, there are people counting on me, thank you, thank you that's very kind.' Then, as if calling from a distance: 'Paul will sort you out, won't you Paul? Do make sure Elaine finds a decent hotel, then we'll tackle the problem of John tomorrow.'

Paul burst out laughing. 'Fantastic! You've got her to a tee. I can't believe you only saw her once.' Simultaneously, he recalled Helen as she had been this afternoon, distraught, convulsed, then immediately composed again when the doorbell rang. It was reassuring, he thought, that however upset she might be, Helen James was not the sort of woman who would ever ask to be looked after; she would never make you feel guilty.

'You've got a real talent,' he encouraged the girl.

'But that's exactly what Hanyaki hated! You see. He said it was too obvious and I was condescending to the person I mimicked. He thought I had a superiority complex. I sort of pointed at them, rather than really *being* them.'

Paul wondered if the girl was more upset about her job situation or her boyfriend. 'Maybe it's just a problem with this director,' he reassured her. 'Some actors have that, I've heard.' Then on instinct he asked. 'It wasn't the guy John thought you were having the affair with?'

Elaine stared. 'How did you know?'

Paul shrugged. The girl had put down her knife and fork and lifted her hands to her cheeks. There was something very underage about the bitten nails. Then, rather deliberately, Elaine looked around the restaurant. 'How elegant the fat women are!' she said. With conscious aplomb she mimed the gesture of tossing a shawl over her shoulder, wobbling her head a little, Indian fashion. Immediately she seemed adult, even old. And I thought she wasn't looking, Paul thought.

Elaine turned back to her food. A moment later, she told him: 'The strange thing with John's family, you know, was that though they never phoned or emailed and hardly ever saw each other, he was incredibly attached. He was always talking about them. I mean, like I never would with mine. Nobody could ever meet John without knowing inside two minutes that he was Albert

James's son. And his mother too. He was so proud of them. That's why I was sure he'd be here.'

Paul agreed it was strange. 'Would you like to go into town,' he asked, 'if the rain has eased?'

'And I feel so stupid,' Elaine protested. 'Like, if I'd behaved just a bit differently, just a bit, or, I mean, if I'd seen it coming, you know, him running off, if I'd had any idea, none of this would have happened. None of it.'

'If people saw things coming,' Paul consoled her, 'we wouldn't have any history, would we?'

In that split second it occurred to him that this must have been Albert James's project in the end: to have no more history.

CHAPTER TWENTY-NINE

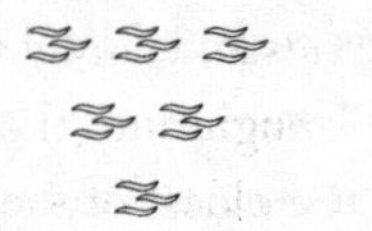

Tonight would not be an ordinary night. Helen was not so blind she could not see a change of colour in the air, a change of weather. But nothing was decided. She sat in her taxi looking at the havoc left by the storm, the broken branches, fallen signposts, spilled rubbish. She watched the rain teeming on the mess, dogs skulking about blocked drains. She had seen it all before. She thought of nothing and at the same time she knew the night would be full of thoughts. She should not have spoken so openly to Paul. A line of defence had been swept away. An army of regrets was preparing the final assault. Go on regardless, Helen told herself.

She paid the driver outside the clinic and, as usual when on night duty, signed in a full hour early. She performed a series of reassuringly mechanical actions. She removed her shoes, opened her surgery and put on her hospital clothes, her work slippers. She checked the admissions register, went to the ward and walked between the beds, nodding to those she knew, checking the records of those she didn't, listening to the afternoon nurse, a middle-aged Muslim woman who was angry with visitors bringing in food and making a mess.

'We must be having some discipline in here!' the nurse insisted. 'You please speak to them, Dr James; if you could remind them of our regulations.'

Helen noticed that Than-Htay was in a bed this evening.

'He has been coughing,' the nurse said. She lowered her voice, 'Blood.'

The boy followed Helen with his eyes but didn't speak.

She went to the noisy Hindu family with their assortment of sweets and cards for a sick auntie. She smiled and they fell silent.

'Good evening, madam,' one of them said.

In a quiet voice, Helen reminded them of the rules, the visiting hours, the number of friends and family members permitted, what could and could not be brought into the ward.

'Very sorry, madam,' the oldest of the group began at once.

'We are leaving only,' another promised.

'It is my fault, madam,' the sick woman said. 'Today it is the anniversary of my poor husband's decease and we were saying puja for him.'

The nurse shook her head as the family bundled out of the door, laughing and hushing each other. 'They were just rude to me,' she complained.

'I'll send you someone to sweep up,' Helen said.

She went back to outpatients now and watched as an elderly doctor in a white cap distributed pills and gave injections to those who came to the clinic after their day's work. Not many had turned up, he said, in this weather. A boy who had lost an arm looked away and talked loudly while his stump was medicated. There were strong smells of damp clothing and disinfectant. Helen went off to have tea with Martin, the Dutch aid worker, who told her about a case sent on to them by a local state hospital during the afternoon. The woman had cancer of the bowel. The state doctors had opened her up to operate, taken one look, sewed her up again and sent her here to die.

Helen liked Martin. She liked his Dutch accent, his seriousness. She noticed he seemed reluctant to head off home after his hours were done. Perhaps he would like to meet Elaine, she thought. He could show her the city. She would not think of John. If his girlfriend didn't know where her son was, she certainly didn't. Obviously he didn't want anyone to know. Helen fervently hoped he was not in Delhi. There is nothing for John in Delhi, she thought. He is much better off far away from me.

She asked Martin what he would be doing this evening. He was going to the cinema. 'Some Bollywood thing.' He was trying to learn a little Hindi.

'You've been here a long time,' he observed. 'You know the language and everything.'

'Only five years. I came with my husband. He was doing research. Anthropology.'

'How interesting. I'd love to meet him.'

'He died just after New Year.'

It seemed extraordinary to Helen that another member of staff didn't know these facts around which her existence revolved. But in the end why should he? Martin had arrived in March.

'No, don't worry, please,' she reassured him. 'It's just that now I can't decide whether to stay here in Delhi or move on.'

'I suppose you have earned the right to go back home.'

Helen shook her head. The young man had a charming solemnity about him. His bare arm on the table was thick with soft blond hair. A teaspoon seemed very small between his fingers.

'I never think of work in those terms,' she said. 'It had crossed my mind I might go out to Bihar to help with the kala-azar they've got. It won't be hard to replace me here and I know kala-azar, I could be useful.'

'That's very courageous of you.'

'It isn't courage. It's what I've always done.'

So many aid workers, Helen had observed over the years, came away to prove something to themselves, to do penance perhaps, then they returned home with no money in their pockets but a small fortune in moral capital: all their lives, whenever inequality raised its accusing face, they would be able to say they had given the world's poor a whole year of their time. Helen was never going 'home', as they called it. She would never give her mother that satisfaction.

She said goodnight to the Dutchman and ran the routine supplies check with the departing doctor of the twilight shift. Dr Naik was a dapper little Tamil, very dark-skinned, with a clipped moustache and neat little teeth, neatly manicured fingers. They went through the emergency drugs inventory: antibiotics, anticoagulants, morphine. Every time Helen saw the green and white packs of insulin, she felt an intensification of awareness, a strong tide of self-knowledge rising within her. 'Do it tonight, Helen. Spread my ashes in the Yamuna, right in town, with the rest of the rubbish.'

'Fourteen boxes,' she counted

'Enough to slay a jolly elephant,' the Tamil doctor laughed.

He hurried off and for a while she stood at the window watching the rain in a narrow alley. It fell steadily as though in a doomed but determined cleaning process, streaming down brick and boards, clattering on corrugated plastic. She thought of the water pulling the city's dust and filth down towards the river, towards the sea. It would be raining hard on the monument to the dead children below the Wazi Bridge, washing away shit and ashes, dry seeds and fallen petals. Why had her work in the clinic lost its meaning when Albert died? Was it because she herself had opened the green and white box and administered the drug? He had tricked her into betraying her vocation and she could practise it no longer; was that it? Or had it been a test to see if she would really obey, like Abraham and Isaac? Perhaps I wasn't really supposed to. I was supposed to stop at the last moment. 'Maybe he didn't want your help,' Paul had said. Helen could make no sense of it. 'I miss you, Albert,' she muttered. 'You shouldn't have left me like that. You shouldn't have made me do it.'

At 9 p.m. she took official control of the clinic. Dr Naik was gone. Not that she was alone. There was a night nurse, and half a dozen and more of the menial staff slept in the back courtyard, or, on nights like tonight, on mats in the canteen. I needed Albert all those years ago, she reflected, to escape England and to stay away. To escape mother and brother. Oh, but it was so much more than that. It was inexplicable. All at once Helen was extremely agitated. What a terrible loss of composure it had been, blathering to this sticky American. 'That just isn't me,' she said out loud. 'I refuse to be like that.'

A young man had been admitted in the afternoon with acute pains in his upper legs. At ten the nurse took his temperature and blood pressure and administered another sedative and anticoagulant. The diagnostic process would begin tomorrow. This wasn't a fully trained nurse but a medical student getting experience, another Muslim girl. These were the corners the clinic had to cut. Helen sent her off to the staff office to rest. She spoke for a few minutes to a mother who was stretched on a mat beside the bed of her infant son. 'He'll get well now,' Helen told the mother. 'He's through the crisis.' She had been saying these things all her life. Then she went to sit beside Than-Htay.

The ward lights were dimmed on the twenty beds with their institutional green covers, white sheets. The windows were open to let in what freshness could penetrate the fly screens. The whir of overhead fans and the patter of the rain mingled with the sighs and snores of the patients. One man in his forties lay awake staring at the ceiling, his turban still pinned in turban shape on the low shelf beside him, his long greying hair matted on the pillow. An adolescent girl tossed from side to side. Albert had sat through many night duties in this and other clinics, partly to help when they were short-staffed, partly because he was interested to know how far culture-conditioned behaviour penetrated sleep habits. It was another eccentric project. Muslims who rose in the night to pray, for example. Did they sleep in a Muslim way? Albert was perfectly capable of staying awake all night, watching and taking notes, coming home to mimic a snore or, on one occasion, a sleepwalker. Sometimes he would talk in a low voice to a sufferer who could not sleep; language was not an issue; he was always able to tell the prayerful man which way to look for Mecca. Helen had admired his thoughtfulness and discretion.

But on other occasions she had betrayed Albert during night duties. She had made love to pleasant young doctors like Martin, and even not so pleasant doctors, even downright pigs, selfish, power-driven men like her brother. She liked to do that, to make these men want her, to have sex and feel nothing for them, nothing at all. Why had she told Paul that? Why expose your life to the very man who could pick up a pen and write everything down? Or was it *because* he could do that? She would never go home to her loathsome mother, her bragging, disgraceful brother, the whole ugly, conspiratorial, profoundly hypocritical ethos of her childhood world.

But why *did* I hate it so much?

Sitting on a stool in the dim ward, by the bed of this sick young man, Helen was struck by a kind of amazement at how she had grown up, the person she had become. How *had* it happened? 'We talked about everything *in theory*,' she murmured out loud, 'didn't we Albert? We talked endlessly about how people develop different personalities in their different countries and different circumstances, how each mind is integrated with its origins. But we never talked about *us*. We never really talked about my family, about my war with Mother and Nick.'

Helen murmured these words out loud as if her husband were there beside her. 'And we never talked about your brother's room either, come to think of it.' For all Albert's interminable analysis of every possible form of communication, they had never actually spoken about the freshly wiped photograph of the fatal girlfriend.

'I have shown you,' he had said, closing the door, and the conversation was closed forever.

At no point had it crossed Helen's mind to leave Albert for the other men she had sex with, the doctors, administrators, occasionally even patients. None of them had had a tenth of her husband's intelligence and tenderness. None of them knew how to combine knowledge and silence. They were chatterboxes. They wanted information without understanding. Talk talk talk. Mother talked endlessly too. Helen hated talkers. Nick had boasted interminably about his girlfriends, his cars, his money. Her brother was a fool. It was Albert's silence that held me, she realised, his determined quietness. How strange.

I must not chatter to the American, she decided. 'Don't,' Helen ordered herself. 'Don't talk to him.' Albert had known so much, but kept silent. It was his silence together with his knowledge that was so compelling. Albert had understood her relationship with her mother and brother. Without discussing it he understood she must leave that battlefield. She must leave England. There was no need to discuss why. Otherwise I would have done nothing but fight them all my life; it would have eaten me up. I would have achieved nothing.

Yes, Albert understood, Helen remembered. Actually, it was hard for her to think of anything he *hadn't* understood. His knowledge encompassed mine. The only irony was that at the end of the day none of that extraordinary intuition had been turned into a real scientific breakthrough. At the end of the day Albert had failed. 'All important communication,' she had read from one of his papers to a conference in Los Angeles, 'takes place without language, or behind language, or in spite of language.' She could see the professors didn't understand. These things were hard to demonstrate. They weren't like a room you could show full of cobwebs, a photo on a bedside table.

'You wrote your papers for me,' Helen said quietly, 'didn't you Albert?'

All their married lives Helen had been convinced that her husband would go down in history as one of the great thinkers of his age. She had felt safe with him, proud of him, proud she had married him. And instead he had achieved nothing. All Albert's thinking had come to nothing. The slut in Chicago had destroyed him, Helen decided, drained him of his energy. A man with that dusty room behind him would never have touched an underage prostitute. She knew it. She knew it was his father who had wiped the picture. He hadn't needed to tell her. What else could she do but work like mad to have his name cleared? Then just as the battle was won he had stopped making love. He had stopped all physical contact.

'Why? Why did you do that, Albert?'

Helen sat still on Than-Htay's bed, listening to the breathing and turning and sudden sighs of her patients, clasping and unclasping her hands. Albert never spent a night in a hospital bed, she remembered. Not once. Wasn't that extraordinary?

She closed her eyes. Here it came again. The thought was returning, the thought that all this other thinking led to: it was not for fear of physical suffering that Albert had asked her for death. That's the truth and you must face it. It wasn't for fear of pain and drugs.

'It was our marriage ending,' Helen whispered. 'Wasn't it, Albert?'

Or rather, it was Albert not letting it end, not while he was alive. That was the suffering he didn't want to go through, or her to go through; that was the thing that must not happen. Their marriage mustn't end. If we ever had a real wedding ceremony, she realised, but now she didn't speak the words out loud, it was when he had said, 'Let's do it now, Helen. Let's do something that can never be undone.'

Than-Htay coughed. His coughing woke him. It became a fit. Chest jerking with convulsions, the adolescent pulled himself up on his elbows in the half-light. Others in the ward stirred. Helen stood and reached a hand behind his head, propped him up, wiped his mouth with paper towels. Breathing again, his eyes registered no surprise to find her there. His whole expression was one of resignation and defeat.

'Are you okay?'

The boy coughed. His ribcage stiffened.

'Are you all right?' She asked in Hindi, in Gujarati.

He didn't respond. He spoke no words and made no signs.

Even if he doesn't hear much, he must have seen my lips move, Helen thought. He must know what I'm asking.

The boy lay back on the pillow. There was a look of reproach in his eyes. He wants to die, she thought. Or he is waiting for death. He has nothing. No family, no energy, no future. All his memories are bad.

Helen stood up, crossed the ward and turned left into the corridor. She walked briskly down to her office at the end, let herself in, unlocked a cupboard and drank directly from a bottle of Royal Challenge. She paused, holding the cap over the neck of the bottle, as if about to screw it back on, then drank again. She and Albert had both become regular drinkers over the last few years. Routine got them through the day, then there was that gap between work and sleep when one drank. They talked a lot when they drank, but never about the things that mustn't be talked about.

Helen took another long slug and looked at herself in the cheap glass of the cupboard. She saw the bottle pressed between her lips, her eyes gleaming softly above it.

'You treated me as a god, not a man,' Albert whispered.

Helen stiffened and lowered the bottle. When had he said that?

'Albert?' she called softly.

She couldn't remember. Had he? Or is it now? Did he say that now?

'You treated me as a god, Helen.'

The drink has gone to her head. But it was true I put him on a different plane. I always did, from the beginning.

Is he standing in the shadows behind her? She didn't turn. Could he be watching?

She had treated Albert as a god. Yes. Above morality, above conflict. All other men were nobodies. Paul is a nobody, she thought. Paul was looking for a god when he turned to Albert. But Albert always turned such people away.

Now the American was trying to make a saint of her.

She had wanted John to worship Albert. Instead the boy criticised. John was petulant and resentful. He clung to me and criticised. I mustn't live with Paul, Helen decided. I will start to blather. I will start to undo everything we did together. She saw now that actually that would be the only way to give a future life meaning: she must undo what had been done with Albert. She must let him go, let him shrink into something smaller and more human. 'Well I won't,' she muttered. It was ugly. It was farce. She lifted the bottle again, again took a long slug, screwed the top back on and locked it away in its cupboard.

Than-Htay doesn't want to live, Helen told herself. It was curious how Albert hadn't wanted children of his own but found surrogate children everywhere, boys and girls. He had made friends with Than-Htay at once. He liked to make friends with people who couldn't follow him, people who wouldn't push themselves forward as intellectual disciples. Disciples embarrassed Albert.

Since the patients were quiet now, Helen could have lain down; she had a mattress in her office. The nurse would do her rounds at midnight, at two, at four. Then there would be the call to prayer from the Jama Masjid, the call to another day without Albert. At six Dr Devi would come. But all that seemed very far away. These thoughts had brought an idea. No, it isn't a new idea; not new at all; on the contrary Helen is aware that she has been thinking about nothing else since her husband died.

She walked through the ward and unlocked a small service room that opened onto the courtyard behind the clinic. She unbolted the main door, pushed it an inch or two and looked out. The rain showed no signs of relenting. The big plants in their pots were taking a beating. There were bougainvillea and jasmine. There were fresh herbs for the clinic's kitchen. Between four high brick walls, the yard was dark and separate, but infiltrated by the noise of the city. Delhi's interminable horns had begun again after the storm; there was the splash of a broken gutter, cries and laughter from the building opposite where lights flickered behind coloured drapes on the second or third floor.

Helen listened. Behind this courtyard, she knew, was a huge pressure of population, Old Delhi, so many people living in poverty, many of them Muslim survivors of Partition. 'One day's sectarian violence can wipe out all the lives you saved in thirty years,' she muttered. But such accountancy was pointless. It is pointless to look for reasons for what you've done. You did it and that is that.

I don't want to see John, she decided. I mustn't. Helen senses now that her son is near. She feels he is in Delhi. He has come. What's he doing here? she wondered. Why is he persecuting me? 'John is a burden,' she said out loud. For his own sake it would be better not to see me. He needs to be free from these roots, or this rootlessness. Explaining wouldn't help. With Albert's death, I've lost the faculty to keep silent, she realised. She had lost her equilibrium. I've started chattering. Well, she mustn't chatter to John. You absolutely mustn't.

All at once a loud shrill laugh rang out from across the courtyard. A voice rose over the patter of the rain, then another. It was a piercing woman's voice, then a man roaring his appreciation. A moment later someone put on some music, a twanging sound. People were having fun, they were living, perhaps they would soon be making love.

Than-Htay will never make love, Helen thought. The idea came with the force of something you just knew and that was that. The boy will never make love. And nor must I.

Than-Htay has lived through things, Helen realised, that stripped him of all desire to live, all desire to talk. It was in the past. It was incurable.

How strange that she had betrayed Albert so easily when he was alive and struggled so hard now he was dead.

It was because Than-Htay had no desire to live, Helen thought now, looking out at the rain, that Albert had not pushed him to return to the clinic for treatment. Obviously. Albert wasn't afraid of other people's despair. Had he been alive now, Helen would have attacked him fiercely for that decision. We would have argued fiercely. But now, without his presence to fight against, she realised that part of her had always agreed with Albert, part of her had always suspected he was right.

Was that why he mocked me? He knew my protests were pointless; I could never really fight clear of him. Now it was as if Helen must be both people in one, she must argue with herself inside her head the way Albert used to argue with her, she must watch herself the way he watched, mock herself as he did. She must mock herself.

It was exhausting.

In the darkness a crow had started to caw. The sound was uncanny in the black rain. It rose and fell monotonously, caw caw caw, until it was hardly a sound at all, but a rhythm, an invitation to darkness and rain. The twang of the sitar faded. A window had closed. Instead the bird animated the darkness, perched on a ledge somewhere. It gave a pulse to the rain. Helen imagined its throat swelling and shrinking. Caw, caw. Then she heard a beating of wings. Another bird arrived. The sound doubled. The rhythm strengthened like gathering waters. Caw, caw, caw, caw.

If only Albert really were beside me, she thought. Those were the moments she had felt strong and, in his strange way, loved, the moments she felt truly herself in opposition to him; not when she had to pit herself against lesser men who only fought for pleasure and power. I went with other men in order to go back to Albert, she murmured. How strange. 'You were a god,' she told him 'that's the truth.' Always watching, always turning a divinely blind eye. Helen remembered closing his lids for the last time. 'Seeing for both of us is hard,' she murmured.

She stepped out into the rain of the yard. She would like to shower in it. 'I want to dissolve in the river,' Albert had said. The tide carries off the day. He had mentioned some dreams but she hadn't listened. He didn't want her to listen to everything. Dreams of flood and creation, dreams of water rising, the slate washed clean. She turned her face to the sky and the chill rain told her how inflamed and tense her cheeks were.

'Dr James?'

'Souk.'

'I have been looking for you everywhere. The young man is coughing, Doctor.'

Helen shut the door on the crows and hurried back into the ward. Than-Htay was lying on his side, knees pulled to his chest as he coughed convulsively into wads of paper. Helen felt his forehead, checked his pulse. The skin was yellow, the eyes bloodshot. 'I'll put him in my office,' she said. 'Or he'll keep them all awake and frighten the younger ones.'

The nurse was surprised. 'How will you rest, Doctor?'

'It's not a problem,' Helen said. 'I'm not sleepy. I'll find a mat.'

'Than-Htay,' she said in a low soft voice. She wrapped a blanket round the boy, put his pillow in his hand, found his slippers and walked him slowly down the corridor to her office.

She was aware, as she supported his arm, of the frailness of his shoulders and the smell of illness on his damp skin. She was aware of having more time and attention for this sick boy than she had had for her own son, though in return she never got a single word. Perhaps it was because of that. The boy was just his illness, his silence. She was drawn to that.

In her office she unrolled the thin mattress she used for night duty. He was sitting on the edge of a chair, shivering violently. 'Lie down, Than-Htay,' she said. She had to release his pillow from a clenched fist.

He lay there trembling and coughing. Helen turned out the light. For a few moments she watched, then kicked off her clogs and lay down beside him. Only now did she realise she was wet from the rain. Her doctor's coat was drenched.

The mattress was narrow and there was hardly room for both. The boy was in a stupor of fever. All the same he suddenly wriggled round and embraced her blindly, hugged her soaking clothes.

She was face to face with him, embracing his bony, adolescent body and the disease that sweated from it. Who is he, really? Helen wondered. Who did he imagine was beside him?

Her cheek was against his cheek. His breath was bad. Well, she had had more than one lover with bad breath. My own must smell of whisky, she thought. A hand clasped her fingers and as it did so she felt more powerfully moved than at any moment with Paul.

Helen sighed deeply and tried just to be there for the boy, to be present. This is the suffering she has given her life to fighting: 'An enemy that will never disappoint you,' Albert had remarked, 'by conceding defeat.'

Albert is here in the shadows. Yes. 'Our marriage is still not over,' Helen whispered. 'You kept it alive with your death.'

Paul on the other hand had soon conceded defeat. Paul had agreed to do exactly as she suggested, and somehow that led her to start chattering, stupidly, stupidly unburdening herself. Her son always conceded defeat too and, again, when he did so, she always felt the urge to say things she mustn't, to open her heart to him.

Thank God she hadn't spoken to him when he came for the funeral. There had been a moment.

'I never will speak,' Helen muttered, clasping the mute boy tight.

She unbuttoned her doctor's coat, slipped it off and drew Than-Htay against her skin. He was burning. She would never go to the places that must stay sacred and silent. She didn't want to change. She would never say, Albert and I were only like this because of this or that trauma, because of this mother, this brother. No.

'I don't want to love again.' That decision was made now. Rather Helen James would melt into this boy's illness, his sick body and foul tubercular breath. Outside she could just hear the rain and the crows; she sensed the distant hubbub of the city and the pull of the river with its laundry wallahs and cremation fires.

CHAPTER THIRTY

Paul had expected the rain to ease, but it hadn't. Thinking Elaine needed some distraction, he got the taxi to take them past India Gate, then up and down the parliament complex. Seen through smeared windows across a steady downpour, remote in its floodlit pomposity, the vast sandstone pile of the Raj seemed to be dissolving into the warm wet Indian night. Then they turned again and proceeded towards the old town via the ghats, the ancient taxi rattling and splashing on the uneven asphalt.

'That's the monument to Rajiv Gandhi,' Paul pointed.

The traffic was heavy and the rain sparkled slantwise in the illuminated air. More curious to Elaine were the bedraggled animals by the roadside, the men lighting fires under makeshift bivouacs. But even these sights held her attention only intermittently. After a few minutes she grabbed the older man's wrist: 'Do you think we should tell the police?'

The girl's hand was tense and alive and it was a pleasure for Paul to feel its grip on his skin. Sitting beside her in the taxi, he might have been travelling with any of a score of young women he had dated during his two marriages and since, all more or less Elaine's age, all infinitely desirable.

'I mean, really, he's a missing person.' Elaine was insisting. 'Isn't he? He walks out on everything, leaving a note with a false destination so nobody will go looking for him. The police should be told.'

'We'll talk about it with Helen tomorrow,' Paul said. 'Check out the dome on the left. The Jama Masjid, Delhi's main mosque.'

'What if he's killed himself, though?'

'I'm sorry?'

'I know it's stupid, but what if he's done something desperate, because he thought I was cheating on him?'

Paul reassured her. 'People don't do that, Elaine. Take it from me. They threaten to, but they never do. You know, I stayed with my second wife at least a year longer than I should because she kept saying she'd kill herself. Take us to the left, along the railway,' he leaned forward to tell the driver – the car was reduced to a walking pace now – 'then back through the side streets towards CP.'

With or without umbrellas people were jostling through the traffic. Men were working to clear a huge billboard that the wind had brought down with all its scaffolding. The night was a din of horns and animated clutter.

'Take a look at the pile to the right,' Paul told Elaine. 'The Red Fort. Moghul stuff. Huge.'

But Elaine was not to be distracted. 'His uncle did,' she said dramatically.

'I beg your pardon?'

'His uncle committed suicide. It runs in his family. I mean, why would he disappear and not answer a single message for weeks? He always answered messages. Even if only to argue. Maybe he's been dead all this time.'

'Elaine,' Paul said firmly. 'Don't be so gruesome. It takes a pretty unusual mindset to want to die. Then a hell of a lot of courage actually to do it. I never knew anyone who did. In the end, it doesn't matter how depressed they are, most people love life.'

As he spoke these words, Paul realised that to all effects and purposes John's father had also committed suicide. And he had done so, Paul felt sure, loving life and perhaps not depressed at all, or not in the ordinary sense of the term.

'And even if he did do it,' he went on, 'just to look on the dark side, it wouldn't be your fault, would it? I don't want to be insensitive, I'm only saying, since other people's decisions are beyond your command, it's pointless to agonise. Right? Don't torment yourself.'

The driver looked over his shoulder. 'I take you to craft emporium, sir? I think your daughter like jewellery? Only five minutes look. It is good for you, sir – rain is very heavy.'

'No, it *would* be my fault,' Elaine announced in a flat voice. 'It would. It really would.' She didn't appear to hear what the driver had said. Looking out of the window she didn't see the milling crowd, garish in neon, the curious clothes streaming with rain.

'But why? How could it be?'

'Very beautiful things in this emporium. Just five minutes look, sir.'

'Because I *was* having an affair. I *was* cheating on him.'

'Real pashmina, wooden carvings, very unusual. Silver earrings and necklaces.'

Elaine had begun to cry. Paul caught the quiet shudder of her body. He took her hand and squeezed it as the taxi fought its way past the turn-off for Chandni Chowk, then accelerated towards Mukherji Marg.

'No shopping tonight, I'm afraid.' he told the driver.

In an expensive bar right on Connaught Place, Elaine made an elaborate confession. Paul sat the girl in an alcove with candles and kept her supplied with small spicy candies and iced vodka. In the chiaroscuro of two nervous flames and twisting wax-smoke her breasts, under their tight black top, seemed even larger and, Paul thought, vibrant.

'It would never have happened if John hadn't been away,' she told him. She had been feeling desperate at the time, about her career and so on, her lack of career, but somehow mischievous too. 'Do you know? I'm different around John and then away from him. I change.' Actually, she was rarely sure how she was feeling at all, Elaine said, or not exactly. She sighed. 'Often I just don't know.'

Anyway, she'd gone to an audition. The nth. She'd been to so many. And she'd performed badly, she thought. Sometimes you do. The candidates were given a few routines to perform: mime a person discovering they are all-powerful, a woman who has just lost her baby, a boy putting on make-up – that was fun – a fanatic preparing for martyrdom.

'There was a speech to read too, a sort of day-after scenario, with a lone survivor surveying the catastrophe.' Elaine pouted. 'God, I was terrible.' She had been really surprised when the director's secretary called her the following day.

Paul listened. He enjoyed hearing people's stories, girls' stories that is. He enjoyed listening to their troubles. In the end he had never really done anything to seduce any of his women, nor really understood why they were attracted to him. He would listen to them; young women were almost the only people Paul did listen to. He would give an older man's avuncular advice, perhaps drop hints of a fraught and complicated private life which he was nevertheless coping with. And somehow it always happened. They turned from their worries to him. If only briefly.

Now, as Elaine described her first meeting with the Japanese director, the small man's abrupt manner, his weird apartment – 'black furniture and white carpets!' – Paul tried to imagine what a volatile state of mind the English girl must be in: first she had taken this extremely rash decision to come to Delhi, a desperate decision, it seemed to him; she had survived a very long and very bumpy flight; then she had found her boyfriend wasn't here after all, he had misled her; then she had been hastily ditched by the boy's mother and passed onto an overweight but moderately handsome American who was now plying her with drink.

She's in a state, Paul told himself.

Hanyaki had been very flattering that afternoon, Elaine said.

'He kept saying I had something unusually fluid about me. Obviously, I was pleased. I mean, I've staked everything on making it as an actress. We talked for hours.'

Elaine thought for a moment. 'He's a special man. Hanyaki. Very sophisticated. Knows everything. I love his accent. It's so strong, he never really learned English properly and he just doesn't care. I love how he doesn't care. Anyway, it made me think how young John was. Too young for me. Not even a man really. The second time I saw him there was a bottle of champagne and I just thought, what the hell. I was in such a good mood because he said he'd give me the part. I was euphoric. Like I'd arrived.'

Paul nodded understandingly, sipping his drink. He offered a cigarette and the girl accepted, though he could see at once she wasn't a smoker. Eventually, he said: 'However, the rehearsals didn't go so well.'

Elaine's eyes gleamed in the candlelight. 'Actually, I'm not sure why I'm telling you this. I mean, I haven't told anyone else, no one, and I don't even know you.'

Paul inhaled. 'It's *because* you don't know me, obviously.'

There was a short silence. Elaine fished an olive from her vodka. Paul watched her put it on her tongue.

'So?'

'Well – how can I say it, it's mad – the more passionate he was in bed, Hanyaki, and he was – he has a flat on Gloucester Place, if you know where that is – the more unpleasant he became at rehearsals. It was like two different people. He was so . . . I've never had sex like that. Well, I haven't really had that many boyfriends. Miles better than John.' She frowned. 'John is a bit quick to be honest. Then he was horrible on stage, in front of the others. He was just unpleasant.'

'Odd.'

'It made me frantic.'

'I can imagine.' Paul reflected. 'Perhaps he didn't want the other actors to know you were his favourite.'

'But they all knew! They knew we were going to bed. He didn't hide it at all. On the contrary.'

As she spoke, it occurred to Paul that this was just the kind of communication conundrum Albert James had loved to analyse. He shook his head. 'So maybe he was angry with himself for mixing pleasure and work. He was reasserting his authority.'

'Oh, I don't know.' Elaine came out with a groan that appeared to come from deep in her stomach. 'The fact is that the very day I started it, or rather the day before, John asked me to marry him.'

Paul laughed. 'Good one. So how did he find out? John, I mean.'

'He saw Hanyaki put his arm round me when we were going into a pub. Or that's what he says.'

'And that's all?' Paul raised an eyebrow. 'You denied it, I presume.'

'Of course. Endlessly.'

'So, John doesn't really know anything, does he? An arm round the waist doesn't mean anything. I could put my arm round you going out of here,' Paul said, 'or standing at the door looking at the rain, and somebody might see us and imagine all kinds of things, but it wouldn't necessarily mean anything. Nobody's going to kill himself because he saw someone put an arm round your waist.'

'No,' Elaine agreed vaguely. With a deep sigh she added: 'But he seemed to know. Really to know. He was very sure.'

Paul glanced into her eyes. 'And it didn't occur to you to take this opportunity to leave him?'

'John?' She stared and frowned. 'It did occur to me, yes. But, I don't know, I really . . . I sort of *like* John. There's something *us* when I'm with him. Then Hanyaki himself kept saying I'd be crazy to leave him, John, I mean. He said it was so unusual to find a young man with a strong vocation.'

Again Paul smiled. How well he knew this terrain.

'But now he is sending text messages from London begging you to go back.'

He nodded at her shiny red phone which she kept on the table beside her elbow and snapped open and closed every few minutes.

'Not for me!' Elaine wailed. 'For his play. We're due to open the Saturday after next. In Hammersmith. And by the way, it's terrible.'

'The play? Who wrote it?'

'He did. With another Japanese guy. A famous novelist apparently. It all happens in an airport, though you never know which. There are five or six plots all running into each other – passengers, cleaners, check-in staff; there's love, lost luggage, you name it – then a suicide bomber blows them all up. Everyone's writing about suicide bombers at the moment. It's awful.'

'If he wants you back for the play, you can't be that bad, can you?'

'I don't know,' Elaine wailed. 'He wants me for the play, but I only have a minor part, I'm the woman who loses her baby in the explosion, and then he'll want sex as well, won't he? And I won't be able to say no or he'll chuck me out and I'll be back at square one with nothing done. And everyone will hate the whole performance anyway.'

Paul thought about it. 'Maybe you don't want to stop the affair. Maybe you enjoy it.'

'Oh, I don't know!' Elaine was in pain, yet she found herself laughing too. She tugged hard at an ear. 'Of course I enjoy it. But first I want to see John. If I just see him, then maybe I can go back and do the play. But I need to see him first and understand about us. And instead he isn't here! God, why didn't I say I'd marry him when he asked? Why!'

'Because you didn't want to.'

Paul relented and took her hand across the table in a fatherly way. 'I'm sure if you and John love each other it will work out in the end. Won't it? For the moment, why not go back and do the play? The important thing is that the guy wants you on stage. At least you'll have achieved something. John will come back. As for the affair, you can take or leave that pretty much day by day.'

'I want to tell him the truth,' she said.

'Don't,' Paul answered quickly. 'You didn't tell him by text, I hope?'

'I want to tell him to his face. That way I can put it behind me.'

Paul kept his hand over hers and pressed with a certain urgency. 'You really mustn't, Elaine.' It was the first time he had used her name. He began to tell her about the time he had told his first wife he was having an affair. 'Later I realised I just wanted to hurt her. It was a kind of punishment. I made her unhappy for nothing.'

'I just don't know,' the girl repeated. 'Life is too complicated. I never thought it would be like this.'

'Let's smoke a hookah!' Paul suggested, withdrawing his hand. He smiled and had ordered one before she had even understood what a hookah was. While he was still explaining, a waiter brought the heavy pipe over from the bar and made an elaborate show of cleaning the mouthpiece. The bowl was already lit.

'Just suck deep through the bubbles,' Paul told her. 'The smoke goes through the water, you see. It's nicer than a cigarette, especially if you're not used to smoking.'

Elaine made another attempt to cheer up. 'It looks like a cross between a candlestick and a vacuum cleaner,' she laughed.

The bar was getting busy and they had to raise their voices. She took the mouthpiece between pouting lips and made Paul laugh sucking in her cheeks and going cross-eyed. As she let go, a great dizziness passed over her.

'God!' she had to shake her head and sit back. She closed her eyes for a few moments, then opened them laughing. 'You've still got my pink scarf on. You look really funny.'

'I'm getting used to it,' Paul grinned.

Then almost indignantly she told him. 'I've talked too much about me. I feel like I'm giving myself away and you haven't said anything about you. It's not fair.'

'So what do you want to know?'

Elaine sucked on the pipe again. 'Who you are,' she said evenly.

'That's a long story.'

'Tell me.'

Paul ordered two more drinks. 'You'll be bored,' he warned. He took a rather melodramatically deep breath. 'In a nutshell, I was a mother's boy in an extremely religious family. When I was small they expected me to be a clergyman. But really, it was a sort of school for lying. I mean, when people demand perfect behaviour, what can you do but pretend you're better than you are? To please them. Then there comes the day, of course, when you want to punish everyone for all the effort it's been.'

Because Paul had said all these things so many times before to so many girls, he had the feeling as he spoke that he was simultaneously both present and not present, honest and dishonest. He was in the bar with Elaine, smoking a hookah, drinking vodka, very aware of the girl's breasts and the scaffolding of her bra, but he was also at a considerable remove, he was calmly observing himself with her, or with some other girl perhaps at some other moment in the past. With Amy even. And quite probably Helen James was beside him in that observation post, wherever it was; yes, Helen was at his elbow as he listened to himself talking so charmingly and persuasively to Elaine; and while he talked, the older woman was passing ironic remarks, sarcastic remarks, because she saw through everything; she saw through his spiel, and she kept warning him to cut the bullshit. But she was enjoying it too, Paul thought. And he was enjoying her remarks, however cutting they were. He knew that deep down Helen didn't really want him to change at all, she didn't want him to become a good man. It was a sort of competition and Helen was actually using those ironic remarks as a way of getting control of him, a form of seduction maybe, just as he in a quiet way, almost against his will really, was casting nets for the girl. 'Liberation from what into what?' Albert James had written in that early email. Perhaps there is no space, Paul suddenly found himself thinking, beyond compulsion and persuasion. Unless death maybe.

'I suppose it'll sound like I've had loads of girlfriends,' he wound up a few minutes later, amused and apologetic, 'but the truth is, in a funny way, it was always them who had me. You know? Really. Then as soon as I'm with someone, as soon as I'm supposed to be faithful to them, you can be sure I'm planning to betray them already. I guess it's just a way of behaving I learned.'

'You could unlearn it,' Elaine said, sucking on the hookah again.

'Easier said than done,' he sighed. 'Though, actually, that's pretty much why I was thinking I'd do this aid work out in Bihar. I'll live like a monk for a while. Out of harm's way.' Paul meant it and simultaneously saw at once what a good line it was.

'Sounds like a cop-out.' Elaine protested. She was speaking in a louder voice now. The alcove was blue with smoke and her hair was mussed from constantly pushing her hand into it. She had drunk a lot. 'I think you should go back and marry this Amy,' she told him seriously, 'and force yourself to make a go of it.' Growing more heated, she didn't appear to be aware when their ankles brushed against each other for a moment under the table.

Towards one Paul called for the bill. 'You must be tired,' he told her. Outside, a doorman held a huge umbrella and steered them arm in arm into a taxi. Elaine slid across the seat. 'The India International Centre,' Paul announced.

'International Centre, sir. Where is that sir?'

'Lodhi Gardens,' Paul said.

The taxi was an old Fiat. The rain drummed on its thin roof. The engine had a hoarse, rasping sound and the suspension slumped alarmingly to the driver's side.

'Typical,' Paul murmured.

They had barely got to Tolstoy Marg before the vehicle coughed and died at a traffic light. Elaine giggled. She was sitting close to him. The driver turned the ignition key, muttering to himself as the starter motor turned and turned. After four or five attempts the thing shuddered into life. At the next traffic light it stalled again.

'Everything okay?' Paul enquired.

'Very okay. Very normal, sir. Older car, sir. Carburettor.'

'What a darling rattletrap,' Elaine laughed. In a low voice in Paul's ear she did a perfect imitation of the man 'Very okay, very normal, sir. Older car for older man, sir.'

Paul squeezed her arm. They proceeded along a broad road glistening with muddy water and littered with broken twigs. The driver had a young, rather sullen face under an untidy blue headcloth. He seemed offended that Paul had doubted his vehicle. Perhaps he had caught a snatch of Elaine's imitation. 'It is always starting again, sir,' he pronounced with sour dignity. 'You are not worrying now.'

Elaine burst into giggles.

The girl half leaning against him, Paul wondered what would happen when they arrived at the International Centre. He didn't greatly care. My career is at sea, he thought. He had never started a project and given up before. It was curious that he wasn't more concerned. And I don't miss Amy at all, he reflected.

Then, as they passed India Gate, the park empty tonight in the heavy rain, he remembered something Helen had said when they had sat together on the grass that evening: 'It would be dangerous, for someone like you to follow Albert too far,' she had said.

The car was coughing and shuddering again. All at once Elaine's fingers were at his neck. 'You look too silly with that scarf.' She couldn't shake off this attack of the giggles. 'I can't believe you're still wearing it!'

Her face was very close to his as she sat up and leaned over to untie the pink silk. He could feel her drunken breath on his lips. He was protesting half-heartedly, 'Don't pull, Jesus, you'll strangle me! Ouch.'

Their mouths were really very close. Then the car cut again. Not at a light this time but while they were accelerating away from one. The driver steered the vehicle through a deep puddle towards the kerb.

Elaine sat back with a jolt, still laughing. Cursing under his breath, the driver began to punish the starter motor. After a dozen attempts, Paul said: 'I think we'd better find another car.'

'Not at all, sir. All very normal.'

'God,' Elaine returned to earth, 'I'm so exhausted.'

'Just one moment, sir. Old car. Always starts.'

They waited while the man sat turning the key. Then Paul had had enough. 'You know, it's only about half a mile to Helen's flat now,' he said. 'Let's walk and call a cab from there.'

'It is raining very hard, sir,' the driver said.

Paul paid him up to this point and they got out. They had no umbrella but the rain was warm. By the time Elaine had walked round the car and slipped an arm under his, they were already drenched. 'Old car!' she mimicked giggling. 'Always starts!'

CHAPTER THIRTY-ONE

'Dear Paul.'

The letter was not addressed to him.

John had had a premonition. He had woken in pitch darkness and for a long time had absolutely no idea where he was. He wasn't frightened. He wasn't concerned. On the contrary, he woke to an intense sense of well-being, of healing. You are not ill, he decided. After all. There has been no catastrophe. Then he realised it was the well-being that follows a nightmare. Yes. He had been reading messages of love, on his phone, but they were not addressed to him. There was another man's name. Elaine was beside him as he read the messages; she knew that he knew, but she wasn't embarrassed. 'I must have sent them to the wrong phone,' she says. They were messages of passion. She wasn't even anxious. She hugged him just the same as if this were a matter of no importance. They were in bed and John kept reading these messages over and over; messages not only addressed to a different person but in a different language, of which he knew not a word, in a different script in fact, made up not so much of letters but of tiny insects, flowers, shoes, animals, a beautifully symmetrical script inlaid in the screen of his phone, beautifully coloured, incomprehensible messages of love – a love I will never understand, he thought – forming and re-forming in the kaleidoscope of his phone. Elaine was beside him, smiling and mocking and he woke into pitch darkness and a huge sense of relief.

Just a nightmare. No catastrophe.

But somebody is beside him. John could feel a light pressure against his back. It's a feminine pressure, he thought. He smelled it. He lay completely relaxed. A great wave of awfulness had passed over him, flowed through and over him, leaving him whole and at ease and breathing freely.

Something bad is over, he thought. The air is fresh. I'm better. The window must be open. Finally he made out the contours of the room in the dark. Yes. This room. The Govind. He was perturbed. He twisted a little, then stopped. His hand felt behind him. The girl. What was her name?

Jasmeet.

Now the passage to reality was as abrupt and cruel as that from nightmare to waking had been healing and kind. He slipped, almost fell out of bed. I'm fully dressed, he realised. What had happened?

He stumbled to the bathroom and turned the light on. His wash kit was all over the place: on the shower plate, in the sink, on the floor. His razor was in the toilet. Somebody has smeared the small mirror with toothpaste.

He stared at the pink scrawl. A terrible thought possessed him and he rushed back into the bedroom. Filtered through the doorway, the fluorescent tube in the bathroom made a ghostly shape of her body on the bed. In a few swift paces he was beside her. She was still. He lowered his head. Still, but breathing. Jasmeet was sleeping soundly, breathing sweetly, fully dressed.

Again he felt a flood of relief. The girl is beautiful. She is a child of God, he muttered. Why did those pious words come to him? John isn't remotely religious. Remembering something, he looked up at the wall. There is no writing. There are no animals or monsters. He glanced at the table, the shelves. The computer was gone. Yes. That had really happened, then. The theft had happened. And my phone, and the pashmina shawl. They had been on the bed. You should have reported it. At least to the hotel.

Suddenly, he rushed round the bed again and bent down to examine her face. There is a small cut on the lower lip, a bruise in the brown skin.

You had some kind of fit, he told himself. You did things without knowing. The thought alarmed him. Violent things. You weren't yourself. You slapped her perhaps. John had never hit anyone. He wasn't that sort of person. But the girl had stayed all the same. She's a courageous kid, he thought. He didn't know what to think. Perhaps she likes you. He saw the shiny red purse belted to her waist. She lay on her side. Perhaps she has nowhere else to go. What a perfect creature! She slept with your father, John thought.

He checked his watch. It is quarter to six. Sure enough the window was greying with light. The day will come quickly. I must have slept, what, twelve hours? Maybe more. I must have collapsed. Jasmeet could easily have left. She could easily have helped herself to whatever she wanted of his. Instead she had laid him on the bed and then laid down beside him. She must be quite strong to have dragged him there. Unless he'd gone himself without remembering. He watched her and it seemed to him now that the girl was taking pleasure in her sleep. She was enjoying sleep like a fragrant bath, or a gentle massage. She sighed and stirred and wriggled and a warm smell of breath and skin filled the air.

John stepped back. He wanted to be out before she woke. He felt lucid now, but fragile, volatile, hungry. He was ravenously hungry.

Where are my sandals?

One lay on the floor beside one of Jasmeet's. He stared at her small elegant white sandal. A child's. Where is his other? He doesn't want to have to talk to her and explain himself. The girl threatened him somehow. That little sandal threatened him.

John hunted about. Where is it? Ah, under the bed. Breathing deeply he crouched down and pulled it out, then slipped the thing on his foot and hurried downstairs. 'I'm just going to a cash machine to get money for my bill,' he told the receptionist. It was the same woman who had asked him to settle yesterday. She didn't raise her head from her bowl of petals.

John found a cash dispenser at the second corner. His fingers tapped the codes. The money came. It was reassuring. Just as on the Edgware Road. The notes were crisp and colourful.

Then, at the first food stand, he wolfed down doughy bread and some kind of yoghurt and three small fried cakes. 'That,' he pointed, 'and this and this and this.' He paid no attention to the names of things, no attention at all to hygiene. He stopped at another stand and ate again. He ate fried things, he ate meat, pastry, again something sweet. The food stuck to his teeth. It filled his mouth. He couldn't remember feeling so hungry, eating so fast.

Stomach crammed, he set off into Old Delhi. The city was bright now, gleaming and steaming in the warm morning dampness. It must have rained hard. Everywhere surfaces were broken and reflected in puddles. Vaguely, he remembered the premonitory lightning. He had looked out of the window, yes, and seen snakes in the sky.

Now he stopped at a fruit stand and bought bananas, peaches. Then at a tea counter. Sweet chai. It was horrible. I'll burst, John thought, but he felt good. Leaning on the counter of the tea stand he saw how every tree and wall and car was lacquered with bright wet light. There was the heavy shape and there was its surface which was dazzlingly bright despite all the dirt. The place was filthy, but dazzling. This is definitely positive, John decided. All will be well.

To his left, a monkey squatted on a step at the opening to a narrow alley. It was pleasingly dark. I'm not far from the Sufi tombs here, he realised. He recalled the street, or thought he did. He remembered the men with the strange alien chant, the hypnotic drumming. Drumming too is a sort of dazzling mesh, cast over heavy things, things that won't move. 'After hundreds of years the tomb of the prophet and poet is still a magnet for the faithful' – he remembered someone saying that, over the beat of the drums, someone talking like a tourist brochure.

I must have had a fit, John told himself. I fell into a fit the way you fall into a hole and wake up in hospital. It was lucky he hadn't done any serious damage. I must apologise to Jasmeet, he told himself. Apologise profusely. Yes, I'll help her get her ticket to London. We can travel together. Mother will come too. They would be a happy threesome.

He paid the chai wallah. Now he felt strong. He walked swiftly past men steering long barrows through the narrow streets. Meat and market produce, bricks and buckets and bicycle tyres. It was extraordinary how long these barrows were. Everything clattered. Everything seemed heavy and painfully bright. How on earth did they push them? And now a man was crossing the traffic with five or six crates on his head.

I had hallucinations, John realised. But all of Delhi is an endless hallucination.

He found the railway station, pushed through a dense, jostling crowd outside, stopped by a wall, puzzled, trying to remember. Eventually he found his way through the early morning travellers, crossed the long bridge over the lines and turned left.

Yes, it was here he had seen the girl picking fleas out her mother's hair. They too had been beating a drum. Where was the name of the street? It was getting seriously warm. Why wouldn't they put the street names somewhere visible? I've eaten too much, he thought.

Then he saw an address on a shop front, 405 Shadhanad Marg. Good. On a corner, Jasmeet had said. It was a long road, stretching off in a bright haze by the railway line. Mum will arrive around seven, he told himself, knowing her. She started her days early. He wouldn't have long to wait. I feel ready for anything, he decided.

Perhaps ten minutes later he spotted the big red cross on a roughly whitewashed brick wall. The street was a sludge of debris and decay. Here and there dogs and other animals were snuffling and rooting. A small pig was dead in the gutter. Crows were gathering. They perched on the rusty fence by the railway line.

I must see her before I have another attack, he was telling himself. He had lost any sense of what was to be said or why. Salvation lay in finding Mother, in confronting her, in taking her back to England. Then he will never lose himself again.

There was a padlocked gate on the corner and already a dozen people were squatting outside, trying to keep clear of the mud. This must be it. They are waiting for outpatients, John told himself. They are waiting to visit their sick relatives.

He went straight to the gate and rang a bell. He waited. Perhaps this madness is an old illness recurring, he thought, the way TB recurred after years of dormancy. The dormant madness keeps itself alive in dreams and then breaks out into your daylight world. In the end it hadn't seemed so unfamiliar. It hadn't really surprised him to see snakes in the sky and drawings on the wall. Maybe it's sanity that is the parenthesis, John thought. The other people at the gate paid no attention to him.

A sort of vapour had begun to steam off the muddy street. The air had grown milky. The morning's brightness was fading. John rang again. Madness is alive in dreams, he thought, waiting for a moment of weakness to break out. It waits for a crack in your defences. Then it bursts over you like a river in flood. Your ordinary self is overwhelmed. A lab is a parenthesis within a parenthesis, John thought. Why was his mind racing so much?

Why am I telling myself these strange things? What he remembered most of all was a sense of acute suffocation. Please God, don't let it come back. It had begun sitting in the rick with Jasmeet, it had risen and risen, then overwhelmed him as he stepped into the hotel room. He'd been knocked over and suffocated. There had been the pressure of an enormous wave breaking. He was in the surf. Whatever he'd done afterwards had just been an attempt to fight his way out.

'Hello. Sir?'

The gate was ajar. A small face looked out and up at him. 'The clinic is opening at seven, sir.'

Others had jumped to their feet and were crowding around.

'I'm John James,' John said. 'My mother works here. Dr Helen James. I have to see her urgently. It's very urgent. Perhaps I can wait inside, if she isn't here yet.'

He was an elderly man with a loose red Rajasthan turban, his jacket unbuttoned, eyes bloodshot but alert.

'Dr James has done the night duty,' he said. 'Come in, sir. You are welcome.'

Mother is here. John's heart leaped. Now! He would see her now. The adventure was over.

The old man padlocked the gate behind, though it was only a few minutes till seven. He was bent, bow-legged.

'You must take off your shoes, sir.'

'Yes, sorry.'

Why did he always forget? To the right of the door were three shelves of green cotton slippers. He took off his sandals. The doorman waited. There was nothing large enough for John's big feet. Numbed with excitement, he squeezed into two odd things and stumbled after his guide.

'I don't know if you are finding her in ward or in surgery, sir.' The man scratched a tangle of hair below his turban. He looked at his watch. 'In ward,' he decided.

They began to walk along the corridor. Suddenly, John wanted to flee. The place stank of disinfectant. He wants to flee, but only because he knows it is too late to flee; he is already in. Everything tugs towards the decisive moment. There are no more distractions. There is no more India between himself and his mother. Only a short stretch of corridor.

John had to shuffle his feet to keep the slippers on. He hadn't been able to get his heels in. To his right the wall was plastered with notices in Hindi, to the left dirty windows gave onto a drab courtyard. It was squalid and alien. But it is Mother who will be caught by surprise, he thought. I have got things to tell her that will change her life. She will have to listen to me now. It was Mother who couldn't escape.

The porter pushed open a swing door. Daylight was broken into a mesh of thin beams by the half-raised blinds. It lay in streaks on the green beds where patients were stirring or sleeping. John saw a little boy turning fitfully this way and that, his mother sitting beside him. A tall young woman in white coat and headscarf came towards them. The porter spoke to her in Hindi. She too glanced at her watch.

'I didn't know Dr James had a son,' she said.

'I live in London,' John told her.

'That is lucky for you,' the nurse smiled. 'But Dr James is still in her surgery,' she told the porter. 'I think she has had a bad night. There was a boy who was very sick.'

'It's urgent,' John muttered. 'About my father.'

'I am taking you to surgery,' the porter said. 'This way.'

There was a sweeper at work in the corridor now, then three boys hurried past carrying pans of steaming dough with oven cloths.

'Rashid!' Someone was calling.

They turned a corner. 'Dr James's surgery,' the porter announced. He knocked and stepped aside to let John enter.

'Rashid! The bins!'

John pushed the door. Inside, the room was dark.

'Mum?'

There was a strange, stuffy, sweetly medical smell.

'Mum, it's John.'

Suddenly alert, he stepped back. She isn't here, he decided. No one was in the room. But he was on his own. The doorman had hurried off, rattling his keys.

John went in again. His hand felt for a switch on the wall but didn't find it. A thread of light penetrating the space at floor level began to reveal the furniture in shadowed relief. There was a large desk directly in front of him. To his left a glass cabinet gleamed and there must be a fan turning slowly overhead, unseen.

Above all, there was the smell. A thick smell. It was strange. The air was thick. John took a step forward and put his hand on something white. A sheet of paper lay on the desk with a slim black pen placed across it. How purposeful it looked! Like a knife. John pulled his hand away and, turning, saw that the light came from under a blind drawn down over a French window. Beyond the desk now he glimpsed the corner of a mattress.

'Mum?'

Moving his head a little, he saw a foot. John stood still. No, he didn't wish to wake her. There was a bare white ankle. He stepped back and picked up the paper from the desk. He didn't want to disturb his mother if she had had a bad night. Standing very still, he was aware of that unhappy moment in her bedroom with the elephants in his hand. I should have apologised.

'Mum?'

She didn't reply. She has had a bad night, he told himself, and is sleeping soundly. It was that deep regenerating sleep of early morning. Jasmeet too had been enjoying her sleep. You could see how her body was cuddling into itself, savouring itself.

Uncertain how to behave, John found he was picking up the paper from the desk. He moved instinctively and suddenly. He snatched it up. The pen rolled off and clattered to the floor. It was amazing how much noise it made. He held his breath. Had she woken? Mum worked so hard. There was only the click and whir of the fan slowly turning.

John looked at the piece of paper in his hand. It was covered in writing. He lifted it to his face. The lines were very neat. It was definitely her writing. 'Dear Paul,' he read. The letter wasn't addressed to him. 'After much . . .'

But it was too dark to read easily. The light is coming from below rather than above. The floor by the window is bright and everything else is shadowy. Who was Paul? he wondered. I really mustn't wake her if she has had a bad night. What did it matter if he put off the meeting by an hour or two? Why am I scared? he wondered: 'You are always afraid to ask, John.' He seemed to hear her voice. 'You never ask.'

'Mum?' he called softly. He knew it wouldn't wake her. But if she was awake she would hear. Then I will ask. I will ask to know everything. That's what I'll ask.

John waited. And he would ask if she cared for him, he thought; he would be direct and open; he would ask her to come back to London with him.

'Mum?'

When she didn't reply he withdrew into the corridor, the letter in his hand. 'Dear Paul,' he read. The handwriting was definitely his mother's, neat and controlled and purposeful.

Dear Paul,

After much thought I have decided to give you my support for a biography of Albert. It will be easier to write when I am not around. Albert's life deserved a biography, if only because he did everything to avoid the limelight and to hide his genius. He had seen his own family torn apart by a struggle between his brother and his father, a struggle in which a girl became involved in a rather ugly way, and though he never spoke of the details I know that all his anthropological and behavioural research was driven by the question of how such catastrophes come about and how they might be foreseen and avoided (perhaps this explains his enthusiasm for taboos).

By some strange chance – because at the bottom of everything there is always a casual meeting – by some odd chance, Albert became my destiny and I his. To be honest, I could never understand why the world wouldn't worship him. He was a man who helped me a great deal, forgave me a great deal and even brought up as his own a son he must have known was not his. Though he believed in nothing beyond this world, his profound wish was for life to be graced with ceremony and beauty and I believe, in his death, we did create a ceremony of some kind, an act of love, as you, with an intuition I confess surprised me, immediately described it.

Over these last few months I have tried to free myself from that ceremony and from Albert, but the more I try to go on with my old routine and recover my appetite for life, the more I feel that these things were possible for me only when Albert was there. I also discover that no ceremony exists alone. Each calls to the next, like festivals in a calendar. Tonight it is raining hard after a long dry spell. It was raining that night in January too. Here beside me there is a young man who knew Albert and who I know is longing to follow him down the river of forgetfulness. Before I get too poetic I shall show him the way.

So you have your story, Paul. You have your book. It will serve you much better than a trip to Bihar. You have girlfriends and children to get back to. You are not cut out for my kind of work. You are too vain and you would be doing it out of an inverted vanity, to do battle with yourself. In parting, many thanks for the flattery of your attention. I bequeath you all Albert's papers, videos and audio tapes. You can have everything you find. In return I would be most grateful if you would attend to the cremation. There are no financial assets to dispose of.

With fondness,
Helen

Ps. I have sometimes felt that Albert sent you to me to point me in this direction. I know that this is an odd and irrational thought, but I wanted to share it with you. Albert always believed a task is best performed by he who does not know it has been assigned to him. Ashes in the river by the Wazi Bridge, please.

John read and reread this letter three or even four times. What was it about? He didn't seem able to read it right through slowly and carefully as he always did with any work that mattered. The words repulsed and deflected his eyes so that he found himself skipping up a couple of lines, or down three, now to the left, now to the right; his gaze wouldn't settle and he was labouring to piece together glimpses and snatches: the rain, the river, the Wazi Bridge, a family torn apart by struggle.

John shook his head in frustration. The corridor was getting busy and he was in the way. A heavy trolley passed, laden with small portions of rice in tinfoil. There was a huge pewter teapot. People were hurrying to get in line. A man carried a child in his arms, while another trotted beside him clutching his trousers.

John stepped back into his mother's office and closed the door after him. There was a key in the lock and, by some unhappy instinct, he turned it. Again he was struck by the powerful smell, sweet and medical and unpleasant. What did she mean, when I'm not around? Was she returning to London? *A son he must have known was not his*. What on earth was that about? Do I have a brother? Why can't I read it properly? It was written clearly enough. There wasn't a single correction on the page. Again he lifted the letter to his eyes, but again there wasn't enough light here in the surgery. His mother's assured and upright handwriting blurred in a web of hieroglyphics. Cremation? Financial assets. He did not understand who it was all addressed to, or why.

John stood between the door and the desk. There was nothing on its surface but a stethoscope, some printed papers in a big stack, and a shallow box with pairs of sterilised gloves. John touched one. It was a rubber the colour of condoms, a stretchy, sticky transparent grey-brown. There had never been anything particular in his parents' cupboards, he remembered, when he had searched through them with adolescent inquisitiveness: the bedside table, the drawers and stored boxes. He had gone through everything any number of times. School friends had boasted of their discoveries, of revealing letters, pornography, even a gun. But John's curiosity had come up against the cool opacity of his parents' perfect marriage, their irreproachable lives.

Still standing by the desk, the letter in his hand, John felt incapacitated, paralysed. He was staring at the stethoscope now. It definitely had a rubbery snakey look. 'In a moment you'll be ill again,' he muttered. 'Snakes make you ill.' I must wake up now, he thought. He was close to panic. No, I must wake *her* up. Come on, get going, get talking, shouting, doing, before your mind gives way again.

Everything was so fragile. John is sure now that there is something he must understand, something he must absorb into himself, but without breaking apart, if possible, without going to pieces. If only he could read whatever it was, like a graph in a report, he thought, like a printout in the lab. If I could read what I have to learn coolly and calmly. Instead it is bubbling up inside him, it will shoot out like vomit. Why on earth had he eaten so much? John is intensely afraid that at any moment consciousness will be drowned in convulsion.

'Mum?'

Once again he began to move round the desk to where she lay asleep. Immediately there was the foot again. She hasn't moved. There was a slim white calf. But it was darker here.

He stopped. Now that he had seen where the light came from, John could easily have gone to the window and yanked up the blind, thrown everything open. He knows that. Surely Mum will be delighted to see her son, even if she hasn't slept well.

Why does he hesitate, then, moving inch by inch round the bulky desk?

Because I'm afraid to disturb of course. On the floor by the mattress, he sees a half-dozen small boxes, green and white, yellow and white. His eye takes them in but they mean nothing.

'Mum?'

John crouched, but jumped back at once.

She was naked. It's the first time he has ever seen his mother's naked thighs and buttocks. He was frightened. He had seen something else too. He feels sick.

John retreated round the desk and stood leaning on it, his hand pressed over his mouth. You're dreaming, he told himself. He definitely felt nauseous. He waited. He began to breathe hard, deeply. Don't vomit. Wait. Breathe. I'm dreaming.

John was panting now, panting and waiting. It's the waiting of someone preparing to plunge. He understood that. Someone shivering on the bank. Get ready for the shock when the water hits you. If he didn't plunge, the banks would burst anyway and he would be overwhelmed.

Or maybe you should just go, he told himself. Go. Leave the room. Mum won't want to wake up and find you've seen her naked, will she? Go and wait outside till she wakes up. That's what a good boy would do.

'Mum!' he yelled, and stumbled round the desk. These stupid slippers he picked up don't fit. He tripped. He caught a loose toe on the corner of a mat and almost fell over their two bodies. He banged his knee. The noise will wake her.

It hasn't.

John looked. Again he had to put his hand over his mouth. His mother was quite naked clasped around a thin, long figure with a head of cropped black hair. John stopped and stared at the woman's luminous skin in the deep shadow.

'Mum?'

She was embracing the man on the narrow mattress. Her arm was round his shoulders, her knee was round his thighs. 'Mum! For Christ's sake!' Why won't they wake up? He got down on his knees, grabbed her shoulder and pulled.

The skin is cold and slightly damp. John stopped. He was breathing hard again. What is she doing? This is different from Jasmeet's sleep, he thought. There isn't the same hum, there isn't the same pleasure.

'Please wake up,' he muttered.

It was a boy, he saw now, not a man. Who is it? Is this Paul? Then he stood again. They wouldn't want him to be there when they woke up, would they? That would be a shock for them. To be discovered. No, he must wake them up and disappear in the same instant, so as not to offend.

Then he was angry. When did Mum ever embrace me like this? When had he ever seen her naked? It's the son the letter mentioned, he thought. *A son he must have known was not his*. The boy is brown-skinned. He can't be Dad's. Was that why they never wanted you to visit?

His mother's smooth back and buttocks looked so finely curved, so strangely young. She was a girl. How could she look so young?

'Mum, wake up!'

He yelled the words now at the top of his voice. He was exhausted.

'She'll never wake up, John,' a voice said.

John stopped shouting and listened. There was nothing. The light under the shutter had grown more intense. There was a deep silence in the room now. But it's the silence of people who have deliberately fallen silent. Not of absence. It is shadows brooding. Or as when you arrive in a place, a clearing, a wood, the upstairs bedroom in the abandoned house, and you know someone is hiding here. Yes. Maybe more than one. They hurried to hide here when they heard you coming. They managed to disappear exactly as you arrived. It's you they hide from, John. Always. They were hiding in the shadow, hiding and mocking.

'Dad?' he called. John swayed on his feet. 'Dad, is that you?'

He was shaking now. But I haven't gone crazy this time, he realised. The room was silent. Not yet at least. They are dormant, he told himself of the two figures on the mattress. It wasn't the same sleep as Jasmeet's sleep, it wasn't a sleep of presence and soft sighs and a forehead that puckered and smoothed. They are dormant, then they will spring to life.

He looked at them. The man was a boy, an adolescent, foreign, horribly thin, not attractive at all. Any moment now they will sit up and rub their eyes and be ashamed.

John stared, frowned. You don't lie naked beside a son, he muttered. He had no memories of closeness with his mother, no remembered smells of bedtime embraces. There were two syringes on the floor beyond the pillow. His mind clouded and unclouded.

John still doesn't want to understand, but very soon now it will be impossible not to. He senses that. He senses the crisis coming. The boy was wearing shorts. He was skeleton-thin. His frail arms lay along his sides, but hers were clasped around him, their heads pressed together on a single pillow. John clutched his hands in his hair. Their bodies are a knot he can't untie.

Someone knocked at the door. John stood still. The handle turned and pushed. The door was locked.

'Please, ma'am! I am bringing some chai.'

He must see her face. Again John got down beside her. He put his hand on her shoulders. He must pull them apart. The cold skin made him shiver. It was stiff as putty. The arms were clasped tight, damp and stiff. Now he knows it's not sleep. Suddenly, he grabbed her hair and yanked it. 'Mum, for Christ's sake!'

'Sir!' shouted a voice from outside.

The head jerked back and the body half turned. His mother's

eyes were open, glazed, the mouth twisted in a mocking smile. Immediately he let go. But the body stayed there, suspended. Her breasts, he thought. He was seeing his mother's breasts. He had asked to see his father's body not his mother's. They were round firm breasts. They weren't old at all. The nipples are distinct. She is laughing at me. John heard his mother laugh. He definitely heard it. A chuckle gurgled from her lips with a trickle of grey fluid. In a split second, he understood; he saw it all with the clarity of the perfect experiment and before he knew it he had slapped her, he was slapping his mother's face. 'Damn you!'

'Sir, madam!' There was more than one voice now. The doorknob rattled furiously. John had no idea what he was screaming, only that his arms were a fury of blows, his hands were aching.

CHAPTER THIRTY-TWO

Paul woke from an intense dream. It seemed he had only just fallen asleep. A phone was trilling, drilling. Paul never dreams, he rather prides himself on never dreaming. He had been in bed, in Boston, with his second wife, their tiny baby, when a voice called. He had pushed the quilt aside and started downstairs, barefoot, listening. Paul! It had been a man's voice. As he descended the stairs, the baby had begun to cry. He heard his wife murmuring comfort. Paul hurried on down flight after flight of stairs. He was naked. He would never reach the bottom. The thin infant whimper, the woman's soft words, grew distant behind him. The steps in front were darker now, darker and narrower, plunging deeper and deeper. His chubby thighs grazed the walls both sides. Paul knew it was no longer his house. How could it be? Then his feet splashed in water, he felt a breeze on his cheeks. A river was running deep in the stone and again a voice called across the darkness.

Paul!

The phone rang. Paul sat up and looked at his watch. 7.25. He had indeed slept only a few minutes, only the time of the dream perhaps. How long do dreams last? Feeling shaken, he waited for the caller to give up. Helen wouldn't phone at this hour, surely. He needed to sleep after a long and very stupid night. At my age. But the noise went on. Paul dragged himself to the sitting room.

'Hello?'

'Hello. Hello. Who is that?'

'Paul Roberts speaking. I'm afraid Helen—'

'You are a relative of Dr Helen James?'

'Who is this calling?'

'This is the police. Delhi police. Are you a relative of Dr Helen James?'

'I'm a friend,' Paul said. He tried to clear his thoughts. 'Has something happened?'

'You are not a relative, sir?'

'I said, I'm a friend. A friend of the family,' he added.

'There is no relative of Dr James at this number?'

'There is no relative staying here, no. Only myself.'

'You are a friend of Dr James?'

'Yes.'

'Please to come to the Sudha Dutta clinic at once. Do you know where that is? Shadhanad Marg? You know? Yes. Very good. I will explain on your arrival. No, please come now. This is a police order. Now. Without delay.'

Returning to sit on the bed, Paul wondered why he felt so . . . what? Upset? Guilty? Or just oddly adrift. It was a physical feeling, a hollowness. What on earth did the police want? Did the phone cause the dream perhaps? Looking for his shoes, he was aware of envying Elaine her youthful misery, of envying Helen her intense adult anguish. These women. 'I have no intensity,' he told himself out loud, and he remembered what the girl had said only a couple of hours ago: 'It just didn't seem real.'

For the evening had finally produced a kiss. Entering Helen's flat towards 2 a.m., soaking wet, laughing from the adventure of tramping through the warm rain over pavements strewn with storm debris, he had turned to her and she had appeared to welcome his advance. They had kissed.

So?

All his experience told Paul that a kiss would settle things one way or another: two personalities met naked on the lips and you knew immediately who the other was, or at least who they would be for you. You knew if there would be sex.

Paul had turned to Elaine, perhaps on impulse, perhaps calculating (but these categories had become meaningless a very long time ago). The girl's mouth came to his; they were tasting each other, opening to each other; there was a nervous urgent warmth about her; the anxiety and confusion of the evening were concentrated on her lips. And she hadn't hung back. She allowed his arms to surround her, allowed their bodies to be pressed together. There was no resistance. It must have gone on at least a couple of minutes.

'We're soaking,' she said then.

'I'll get you a towel.'

He had hurried to the bathroom, his mind full of logistics. Here? Now? What time would Helen be home?

He came back with a bathrobe. There would be the problem of her hairs on the pillow. Her perfume perhaps. Paul liked these details.

Elaine was still standing on the mat by the door where Helen left her indoor slippers.

'I'd better go to the hotel,' she had said.

Paul handed her the robe. 'Get dry,' he told her. 'What's the matter?'

'Please,' she said. 'Call a taxi.'

Paul was not the man to insist. Yet he was surprised.

'It was a nice kiss,' he said quietly.

She managed to smile and bite her lip at the same time. She opened her mouth, hesitated: 'I came to find John.'

Paul handed her the towel. 'Beautiful and elusive creature,' he said with mock gravity, 'give me a moment to change, then I'll call a cab and take you back.'

He had gone into his room. Drying off and dressing, he had been very aware of being overweight, over forty. All around were Albert James's books with their enigmatic scribblings. James's problem, he suddenly decided, was he never had fun.

When he went back, Elaine was still in her wet clothes, her head to one side as she towelled her hair.

'Your pretty pink scarf,' Paul said.

It was sodden, which made the pink darker, almost crimson. She took it, grimaced, pushed it in a pocket. 'You really looked cute in it, you know.'

'Sure you want to go?'

She nodded. But then the taxi company didn't answer. A recorded message explained they were closed on week nights from 2 a.m. to 6 a.m.

'So?' Paul asked. 'What do we do?'

She agreed to strip off her wet clothes, wear the bathrobe, sit on the sofa. 'I'll wait up till six,' she told him. 'You go to bed.'

Paul was too gallant to leave her. And she might change her mind.

'Whisky or tea?' he offered.

She wanted tea. She sat cross-legged in the bathrobe, careful to keep herself covered, pulling the lapels across her chest, tucking flaps between her legs. The movements intensified an atmosphere of domestic intimacy, as between father and daughter.

'God, it's quiet here,' she said. Then, as if engaged in some other ongoing conversation, she went on: 'I won't decide anything till I see John.'

'What if you can't find him?'

She began to explain that she had said no to John's proposal when he made it because it seemed too soon, it didn't fit in with becoming an actress. She was ambitious and he had seemed overwrought, not really himself. He was so young. Now she had lost John and maybe her ambition too.

'As soon as you get back to London you'll feel excited about it all again,' Paul assured her. 'Especially when you hear your parents telling you to get a proper job.' He laughed. 'For example, if I went back to Boston, instead of going out to Bihar, you can bet your life in a few days I'd be drafting a proposal for some new book or other. I'd be back with my girlfriend there.'

'So it's just a question of where you are?' she protested.

'Where you choose to be,' he corrected.

Paul was playing the gentleman and at the same time enjoying the sight of that flushed skin at the base of her neck, the paleness of her small feet, her tight little nail-bitten fingers clutching her mobile in the hope of a response from her boyfriend.

'Speaking of choosing to be places,' he said, 'if you're feeling tired, we could lie down on the big bed. I won't touch you. Promise.'

She shook her head.

'You don't trust me,' he grinned.

'Maybe I don't trust myself.'

Encouraged, Paul grew earnest. It was a while since he had stayed up all night. Perhaps personality shifts in the small hours. Or perhaps he didn't really have any personality at all. Albert James had suggested, he began to tell her, that we can only understand ourselves in relation to the communication systems we are locked into. 'It's a pessimistic position, but there's also the hint of a possible way out: if you suddenly change the way you behave, the system is exposed, the other people in it get confused, and the self-perpetuating machinery seizes up. If you follow me.'

Elaine shook her head. She had understood nothing about John's father, she said. Paul jumped to his feet, went to the shelves and pulled out a few books. He was genuinely enthusiastic and at the same time felt a powerful physical desire to be near the girl, to smell her skin up close.

'See how he wrote over everything he read?'

He sat beside her on the sofa and opened a heavy volume. She looked at the scribbles in the margin and managed to decipher: 'Reconciliation is ever spectral.' What on earth could that mean? The book was about Partition. Still shaking her head, she remarked: 'John thought he was a genius.'

'No doubt about it.'

'But that he'd thrown it all away by not getting involved in a proper research team.'

Beside a page discussing the negotiations that led up to Indian independence, James had written, 'Syntax and semantics dissolve in contemplation.'

Elaine had to turn the book round to follow the scrawl round a photograph of Nehru. 'Art's lively death wish . . .'

'Well, I hope *he* knew what he meant,' she sighed.

Then she twisted her lips in an expression that might have been wry, or just sardonic: 'I'll tell you what, though: whenever John, or now you, start talking about him, you always get exciting and,' she hesitated, 'sexy somehow?'

'I'll bear it in mind,' Paul smiled.

Three hours later, unexpectedly, as he walked her down the stairs to the taxi in the early morning, she kissed him again. She didn't want to be accompanied as far as the hotel, she said. She had put on her damp clothes with no more than an amused grimace and shiver. But as they arrived in the entrance she turned to him and opened her arms. It was recognisably the same kiss as before, but also unmistakeably valedictory, as if promise and goodbye had somehow been superimposed. In his ear she whispered, 'I'm sorry, it just seemed unreal.'

Paul had hurried back upstairs and lain in bed. He was angry with himself. Over the last week or so he had resolved to change and now, almost immediately, he had betrayed that resolve. He felt confused. 'You must go to Bihar,' he muttered. He repeated the words. In all of this adventure, he told himself, the only person with any solidity and consistency has been Helen. Helen was the same in every time and place; Helen lived and saved lives while Albert did nothing but watch and take notes. 'Go to Bihar,' he whispered. 'Life has brought you to a big change.'

Unable to sleep, Paul had found himself repeating these fragments. 'Life has brought you to a big change. You must go to Bihar. Enough of collecting women. Enough of *playing* at living. This failure with Elaine is the turning point. Go to Bihar. Go with Helen. Life has brought you to Helen and Bihar.'

Whichever way he turned on the pillow, after a few seconds a pulse began to thump in his ear. Bihar. Bihar. He lay on his back. Bihar was a poverty-stricken, miserable place. So he imagined. I had life sewn up, Paul thought: the books, Amy. Why do I have to do this?

He turned this way and that, but the words went on automatically. 'Go to Bihar. Change your life. Go to Bihar.' Then suddenly he was in a different bed; he was back in his house in Boston, back with his second wife, their baby daughter, and a voice was calling his name from the basement, from somewhere deep below the ground: Paul.

'Go figure,' Paul muttered, putting the phone down and heading to the bathroom for a pee. The Delhi police. He had never had a high regard for dreams. No need to hurry, he thought. He had never had a high regard for the police forces of developing countries. Years of journalism had acquainted him with their appetite for melodrama and red tape, especially where foreigners were concerned. It would be some stupid quibble over someone's immigration papers or permission to work. Paul prepared himself a coffee, then called a cab.

There were two police vehicles in the street by the clinic. Still uncertain whether to be alarmed or irritated, Paul was led to the outpatients' waiting room. 'Please stay here,' he was told abruptly. 'We are coming to talk to you very soon.' Before he could think to object, the men were gone.

Paul looked around him. The benches against bare walls were all taken and a dozen and more men and women sat patiently on the floor talking quietly, chewing, scratching, in a warm but, for the American journalist, alien togetherness.

He went to stand at the window, looking out of the room through vertical bars and smeared glass across the brick and mud path between entrance and gate. It was all very unlovely, but better than meeting the quietly curious eyes of the Indians in the waiting room. It irked him the way they were all looking at him, in a quiet collective way. Then, with a muffled clatter, four policemen banged out of the main entrance to the building some twenty yards away to the right. Two were holding a young man by the arms, a white man with flaxen blond hair. His head was swaying and he walked uncertainly, as if in some kind of trance. Another policeman walked ahead and another behind.

Paul watched and frowned. The policemen pushed the blond boy through the gate and into a car. Something has happened. He turned and looked for someone in the room to speak to: 'Do any of you know why the police are here?'

'What is that, sir? Sorry?'

It was a gaunt man leaning on crutches. Paul repeated the question a little more loudly. 'Do you know why the police are here?'

Everybody began to talk. In Hindi. Some of them were obviously joking at his expense. Finally, a younger man sitting on the floor said: 'Nobody knows. Perhaps a crime, sir.'

A nurse arrived at intervals to call the patients by number. They were all holding numbers. It was almost an hour before a policeman came and told Paul to follow him to the other end of the building. In a room that was little more than a cubby a senior officer was speaking on his mobile.

'I'd be grateful if you could tell me what all this is about,' Paul began the moment the man closed his conversation. 'Where's Helen? Helen James?'

The man wore a khaki uniform and peaked cap. Thickly framed glasses gave the pockmarked face a certain poise. His moustache was a badge of self-satisfaction.

'Mister?'

'Roberts.'

'Ah yes, my colleague spoke to you on the phone.'

'Please, I've been waiting—'

'Mr Roberts, I must ask one or two questions.'

The man was abrupt and authoritative. Paul was given a seat across the desk from a young policeman who was taking notes. Telephone still in his hand, the officer preferred to stay on his feet. There was much coming and going of men in uniform; a doctor looked in and hurried out.

'You are staying in Dr James's apartment. That is right?'

'Yes.'

'How long have you been staying there, Mr Roberts?'

Paul tried to remember. 'Three weeks, give or take a day or two.'

'You are not resident in India?'

'No.'

'And what is the purpose of your visit?'

Paul was patient. 'I'm researching a biography of Albert James, Helen James's husband.' He hesitated. What other explanation could he convincingly give of himself? 'He died recently.'

'Ah.' The policeman frowned. 'A biography. You are a writer, then?'

'I wrote a book on Gandhi.'

'Gandhi,' the man raised an eyebrow. 'You are a pacifist?'

'Not especially.'

'You are not a pacifist.'

Paul was exasperated. 'Listen, could you tell me what this is about?'

The request was ignored. 'When did Dr James's husband die exactly?'

'January. I think the 17th of January.'

The officer went to stand over his younger assistant's shoulder as if to check what he was writing. Perhaps his English wasn't perfect. Without looking up, he asked: 'And what were your relations with Dr James's son?'

'John James?'

'I didn't know his name, Mr Roberts. I asked you what were your relations with him.'

'None. I've never met him.'

'You've never met Dr James's son?' The policeman raised a heavy eyebrow and smiled with self-conscious sarcasm, as if he had caught Paul out. 'You are a guest of the mother, but you don't know the son.'

'John lives in London.'

'Does he? Does he indeed? Yet right now he is in Delhi.'

'He is?' Only now did it cross Paul's mind that it was John whom the police had taken away. 'Helen didn't know her son was in India,' he said quickly. 'They hadn't been in touch.'

'Ah. Is that so? The mother and son were not in touch?'

'No.'

'And he wasn't staying at his mother's address?'

'No. But . . .' Paul stopped.

The policeman watched him. 'And you don't know where he was staying?'

'How could I, if I didn't know he was in Delhi?'

With an abrupt change of tone, the officer asked, 'Where were you last night, Mr Roberts?' He started to tap his fingers on the desk.

Paul hesitated. 'You need to know where I was? What on earth for? What—'

'Mr Roberts, you must cooperate. This is a most serious matter.'

'Okay.' Paul took a deep breath. 'So, yesterday afternoon a guest arrived at Dr James's apartment, the son's girlfriend from London.'

Realising the officer was looking at him blankly, as if 'girlfriend' were not a category he recognised, Paul explained: 'A young woman who is a close friend of John's and of the family came to Dr James's apartment because she believed John was in Delhi and thought he was staying with his mother. In fact, that was our first inkling that John might have come to Delhi. Then, since Dr James was on night duty here at the clinic, I took the young lady to her hotel, and to dinner, and then, because she had never been to Delhi before, I drove her round the old town.'

The policeman was in some difficulty with this. He had taken his glasses off and was rubbing them with a tissue, frowning, as if clean lenses might help him grasp the point of what Paul was telling him. After a moment, he asked. 'Why did this woman come to Delhi, where did she travel from, how old is she, why did you take her to dinner and round the town?'

'As I said' – Paul realised that the story might not make much sense to a man of the policeman's background – 'the girl, her name is Elaine, is a close friend of the family. Maybe she will become John's wife. Anyway, she came from London to visit him. He had told her he was in Delhi, but not where he was staying.' When the policeman still seemed unconvinced, Paul added, 'In these circumstances it was a normal courtesy on my part to take her out. She doesn't know India.'

'You drove her around the old town also? In the rain?'

'Yes. Then we had a drink. Off Connaught Place.'

'The lady will verify this?'

'Of course. She is staying at the India International Centre. Her surname is Harley, I think. I can't remember the name of the bar, but I could certainly take you there.'

'And what time were you taking this lady of yours home?'

'Not my lady,' Paul corrected. 'Let me see,' he made a show of thinking. 'I was back in Helen's flat at one-thirty, as I recall.'

'One-thirty? You are out with a girlfriend of the family until one-thirty!' There was a decidedly unpleasant sarcasm in the officer's voice. He scratched at one corner of his moustache and exchanged a smile with the young man labouring with his pen. Then his phone rang again. 'Hello?' He hurried to the door and spoke in a low voice in the corridor. An elderly man in a white coat knocked, came into the room, handed a file to the young policeman behind the desk, said a word or two in Hindi and hurried out.

The officer returned and spent a few moments looking through the new file. He grunted two or three times, as if hardly satisfied. 'So,' he looked up, 'what did Dr James say when this family friend arrived.'

Paul was aware of feeling extremely tense. 'Helen was very surprised,' he said carefully. 'She had no idea John was coming to India. She didn't expect this young lady to visit. She didn't know what exactly the relationship between them was.'

'Was Dr James happy that her son was in Delhi?'

'She still didn't believe he really was.'

Very abruptly the policeman said: 'There was a quarrel between mother and son, wasn't there, Mr Roberts. Don't equivocate. Dr James was afraid of seeing him in Delhi.'

'No,' Paul protested.

'Why didn't somebody use the telephone and call the son also? This situation is not credible, Mr Roberts.'

'His phone was turned off . . .' Paul began.

But now the officer's own phone buzzed again, and again the man hurried out of the room to talk. Feeling extremely anxious now, Paul sat still, aware of the low voice out in the corridor and the young policeman intent on his notes, making corrections, occasionally glancing at this file that had appeared. The room was lined from floor to ceiling with wooden shelves and boxes of medicines. Then, from the one small window, came the sound of a peddler crying his wares in the street. 'Pa-tai-yei, pa-tai-yei.'

Paul listened, understanding nothing. 'Ma-tai-yei!' Why did I dream of a voice calling? he wondered. India was full of urgent voices. Some residue from religious infancy, perhaps? Calls, duties. Then, as if physically nudged, he remembered Helen's story about the dent on the table, the stone elephants, her son's weird behaviour. He was in Delhi after all. Suddenly, Paul was terrifically alert. The candle had tipped on the table and burned his hand. 'Do you think he meant to kill me?' Helen had asked. The question had struck him as absurd, melodramatic, definitely out of character. But now something had happened. A very serious matter. 'Ma-ti-alli-yei!' came the voice. 'Pa-tai-yei!'

Five minutes had passed. Listening, Paul realised that the officer was no longer talking in the corridor. What the hell is happening? He jumped to his feet. The young policeman looked up. 'I have to go to the bathroom,' Paul said.

The man seemed to hesitate. 'You must wait,' he said.

'Delhi belly,' Paul told him. 'It's urgent.'

He hurried out into the corridor. People were jostling in lines or hurrying back and forth but there was no sign of the officer. I must find Helen, Paul decided. He opened a door and saw a dark cupboard, closed it again.

'Where is the main ward?' he asked a man with a broom and trolley. Without stopping, the man pointed. Paul hurried along the corridor, turned a corner and saw a larger double door. She would be here, surely. He should have come straight to her the moment he was in the hospital. Paul pushed the doors open.

On each side of the big room was a row of beds. The air was sour with powerful smells. Chemicals and vomit. On the third bed to the left a man was retching. At his side a nurse, a rather fat young woman, was holding his head over a plastic bowl. The man was in his mid forties, thin hair plastered in sweat, eyes bloodshot, neck straining with each spasm, each attempt to throw up. The nurse was speaking in a low voice, her face quite close to his.

Again the man retched. A trickle spattered from the corner of his mouth, dribbled down his chin and onto his sleeve. The nurse spoke softly. Other patients had turned away from the scene, lying on their beds. Someone was reading a magazine. An elderly woman had propped herself up to work at some kind of embroidery, a broad silky weave of blues and greens. She seemed indifferent to the coughing and rasping.

Suddenly, the man's whole body jerked back then forward again and the vomit poured out of his mouth. It was unexpectedly dark. Paul heard the clatter and splash in the plastic bowl. It must have splashed in the nurse's face, he thought.

The patient retched yet again, in vain this time. The nurse was young and held his head tight between puffy hands, speaking kindly. Bihar, Paul thought. He was fascinated and repulsed. In Bihar, *you* will be holding that head. You will be splashed by vomit. Why? Why do you want to do this?

'Mr Roberts?'

At last aware of his name, Paul turned.

'Mr Roberts, I was questioning you about a crime. Why did you leave? Do you want me to put you under arrest?'

'I need to speak to Helen,' Paul said.

The officer's eyes narrowed. He seemed to be weighing the American up. 'Follow me,' he said.

Again Paul was taken down the corridor. This time they turned to the left. In a few moments he recognised Helen's surgery and saw at once that the wood of the door was splintered around the lock.

'What's going on?'

A policeman with a rifle allowed him to cross the threshold.

'You can approach the tape, but do not go further,' the officer told him. 'We are awaiting an expert to examine this.'

With the blinds raised, the room was in full sunlight. Paul stepped to a red and white plastic tape that had been stretched from a cupboard on the left to the handle of the French window on the right. Beyond the tape was a large desk, but stepping to the right of that Paul saw two bodies, one each side of a low mattress. On the far side was an emaciated teenager in grey-white underwear; his head was thrown back, eyes closed, mouth twisted in a painful smile. On the near side, in a beam of sunshine, Helen's body was obscenely outspread, as though for some particularly unpleasant form of pornography. From face down to knees, the white skin was oddly mottled, the outflung limbs seemed contorted, the belly slightly swollen.

Involuntarily, Paul brought his hand to his mouth. He couldn't look and he couldn't look away. Above all he couldn't understand. The body demanded his gaze and repelled it. It seemed so much bigger, longer, whiter, more present – immediately, materially present – than a living person could ever be.

'Helen,' he muttered.

'What was that?' the officer asked.

The man's voice was sharp. He was observing Paul carefully, but Paul paid no attention. He couldn't see any way forward from here, or back for that matter, away from this body. The shiny plastic, police-incident tape prevented him from getting closer. But he couldn't turn round and walk out. He couldn't think at all. Her breasts were flat and misshapen, her pubis brutally exposed to the bright morning light. Only yesterday they had been in bed together.

'Her son was slapping her face when we broke in,' the policeman announced. He seemed satisfied to see the American shocked. 'He refused to open the door.'

'Her son was here?'

'Yes.'

'Slapping her face?' Paul couldn't understand. 'But who's the boy? What happened?'

'The young man is a patient at the hospital.'

'A patient?'

'Mr Roberts, any son would be upset to find a mother in this undressed state with an unknown man also. Don't you think? It is too clear what has happened. Unfortunately John James refuses to answer our questions. Now—'

'But how did they die? He couldn't just have—'

From along the corridor came the sound of angry voices. They both turned. There was a clatter of footsteps and something banged. Even in Hindi Paul recognised that it was someone he knew. He knew that voice. A man was shouting, objecting, insisting. Other voices were raised against him. The corridor echoed. The argument was hurrying towards them. There was a yell, then Kulwant Singh pushed in. His bearded face was distraught, his eyes gleaming, his black turban not quite straight on his round face. Fending off every attempt to block him, even taking a knock from a rifle butt, he hoisted up the plastic ribbon, ducked under and at once let out a roar of pain. 'Helen!' he shouted, 'No!'

Three policemen grabbed at him, but Kulwant was already down beside the body. He was shouting. He had his head beside hers. He grabbed her wrist for the pulse, threw it down, clasped the body against his own. 'No!' he yelled again.

Paul watched, humiliated by the bigger man's energy and

evident grief. Kulwant was embracing the nude body in a frenzy of denial. 'No, no, no!' he went on. The officer shrieked at him. He was spoiling a crime scene. At last, the two young policemen had hold of his arms, forced him to let go of the body and pulled him back. The Sikh was trembling violently, his strong fleshy mouth alive in the grizzle of beard. A torrent of Hindi poured out. His eyes were thick with tears.

Paul listened. He understood nothing, only that Kulwant was profoundly emotively involved with Helen in a way he himself had not been. The man cared enormously. There was a back-and-forth between the officer and the Sikh now. Kulwant seemed to be explaining who he was and why he was there. When the officer interjected, Kulwant snapped back, his voice full of contempt. The man didn't intimidate him at all. For a moment his powerful wrists wrenched and struggled. Then he rounded on Paul.

'These idiots are asking me questions about her son. They don't understand anything.'

Paul was unable to respond.

Kulwant made another lunge, shook off his minders and grabbed one of four or five small plastic bags from the desk. There was a syringe inside and he waved it in front of the officer shouting excitedly. Again Paul couldn't follow. His eyes were drawn back to Helen's body. The combination of outflung arms, ugly exposure and wax-white stillness was uncanny.

'The American will confirm every word I am saying.' Kulwant turned on Paul again. 'This is a terrible terrible tragedy. Her husband got her to kill him six months ago, isn't that right? She killed her husband at his request. He wanted to die. And no doubt he asked her to do the same to herself. He incited her. I have seen her thinking about this for many months. I have been warning her, many, many times. Her husband was a sick man, isn't that right, Mr Roberts? You are writing about him. You must be aware of that. He was a brilliant man, but sick, with sick impulses, very sick, very contorted, very afraid. I have been telling Helen for many years. Oh I can't believe this. It is my fault.'

Weakly, Paul said, 'I am sure Albert James would never have persuaded anyone to kill themselves. Let alone his wife. That was quite the opposite of his character.'

'But all his thinking was going that way!' Kulwant cried. 'Anyway, what is this?' Again he waved the syringe and turned to the policeman. 'You will find a deadly mixture in this syringe. I am sure. Probably insulin and Valium. It is very swift.'

'That is enough now,' the officer said sharply. 'A man who is dead six months cannot incite anyone to kill themselves. I said enough!' he repeated, when Kulwant opened his mouth again. 'It is true we have found four syringes on the floor. They will be examined of course.' The officer left a short silence. 'However, there are other questions also to be answered.' He touched his moustache for a moment. 'Why did the son not tell his mother he was in Delhi? Why has the woman left no note, if it is a suicide? If he found his mother already dead, why did the son lock the door behind him? Why did he refuse to speak to us?'

Kulwant suddenly seemed exhausted by his emotions. 'Perhaps there is a note,' he said lamely. 'I still can't believe this. It's too horrible. Perhaps she has sent an email to someone.'

The officer turned to Paul: 'Do you think Dr James could have killed herself? Was she talking about such matters while you were staying with her?'

Very slowly, Paul's mind was beginning to function. Had Helen said anything? Perhaps she had and he hadn't understood. 'What about this boy here?' he asked carefully. 'Why would the boy be dead if it was suicide?'

Kulwant turned back to the bodies. He crouched down but without trying to get closer this time. 'Dear God,' he muttered.

'Helen!' He raised a hand to his forehead, adjusted his turban, stood up again. 'I see no marks on him,' he sighed. 'There is no blood. You will see he also died from an injection.'

Then in someone's pocket a phone began some urgent melody. A bhangra dance tune. It sounded rather merry.

'There must be an autopsy,' the officer was saying.

Kulwant dug into his trousers, pulled out the phone and checked the illuminated screen. 'Jasmeet!' He pressed a button, lifted it to his ear and demanded, 'Where in the name of God are you, Jasmeet?'

CHAPTER THIRTY-THREE

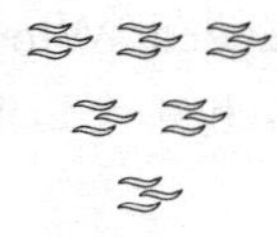

John was held in a police cell in Naya Bazar Road, not half a mile from the clinic. He denied that he had struck his mother. Perhaps he had slapped her face in an attempt to wake her. His last memory, he was finally able to explain to the police after more than twenty-four hours' paralysed silence, was that of crouching to pull her up from the floor and get her to put some clothes on. What most upset him was to find her naked. No, he could not say at what point he had realised she was dead. Perhaps even now he hadn't taken it in.

But yes, he did remember the questioning, John said, and honestly he had tried to respond, but he had been 'under water', he told the officer. He couldn't open his mouth. The receptionist of the Govind Hotel, John stated, would confirm that he had spent the night in his room there and left shortly after 6 a.m. He had come to Delhi, it was true, to see his mother, but then hadn't gone to her at once because the meeting frightened him. He hadn't been feeling well. He couldn't say why. There were important matters to discuss between himself and his mother. No, he couldn't really say what.

'Maybe I just wished he was still alive,' John muttered.

'Why did you lock the door to your mother's surgery?' the officer asked.

They sat across a table in a police interrogation room. A recording device had been switched on. John declined the offer of a lawyer. He had done nothing wrong.

'Did I lock it?'

The officer was exasperated. It was the first time he had dealt with a crime involving Europeans.

'Since there was no one else in the room, Mr James, no one else who was alive, you must surely have locked it. It was locked, from the inside.'

'I suppose I wanted her to myself,' John eventually said. He hesitated: 'There were so many patients in the corridor, you know? My mother was always very busy helping people.'

'Did you recognise the boy who was with her?'

John was silent. He looked down at his knees. Finally he said: 'I have never seen him before.'

'You don't know what was his relation with your mother?'

'No.'

Returned to the cell after questioning, John was not unhappy. The suffocating heat in the narrow cement space didn't concern him. Nor the powerfully unpleasant smells. He didn't feel it was a scandal that they were holding him. He didn't yearn for company. He lay on a bunk. The flies are free to settle on my face, he thought, on my lips and hair. They don't bother me. He felt safe here, removed from danger, released, above all, from any obligation to think. I will not think, he decided. I don't care.

Instead he listened to the other men who were brought in and out. He kept his eyes closed, as if sleeping. He lay still on his back on the thin mattress with his hands joined on his stomach. There were bunks for six. At one point there were eleven men in the room. The beds creaked. A key turned the lock with a clank. Prisoners came and went, protesting. It was pleasant not to understand a word they said. They chattered and farted and argued and sucked up catarrh. My stomach feels good, John noticed. The dysentery had gone. The worst possible thing has happened, he thought, and is past. At a certain point he remembered with a jolt that there was a letter in his back pocket, a letter that wasn't addressed to him. Dear Paul . . . Who was this person? His mind clouded. He felt anxiety rising. What if they took his clothes away? So far they had only frisked him for weapons. Anyway, he would not take that letter out or think about it at all. I will drift, he decided.

Breathing softly in the suffocating afternoon on the hard bed, and then through the long night that followed, John began to feel that his body was not on a solid bed at all, but floating on air or water. He had the impression he was turning this way and that, propelled, as if following a current or swinging with a tide. During the night he became aware that his hands, joined on his belly, had sunk deep into his body; they were one with his gut and organs. His hands were inside his belly. And his feet and calves and knees and thighs had fused together. I am a cocoon, he whispered. His entire body had liquefied and was becoming one warm cosy fluid.

John James was held in the police station for forty-eight hours then released without charge after an autopsy had established the time and cause of his mother's death. Various powerful blows had been delivered to the woman's body, the examining doctor reported, but this had occurred some hours after her decease. In a brief morning meeting, two senior officers decided that the Delhi police had better things to do than to pursue such an obscure misdemeanour. The boy was disturbed. Both the victims were foreign nationals. No relatives were demanding justice.

Led to the entrance of the police station toward 11 a.m., John was amazed to find Elaine waiting for him. I'm sick again; he thought.

Elaine was demanding to know if he was okay. 'John! Oh John!'

She was smiling and crying and hugging and kissing. Her quick little mouth pressed against his cheek, his nose. 'It's so great to see you.'

Overwhelmed and wooden, John couldn't understand how his girlfriend had arrived so soon. Who had told her? Her name formed on his lips but he couldn't speak it.

'Hi, I'm Paul Roberts,' the man beside her introduced himself. He stood for a moment offering a hand that John didn't take. 'You don't know me but I was planning to write a biography of your father. I've been staying at your mother's apartment these last couple of weeks.'

Finally, John found his voice. 'Can we go, please?' he asked.

In the taxi, sitting between the others, he was on his guard.

'John,' Elaine repeated. 'God, I'm so glad they've let you out. I was so worried.'

But now John had remembered the Govind. 'Take me to Bhavbhuti Marg,' he leaned forward to explain to the driver where it was. 'Now please.'

When they arrived, he insisted on going up alone. He just had to get his things, he said, and pay his bill. There was no reason for anyone else to come. He asked if either of them could lend him 2,000 rupees. Paul immediately pulled a wallet from his pocket and counted the notes.

Climbing the stairs to the hotel, John became concerned that Jasmeet might still be in his room. He had treated her badly and she had nowhere to go. She would make demands. She would talk about air tickets. She would run out and confront Elaine.

He stopped at a dusty landing where a small Ganesh had been fixed to an old brown door. The god smiled his inane elephant smile. Behind the door someone laughed. John distinctly heard laughter, and music too. He stared at the stupid image with its jumbo trunk and chubby grin. Why had he lashed out at Jasmeet?

It wasn't her fault. And how could you be so cheerful when your father cut off your head and replaced it with something grotesque? Three elephants, sir! He heard the hawker's chirpy voice. Happy family, sir. *A son he must have known was not his*, his mother had written. Inside John's thinking, right at the liquid core where ideas bubble up, a dull ache set in. 'Cement,' he found himself muttering. And then unexpectedly: 'Carry on regardless, John.'

'What lady?' the woman in reception asked coolly.

'You remember, the girl who waited for me. She spent one night in reception.'

The receptionist busied herself with some papers. 'The lady left the hotel a few hours after you, as far as I can remember.'

'She didn't leave a message? She hasn't been back?'

'No, sir.'

At once John was disappointed. He now felt he needed to see Jasmeet quite urgently. He couldn't remember why, but there was a reason. Had he really hit and kicked his mother as the policeman said? How could he have kicked anyone with those stupid hospital slippers on? The ache flowered in his mind. It had a purplish colour, like a flower opening on water, blocking reflection, clogging the flow. There was no question of giving the letter to the American.

'I must settle my bill,' John announced calmly.

'Very good, Mr James.'

The woman opened a folder and produced a paper with various scribblings: his breakfasts, the dysentery pills they had bought for him, bananas. She tapped in figures on a little calculator. Her fingernails were green, her sari a soft peach against the milk brown of her wrists. As always the bowl of water with the trembling petals was on the counter by her elbow. Even when they were different, John thought, the coloured patterns were always the same. Waiting while the hotelier counted the banknotes, he stared at the pointillist geometry hovering on the transparent skin of the water. What was the logic of it? What if the petals hid something ugly beneath?

Putting his money in a drawer, the hotelier smiled. She must have expected the worst when he disappeared. Now she was in a generous mood. 'Your room has been cleared for another customer, Mr James,' she said. Her plump face was warm and motherly. The generous lips pursed and smiled. 'Everything has been packed in your bag. You will check it please before you go. You must say if something is missing.' She lifted the phone and spoke briskly in Hindi.

John felt he would have liked very much to stop and talk to the woman. He had always been attracted to her he realised now. Polite and businesslike in her sari and elaborate bracelets, her very discretion was a form of intimacy, as though, precisely by not mentioning the troubled nature of his stay, she were gently suggesting her awareness of it, her readiness to help. John watched her jotting down a last note, brushing strands of fine hair from her nose – how pretty the bright jewel sunk in the dark skin – but in the end he said nothing and now an elderly man had appeared from the corridor bringing his bag. John gave him twenty rupees. 'Please check everything now, sir,' the hotelier warned. 'I would not like to hear something is missing.'

John sat on the reception's low sofa and opened his bag. His clothes, though unwashed, had been folded. His washing kit had been gathered together and zipped into its pouch. Perhaps now would be the moment to mention the computer, he thought, and the phone and the pashmina shawl. He didn't. Glancing distractedly through his few things, he realised that he had actually been looking forward to going to the room and sorting it out himself, or maybe just lying down a few minutes on the bed.

Then, opening the bag's side pocket, John came across the laundry-order paper with the drawing of his father's face. So it hadn't been taken! He looked at the rough little sketch. He had forgotten that he had put his father in his coffin; he had even sunk him under snaky lines of water. I didn't see the body but I drew it. I buried it. Disturbed, John quickly folded the paper and pushed it in his back pocket together with his mother's letter. He zipped the bag shut and got to his feet.

'Thanks for packing my clothes,' he told the hotelier. 'That was very kind.'

'You are welcome, sir,' she said.

At his mother's apartment John simply waited for the American to go. He wanted him out. Paul had mentioned moving into a hotel. 'I don't want to be in you young folks' way, but I'm right around the corner if you need help.' His mobile and hotel numbers, he said, were on the pad by the phone.

'John, I can imagine how upsetting this all is,' Paul added quietly, standing at the door about to go, 'but there's the question of funeral arrangements. You mother's body is being released this morning. I told them to send it to a funeral parlour. Let me give you their number as well.'

John didn't reply. He was standing at the table, looking across the room at the shelves of books and videos. How dusty it all was. As if attracted to it, his fingers found the dent where he had banged down the stone elephant. Mum and Dad both escaped me, he thought.

Meantime the elderly maid was carrying in tea on an English tea tray. John had forgotten her name. She set mats and cups and the big white pot on the table.

'So, would it be okay?' Paul asked with gentle practicality, 'if I arranged the same sort of ceremony that she arranged for your father? At the Christian crematorium? You have to do things quickly here you know. It will be for tomorrow. At most the day after.'

John must have nodded. The American said something in a quiet voice to Elaine, then left.

They finished their tea. After a few moments' silence, Elaine started to explain how she had abandoned the play she was working on and decided to come out to Delhi to find him. 'It was a premonition maybe,' she said. 'I suddenly realised how important you were.'

John was staring around the shelves, at the weight of his father's books, the strange bareness of his parents' world. They were both gone.

'You don't want to talk?'

The doorbell rang. It was a sharp old-fashioned buzz. Lochana's daughter and granddaughter had arrived. The elderly maid opened the door for them. Vimala went to shake John's hand, then Elaine's. The girl seemed anxious to speak, but then simply sat down at the table, opening and shutting her knees in pink trousers, while her mother tried to talk to John about Lochana.

'You will return to England now, I think.' The woman spoke brusquely in a low urgent voice. 'And what will become of my mother, sir? She is working for Mrs James for five years now. It will not be easy for her to find another place at her age.'

'I've really no idea,' John said. He had sat down again. 'I have no money and my parents left nothing at all.' He opened his hands in a gesture of destitution. He was secretly pleased that Mum had made no arrangements for her maid.

Standing to leave, Vimala asked in a low voice. 'Can I take a book, Mr John? To remember your father. You know I helped him also in his research.'

'Take what you like.'

Without hesitating, the girl walked to the far wall and stooped to the bottom shelf. She had a natural liquid grace. A slim hand moved rapidly across the book spines, then she sighed and pulled out a copy of *Through the Looking-Glass*. 'That is so kind of you,' she said, standing up. 'Thank you, Mr John.'

When the Indians had gone, John told Elaine he needed to rest. He stood up and went to the small bedroom, the guest room. For perhaps an hour Elaine sat alone on the sofa. She read a message on her mobile but didn't reply. She moved to the window and looked out at the sullen heat. Apartment buildings were scattered at random across dark scrub and unmarked roads. The sky was low and still, the landscape an empty reddish brown.

Elaine turned back to the room's shelves and looked for something to read, anything. *Homus Hierarchicus*, she found, Louis Dumont. She sat down again, leafing through the pages, unable to concentrate. The index pointed her to a section entitled 'Conjugal Unions'. She tried to read the opening lines: 'Let us recall that neither premarital sexual relations nor adultery is tolerated.' She twisted the page round to follow a scrawl in the margin. There was a spooky constrained urgency to the slanted handwriting: 'To live is to punish.' Elaine frowned. John's father was weird. She put the book down and, without knocking, went into the bedroom.

'Why did you come to India, John? You haven't told me anything.'

She kept her voice as calm as she could. 'Why didn't you answer my messages? Why didn't you go to see your mum till yesterday? What have you been doing all this time?'

John was on his back, his hands behind his head. He pulled himself up a little and opened his mouth, then closed it again.

'You know she had no idea you were here. Your mum. I saw her. Maybe you didn't realise. I arrived thinking you would be here. I saw her just before she went to the hospital. The last day she was alive. It makes me shiver. I know I'd never met her before, but she seemed completely normal to me. What happened John? Why did she do it?'

Her boyfriend stared at her, but in such a way that their eyes couldn't meet. He was looking at her neck, at her waist, at someone who had pushed in through the door.

'John! I know it's terrible, I know you must be so shocked, but, please, let's talk a bit. Please look at me, I'm going crazy.'

He sighed, still hesitated, then at last glanced into her eyes and said: 'I want to pack all Dad's books and tapes. I want them all put in boxes and sent back to London. We'll have to find some boxes, or maybe call a freight company. We can do it this afternoon.'

Elaine was still standing at the door. The small room was quite unfurnished aside from bed and heavy home-made bookshelves.

'Don't you want to give the stuff to Paul?' she asked. 'At least for the moment. In case he writes his biography maybe. It would be easier to let him handle them.'

John shook his head. 'Mum didn't want him to write a book. And nor do I.'

'Oh.' Elaine was surprised. 'I thought you said it was a good idea.'

'No.'

'But where on earth will you put them?' She really didn't want him to send those books to England.

'Somewhere. I'll store them somewhere. Maybe at my grandmother's. She has a big house.'

The girl came and sat on the corner of the bed. She spoke practically. 'Listen John. I have to decide whether to go back soon, in the next day or two, and do my play. I said I'd resigned but they're insisting I do it. They're sending messages. I've got to make up my mind.'

John didn't reply. She put a hand on his where it lay on the blanket.

Then he sat up abruptly. 'I have to pack those books. I have to contact the owner of the flat here and cancel the rent contract. We have to check when the funeral can be held and make sure we get the first flight afterwards. And we have to find someone to pay for it and to pay to put the books on it.' He looked at her. 'Let's go.'

'Helen James was by far the most remarkable woman I have had the honour to meet,' Paul said from the podium at the funeral the following morning. John noticed Jasmeet sitting beside her father to his right. From time to time the girl turned a dazzling smile his way, as if this were a happy event, as if there were a special complicity between them. She was wearing a pale yellow sari with a blue blouse. Kulwant looked distraught and frequently put his arm round his daughter's shoulders. Sharmistha and Heinrich were side by side behind.

'I came to Delhi, as you probably know, to study the work of Helen's husband, the anthropologist Albert James, but more and more I was forced to realise that Albert could not be talked about separately from Helen. Their different, sometimes contradictory vocations had to be seen as stems twisting around and supporting each other. I know that more than once I felt a deep envy for the wonderful marriage they had, a partnership that took them all over the world and held them together through so many difficult situations. We can all imagine, I think, how hard it must have been for Helen after Albert's death.'

It was the first time Paul had addressed anything similar to a church congregation. He felt quite at home, even rather moved by his own words.

'Still, I cannot believe that her untimely departure was planned. On the very day she died Helen was telling me of her plans to go out to Bihar and work in a small hospital there. She even made a considerable effort to persuade me that it would be right and exciting if I were to give some of my time to help there too. I have no doubt that she was serious about the project and that whatever happened on the night of her death must have been the result of a moment's despair.' Paul hesitated. 'As a tribute to Helen, I have pledged that I will do as she proposed and spend at least a year in Bihar. Obviously I cannot be the help she would have been. But I will do my best.'

'Crap,' John whispered to Elaine. He didn't join in the small clatter of applause as Paul stepped down.

'Aren't you going to speak?' Elaine asked. The American was the third to have been to the podium. The girl seemed anxious about the form of the ceremony in exactly the way John had been at his father's funeral six months before.

'No.'

'Don't you think people will see it badly?'

John shrugged his shoulders.

Now Dr Coomaraswamy was saying that when two great spirits lived together on earth they tended to become different in order to complement and complete each other. When one died there was imbalance and yearning on both sides of the great divide, on the earth below and in the ether above.

'Crap,' John whispered again.

'No, it was a beautiful thing to say.'

'With regard to the strange nature of her departure,' Coomaraswamy concluded and he lowered his head to look at the small gathering over his rimless glasses, 'I am not sure that this was an act of desperation. I am not sure we need regret it. Theosophy teaches us that the Masters guide our actions and are attentive to our most profound needs.' He paused. 'Now this river too has flowed to the sea.'

'Beauty's got nothing to do with it,' John muttered.

'You should say something, John,' Elaine repeated. 'She was your mother.'

'No.'

Kulwant Singh strode to the podium with the rapidity of a warrior. 'Ladies and gentlemen.' He turned this way and that, his fists pressed together and against his chest. 'Friends. I am very upset by what has happened. And I'm very angry. I cannot tell you all how upset I am. Helen was a very beautiful woman. Yes, she was very funny also. Full of living. Sometimes we drank whisky together after our work. I have known her a long time. Five years. Sometimes we had breakfast after a night duty. Helen liked to laugh and she liked to hear good jokes. She was not a snob. She was not squeamish. For many many years this woman worked very hard to help people, she helped the poorest people, and she asked nothing. I think she was paid nothing also. She did not even ask for admiration. It is unusual. She did not ask for medals. How many people will give so much and ask for so little? For nothing even. Her death is really very sad and very stupid. And I am very angry that I, you, all the people who knew Helen, did not see this coming. We should have prevented it. Helen was a private woman, yes. She was very discreet. She didn't often say what was in her head, she seemed a very strong woman, she didn't ask for help or sympathy, but we should have understood. It is a condemnation to all of us. Helen still had much to live for. She had a fine son, John James. He is here today. He is a fine young man. Very intelligent. We can imagine his grief. She had warm friends. There are many of her friends here today. I wish only that Helen had leaned on us the way other people were leaning on her, always. God could not have wanted this,' the Sikh said with sudden conclusive vehemence. 'God does not like these ugly deaths.'

For a moment Kulwant seemed unable to go on. He opened his mouth, closed it, opened it again. 'I shall miss Helen very much. Very much.' The big man suddenly swung round, knelt down, pushed his face against the coffin and kissed it.

John bowed his head in his hands. He was stung and paralysed and tongue-tied. He did not look up when the Sikh stepped down and again the small congregation applauded warmly. He did not look up as the elderly Dr Yellaiah began to explain how, when the cost of medicines had gone beyond the clinic's budget, Helen

James would pay for a patient's treatment herself. 'She used her own money, or her husband's. Even in the case of the poor boy who died with her,' the old doctor went on in a thin, high-pitched voice, 'Helen James had paid for special antibiotics to be procured in the hope that these would overcome the resistance that the boy's strain of the disease had developed.'

John did not look up. Caught in the tangle of it all, the déjà vu, he sat still and numb as the man from the British Council said a few quiet words, then while Aradhna Verma spoke for fifteen interminable minutes about Helen's commitment to the rural poor and various ambitious projects presently being sponsored by the Gandhi Society to which those present might wish to give generously. Even for the awful moment of the coffin's departure, John would not look up. He sat rigid.

'It's time to go,' Elaine tugged at his wrist.

He wouldn't move.

'There's a girl wants to talk to you.'

John was stiff as stone. Elaine smiled at the Indian girl and shrugged her shoulders and Jasmeet turned and hurried after her father.

'John, there's another group to come in. We've really got to go.'

John would stay for that funeral too then. He would stay for all the funerals.

Everybody had got to their feet now. Most had reached the door and were walking out into the stifling day. Then Paul Roberts came back in, hurried up the aisle and along the bench to where Elaine was still beside her boyfriend. 'We should be going now,' he said. Elaine made a face of desperation. John just sat. His neck was bowed, his cheeks buried in his hands.

'If John agrees,' Paul said carefully, 'when the ashes are ready I'll see they're sprinkled in the river where she put Albert's, I think.'

'No,' John sat up and turned to him. 'No. John doesn't agree. The ashes stay in the crematorium.'

The remaining hours before the flight were ones of extreme anxiety for Elaine. Events had deprived her of every sure reference. On leaving for India she had told her parents not to phone, not to meddle in her life any more, and they hadn't. She imagined they must be furious and while, on the flight out, this thought had afforded some pleasure, now it made her apprehensive. Hanyaki on the other hand had texted her almost hourly for days. He needed her for the opening night. But the day of the funeral his messages stopped. He had found someone else perhaps. And now John wouldn't speak to her at all. She had come out here for him, but he was no longer the boy she had known in Maida Vale; he was no longer the young PhD, the safe bet, the steady friend. 'What happened, John?' she asked him. She felt vulnerable. 'What was it?' He set his lips and clenched his jaw.

Elaine was lost. John moved from room to room in a desultory, angry way, muttering to himself. He grabbed a broom and swept. The books and videos were packed and gone. Paul had arranged for a freight company to come. The men had filled three packing cases and left behind a mess of dust and cobwebbed corners. John swept up dead flies and assorted debris. He even swung the broom along the curtain pelmet. 'What for?' Elaine protested. Whoever came next would do a thorough clean anyway. He looked up at her, but would not speak. He shifted the fridge and swept out the filth behind. 'John,' she asked, 'please. Why am I here if not to be with you? Why don't we talk?'

Returning from the crematorium, Paul had sat with the young couple in a taxi. He found the young man's behaviour embarrassing. He had paid for their flights to Heathrow and was yet to be thanked. He had paid for the funeral too. It was not cheap. He would have liked to talk intelligently to John about his father, his mother, about what had happened, about how the two of them would be remembered by posterity, about the papers being shipped to London – where would they be stored? – about an eventual book – who could tell what the future might bring, after his return from Bihar? But the boy was hostile, even rude. I've done nothing to deserve this, Paul was sure. He rather pitied the charming Elaine.

The afternoon dragged on. John paced. He banged the broom against the skirting. I should go out, Elaine decided, but she felt intimidated by the prospect of adventuring into the town alone. Perhaps she could call Paul now, she thought. He would take her into the old centre again for this last evening. At least she would see something. She hadn't seen India at all. He was an interesting man, full of stories. John's refusal to acknowledge her and his angry back-and-forth through the two or three rooms was a constant friction on her nerves.

Towards seven, with darkness already fallen, the phone rang. Heinrich and Sharmistha were inviting them to dinner. 'No thanks,' John said and put the phone down. When it started ringing again, he bent down and unplugged its wire.

'For Christ's sake!' Elaine demanded. 'I exist too, you know!'

John carried the phone into the kitchen and put it away in a cupboard.

'We need to eat at least,' she called after him.

John didn't need.

Elaine watched him. What had happened to John was truly awful, but all the same he was behaving badly. She turned on the television and tried to follow a programme. They were talking about removing food vendors from Delhi's streets. At least we are flying back tomorrow, she thought. Then I'll leave him.

John had sat beside her now. It was evening already and with the daylight gone the TV colours played across his face. She turned and saw how tense he was. And as she watched his lips moving, the muscles working round his jaw and a nerve that twitched by his eyebrow, she knew she hadn't quite given up on him yet. His mum killed herself, she thought. Together with a teenage boy. How disturbing must that be?

'John?' she tried.

He didn't reply.

They were showing a soap opera in a mixture of Hindi and English. John stared without laughing. She said softly: 'Actually, I came out here to accept that offer of marriage you made. Remember? When you texted me?'

John breathed deeply.

'Why else do you think I'd have got a plane to come to India? That's why I gave up the play. To accept your offer.'

John's face remained blank. He doesn't care, she decided. He's forgotten even. It was months ago and she had given him a determined no. What a lesson in life this was!

Now John stood up and wandered off again, this time into the kitchen. Elaine felt scared and angry and stupid. But she had decided to hold onto him. It's a spell and he'll snap out of it. Or she herself was caught in a spell.

John was suddenly back in the room. 'Let's walk,' he announced abruptly. He was already heading for the door. 'Let's get out of here.'

She pulled on her sandals and ran down the stairs after him. Away from the apartment block, the road wasn't lit. The cement pavements were rough and broken. Elaine tripped. 'Where do you want to go?'

'Nowhere.'

The air smelled of burned cloth and oil. It was still hot. The cars passed in gritty, frenzied surges released by some distant traffic light. After a few minutes they passed an animal dead in the gutter. John crouched down and poked it. A dog.

'Don't touch it, John.'

'It's only dead.'

'Look at the ants.' Thick lines of insects marched across the pavement, tails in the air. 'God knows what infections there must be.'

He stood up and began walking again.

'Do you know where we're going?'

He didn't reply.

'What if we get lost?'

He shrugged his shoulders.

They passed a huge billboard with a shabby kiosk beneath. Cars had pulled over onto the mud and men were leaning on a fence drinking from bottles. A couple of autoricks slowed to offer rides but John ignored them. Then, in a lull, a peacock shrieked. It shrieked again. 'Oh Jesus!' Elaine muttered. The cry came from behind a low wall. John didn't turn. He wouldn't speak.

But very slowly, and despite the heat and sweat, Elaine began to feel better walking. She began to feel they were together at least, the two of them. Even without talking or touching, still they were moving together, walking together in the same direction along the same road. She decided just to trust and walk, trust and walk. Taking her somewhere, he was taking responsibility for bringing her back.

Meanwhile, the length of the streets was surprising. Elaine hadn't thought of India like this. The streets went on forever in discouragingly straight lines past shabby apartment blocks, scrapyards, empty plots with leaning trees and washing on wires. The occasional junctions were open and dark and there seemed to be nothing to distinguish one from another. Dark trucks rumbled in small convoys. There were no signposts. A bus threw out clouds of smoke. Two boys hung from the side, shouting. They passed a dozen or so older women squatting together on the dry mud beside the pavement, eating. They had a goat tethered to an old block of cement. One of the women lifted her head and called, but John walked on.

'If we got a taxi we could go to town and have a drink or something,' she said. 'I'm famished.'

Now at last he stopped; he looked at her. Finally he said, 'Please, Elaine.'

From then on the silence was easier.

They tramped through the empty roads of southern Delhi. They turned neither right nor left, just walked, Elaine had no idea in which direction, away from everything it seemed. A pale moon was out, but the ugly landscape seemed to have a sick glow that was all its own. She began to count the telegraph poles, the leaning bus stops by tiny side roads. The thought that they would have to walk the same way back began to oppress her. He is walking himself to exhaustion, she thought. He is walking away from talking, away from life.

The road had been climbing slightly for a few minutes and now they realised they were on a bridge. The asphalt had lifted away from the land below. To their right a single iron rail passed through cement posts.

'Water,' John said.

Elaine looked down. Sunk into steep banks she could just make out a glassiness in the dark. There was a dank smell.

'Is it the river?'

'I don't think so.'

They stood looking down. Precarious on the steep banks, a half-dozen shadowy animals were grazing in clumps of grass. It was hard to make them out. Buffalo perhaps. About fifty yards beyond, a light flickered inside a tent or shack.

'The Yamuna is wider,' John said, 'with big sand-flats either side. I don't think it passes here.'

He searched along the edge of the road, found a small stone and dropped it beyond the rail. There was a dull plop, but they couldn't see anything. The moonlight didn't seem to reflect on this water. It was quite a way below. John dropped another stone and another. She was grateful he had stopped walking. Then she grew anxious again when he just stood still leaning over the rail.

Without thinking, she asked: 'Why didn't you want your mum's ashes put in the river?'

John didn't reply, but turned to her. She saw his face cloud and then, in a rapid movement, he felt in the back pocket of his jeans. He pulled out a couple of pieces of paper and, without unfolding them, tore them up with quick nervous fingers, first in half, then again. Reaching over the rail, he let the pieces flutter down through the still air.

'It must be a canal, or drain,' John said now. He leaned over, wondering if he could see the paper on the water. Yes. Its whiteness picked up occasional flares of passing traffic in scattered scraps.

'Litterbug,' she said stupidly.

John hung over the rail. 'Is it moving?'

She watched. 'No.'

The scraps of paper hung quite still in the dark below them. The water had a rank, low-tide smell.

'Remember . . .' he began, but then had to wait while a slow truck rumbled by. A blast of warm air passed over them. 'Do you remember that night when we went swimming in the river?'

'The water was disgustingly slimy,' she laughed.

'Better than here, though.'

She looked down at the flecks of paper. 'They have moved. Look. A tiny bit. Away from us. It's moving that way.'

'Would you swim in here?' he asked.

'No way.'

'For me?'

Elaine was puzzled. His voice had altered.

'What good would it do?'

He was silent.

'And you? You'd swim in this sewer for me?'

John reached out his hand and touched her. 'Let's go back. It's a long walk. Tomorrow's an early start.'

In the Jameses' flat, John stripped to his underwear and lay on the sofa, ready for sleep. He didn't want to sleep with her. Elaine went to the bathroom, showered, washed her hair carefully and wrapped it in a towel. She cleaned her teeth. Lifting a glass of water to her mouth, finding her face in the mirror unusually pensive and concentrated, she had an image of herself setting out to carry the glass all the way back to Maida Vale without a spill. Why not? That would be a nice mime, she thought vaguely, crossing the world with a full glass of water in your hand. It could be a comedy, or rather frightening. She filled the glass again and held it at arm's length. Her hand was rock steady. The liquid didn't even tremble. The whole glass was perfectly transparent. Then she thought that if they departed tomorrow, there was no reason why she shouldn't appear in the play after all. They couldn't possibly have found anyone to take her place and learn everything in a matter of hours. Still carrying the water, she walked back into the sitting room and across to the small bedroom where she had slept the night before.

'Goodnight, John,' she said quietly.

John had his eyes shut.

'Ellie,' he said.

She stopped.

Without opening his eyes, he said quietly: 'You know Dad had a girlfriend before he died. I read some letters. She was very young.'

'Oh?' Elaine turned to him. He seemed very still. She hesitated. 'Did that upset you?'

'Well,' he lay still on the sofa, he seemed to be concentrating on staying very still, 'I just can't imagine what he thought he was doing with someone nearly forty years younger. Or why on earth the girl would want him.'

Something in his voice made her tremble and she felt a drop of water spill over her fingers. Eventually she asked: 'Did your mum know?'

His face was perfectly smooth. 'I've no idea.'

'Maybe it wasn't important. Just a sort of accident.'

'Then her dying with this really young guy beside her.' John spoke calmly and softly. 'It's so weird, isn't it?'

Elaine said nothing now. She was aware of concentrating on keeping her arm steady and simultaneously thought that actually it was pointless, since she had already spilled a bit, before even crossing the room, never mind the hemisphere.

John opened his eyes. He looked at her standing between sofa and guest room, then suddenly smiled. 'God, what tiny feet you have!'

She tried to laugh. 'So you always said.'

'I'm sorry,' he said, 'but for months now it's been like I'm constantly trying to wake up from something.' He thought for a moment. 'But before I wake up I have to remember the dream I've been having, and I can't. When that Sikh bloke gave his speech, I don't know why, but I was sure it was going to happen. Something horrible. Then it passed.'

She waited, holding the glass more calmly now. After a moment, she said: 'I thought it was really nice what the Sikh man said. What was his name? I mean it showed how much people loved her.'

John closed his eyes again and lay quite still.

'Want some water?' she asked.

'No thanks,' he said.

The following morning, no sooner were they through the airport check-in than a delay was announced. Someone had hidden a bomb in a child's buggy at Heathrow. They waited for three hours while British Airways ran their own security checks. Even with the air conditioning, the heat was unpleasant and they had to give up bottles and liquids of every kind.

'We'll have to pay Paul back, though,' she said, when eventually they boarded the plane. 'He's been incredibly generous.'

'I don't like him,' John said

Elaine buckled her seat belt. She didn't pursue the matter. There was something sharp and unyielding in John that hadn't been there before. But as the flight staff began the safety rigmarole, he laughed and shook his head. 'You know, though, now that I've thought about it, I can't believe you came out to Delhi to tell me you would marry me. I can't believe you did that. It was mad. You're mad.'

'Well, I did it.'

'You appreciate I am penniless.'

'I know.'

He hesitated. 'Maybe it was stupid, but I was sure you were seeing that Japanese bloke.'

'Well, I'm not.'

As the plane took off John looked down from the window and tried to find the river. It was early afternoon and the city was drenched in humidity. It was hard to make anything out. 'I bought a shawl for you,' he eventually said, 'pure pashmina, but it was stolen, along with my mobile. I don't have much luck with presents, do I?'

'Sounds like me who's not getting the luck,' Elaine said.

The passengers settled down. The screens above them began their graphic representation of the plane's progress on the long journey to London. *Plagued, perhaps blessed*, John remembered his father's angular handwriting, *by dreams of rivers and seas.* For a moment he imagined Albert James holding Jasmeet's hand as they descended flight after flight of steps into the ground. A temple upside down, she had said. The well had dried up centuries ago. The girl has gone back to her family, John thought. Then he remembered his mother arm in arm with that dark young figure on the mattress.

Staring at the screen, at the red line pushing out from Delhi northwards, at the figures giving the wind speed, the outside temperature, the estimated arrival time, John suddenly felt calm. These are things you will think about for all your life, he realised, things that will lie dormant then wake up again from time to time. It was definitely a good thing, he decided, that he had taken possession of Dad's papers. At least he had got control of those.

A meal was served. The usual, improbable Indian love film began. A crusty Brahmin family was insisting on caste niceties. Their handsome, rather fatuous son couldn't care less. He was courting an improbably beautiful supermarket cashier whose father was an alcoholic. It was a potential tragedy that would end in comedy and laughter. John motioned for Elaine to remove her headset.

'I think I'll write Dad's biography,' he said.

'Sorry?'

'I'll write a book about him. Not now, but someday.'

She frowned inquisitively. 'Well, he was your dad.'

'Might even make some money,' John added.

'Was the shawl you got like that?' she asked, indicating something on the screen.

He looked. The lucky supermarket girl was dancing alone on a mountain terrace, in love, waving an expensive shawl that her Brahmin boy had given her to disguise herself for their clandestine encounters.

'Oh, much prettier,' he said.

'Describe it, then. Tell me what it was like.'

John thought. It was actually quite hard to visualise what the shawl had been like, and even harder to remember the state of mind in which he had bought it. He did remember, though, that moment when he had spread it on the bed at the Govind and put

Father's computer on top; there were some things you did as though obeying orders or performing rituals. It was odd.

'If you can't describe it, how can I believe you ever bought it!'

'Okay. Hang on.'

John made an effort now to remember the situation in the shop when he had chosen it, the shopkeeper shaking open one dazzling pattern after another before his confused eyes.

'Right, I think I've got it. So, let me see: it had a sort of lilac colour, a soft pale kind of lilac, with tiny gold embroideries; that's why I bought it. The colour. I thought pale lilac would look great with your hair and skin. I saw it and just thought, Elaine.'

'Even though you weren't answering my messages at the time?'

He shrugged.

'Lilac is a good colour for me,' she said.

'Actually' – and now he remembered a little more – 'it was only when I opened it, later, in the hotel where I was staying, that I saw how nice the embroideries were. You know? I'd seen them, but I hadn't really taken them in. They were tiny snakes round the edges all entwined, with a baby elephant in each corner. Clichéd, I suppose, but very pretty. And the cloth, it sort of ran through your fingers, like water. It really felt like liquid, slithering over your hands. Like liquid you can hold.'

'Give it to me,' Elaine said suddenly. 'Come on. I want my present. I need a pretty scarf. Give it to me.'

'I told you, they stole it.'

'Stupid, give it to me.'

He looked at her. She was almost belligerent, but smiling.

'Okay.' John hesitated, then said rather severely: 'Actually, I had meant to wait till we got back, Elaine. I'm not sure this is a good moment for presents. You know, with everything that's happened.'

'No, I want it *now*,' Elaine told him. 'I want to be spoiled.'

With apparent reluctance, John leaned forward in his seat and rummaged in the pocket with the in-flight magazines. 'Wait a moment,' he said. 'I can't remember where I put it.' He looked puzzled, rummaged. 'Where is the damn thing? Ah,' he sighed with relief, 'here we go.'

Carefully, he lifted out a soft package and handed it to her. Elaine took it from him, brushing his fingertips as she did so. She caressed the crinkly paper, felt the parcel's weight, its floppy bulk, smelled it with an enquiring, twitching nose. 'What lovely purple paper,' she said. Then she set it on her knees and very delicately started to untie a bow of yellow ribbon. She had trouble with it because the knot was tight. She looked more closely. She frowned. 'Ah.' Then she found an end and pulled it through its loop. She looked up and smiled. John watched her slender wrists with their light down of hair, her sly little mouth, the upper lip set in a curl of mild surprise.

'Is it really for me?'

She removed the ribbon, coiled it round a finger and slipped it in a pocket, as though to use it again for some future package. More urgently now, she unfolded the paper, which made a happy crackling noise; then she stopped and gasped softly with pleasure.

'Oh John. Johnny!'

She lifted the invisible shawl from its wrapping. It was very beautiful. She held it to her cheek and shut her eyes as her skin met its softness. She sighed and opened it out now, fold by lilac fold, a huge flower blossoming, until her arms were spread wide and draped in beauty.

'Handwoven,' John murmured, 'by the girls of Kashmir.'

She took two diagonal corners, brought them carefully together, and, consulting a mirror that had appeared in the back of the seat in front, eyes narrowing, shrewd lips pouting, began to tie it round her hair and under her pointy, English-girl's chin. She patted it over the ears and pulled out a wrinkle and smoothed the embroidered ends where she had made the knot.

'And the elephants,' John asked, 'the snakes. Do you like them?'

Elaine pulled up a corner of cloth beside her mouth, squinted downwards, and shivered a little, as if exotic creatures were wriggling in her clothes.

John laughed.

Still smoothing the scarf on her hair, admiring herself in the mirror, moving her face first to this side then to that while the bright eyes stayed locked on their elfish reflection, Elaine suddenly turned to him. In a glow of amusement, her eyes went deep into his. He tried to understand. She raised an eyebrow, cocked her head. Now she frowned. Why did he like that curious lopsidedness she had so much?

Very quickly, Elaine pulled off the scarf and shook out her hair. She unfolded it again and, lifting the liquid cloth above her head on elegantly raised wrists, beckoned him to join her underneath. It might have been a tent she was holding up, or a net, or the silky sheet of a marriage bed. 'Kiss me, John,' she said. 'Kiss me underwater.' Her voice was businesslike. Taking a deep breath, John shut his eyes and dived right in.

ACKNOWLEDGEMENTS

My warmest thanks to Rana Dasgupta for his swift and patient assistance.

www.vintage-books.co.uk